THE
DASTARD

PIERS ANTHONY

THE DASTARD

A TOM DOHERTY ASSOCIATES BOOK

NEW YORK

THE DASTARD

Copyright © 2000 by Piers Anthony Jacob

This book is printed on acid-free paper.

A Tor Book
Published by Tom Doherty Associates, LLC
175 Fifth Avenue
New York, NY 10010

www.tor.com

Tor® is a registered trademark of Tom Doherty Associates, LLC.

Library of Congress Cataloging-in-Publication-Data

Anthony, Piers.
   The Dastard / Piers Anthony.—1st ed.
      p.   cm.
   "A Tom Doherty Associates Book"
   ISBN 0-312-86900-2 (alk. paper)
   1. Xanth (Imaginary place)—Fiction.   I. Title.

PS3551.N73 D37 2000
813'.54—dc21

                                                                00-031679

First Edition: October 2000

Printed in the United States of America

0 9 8 7 6 5 4 3 2 1

Contents

THE
DASTARD

Prolog

D raco Dragon oriented on his prey. He saw it fleeing across the plain, having foolishly exposed itself by daylight here in dragon country. Foolishness had but a single reward: to become food for a moderately hungry predator.

He angled his wings, banked, and sailed downward. There was a small cloud between him and the prey, and he maneuvered to keep it in the line of sight as long as feasible, so that the prey would not realize that it was in danger. But such cover was only temporary; soon he was in the final lap, and had to depend on sheer velocity. He folded his wings halfway and dived, making fantastic speed.

Now the prey spied him. It screamed and dived sideways into a pool, surprising him, so that he missed his first pass. Disgusted, he nosed up, made a looping turn, and came in for the second pass. The pool was hardly more than a puddle, too shallow to provide much protection. He could still nab the meat.

But the creature dived under the surface of the water, barely escaping Draco's reaching talons. He missed again, losing track in the stirred muck. Disgusted, he let fly a belch of fire, vaporizing a gout of water ahead of him. Then he banked again and came in for a landing. He would pull the creature out from under and eat it right there.

He landed with a splash, holding his wings high to avoid getting them dirty. The water felt good on his legs, cooling them, and a pleasant drop landed on his tongue. This was a tasty pond.

He settled in place and waited silently. The creature would have to come up for air soon. Then there would be a surprise.

The prey popped up. It was a young human woman, very nicely fleshed; she would be delicious, once he toasted her and burned off her clothes. He took a breath as he met her frightened gaze. There was a shimmer, and suddenly she looked twice as good, but in a different way.

Then something amazing happened that entirely took away his appetite for food.

Only after he dragged himself away from the pond, exhausted, did Draco figure out exactly what had occurred. He had blundered into a love spring. His intended prey had become his love object. Oh, the shame of it! He would never live it down if the other dragons heard about it.

PART 2
DEAL

Anomy was eighteen, and the last thing he wanted to do was settle down on the farm and work for a living. But not much else seemed to offer. Only if he made a good living would any of the village maidens be interested in marrying him, and what would that lead to anyway? Storks and babies and more work.

He wished he could go somewhere interesting and be someone exciting. But he couldn't, because his magic talent was having stupid ideas. Anything he thought of was stupid, no matter how smart it seemed at the time. For example, he had once seen a lovely young woman on a beach, and had the idea to embrace her. But she had turned out to be a sand wench, trying to lure him into a sandy grave. He had barely escaped. Another time he had found an interesting pot, and thought to clean it up and give it to a pretty maiden, thereby winning her favor. But it had turned out to be a crack pot, that had not only had a bad crack on its side, it had made things around it really weird. The maiden had not been favorably impressed.

"I detest my stupid life!" he exclaimed angrily.

There was a flicker before him. A cloud of smoke puffed out, and a face formed in it. "You called?" it inquired.

Anomy halted just outside his tracks. "What are you, smoke-face?"

The smoke extended downward, forming a vaguely manlike figure. "I am the Demon Test," he said. "Did you not speak my name?"

"Listen, jerk-cloud, I have problems enough without being bugged by demons," Anomy said politely. "So why don't you go suck your foot up your nose and leave me alone?"

The demon solidified, barring his way. "There is something about you that appeals somewhat to me," he said. "You seem to have the attitude of a demon."

"And you have the attitude of a person," Anomy said. "Now that we've exchanged insults, how about getting out of my way, you bag of dirty smoke?"

"Not until we settle with each other," the demon said. "You summoned me, and so we have to deal."

"How did I summon you, you waft of foul air?"

"You spoke my name. D. Test. So I was duly conjured here, and now we must deal. Name your terms."

Anomy was not much of a human being, but neither was he entirely stupid. "I want a really good magic talent."

"Fair enough. I want a grungy soul."

Anomy had not gotten much use from his soul, so he figured he could live without it. "So let's trade. What kind of talent do you offer?"

D. Test considered. "In my wanderings I have scavenged a few things. Let's see if I have any good talents in here." He formed a large bag and opened it. He pulled out a small object in the shape of the letter P. When he squeezed it a thin yellow stream jetted out. "Yes! How about this Pee nut, that can make a person—"

"Forget it; I already have a stupid talent like that."

Test reached in again. "Here is the talent of time travel." He pulled out something that looked vaguely like an invisible hourglass.

"Time travel? You mean I can go to the future?"

"No, this is more limited. You can go to the past, and change things. So it's really the talent of unhappening. But there's a catch."

"A catch?" Anomy asked suspiciously. His whole life seemed to have been a series of catches.

"You can go back only as far as right now."

"Right now? But this is the present. That's not time travel."

"It gets better. Tomorrow you can come back to now. Next year you can come back to now. You just can't go back to before you got this talent."

Anomy thought about that. "So I could come back to now. What could I do with now?"

"I told you. You could unhappen events. You could change something to suit yourself better."

They talked about it, and finally Anomy was satisfied. He handed over his soul and took the talent, and the deal was done. Neither of them thought about the possible long-term consequences.

PART 3
RULE OF TEN

The ancient old wizened little man pored over his huge tome, searching for an Answer. "There has to be a way!" he muttered grumpily.

A woman appeared in the doorway, locating it by memory and touch. "What is it, Magician?" she inquired.

The Magician looked up. Ordinarily he hated company, but his son's wife had a benign effect on him. "Come in, Wira," he said, already feeling slightly less grumpy.

She entered the dusky chamber, touching a wall lightly. The lack of sufficient light did not bother her. "Is everything in order?"

"There is a crisis coming, which will require the cooperative effort of a number of people. The effort must be kept secret, which means no more than ten people may know of it. This is the Rule of Ten."

"That sounds sensible," Wira said.

"It is sensible. But in order to handle this crisis, eleven people and a bird will have to know. That means it won't be tight, and the opposition will have a chance to discover it and interfere, so the outcome is by no means certain."

"One of them can't be excluded?" Wira asked.

"No. All are necessary. I have gone over the list repeatedly, and all must know. I have tried to find a way to extend the coverage to eleven or twelve, but the magic won't stretch. The Rule of Ten is inviolate."

"That's too bad, Magician. What will you do?"

"I will try to find some other way to handle it. There is an element that relates to a small flying dragon. It is peripheral, but if it should fall into place, the day may yet be saved."

"But Magician, suppose it doesn't fall into place?"

"Then I will sweat," he said grimly.

Wira shuddered. The Good Magician had never sweated in the time she had known him. She hoped he would find a better way, so they wouldn't have to fumigate the castle.

There was a ding. The ding bat was signaling an event. "Oh, someone is coming," Wira said. "I should have been more alert."

It was true, but the Magician was never in a mood to blame her. "Show her in."

Wira departed, and he turned pages in his tome, which was the *Book of Answers*, reviewing what he would tell the querent. Giving Answers was such a bore, but it was a service he was more or less committed to, so he acceded grumpily. According to his research, this one was a girl, fourteen years old, who wanted to know her Purpose. The purpose of any girl was to settle down after a few more years and make some unworthy man moderately happy for a time. To provide a decent home for the surplus babies the storks had to deliver somewhere. The girls might see it somewhat differently, of course, but the *Book of Answers* wasn't asking them.

Yet the *Book* had a question mark by her name. Her destiny had not yet been decided, oddly. What was the problem? Was he going to have to find a special purpose for her? This promised to be more work than her payment of a year of service would be worth.

The Magician sighed. What use could he make of an innocent girl without a Purpose? He already had someone to wash the dishes and to pick up dirty socks. In any event, this girl was a crossbreed, half-dragon,

and would require considerably more challenge. A bored girl could be
mischief; a bored dragon could be worse. The combination could be
dangerous; the castle furnishings were flammable. What did he have for
her to do that would be sufficiently challenging and, preferably, away
from the castle? It was bad enough trying to fathom the manner a small
flying dragon related to the coming crisis of Xanth, without having to
guide a dragon girl.

Dragon—dragon girl. Suddenly a bulb flashed, illuminating the dingy
study for an instant. She could be the connection!

He heard footsteps on the winding stair. Wira was bringing her in.

Feverishly he turned pages of the tome, finding the place. Yes-she
was the daughter of Draco Dragon and an anonymous nymph or maybe
human girl caught at a love spring. And she could be the key to the
solution of the crisis, if properly placed. It was no sure thing, but it
improved the chances of success by a significant fraction. Maybe enough
to overcome the liability of the Rule of Ten.

Wira and the girl entered. The Magician looked up from the tome.
"Yes?" he inquired grumpily. He wasn't actually feeling grumpy at the
moment, but the forms had to be followed.

"Good Magician, this is Becka," Wira said. "She has navigated the
Challenges and has a Question for you to Answer. She understands that
she will be required to give a year's service."

The girl stood shyly, not speaking. She was cute, with blonde hair
and brown eyes.

"Let's see your natural form."

Her human aspect became a front; the rear was the body of a dragon
with bright green scales, with purplish tinges at the ends. There were
large folded batlike wings. Overall, handsome enough, and definitely
reminiscent of Draco.

"Out with it," Humfrey said, pretending indifference.

"Please, Good Magician—what is my purpose?"

And now he had an Answer. "To effect the welfare of Xanth."

Her human front looked perplexed. "But how can I affect it?"

"Effect, not affect," the Magician snapped. "Now, for your Service,
you must go in girl form to the monument commemorating the Sea Hag's
life story, and wait there until a man passes. You will accompany him
and try to help him in whatever legitimate way he wishes. In this manner,

in due course, you may thus effect Xanth's welfare, and your Service will be done."

The girl was not entirely innocent of the ways of men. "But suppose he tries to—?"

"Then turn dragon and chomp him."

"Okay," she said, faintly reassured.

"Take this." He lifted a little globe.

She took it from his gnarled old fingers. As she touched it, it puffed into a little ball of vapor and dissipated. "What is it?"

"Awareness. You'll need it."

She nodded, though evidently perplexed. "Thank you so much, Magician."

But the Good Magician was already looking through the *Book of Answers* for the next situation, which would involve three little princesses and a bird. Wira guided Becka out.

1
DASTARD

The Dastard walked through the forest, looking for mischief. It had taken him a while to get the hang of living without a soul, and to learn to use his talent effectively, but now it had been four years since his deal with the demon, and he was ready to make more of an impression on the Land of Xanth. He had cast off his old nothing-name of Anomy and perfected his new one, for the dastardly deeds he was doing. So he was emerging from his secluded neck of the woods and searching for greater challenges.

He was well equipped to search, because an aspect of his talent was to have a sense of place/time. He could tell where and when there was something significant, and so could go there to discover what it was. His sense informed him that something interesting was headed toward him on this path. All he had to do was keep going the way he was going.

He encountered a little girl walking the opposite way. "Hi, mister," she called. "Is this the way to the Good Magician's castle?"

One thing the Dastard had discovered in the course of his restricted practicing was that significant mischief could come from seemingly minor situations. He had also learned that lies were precious and vulnerable; it was best not to use one where the truth would do. That way he could save his lies for the best opportunities. So he told the truth: "No, this is not. But I can show you the correct route."

She squealed in girlish fashion and clapped her hands. "Oh, thank you so much, mister! Where is it?"

"First we have to go this way," he said, indicating the way he was going. "For I am just now emerging from the hinterlands, where there is nothing interesting." That was in part because he had abolished anything interesting in that region, but he didn't feel the need to clarify that aspect. Now he needed to find out what was significant about this dull child. "Who are you, and why do you want to find the Good Magician's castle?"

"My name is Melody Irene Human, and I'm from Mundania," she said proudly. "I was named after a princess and her grandmother, I think. I want to ask the Good Magician how I can stay in Xanth."

"You think you are named after a princess? Don't you know?"

"Well, you see, I'm older than Princess Melody, so I'm not sure I was named after her. But maybe she was named after me."

"That makes sense," the Dastard agreed. That wasn't even a lie; the princess could conceivably have been named after a Mundane girl. There were three little princesses, four years old, named Melody, Harmony, and Rhythm. Their parents might have had trouble coming up with three names at once. "If you are Mundane, why do you want to stay in Xanth?"

"I've always loved Xanth," Melody said. "I've always wanted to be here. But my parents don't believe in it. So I'm going to ask the Good Magician, and even if he says I can't stay, I'll still have to remain here a year to finish the service for my Answer. That's a lot better than nothing."

This didn't seem to have much potential for mischief, but his sense of significance was seldom wrong, so he gave it another try. "How did you get here?"

The child launched into her story. "My folks were coming to Florida to visit Disney World. We were driving south from Virginia. We stopped to eat in Georgia, and there must have been something wrong with the food my big sister had, because suddenly she was ready to burst with indigestion and had to get out of the car before she exploded. Dad didn't want to stop, 'cause we were on Interstate seventy-five you know, and there was no rest stop near. But my sister wasn't fooling, and Mom said if he didn't want it to happen in the car he'd better pull off in a hurry.

I thought it might be sort of fun to have it happen in the car, you know, having a really big stink, but I guess Mom wouldn't have seen the humor. So we were passing this section where the north and south lanes separated, and there were trees growing between them. In fact, there was a whole little forest there. Dad saw a little trail going in, so he braked and slowed the car to the left and got onto that trail, into the forest, and out of sight of the highway. Then he stopped, and Mom pretty much dragged Sis out and they disappeared into the ferns. So I got out and looked around, and you know, it was different. In fact, it looked sort of magical. I really liked it. But then Mom and Sis were done and we had to get back in the car, and Dad turned it around and we drove back out toward the highway. But we couldn't find it. I said 'Hey, maybe it's a magic forest, and soon we'll find a house made of candy, and a nice old woman saying ' "Come in, the oven's hot." ' I thought it was funny, but nobody laughed. Adults don't have much of a sense of humor, and Sis wasn't feeling all that good at the moment. I learned about the adult deficiency in humor the time I joked that if Mom had a phantom pregnancy, she'd give birth to a ghost. Not only did she not laugh, she sent me to my room without dessert. Can you believe it? But when Dad still couldn't find the Interstate, Mom started yelling at him for making a stupid wrong turn, and he said he hadn't, he was just coming straight back the way we had come. Then I saw what sure looked like a tangle tree and I said 'Hey, this must be Xanth!' But they didn't know what I meant, because I'm the only one in my family who reads the Xanth books. The others are just sort of back in the stone age when it comes to reading. Dad drove right by that tangle tree. But I kept telling them 'We're in Xanth! We're in Xanth!' and finally Mom said that if I could show them something truly magical, then they would believe me. The trail kept on, in fact it became a trollway, but Dad thought the sign was a joke. Then I spotted a centaur, and I yelled 'Stop the car! Look out the window to the left!' Dad and Mom and Sis looked out, sort of sneeringly, but then they saw it, and their mouths dropped open. The centaur saw the car and spooked; I guess he never saw a car before. He ran off. But now my folks had their minds halfway open, for a change. Then we came to the Gap Chasm and had to stop. I told them to turn in the direction of the bridge and Castle Roogna, and when we crossed the Gap they really believed, 'cause it was so wide and deep. So we got there and I wanted to see the king and queen so maybe we could get a house to live in, but my folks just wanted to find the way back to dreary Mundania. But nobody's figured out how to return yet, so while they're thinking about it, I'm on my way to see the Good Magician, to find out how I can stay here. I mean, I may never get another chance, 'cause I don't think we'd ever find that one trail that led into Xanth again."

The Dastard considered. A whole Mundane family stranded in Xanth, and the youngest member eager to stay. The Good Magician would probably find a way for her, too, and she would surely be endlessly happy, having lucked into her dream. This did seem like a worthy project.

The Dastard didn't say another word. He slid into limbo and traveled back in time two days. As he did, he guided himself toward the north, looking for the area where the Mundanes had entered Xanth.

It took a while, but it didn't matter, because he remained in limbo during his excursions in place/time and it didn't affect his real life. He slid back and forth between one and two days ago, and canvassed the general region. His sense of significance got a bit fuzzy in limbo, but he knew he would get it straight eventually. He finally saw the family enter, passing through a glitch in the magic boundary without knowing it. Good; he had it spotted.

He slid to the time one hour before their arrival. Then he emerged into real existence at the boundary. He dragged fallen branches to the trail and formed a pile that blocked it off. He laced the branches with brush to make it look entirely impassable.

He finished just in time. The odd Mundane vehicle was just arriving. It would have to stop outside Xanth, and would never know what it had missed.

He relaxed, and the place/time vortex pulled him back to the present. He emerged in the precise place and time he had left it, on the path he had been walking with the girl. But now there was no girl. Melody Irene Human had never entered Xanth.

The Dastard rubbed his hands together in glee. He had just performed another dastardly deed. He had deprived the family of its phenomenal experience, and the girl of the accomplishment of her dream. That made him feel good.

He continued in the direction he had been going, where his sense informed him that there was more significance ahead. Soon another traveler appeared. This was an old woman. "Pardon me, young man," she said. "Could you tell me what this year is?"

"It is the year eleven hundred," the Dastard replied, finding no good reason to deceive her. The woman looked old enough to have misplaced a few years, which was probably why she was uncertain.

"Eleven hundred!" she exclaimed, surprised. "Is Castle Roogna still in existence?"

For some reason, this question struck him as odd. But there still seemed to be no harm in the truth. "Yes."

"That's good. I was afraid it might have fallen or been deserted in eight hundred and fifty years."

This seemed even odder. "If I may ask," he said politely, for politeness was always best until he knew enough to make rudeness really count. "Who are you?"

"I am Sorceress Tapis. I make magic tapestries. Because of a complicated situation that I need not bore you with, my body became a magic seed, and it recently sprouted, returning me to my former state. Now I shall do my best to make do in the Land of Xanth as it is presently constituted. I trust there remains a market for magic tapestries."

The Dastard remembered the Sorceress Tapis from his centaur-school history lessons. They would certainly be glad to see her at Castle Roogna. One of her magic tapestries still hung in the children's room there. It showed all of Xanth geography and history, and was a prime source of entertainment and amusement. There would surely be a rich market for more tapestries. The Sorceress would be highly successful and renowned.

So the Dastard re-entered place/time. He quested until he found the time and spot where the Sorceress had sprouted from the seed. A heavy rain had wet it, making it come to life. He moved to one hour before that. He picked up the dry seed and put it in the dry hollow of an acorn tree. He sealed the hollow with a fragment of wood, so that no water could get in. It would not get rained on, and would not sprout this day, or for many, many days to come. In fact, maybe never.

He relaxed, and was drawn back to his place/time in the present. He resumed walking along the path. The Sorceress Tapis was gone; indeed, she had never been there. He had performed another gratifyingly dastardly deed. He felt great.

This path had been worked out, but his sense informed him that there was another significant nexus not far away, along a side path. He took that route, and continued until he encountered another female. She was twelve years old, and suddenly appeared before him on the path. "Who are you?" he inquired.

"I am Surprise, the child of Grundy Golem and Rapunzel. I have many talents, but can use each one only once. Then it is gone. I just discovered that eventually my used talents will replenish, so I can use them again, if I just have enough patience. Isn't that wonderful?"

"That should make you very happy," the Dastard said. "How did you discover it?"

"I was sitting by a pleasant pool, looking at my reflection in the clear water, and I remembered how I had once made a ball of water. Before I thought about it, I did it again. Then I remembered that I couldn't use a talent a second time. I was amazed. So I tried another old talent, and a third one. I discovered that my oldest talents had recovered, but the ones I had used recently were still gone. So I figured it out. I'm really, really pleased. I just had to tell someone, and you're the first person I've seen since it happened. Well, farewell." She spread her arms and flew away without wings.

The Dastard went back into place/time travel. He explored until he found the clear pool where the girl had seen her reflection and made her discovery. He went to the time just a few minutes before her arrival there. He scooped up handfuls of mud and stirred them into the water until it was impossible to see any reflection. It would be hours before it cleared. The girl would not see her reflection, and not think the thoughts that had led to her discovery. She would not know what she missed.

He returned to the present. Another dastardly deed accomplished. This was turning out to be a great day.

But it was not over. If he hurried, he could nab yet another significant nexus. They were thick and fast, out here in unmolested Xanth. He ran back along the path to the main one, found another side path, and followed that. He encountered a man, an adult of moderate age, and handsome. "Who are you?" he inquired.

"I am Ho," the man replied. "I am traveling to see the Princess Ida, hoping she will find my talent useful. I think she will. I might even marry her, if she likes me well enough. Maybe we'll have a child named Idaho who will have a talent with potatoes."

Princess Ida was Princess Ivy's twin sister. Her talent was the Idea, and she had whole worlds of ideas. She could make any idea come true. But it had to originate with someone else, who did not know of Ida's talent; Ida could not make her own ideas come true. That was the one limit on an otherwise extraordinary talent.

"What is your talent?" the Dastard asked Ho.

"It is selective amnesia. I can make a person forget any particular thing he or she wants to. This would enable Princess Ida to forget the nature of her talent, and it would thus become far more useful to her. I think she should be very pleased."

The Dastard nodded. This could make an enormous difference. Probably Ida and Ho would like each other, and would marry, and be happy forever after, and do much good with their new ideas. A wonderful future awaited them. How dastardly it would be to deny them that.

But as yet he wasn't sure how to do it. Ho was already on his way, and had a clear notion what he wanted; it seemed to be too late to change that. But there had to be a way. Sometimes the intellectual quest was more difficult than the physical one. "What gave you the notion of doing this?" he asked.

Ho, like most innocent upright decent folk, was glad to answer openly. "It was sheer coincidence. Last month I was walking along the path from my village when I happened to stumble on a stone I didn't see. I didn't fall, but its sharp ridge caught my shoelace and broke it. So I had to replace the lace. So I turned around and went back to the village for a new shoelace from Lacey, the woman who makes them. This time her new husband was there, a man I hadn't met before. So we chatted, and he turned out to be descended from Ghost King Warren, whose talent after he died he said was making ghosts. He inquired about my talent, and I told him, and he said that might be useful for Princess Ida. I had never thought about that, but the more I considered it, the more intriguing it seemed, until finally I decided to do something about it. So here I am, on my way—all because of a broken shoelace."

The Dastard didn't wait. He phased into limbo, orienting on that place/time where/when Ho had broken his shoe-lace. In due course he found it, and entered regular existence just before Ho came down the path. He picked up the rock Ho was about to stumble on and hurled it into the brush. Then he returned to the present. He was alone; Ho was not making his journey to meet and marry Princess Ida. There would be no child, and no potatoes.

Oh, this was wonderful! The day was yet young, and he had already abolished four significant events.

However, there was nothing remaining in this general place or time; he had used it up. It might be another day before he found anything else.

He was hungry, so he paused at a path-side stand that served freshly harvested pies. There was a small orchard of pie trees behind it, obviously well cared for. The young woman tending the stand was unusually pretty; she practically glowed in a lovely green hue, from her blonde-green hair to her fair-green complexion. The Dastard liked her immediately, so he struck up an acquaintance. "Who are you?"

"I am Jade," she replied. "My talent is to make anything into a jade stone." She indicated a number of jade stone statuettes she had converted from other substances.

"Are you married?"

She giggled, embarrassed by the directness of the question. "Of course not!"

This looked promising. One thing the Dastard lacked was a woman to appreciate him. For various reasons that escaped him, girls tended to avoid him once they got to know him, so he had had no serious romantic relationship despite being twenty-two years old. He had thought his acquisition of his wonderful talent four years before would change that, but it hadn't. So he was still looking, and maybe Jade would do.

"How about marrying me?" he asked.

"Oh, I couldn't possibly do that," she said.

"Why not?"

"Because I'm in love with Mac."

Oops. He had forgotten to ask whether she had a boyfriend. Pretty girls usually did. But maybe the situation wasn't wholly hopeless. "Who is Mac? What's his talent?"

Jade was happy to talk about her boyfriend. "He's just the most handsome, smart, wonderful person I know. He's different. He can split into three likenesses, called Mac, Mike, and Mal, and each is a bit different in looks and temperament, so it's never boring. We met three years ago, and it just got better, so now we're going to marry and be happy forever after. Oh, it's just so utterly thrilling!"

The Dastard was really getting to dislike this Mac/Mike/Mal. But maybe if he could get rid of him, Jade would be available for himself. Three years was within his range. "How did you meet him?"

"Well, I was baby-sitting for Okra Ogress three years ago. Her twins were Og and Not-Og, five years old. Og was already getting really stupid, even for an ogret boy, and Not-Og was getting really ugly, even for an ogret girl. He could lose track of how many toes he had, and she could curdle cream with one smile. In short, they were wonderful ogre children, and Okra was really proud of them. But her husband Smithereen had gone on a boulder-smashing expedition and not returned, so she knew he was lost, and she had to go find him, and so she left the twins with me, the neighbor's daughter. It was a few weeks before she returned, and the ogrets were getting bored, so I took them for a walk in the woods, where they could practice being really stupid and ugly. I didn't have to worry about safety, because nobody who isn't duller than an ogre—and there are none such—ever bothers an ogre. Or an ogret. The very greensward cringed at their approach, and the sun dimmed when they glanced at it. They both had fun twisting small trees into pretzels and teaching young dragons the meaning of fear; these are just things ogres naturally do. They are so justifiably proud of their strength, stupidity, and ugliness.

"Then Fracto drifted by. That's Cumulo Fracto Nimbus, the worst of clouds, always looking for picnics to rain on or valuables to blow away. He thought he would have some fun with the ogrets, because he figured they couldn't do anything back to him. He made a foggy face and started blowing up a storm. But it didn't turn out the way he expected. The wind stirred up half a soul that had been half buried somewhere, and as it flew by, Og grabbed it, and held it, wondering whether to eat it or squeeze it into pulp. Just then a stone gargoyle happened to pass by, and Not-Og smiled at it, for a moment petrifying it with her un-beauty. When it stood immobile, she pulled off one of its gargoyle socks, admiring its colors. Og saw that, grabbed it, and stuffed the half soul into it. Not-Og snatched it back. Og grabbed it again and hurled it into the cloud. The half soul escaped and found Fracto. That made Fracto turn halfway good. He collapsed his storm front and sailed rapidly home to the Region of

Air where his partner Hurricane Happy Bottom lived, and they did whatever clouds do to summon the stork, and after that Fray came on their scene, and she got the half soul. Just what sort of a cloud she will turn out to be we don't yet know."

"This is all very interesting," the Dastard said, expending a fair sized lie at this point, because it was really all very boring. "But what does it have to do with your meeting Mic/Muck/Mock?"

"That's Mac/Mike/Mal," Jade said sharply. "I'm coming to that." She gave him a brief green stare, then resumed her how-we-met narrative. "The day was getting on, so we started back toward home. But the ogrets heard someone declaiming heroic poetry and ran to see who it was, and I had to follow. It turned out to be a woman polishing a freshly waxed statue. It was the statue doing the declaiming. For a moment I was mystified what it all meant, but then I realized that she was waxing poetic. Fortunately poetry bores ogres, unless they are speaking it themselves, so that didn't hold the twins long. We resumed our trek, and encountered a group of big furry animals. I hadn't seen anything like them before, so I inquired: 'What kind of creatures are you?' And two of the biggest ones, who seemed to be males, replied 'We are bears. We are Bears Noting, and these are bears mentioning.' They indicated two females. 'And we are bears repeating, bears repeating,' two small ones said. That left one more, who was busy scratching figures on a pad he carried. He looked very interesting, but didn't speak. "Do you feel you are of no account?' I asked. 'By no means,' he responded. 'I am an interest bearing account.' So then I understood, and we went on toward home."

"But about 3M," the Dastard said, trying to stifle his burgeoning impatience.

"I'm getting there," Jade said severely. "We had to stop, because there was an imp ass. It was just a little mule, but we realized it had strayed from a settlement of imps and needed to be returned. So Og picked it up, and Not-Og smiled around until most of the surrounding foliage wilted, and there was the imp colony. Og set the imp ass down there, so than it no longer blocked our way. The imps were very grateful, so they told us where we could find some nice varieties of thyme. A person can never get too much thyme, so we thanked them and went there; it wasn't far off the path, but we would never have found that patch on our own. There was 2/2 Thyme, and 4/4 Thyme, and 6/8 Thyme—just a great variety of very special Thymes. So I gathered a timely assortment, and we started back for home again."

"Will you get on with it!" the Dastard said, becoming foolishly impatient. He was beginning to wonder if this pretty green woman was worth the effort. Her endless talk was as dull as she was lovely.

"I'm getting there," Jade said, favoring him with a glare. "We started back—and there, coming along the path the other way, was Mac. I was so surprised that I fell back. Right on my soft bottom, as a matter of fact. A stray gust of wind came at that moment. My skirt flared up and gave him a good flash of my panties. Maybe that was just as well, because he froze in place, as men do, and remained that way until I got back on my feet. I realized that chance had enabled me to capture his attention. He was a handsome man, so I decided to keep it. And that was the beginning of it all, and soon we will be married. Meanwhile, the ogres—"

But the Dastard was already fading into limbo. He went back three years, then zeroed in on the thyme patch. He considered half a moment, then set about fashioning a baffle. He set it up by the path, just upwind of the place Jade would tumble, so that when the stray gust of wind came, it would be deflected before it reached her skirt, and her skirt would not flare, and the man would not see her panties. So she would not catch his attention, and they would pass without noticing each other.

He returned to the present. There was Jade, just as pretty as before. "So how about marrying me?" he asked again.

"Oh, I couldn't possibly do that," she said. "I'm in love with Eck."

"Eck?" he asked distastefully.

"Eck Sray, my fiancé," she explained. "He sees through things. When we first met, he saw right through my skirt to my panties, and—"

Oh, no! He had abolished the incident that attracted Mac's attention to her, only to have her meet another man who was attracted by the same thing. Which meant that the Dastard still didn't have any decent chance to get an indecent look himself.

He was tired of such frustrations. So he decided to snatch what spot of pleasure he could, and move on. His talent had one more aspect that could be extremely useful on occasion, and this might be such an occasion.

He reached across the table and caught Jade's head. He pulled her in for a hot kiss. It was pretty good, considering that her lips were mushy; surprise had made her forget to firm them.

Then she jerked away and screamed. A huge older man appeared from the garden. "What's the matter, honey? This creep bothering you?"

"Yes, Father," she said. "He kissed me!"

"Well now," the man said grimly. He strode toward the Dastard, raising a hamfist.

But the Dastard got out of there by going into limbo and changing his own recent past. He could do that, to a limited extent. He could go back as far as a day, if he hadn't been changing the lives of others, or otherwise as far back as the last change he had made. When he changed others, that fixed his own presence, lest he run afoul of paradox. So in this case he was limited to about five minutes, since he had abolished Mac. That was enough; he went back to just before he kissed Jade, and this time he didn't kiss her. The episode had never happened.

But he remembered it. He was the only one who could remember events that he had made unhappen. So that he didn't lose his awareness of his own dastardly deeds. After all, what would be the point, if *he* didn't remember?

Jade was still talking about how great Eck Sray was, and how they were going to be married soon, and then he wouldn't need to see through her clothing to see her panties, because she would show them to him anytime.

"Uh, sure, thank you," the Dastard said, trying to control a fit of jealousy, and moved on. She was a pretty girl, but as usual he had gotten nowhere. He hated that.

There was another nexus some distance ahead. Maybe that would be better. He needed something to shore up his spirits. He had a great talent, and he had no soul, which gave him wonderful freedom, but it wasn't enough. He wanted a woman, too. A pretty one.

Farther along he spied an animal going the opposite way. Was this the nexus? No, his sense did not respond. But the creature approached him. It was a male canine, but did not seem to be a werewolf. What did it want?

He saw that it wore a mundane collar, from which dangled a little sign. He read the sign: MY NAME IS BOSS. I AM A 90 POUND BLACK

LABRADOR DOG. I LOST MY HOME AND AM LOOKING FOR A NEW ONE. CAN YOU HELP?

"Certainly I can help," the Dastard said. "But I won't. Go away."

The dog walked sadly on. It was momentarily satisfying to frustrate him, but hardly worth the effort.

In due course he came to the nexus. It was at a statue of the Sea Hag, a Sorceress he had always admired. She took the bodies of young pretty girls and used them until they got worn and ugly, then moved on to others. She must have a fabulous history! She was old, in spirit if not in current body, and must have been around since the dawn of Xanth.

Then he saw a girl standing there by the statue. She was sort of halfway pretty, with blonde hair and brown eyes, but young. The Adult Conspiracy could get after a man who tangled with too young a girl; he had had some experience, and didn't need any more. So she was of no personal use to him. Still, she was at the nexus, so this needed to be investigated.

She saw him, "Did you see a big dog? I thought I saw one not long ago, maybe looking for a home."

The Dastard ignored this. "Who are you?" he asked her.

"My name is Becka," she said. "Who are you?"

That set him back. The Dastard was not used to people asking *him* questions. "Why do you want to know?"

"Because I'm supposed to wait here until a certain man comes, and then I'm supposed to go with him and help him in whatever way he wishes. I need to know whether you are that man."

This was interesting. She was at the nexus, and she wanted to help him. Maybe she was what he was looking for, despite her youth. If she didn't tell, who would ever know? So he gave it a try. "Kiss me."

"No."

"If you're supposed to help me—"

"Not that way."

"How do you know?"

"I'm too young."

"Maybe not," he said. He grabbed her and sought to kiss her.

Suddenly he was holding on to a dragon with purple-tinged bright green scales.

He backed off five minutes and tried again. They went through the introduction, and this time he answered her question. "I am the Dastard, because I do dastardly deeds. Do you have a problem with that?"

"I guess not," she said. "You must be going to do something good for Xanth, that I'm supposed to help you with. Otherwise the Good Magician wouldn't have sent me."

"The Good Magician! He sent you to meet me?"

"Yes. Didn't you know?"

"No. Why should that little old wizened gnome want to do anything for me?"

"I don't know. My guess is he wants to do something good for Xanth."

The Dastard pondered. This was a curious business. He hadn't known that Magician Humfrey even knew about him, let alone wanted to help him. Maybe it would be better to slide back through limbo and nullify that connection. But he hesitated, because he knew the Good Magician was a sharp old codger with a lot of information, and if he changed Humfrey's action once, he would not be able to change it again thereafter, because of the rule of paradox. Maybe the Good Magician was counting on that, to mess him up. So he would play along, and learn more about it, not acting until he was sure. Having a good magic talent was one thing; using it effectively was another.

Meanwhile, here was this girl who could become a flying dragon. She was obviously no prospect for any romance, and not just because she was too young. She could defend herself. He hated that. But she might indeed be useful, if he could figure out how.

"Very well," he said. "Tag along for a while. And if you don't like what I do, then you can depart." And that would get rid of her without putting him into any paradox bind with respect to the devious Good Magician.

"Okay," she agreed.

It was definitely a nexus, but not one he properly understood. Yet.

2

THREE LITTLE PRINCESSES

They were four years old, and they were bored. It wasn't all that easy to be a princess. Their mother, the Sorceress Ivy, had the talent of Enhancement, and she certainly had been using it recently. Every trifling wee little inconsequential thing had been magnified beyond all reason. It was said that this was any mother's talent, but that didn't make it easier to endure.

For example, there was the incident of the Pay Phone. Xanth had gotten connected in the past year or so to a magical network called the Mundane Mega Mesh, which folk like Com Pewter and Com Passion tied into. But because it related to Mundania, which it seemed was not quite as stodgy a region as reputed, there had to be a Phone. So a Pay Phone had appeared in Castle Roogna. A person could talk into it all she wanted, but somebody had to Pay. Somebody else took care of that; it wasn't their concern. They had gotten hold of the Phone and discovered how to talk for hours to several people in Mundania, including something called Phone Sects. It had been mysterious but fun. But Mother had magnified it ludicrously, and forbidden them to touch the Phone again.

Then there was the See Saw in the playground. It had eyes to see what it sawed, and they used it to saw through several things, like the door to their bedroom. What was the problem with that? They had discovered that See Saws even had conventions, and had used their Saw to travel from See to shining See. But Mother had claimed they were lost for those three days, and had half a conniption. She had not been reasonable at all.

And the pair-it. This was a pretty green bird that doubled objects it touched. So it made pairs of their toys, beds, potties, and dresses. And pairs of the pairs, unendingly. Soon their room was filled with pairs of things. In fact, they overflowed into the hall. That was when the adults got involved, and there was another awful fuss about nothing much.

So here they were, shut in with absolutely nothing to do except practice their talents. This was to sing and play things real. So far they had used it mostly for illusions, such as fancy castles, complete with secret chambers and moats filled with tasty tsoda pop from the lake, and of course Soufflé Moat Monster. They had even managed to make the castles solid, so that they were no longer illusions, but had to keep them small, like dollhouses, so they would fit in the room. But there was a limit to the interest of conjured little castles, and anyway, Mother didn't like the moat water splashing across the floor and dripping on the heads of visitors in the rooms below. Yet another molehill made into a mountain.

"Maybe we can have a good pillow fight," Melody suggested. She wore her customary green dress, to go with her green/blonde hair. She was most like her mother Ivy, including her blue eyes. "And bash the pillows to splintereens."

"Maybe we can conjure pillows with stink horns in them," Harmony said. Her dress was brown, to match her hair and eyes. She was most like her father, Grey Murphy. "And stink up the whole castle."

"No, we got in trouble the last time we did that," Rhythm said. Her dress was red, matching her hair but not her green eyes. She was most like her big cousin Dawn. "Mother raised almost as much of a stink as we did."

The three burst into titillations of mirth. That had indeed been fun, despite Mother's overreaction. After all, it had required only three days and four fumigation spells to deodorize the castle.

So that option too was gone. The three sat on a bed and settled into half a funk. There was nothing whatsoever to do.

There was a swirl of smoke in the center of the room. In a moment it formed an eye near the top. "You three look door," the eye observed.

"Look how?" Melody asked.

"Sad, dejected, sullen, moody, gloomy, all entrances closed—"

"Dour?" Harmony asked.

"Whatever," the eye agreed, squinting irritably.

"It's the demoness with the speech impediment," Rhythm said.

"Oh, hi, Metria," Melody said.

"Yes, we are dourer than dour," Harmony added.

"Because we have nothing to do," Rhythm concluded.

The smoke formed into a lovely demoness. This was D. Metria, who had married, gotten half a soul, signaled the stork approximately fifteen hundred times in two years, and finally got its attention. Her half demon son, Demon Ted, was the result. He was the same age as the triplets, and could be fun when he chose to be, because he had crazy naughty boy notions.

"How would you like the company of Ted and Monica?" Metria asked.

"Sure!" the three said together. DeMonica was the half demon daughter of Demon Vore and Princess Nada Naga, and she was fun because she had naughty girl notions. She was also four years old. Mother did not really approve of the children's association with Ted and Monica, which made it all the more fun.

Metria dissolved back into smoke. It formed into a ball, and the ball divided into two parts, which drifted to the floor. One part shaped into a little boy, and the other a little girl. The boy wore blue shorts and blue sneakers, while the girl wore a pink dress with pink sandals, and a red ribbon in her hair. "Hi, triples!" they said together. "Why so glum?"

"We're all out of mischief," Melody explained.

"We can fix that," Ted said, smiling so broadly that the corners of his mouth extended into his blond hair.

"Not if Mother catches on," Harmony said.

Monica cocked her head to listen, making her brown hair flop. "She's not close," she concluded. "She won't catch on if we're quiet."

"And if we don't make a smell," Rhythm said.

The others nodded. They had a formula for success.

"So what do you have in mind?" Melody asked.

Ted looked around, making absolutely sure there was no adult within range. "I thought of a way to fathom the Adult Conspiracy."

"OoooOooo!" the triplets said together, putting at least eight O's and some capitals into it. Of all the nuisances fostered by adults, that was the worst. They absolutely refused to let children learn certain potent words, or find out how the storks were signaled to deliver babies. It was a tyranny that oppressed every child. If Ted had truly found a way to get past that, it was the discovery of the millennium. Childhood would never be the same.

But Monica was suspicious. "There have been false alarms before," she said. "Like the time you wanted to form a smoke screen we could hide behind so we could see adults doing it."

"Well, how could I know they would wonder what such a big screen was doing in their bedroom?" That of course was the problem with Ted's ideas: there could be aspects he didn't think of. "Anyway, you didn't do any better spying on love springs."

"It's my talent," DeMonica said. "Identifying springs. I just wanted to be sure they really were love springs."

"And they weren't," he retorted.

"You have a magic talent?" Melody asked, impressed.

"You can tell what kind of magic a spring has?" Harmony asked, similarly impressed.

"Well, sometimes I get it wrong," Monica said. "But I know when one is magic, and I'm getting better at types."

"That's a good talent," Rhythm concluded.

"Well, there are no springs here," Ted said, getting jealous.

"Yes there are," Monica said. "And I can identify them: bed springs."

The triplets laughed gleefully. Then they returned to the subject: the quest to fathom the Adult Conspiracy. They had never made much progress before. Still, it was a worthwhile pursuit. If they ever did manage to fathom the dread Conspiracy, they would tell all other children, and never again would any child be tortured by curiosity. "So what's your idea?" Harmony asked.

"You three can conjure up a grown blind man," Ted said eagerly. "And a grown blind woman. So they can't see us and know we're watching. If we don't make a sound, they won't know we're here. Then we can watch while they signal the stork."

They considered this. "Suppose they don't signal the stork?" Rhythm asked.

"But they always signal the stork, when they're alone together," Ted said. "Twice a day."

"That's right," Monica said. "Your mother does it twice a day. That's why she palms you off on other folk for baby-sitting."

"Twice a day," Ted agreed.

"But that doesn't mean that other grown folk do," Monica said. She was less imaginative than Ted, but more sensible.

"What else would they do, when there are no children watching?" Ted asked.

That turned out to be a good question. They couldn't think of anything else adults would do.

So they got to work on it. Melody began to hum, forming the first part of their magic. Harmony made her harmony-ca appear and played it in time, augmenting the magic. Rhythm conjured her little drum and made a beat, completing the magic.

First they formed the image of a grown man. When the image was complete, they solidified him. He stood there, not doing much other than breathing. They didn't yet know how to give a conjuration intelligence, but trusted it wouldn't be needed here. Then they formed the image of a grown woman, and solidified her similarly. The man was moderately handsome, and the woman was halfway pretty. Not that it much mattered, because neither had any eyes; they had been drawn blind.

Now there was a problem. The figures were blind because the children didn't want to be seen. But that meant they couldn't see each other, either; they didn't know they weren't quite alone. However, after a moment they had the man raise one hand, and the woman raise a hand, and the hands banged together so they found each other.

What would they do next? The children waited in absolute silence.

The door opened. There was Mother. "What are you up to?" she demanded.

The figures popped out of existence, and the triplets assumed an expression of perfect innocence. But not quite fast enough. Princess Ivy caught half a glimpse of the conjured figures. "So you are trying to undermine the Conspiracy!" she said severely.

They were fairly caught. "How did you know?" Melody asked.

"You were too quiet."

What irony. Their very silence had betrayed them. Now they were in trouble. Again. As usual.

Then Mother saw Demon Ted and DeMonica. "I should have known," she muttered. "Little demons."

There was nothing they could say, for she was at least half right. But there was seldom anything to be said when an adult got an Attitude. They just had to wait for the storm to pass.

"It is time you got some education," Ivy said severely. It was obvious that she had never been a child. "Now you sit there and watch the Magic Tapestry until you learn something." She departed, closing the door decisively behind her.

Now they were in for truly awful dullness. The Magic Tapestry hung on their wall, as it had for generations, and showed nothing but animated Xanth scenes, past and present. The little woven figures came to life, in a manner, when they were watched, and reenacted their bits of Xanthly lore. It was very educational, which was what made it so dull. It had a spell on it that their friend Breanna of the Black Wave called a V-chip: it chipped out key sections, which made the scenes very dull. No storks at all. If they watched it enough, it would show them all sanitized Xanth History. What a bore.

They saw an animal wandering. "What's that?" Melody asked.

"Must be a werewolf," Harmony said.

"No, it's Mundane," Rhythm concluded.

They focused on the creature, which had a little sign dangling from his collar. It had words on it, but they couldn't make them out, and anyway, they didn't know how to read.

"He looks lonely," Melody said.

"Maybe we should 'dopt him," Harmony agreed.

"Mom would never let us," Rhythm said. She was obviously right. So, reluctantly, they let the dog wander off the scene, and wished they could wander with him.

But they had no choice. They set it for Recent History. They happened to spy a night mare racing across the scenery with her cargo of bad dreams. The picture she was going toward had a man just settling down to sleep beside a pleasant spring. Obviously the dream was for him; the mare would arrive just after he fell asleep. The moonlight was bright.

But the night mare tripped on a stick just as she got there. The noise made the man wake, and he saw her. She tried to turn and retreat, because bad dreams just didn't work on waking folk. But both misjudged their steps, and fell into the pool. Water splashed up, soaking them—and little hearts flew out in patterns.

"It's a love spring!" Monica exclaimed. "How romantic!"

"Hey—maybe we'll see them signal the stork!" Ted said.

It was too late for man and night mare to escape; they had seen each other and fallen in love. They came together—and at that point a nasty cloud hid the moon, and the scene went dark. That always happened, frustratingly.

When the light returned, both man and mare were gone. There was a blink, signaling elapsed time, and then a young centaur appeared. He was about three years old, black like the night mare, and his face resembled that of the prior man. He was the offspring the stork had delivered to the love-spring folk.

The centaur walked oddly, moving from one shadowed section to another. Soon it was apparent that he was shadow-walking: going between shadows. He was solid, like his father, but walked in darkness like his mother. That was an interesting combination.

Then the centaur encountered a regular man, wearing a dull gray shirt. They talked, but the Tapestry did not give sounds, so what they said wasn't audible. But probably the centaur was explaining how he had come to be. He seemed to have a good future ahead of him, because he could move quite rapidly between shadows, jumping from one to another, yet do something solid when he got somewhere.

The man in the gray shirt did something odd. He turned half real. His form left the scene, and a mere trace traveled backward in time; they could tell because all the other scenes on the Tapestry were now running backward. This was weird; the children had not seen this effect before.

The shirt-man came to the love spring, four years before, where the first man was settling down for the night. The shirt-man solidified and went to the place where the night mare would soon trip on the stick. He picked out the stick and set it in the brush where it wouldn't be in the way. Then the shirt-man faded out and zipped back to the place and time when/where he had encountered the special centaur. But the centaur was no longer there. Satisfied, the shirt-man walked on.

"I don't understand," Melody said. "What happened to the centaur?"

"Oooo," Harmony continued. Four O's was all she could manage alone. "I think I know. That stick—he moved that stick."

"And that means the night mare didn't stumble over it," Rhythm concluded.

"So the sleeping man didn't wake," Ted said.

"And so he received the bad dream, just as he was supposed to," Monica said.

"And there was no meeting in the love spring," Melody added.

"So they didn't signal the stork," Harmony said.

"And no centaur was delivered," Rhythm finished.

They sat on the bed, mulling it over. "That man in the shirt," Ted said. "He did it on purpose!"

"He traveled back and stopped the mare from meeting the man," Melody said.

"He unhappened it," Harmony said.

"What a dastardly deed!" Rhythm said.

Ted for once was thoughtful. "If he did that to the centaur, what will he do to other folk he doesn't like?"

"Suppose he doesn't like *us*?" Melody asked.

That made them all thoughtful. "Maybe we better tell Mother," Harmony said.

"But she always says no," Harmony said.

"Maybe we better do something about it ourselves," Melody said. "That man can travel in time; nobody else can do that, except maybe us."

The more they considered it, the more they thought they should. For one thing, it would alleviate the boredom.

They marshaled their arguments, then called Mother. Princess Ivy listened to them, then watched the replay of the unhappening on the Magic Tapestry. She called Father Grey.

"What do you think?"

"I think they should go ask the Good Magician," he said. "It will be good practice for them, sharpening their talent, and his advice should be good."

"But what about the year's service he charges for an Answer?" Ivy asked.

"Maybe he will waive that, if their mission is important enough."

They weren't saying no! That was almost suspicious, but the girls didn't hesitate. "Yes, we'll go," Rhythm said.

Grey glanced down at them. "But maybe this should be our secret," he said. "So that Queen Irene doesn't hear about it."

Grandma Irene would absolutely, positively, definitely say no. "Secret," Melody agreed.

"That includes you two," Ivy said to Ted and Monica.

"Sure!" the two half demons agreed together. They liked secrets almost as well as mischief. "We'll help!" Ted added.

"It's a great secret," Monica said.

"What's this about a secret?" Demon Vore inquired, materializing. He had come to pick up the half demons and take them home, as usual.

Grey and Ivy exchanged most of a glance. "Can't readily keep secrets from demons," Grey said.

"Perhaps tell only the demon parents," Ivy suggested.

So they told D. Vore, and he agreed that D. Metria would be the only other person told. Then he swept up Ted and Monica and faded out.

So it was that the three little princesses made their first excursion on their own. Next morning they sang and played a large magic carpet into existence, and climbed onto it. It was a bit unsteady at first, and listed to one side, but they kept working on it until it was firm. Then they floated out the window. They were on their way.

They floated not too far above the ground, being nervous about going very high. They also did not go very fast, afraid the wind would blow them off. This was quite enough adventure, for now.

Once they had the carpet stable and moving steadily, they lifted it to just above tree height and headed toward the Good Magician's castle. They knew it would take a while, but they were satisfied.

Then they had time to reconsider. "How come they didn't say no?" Melody asked.

"Maybe they realized we're big enough to do our own things," Harmony said.

Rhythm burst out laughing. After a moment the other two joined her. Obviously the adults had some other reason.

"Maybe they want us out of the way so they can rest," Harmony said.

That seemed reasonable. Then Rhythm came up with the best one: "They must want more time to signal the stork."

That certainly explained it. Satisfied, the three forged on.

A cloud appeared ahead. "Oopsy," Melody said. "That looks like Fracto."

"In a bad mood," Harmony said.

"He's always in a bad mood," Rhythm said.

They tried to avoid the notice of the bad cloud, but Fracto had already spied them. He floated toward them, puffing larger.

"He's going to try to blow us away," Melody said.

"Or wet on us," Harmony added.

"Or lose us in fog," Rhythm concluded.

A huge face formed on the cloud. Wind whistled through the big mouth. "AAAALLL OF THEEEE ABBOOOOVVE!" it gusted.

They pondered, considered, and thought, but time was too short to allow them to contemplate. They had to act quickly.

"Let's each think of something," Melody suggested.

"And each make it exist," Harmony agreed.

"And use it to mess up Fracto," Rhythm finished.

They concentrated. Melody thought of a cold snap. She snapped her fingers, and the carpet and air around them turned cold. That didn't help, because it made them cold without bothering Fracto, who reveled in cold air and hot air and turbulent mixings of the two.

Fracto's mouth blew out more gusts: "HHOOO HHOOO HHOOO!" it laughed.

Harmony thought of a compact disc. She formed it and held it before her. It was small but marvelously shiny. She threw it toward the cloud, and it skated along, whirling, and when it struck the cloud it compacted the cloud flat. Fracto went whoosh and became a big spinning disk. But that didn't stop him long; he whirled so fast he flew apart, and then reformed as a larger, fiercer cloud. Now he was annoyed.

"NNNNOOO   MOOOORRE   MIISSTTER   NNNIICCCEEE
GGUUYYY!"

Rhythm knew she needed something more effective. She conjured
something she had barely heard of. It looked like a line of obscure numbers.

"What do you have?" Melody asked.

"It's a Dow Jones."

"What does it do?" Harmony asked.

"It's supposed to make things rise or fall when certain magic words
are spoken."

"What are the words?" Melody asked.

"I can't remember!" Rhythm wailed.

Meanwhile, Fracto was looming almost over them. In a moment he
would fog them, wet them, and blow them away.

They guessed desperately at words. "Hello and good-bye," Melody
said, but nothing happened.

"Eye Scream and chocolate sauce," Harmony said. Nothing happened.

"Hugs and kisses," Rhythm said. Nothing.

Fracto surrounded them, marshaling his fog.

"Joy and grief."

"Buttons and bows."

"I think it's animals," Rhythm said, almost remembering.

Fracto filled a bowl-shaped cloudlet with water, sailed it directly over
them, and began to tilt it. They were about to be wet on. This wasn't
exactly a fate worse than spinach for supper, but they hated to let the
mean cloud win.

"Dragons and griffins," Melody cried.

"Werewolves and night mares," Harmony called.

"Spiders and bugs," Rhythm shouted.

The water came down on their heads, soaking them. "Eeeek!" Melody shrieked, putting all the E's into it her age allowed. Next year she
would be able to manage five.

"We're all wet!" Harmony cried, pulling off her soaking brown dress.

The others did the same. "We're all bare," Rhythm said, shivering.
Then a light bulb flashed over her head. "Bear!" she exclaimed.

The carpet dropped toward the ground. She had found one of the words. Bears crunched down.

Fracto pursued them, pouring more water.

"What's the other word?" Melody asked as she clutched the sinking carpet.

"Yes, what makes things rise?" Harmony asked as she hung on to their loose dresses.

Rhythm remembered. "Bull! It leaps up!"

The carpet stopped falling and started to rise.

Fracto blew at them. The Dow Jones flew from Rhythm's hand and disappeared into the boiling mist. They had lost it.

But now they had the word. Quickly they got together. Melody hummed, Harmony played her harmonica, and Rhythm beat her drum. "BULL!" they sang together.

Fracto suddenly rose straight up, trailing cloudlets of fog. He rose so high that the weird magic of perspective came into play, making him small. The bright sun was uncovered, and shone down warmly. They sang and played to enhance the warmth, drying their dresses, and soon everything was all right.

"I guess that blew *him* away," Melody said with satisfaction.

"I guess that parade dried up his rain," Harmony agreed.

"I guess that fogged his bottom," Rhythm said, and they all burst out laughing.

Much cheered, they resumed their flight to the Good Magician's castle. They had proven once again that while any one of them might be bested despite being a Sorceress, the three of them together were something else.

Soon the castle came into sight. They landed and let the magic carpet fade away.

The Good Magician's residence was familiar in its unfamiliarity; each time they saw it, it was different. Oh, it had the usual turrets and spires and parapets and all; they were just in a different arrangement. The moat was there, but this time it was surrounded by a garden of S-shaped flowers. A sign identified it: NATURE. There was a fierce looking animal chained before the drawbridge. A sign there said ITION. A woman relaxed on a deck chair at the edge of the garden. A sign by her said A. CAUSE.

"This is a Challenge," Melody said, recognizing the type.

"That means the Good Magician is expecting us," Harmony agreed.

"And will Answer our question," Rhythm finished.

They reviewed the Challenge. Obviously the toothy creature was there to chomp anybody who tried to use the drawbridge. The garden must belong to the woman, who liked the flowers.

"Maybe we can crawl behind the flowers so the beast won't see us," Melody said.

They tried it. But the moment they got near one of the flowers, it hissed "Sig!" and waved violently around.

The toothy creature's sharp ears perked up. "Ition! Ition!" it barked. That explained its odd name.

The woman stirred. "What is it, pet?"

"This isn't working," Harmony whispered.

"The flowers make a commotion," Rhythm said.

They backed away. The flower stopped waving, and the beast settled down. So did the woman.

"We'll have to use our magic," Melody said.

"Is that allowed?" Harmony asked.

"I think so," Rhythm concluded.

They sang and played to make a slumber spell to put the animal to sleep. But it didn't work; instead the animal perked up again and growled, peering all around.

"Maybe not," Melody said.

"We must have to get through without our magic," Harmony agreed.

"By figuring out the Challenge," Rhythm concluded.

They discussed it. It was Harmony's turn to think of something. "Maybe we have to ask the woman to take away her pet," she said.

"Maybe," Rhythm agreed.

They walked around the garden and approached the woman. "Please, miz," Melody said. "Will you take your pet away so we can cross the bridge?"

The woman turned a gaze on them that reeked of adult contempt. "I will not," she said.

"And maybe not," Harmony said.

They discussed it some more. They had tried two ideas, and would run out after the next, so it had to be good.

"We tried going around the flowers, and that didn't work," Rhythm said. "We tried asking the woman, and that didn't work. So maybe we should ask the beast."

"But it's got teeth!" Melody protested.

"We thought the flowers would be friendly, and they weren't," Harmony pointed out.

"We thought Miz Cause would be friendly, and she wasn't," Rhythm said. "Maybe we're wrong about Ition."

The notion of princesses being wrong was formidable, but after some struggle they agreed that it was remotely possible. They were, after all, *little* princesses. So they nerved themselves and walked down the center path toward the creature.

"Hello, Ition," Melody said bravely.

The beast wagged his tail. "Woof!"

He was friendly!

"Will you let us pass?" Harmony asked.

Ition shook his head. It seemed he wasn't quite that friendly.

"Maybe if we do something for you?" Rhythm asked.

The beast wagged his tail.

"Like what?" Melody asked.

Ition strained at his chain.

"Like petting you?" Harmony asked.

He shook his head.

"Like letting you loose!" Rhythm concluded.

The beast nodded.

So Melody nerved herself and went close to the creature. She reached for his collar and found the snap. She unsnapped the chain. She froze, afraid of what might happen next. Normally they could protect themselves against just about any monster, but that was when they had their magic. It was scary being without it.

The creature ran through the garden, picking the peculiar flowers. He gathered a bunch and carried them to the woman. "Why thank you, pet," she said, accepting them. Then she turned to the three little princesses. "What do you suppose is happening here?"

They were taken aback, but they thought about it. "The beast is bringing you flowers," Melody said.

"Not necessarily," the woman said, which was the adult way of saying no.

"Ition is fetching sig flowers for Miz Cause," Harmony said.

"Perhaps," the woman said, which was adult for maybe.

Then a bulb flashed above Rhythm's head, as it had before. She was often the one to get the brightest ideas. "Pet Ition is collecting sig natures for A. Cause!" she exclaimed.

The woman smiled. "Certainly." That was the adult way of saying yes. "You may go now."

They went—across the drawbridge. But at the other side of it was a huge pile of junk. It completely blocked the entrance to the castle.

"I think this is another Challenge," Melody said.

They stared at the pile. There were all manner of things in it, ranging from pieces of paper to a kitchen sink. There was far too much for them to move, unless they used magic.

So they tried magic, just in case. They sang and played, trying to make the huge pile light enough to float away, but it just seemed to get heavier, settling down a notch. So magic was not going to do this one either.

They looked around. To the side was a pit, and in the pit was what looked like a bespectacled man. He was reading a book. That was all; the rest of the pit was completely bare.

"This must relate," Harmony said.

"Somehow," Rhythm said.

"Hello," Melody called to the man.

He looked up. "Do you have something to eat?" he asked.

They hadn't thought to bring any food. "No," Harmony said.

"I've got to eat!" the man cried. Then he took a bite out of his book.

They stared down at him, as he consumed the rest of the book. He was really hungry!

"Junk and a hungry man," Rhythm said. "We have to figure out how it works."

"Maybe he could help us clear that junk away from the door," Melody said.

"If we just had something for him to eat," Harmony said.

"And I guess he'll eat almost anything," Rhythm said.

They looked at each other. There was the odor of a pun in the neighborhood. A bulb flashed over their heads. They couldn't be sure whose light it was.

They fetched some of the smaller debris from the pile and tossed it into the pit. The man grabbed it and gobbled it up. Soon they uncovered an old wooden ladder. They struggled to drag it to the pit.

"Don't eat this!" Melody called to the man. "Use it to get out of the pit. Then you can eat all the junk by the door."

They slid the ladder into the pit. The man managed to control his hunger long enough to lean the ladder against the side and scramble up and out. Then he ran for the pile of junk and began eating. He just stuffed objects into his mouth and chewed them up so rapidly that fragments flew out. It was amazing. Before long the whole pile was gone, and the doorway was clear.

"He ate the litter," Harmony remarked.

"He's litter-ate," Rhythm said, completing the pun.

Then the literate man went back to eat the ladder, and the three little princesses walked into the castle.

Inside they came to a river. They paused, surprised; usually rivers were outside of castles rather than inside. They walked beside it, until they came to an irritable-looking child about as old as the three of them put together. "Go away," he said.

But by this time the princesses did not much feel like being stupidly balked. "Who says?" Melody asked.

"I say," the boy said.

"You and who else?" Harmony asked.

"Me and my tangle tree." The boy gestured, and they saw a tangle tree growing right by the path they had to follow to get the rest of the way into the castle. It was beside the water, growing from the river bank. "That's my talent: controlling tangle trees."

It was the third Challenge. What were they to do?

They tried reasoning with the boy, but he was completely unreasonable, as boys tended to be. He was not about to let them pass, no way, not at all. They tried to approach the tree, but its green tentacles twitched menacingly. They tried to pacify it with magic, just in case, but had no success. They had to figure out the correct way.

"This has all been puns so far," Melody said.

"That's because Xanth is mostly made of puns," Harmony said.

"So maybe this is another pun," Rhythm concluded.

Melody looked at the tree. "Are we getting into a tangle?"

Harmony looked at the river. "Are we all washed up?"

Rhythm looked at the path. "Is this the route to trouble?"

"Oh, put a sock in it, you little twits," the boy said nastily. "You'll never figure it out."

This annoyed them, so they concentrated really hard. There was a boy. What did boys do? They were obnoxious. There was a tree. What did trees do? They grew leaves, except for tangle trees, which grew tentacles. There was a river. What did rivers do? They flowed.

They weren't getting anywhere, so they changed places and tried again from their new perspectives. The boy, the tree, the river. The tentacles, the river bank, the path. Still nothing. They just weren't as good at using their minds as they were with their magic, and now that they couldn't use their magic, they weren't getting anywhere.

So they tried observation. The boy had curly black hair and a perpetual sneer. The river had a gently sloping bank. The tangle tree actually leaned out over the river, but not so much as to prevent it from grabbing anyone who tried to pass on the other side.

"Lean," Melody said, trying to catch a fleeting notion.

"Bank," Harmony said, pursuing another faint idea.

A bulb flashed over Rhythm's head. "Banks take leans," she said. A passing spelling bee looked disgusted. It flew in loops, spelling out LIENS, but they ignored it.

The tangle tree leaned further. In a moment it splashed into the river. "Spoilsport!" the boy said, and walked away.

They had unriddled the third pun. They followed the path to a door. The door led into an anteroom. A woman was waiting for them. "Hello, Princesses," she said.

"Hi, Wira," the three chorused, hugging her from three small sides. Wira was the Good Magician's son Hugo's wife, and she was really nice. Also blind. But she had no trouble in the castle, because she knew exactly where everything was.

"The Good Magician is expecting you."

"We know," they said.

They followed her into the rest of the castle.

3
PURPOSE

If anyone except the Good Magician had told her to do this, Becka wouldn't have believed it. She could tell already that the Dastard was nobody she would ordinarily care to associate with. He was nothing special in appearance, with hair colored hair, eye colored eyes, skin colored skin, and dingy dull clothing. His character was worse. She thought he had tried to kiss her against her will, and she had had to turn dragon to stop him. Actually that hadn't happened; it was just a stupid daydream, but she still didn't trust him.

"Why did you go to the Good Magician?" the Dastard asked her.

There seemed to be no harm in answering. It wasn't exactly a secret. "I wanted to know my purpose in life."

"What did he say?"

"That my purpose was to effect the welfare of Xanth."

"How can you affect it?"

"Effect, not affect. I don't know how."

The man considered. "You intrigue me," he said.

Then nothing happened, but she had the distinct impression he might have wanted to do something dastardly, like pulling up her skirt to see her panties, and she might have had to turn dragon and chomp his hand. He hadn't, of course, and she hadn't, but there was an odd half-memory,

as though it might have been, maybe in some other realm. It was un-
settling. "I'm supposed to help you," she said. "That's all."

"Then fetch me something to eat."

So he thought she was some kind of servant. That rankled. But maybe
that was the way she was supposed to help him, to effect the welfare of
Xanth, far-fetched as it seemed. So she explored the area, looking for
food.

She spied a group of cat tails growing in a swampy section. Some
varieties of those were edible, so she went to pull some off. But the first
one she grabbed made a horrendous screech. Then the cat tore out of
the ground and bounded away. Oh. For some stupid reason she had
thought it was a plant.

She saw a tree with a number of unfamiliar fruits. Those might be
good. She went to pick one that looked like a little bomb, but it exploded
at her touch, splattering juice all around. It wasn't a cherry; it must have
been overripe. She tried another, that looked somewhat wasted, but its
touch made her feel devastated. The third one resisted her pull, refusing
to be plucked. The fourth one was tangled up in vines and thorns, making
it too much of a project to get to it. What was going on here?

Then she recognized the type of tree. It was a shun tree, whose
seeming fruits were really bad seeds. The seeds of destruc-shun, devasta-
shun, opposi-shun, complica-shun and the like. Smart folk shunned this
tree, as it bore nothing worthwhile.

She saw several sleepy looking plants with fruits like buttons. Those
might be good. She picked one, and was about to eat it, when she hesitated; she vaguely remembered something like this, and it wasn't necessarily good. So she merely touched her tongue to it.

Sure enough, she suddenly felt drowsy. It was a snooze button, that
tasted good but put people to sleep. She hardly needed this.

Then she reconsidered, and picked several buttons and put them in
her handbag. They might after all be useful some time—for someone
else.

She went on, and encountered a walking shape. It seemed to be a
book, but it wore a skirt. "Hello," she said uncertainly. "If you don't
mind my asking—what are you?"

"I am Novella," the book replied. "A small female novel. Isn't it
obvious?"

In retrospect, it was. "I guess I'm not much of a reader," Becka said, embarrassed. "I'm just looking for something to eat."

"Food can be a long story," Novella said. "I think the chain smoker knows where there's some. He's right over there." She pointed with a page.

"Thank you." Becka went to the chain smoker, who was a man sitting with his back against a tree-trunk, smoking a long chain. "Sir Smoker, can you tell me where there is some food?"

"My friend the pack-rat has plenty," Chain replied. He patted the head of the rat sitting next to him.

The pack-rat obligingly opened his knapsack and gave her several rocks and what looked like a squashed squash.

"But this isn't food," she protested. "It's pyrite and gneiss and disgusting gourd refuse."

"Yes it is," Smoker said. "That's pie-right, and nice, and a pun-kin pie."

Becka looked again. So it was. "Oh. Thank you very much." She wrapped the pies in a section of sheet and carried them back the way she had come.

The Dastard was not grateful. "What's this sheet?" he demanded.

"That's just a piece of sheet rock I used to wrap the pies," Becka explained. "To keep them clean."

He lifted one of the pun-kin pies. "I recognize this. If I take one bite, I'll be emitting foul puns for the next hour."

Becka had forgotten about that quality of the pies. "Then I'll eat them," she said regretfully, for she was hungry.

"Then I'll have to listen to *you* emitting the stinking things," he complained. "Throw them away."

She realized he was right. It was bad enough when men ate pun-kin; for girls it was downright unladylike. She knew they tasted good enough, but they did cause pundigestion, and nobody else could stand to be in the company of someone constantly letting fly with the filthy things.

Reluctantly she took the pun-kin pies and set them on a small round stone she saw nearby. Immediately they sank into the stone, and an arrow in it spun around to point at the remaining smear. Oh, no—she had converted it into a pun dial! Careless disposal of pun refuse was dangerous; it contaminated everything it touched.

Becka ate a leftover piece of pie, but part of it had hardened into stone; when she unwittingly chewed down on it, it knocked out a tooth. Ouch! Fortunately she had some tooth paste in her emergency kit. She brought it out, spread it on the tooth, and put it back in her mouth. The paste attached it securely back, just about as good as new. There was nothing like being prepared.

By this time they had wandered away from the statue of the Sea Hag, which was a relief; Becka had heard ugly stories about that ugly Sorceress. Why anyone would want to commemorate her life history was beyond her.

Another person was coming along the path toward them. It seemed to be a huge face with little arms and legs. "What in Xanth are you?" the Dastard asked it.

"I'm an Interface," the thing replied. "I can make things easy or hard."

"Make *what* things easy or hard?"

"Well, like relating to something," Interface said. "For example, if you were trying to relate to that girl with you, I could make it much easier—or much harder. That's my talent: to make things relate, one way or another."

The Dastard considered. He glanced sidelong at Becka in a way she didn't like. "So you could make her show me her panties?"

"Now wait a minute!" Becka protested.

"Sure," Interface said.

"Go ahead then. Do it."

"No way!" Becka snapped.

"No."

"What?" The Dastard was clearly annoyed.

"I said no. She's too young."

"What if I say she's not?"

"Doesn't matter. She's obviously only fourteen. Four years before she can show anything like that."

Becka knew of girls who had done it before then, but she decided to keep her mouth shut.

"Do it anyway," the Dastard said.

"Say, what are you?" Interface demanded. "Some kind of pervert?"

"I'm the Dastard. I do dastardly deeds. It's my nature. I'm trying to get this girl to be of some use to me. So are you going to do it?"

"Of course not. Instead, I'll make you relate to that boulder over there. Like head first at high velocity." Interface began to concentrate.

Suddenly Interface was walking down the path toward them. "What in Xanth are you?" the Dastard asked.

"I'm an Interface," the thing replied.

Becka was astonished. This scene had happened just about three moments ago. How could it be happening again?

Meanwhile, Interface explained about its talent. Becka braced herself for the Dastard's dastardly question—but this time he didn't ask it. Instead he said "That's interesting," obviously bored, and walked on by.

Becka was having trouble assimilating this. Finally she asked "What happened?"

"Nothing happened," the Dastard replied blithely.

"Yes it did. The Interface met us twice. It—"

"Oh, that. That's my talent. I make things unhappen."

"You tried to get it to make me show my panties!" she said accusingly.

"Well, it was worth a try."

"You're not even sorry!"

"Of course not," he agreed. "Why should I be? I'm sure they're a fine sight."

"Don't you even have a conscience?"

The Dastard paused, thinking. "I suppose I don't. I used to; I know, because it kept getting in my way. But it hasn't bothered me since I made the deal with the demon, trading my soul for this talent. The conscience must have gone with the soul."

"You have no soul?" she asked, appalled.

"None," he agreed, satisfied.

"But how can you live that way? Everybody needs a soul."

"I don't. I get along just fine without mine."

"So when you tried to see my—you have no morality at all!"

"Right. So why don't you either give up your foolish reluctance, or go somewhere else?"

Becka really wanted to be somewhere else. But the Good Magician had sent her here to help this despicable man, so she was committed. "No. I'm not going, and not showing."

"Too bad," he said indifferently.

But she wasn't through figuring things out. "You tried before! But I turned dragon, so you unhappened it."

He turned to her. "Now that's interesting. You actually remember?"

"Some. I thought I was just imagining it. But it happened, didn't it?"

"Yes. Happened and unhappened. The first time I tried to kiss you. The second time to pull up your skirt. I got a good look, too."

"You did not!" she flared, reddening. "I turned dragon before you saw anything."

He nodded. "So you *do* remember. Nobody else does. You must have a bit of extra talent."

"You're trying to see underage panties—and you don't care at all!" She was so angry she was starting to see around trees.

"Certainly I care. I'm frustrated because my effort was wasted. All I can see is your stupid feet."

"I ought to turn dragon now and chomp you!"

The Dastard was unimpressed. "I'd only unhappen it. You may remember, but you won't get to chomp."

He was probably right. That made her madder than ever. Then she remembered the snooze buttons she had saved. If she sneaked one of those into his food, he would fall asleep, and then she would be able to chomp him. If he ever succeeded in getting a dirty look at her panties, she would do that. But until then she would try to follow the Good Magician's directive, and remain to help this utter cad in some way. She had heard that the Good Magician's Answers could seem irrelevant or crazy, but always made sense in the end. She had to hope that this Service also made sense. Somehow. Eventually. By some incredible coincidence.

Another creature came down the path. This was a busy route! This one looked like a wolf. Could it be that lonesome dog she had almost seen before? No, it looked different.

"What are you?" the Dastard asked it.

"I am a who-what-where-wolf by the name of How?LL," he replied. "I have a real nose for news, and a tail for truth."

"Well, can you tell me how I'll get to see the panties of this obdurate girl?"

Becka shuddered. The man had no shame at all. Shame must be another quality of conscience or soul.

The wolf looked at Becka. "No. She's underage."

The Dastard looked so frustrated he seemed about to burst. He didn't, but she did: Becka burst out laughing. She couldn't help herself. It was so great to see the heel balked.

But this time the Dastard didn't make it unhappen. Instead he continued to question How?LL. "What else can you tell me?"

How?LL took a step forward and sniffed him. "You are a man without a soul," he said. "And a devastatingly devious magic talent."

"Don't bother with the flattery. Will I succeed in my objectives?"

"That depends on what your objectives are."

"To do dastardly deeds, mess up Xanth, become somebody, and marry a princess."

How?LL pondered a moment. "I'm much better at sniffing out the past than the future. It does seem likely that you will succeed, considering the indications, but I can't be quite sure. There is a force gathering against you that may succeed in stopping you."

"What force?" the Dastard demanded.

How?LL pondered again. "I can't quite smell it. It's far away, and secret. It may be fathomable, as there seems to be more than ten folk who know it, but I can't quite sniff it out. This girl has something to do with it."

"You mean to tell me that this balky girl who will neither show me anything interesting nor go away is conspiring against me?"

"No. She's innocent. But she relates in some devious improbable way that no one will ever guess until it happens."

"Can you tell me anything else?"

"No. There is too much vagueness surrounding you, because of the way you change what happens."

Becka blinked. The who-what-where-wolf was coming down the path toward them. "You unhappened that dialogue," she said.

"Of course. I don't want him knowing what I'm doing."

Was there no end to this man's deviousness?

How?LL came close. "Where is there a good camping place?" the Dastard asked him.

"Not far on along this path," How?LL replied.

"Thank you." The Dastard walked on without pausing for further dialogue. The wolf continued in the other direction, unaware that there had ever been anything more.

"So you used him, then unhappened it," Becka said. "But I remember. Are you going to unhappen me?"

"I can't unhappen people," the Dastard said seriously. "I merely change their encounters with me."

"Why do I think you're not telling me the whole truth?"

"Because I'm not. I see you're not entirely dull."

"So you'll find out all you can about how I relate to the force against you, then unhappen our whole interaction?"

"Of course."

Becka decided to gamble. "You're lying."

He was unbothered. "You know, I could almost get to like you, if you showed me your—"

"No!"

He sighed. "If I tell you more of the truth, will you show me more of—"

"No!"

"Then you hardly seem worth my company."

Becka realized that he didn't really want her company. He was trying to make her go away. But why should he bother to do that, when he could readily unhappen their entire association, remembering all of it himself? That would get rid of her most effectively. Yet he wasn't doing that. This didn't seem to make sense.

So she gambled. "Well, I'm not leaving. And I'm not showing you anything. So go ahead and unhappen our association."

"What a mean spirited tart you are."

"And I'll get meaner, if you don't get rid of me. So do it. Why wait? I'll only get in your way."

"You think I won't?"

"Yes, I think you won't. Because I think you can't."

"I don't want to get rid of you until I know exactly how you relate to the force against me. Obviously the Good Magician sent you to me for some devious reason. I need to know that reason, so I can foil it."

"I can't tell you, because I don't know it myself. But I'll be glad to foil you, if I can. So you might as well get rid of me, or admit you can't."

He considered again. "If I tell you the whole truth, will you be my servant without baiting me?"

That was a different offer. She didn't care to be his or anybody's servant, but she did want to fulfill her obligation to the Good Magician, and she was getting really curious about the Dastard's devious magic. "No. I'll help you with routine things, the way the Good Magician told me to, but that's all. I'm nobody's servant." Saying that made her feel better.

"Then how about not interfering with me?"

"Interfering?" she asked blankly.

"Trying to mess up what I do."

"How could I do that?"

"If I tell you, you'll try to foil me. So I can't tell you unless you agree not to."

Oh. She thought about it, and realized that he had a point. The Good Magician hadn't told her to foil the Dastard, however much she might want to, but to help him. So maybe it was better to let that be. "Okay. If you promise not to try to look at my—"

"$$$$!" he swore. "You closed the loophole."

Her ears were momentarily stunned by the bad word. She had never heard it before, but recognized its nature. She refused to let him think he could freak her out, so she concealed her disorientation. "Well?"

"Very well. But you had better be an excellent servant."

"I'm *not* a servant. I'm just agreeing not to try to foil you or mess you up. I do have some pride."

"All right. Here is the whole truth. Once I have unhappened something with a person, I can't unhappen it again, because that would be treading on my own trail, as it were. I can unhappen something else with that person, but I can't go back to the first unhappening. So the first time I unhappened you, at the time of the kiss, I lost the ability to wipe out the rest of the interaction, because that would unhappen the first unhappening."

Becka found this too confusing to digest immediately, but she concluded that he was telling the truth. "Then why did you do it?"

"You caught me by surprise, the first time you turned dragon. I unhappened it automatically. I suspect the Good Magician knew it would be that way. So he stuck me with you."

That did make sense. It was the kind of devious logic the Good Magician was reputed to have. His reason for sending her here was beginning to clarify. "What else?"

"I can unhappen things going back as far as four years ago, when I got my talent. And I can unhappen myself as far back as a day, if I haven't unhappened something else in that time."

"Yourself? So you don't remember what you did?"

"No. I always remember. But sometimes I need to get out of a spot picklement."

"I can't think why," Becka said dryly.

He missed her sarcasm. "Last time it happened was when I kissed a pretty girl, and her brute of a father caught me."

Becka almost laughed. "And you had to get out of there in a hurry!"

"Right. I unhappened the kiss. It remained just as real to me, but not to her." He glanced at Becka. "So if you want to kiss me, I can unhappen it, and—"

"No!" She didn't want to kiss him, and also suspected that there could be a lot more to it, all conveniently unhappened so she couldn't prove a thing if she complained to anyone else. It would be their secret, and the Dastard was a liar, so wouldn't admit it. This also gave her more of a hint why the Dastard hadn't told her to go away at the outset: He wanted to get his hands on a cute girl, one way or another. If she weren't what she was—a dragon girl—she would have been in trouble. As the Good Magician must also have known. She was coming to better appreciate Humfrey's cleverness, though she wasn't at all sure she liked it.

Did she really have the whole truth now? Not quite. "You said you couldn't unhappen people, but I think you were lying. So can you?"

"I hate to waste lies," he said evasively.

She was definitely on to something. "Our deal's no good if you don't tell the whole truth."

He sighed. "Yes, sometimes I can unhappen people, when they're young enough, by preventing their parents from meeting. So I wasn't really using up a valuable lie. I can't unhappen you or anyone over four years old."

Valuable lie? Becka decided not to follow that up, sure she would not appreciate the answer. "Okay."

"And one other thing," the Dastard said. "If I happen to be standing there when you turn over in your sleep, and you show something, that's not my fault."

He never gave up! "That won't be a problem."

The Dastard made a quarter smile. He thought he had reopened the loophole.

They reached the camping place. It was enchanted against dangerous creatures, and there were pie trees growing in fresh abundance. Caterpillars had left two large tents, and there were pillow and blanket bushes. There were even several litterbugs to clean up any litter they might leave. It was ideal.

That night the Dastard retired to one tent, and Becka to the other. She lay down, but didn't bother with a blanket. She knew the Dastard didn't value his given word, and would try to catch a forbidden glimpse of her underclothing as she slept. She wasn't concerned. She changed to dragon form, curled up with her tail across her nose, and slept.

In the morning the Dastard seemed ill of temper. Becka could guess why: He had tried to peek into the tent and see her panties, and spied only the dragon. She suppressed a smile; it served him right. One of the weird things about men was that they were always so eager to see what would freak them out. But nobody accused men of being sensible.

They cleaned up. She did so in dragon form, swimming in the nearby river, then changing back to girl form. She was fortunate in that her dragon scales became her girl clothing; she was never exposed while changing. In her natural form, her girl front was clothed, her dragon rear scaled. She could take off her clothing if she wanted to, but it was easier just to turn dragon, wash her scales, then turn girl with a new outfit.

They ate more pies. Then the Dastard spoke. "There's a nexus."

"A what?"

"A meeting with significant potential. I will discover who it is, and maybe unhappen it, and you won't interfere."

"I agreed not to," she said. "Unlike some folk, I have a conscience. I keep my word."

"I've kept my word with you."

"What, you mean to say you never looked into my tent last night?"

"I mean to say I never saw anything you didn't want to show."

Maybe that counted. The Dastard kept his word when he couldn't help it. "So what makes this encounter different from what I've already seen?"

"All you have seen so far is spot minor unhappenings. This will be a big one."

"If you're going to unhappen it anyway, why bother? Why not just take a different path?"

"Because this is how I get my pleasure in life. By changing things to make other people worse off than I am."

This took more than a passing effort of understanding. "You enjoy making others unhappy?"

"Yes! Because that makes me better off than they are."

"But why don't you just use your talent to make yourself better off without hurting anyone else?"

"I would if I could. I'd like to marry a princess, and spend the rest of my life in useless indolence, much respected by all who meet me. But I haven't found a princess to marry, or even a girl to smooch along the way." He glanced sidelong at Becka, but she turned dragon for just a moment, warning him off. "So it's easier to make others worse off."

He did have a point, of a sort. But she was short on sympathy, knowing his nature. "Well then, maybe you should just find a princess to smooch, instead of messing with unimportant folk."

"If I find one, I will certainly do my best to win her. Meanwhile, I'll continue to seek nexi."

Becka wondered if she was supposed to help him find a princess. But she didn't know any princesses. "Okay, I'll just watch and not interfere."

"Thank you," he said insincerely. "This way." He walked back along the path they had followed the day before.

"But we've already been there," she protested.

"I have a sense about it. I go where there is a nexus. I don't care what direction it is."

So they walked back toward the Sea Hag's statue. Becka would have preferred some other direction, because the statue was creepy, but had no choice.

After an hour they met a young woman walking the opposite way.

She was rather pretty, in a disheveled way, if a person liked that type. She had wild black hair and wild black eyes, and her clothing seemed to have been randomly assembled without regard to color or pattern. But beneath it all she had a somewhat too-prominent bosom that sported more than an eyeful of cleavage, thanks to inadequate buttoning. Naturally, the Dastard's eyeballs were heating. Becka was disgusted.

"Who are you?" the Dastard inquired in his crudely abrupt way.

The creature let out a laugh that was halfway between the squeak of a stuck door hinge and the squeal of a stuck road hog. "I'm Ann Arcky. My talent is absentmindedness."

Obviously true: Her wardrobe and hairstyle suggested as much. But the Dastard's eyes were still glued to her bouncily heaving décolletage.

There was something else: As the woman spoke, a fuzzy balloon appeared over her head, then faded. She was an odd one, certainly.

Since the Dastard was for the moment distracted, Becka asked a question. "What is that bubble over your head?"

"Well, it's a medium-length story," Ann said. "And sort of scattered, or maybe I should say scatterbrained."

"Go ahead and tell it," the Dastard said. "We're listen—"

But his voice cut off in midword, leaving the "ing" cut off and dropping to the ground, for Ann had just inhaled, popping loose a button. Becka didn't want to admit she was jealous of such ability, so she kept her mouth shut, in contrast to the Dastard, whose mouth was hanging open.

"I came from Mundania," Ann said. "I was always sort of disorganized, always losing thoughts. Then I wandered into—what's this land called?"

"Xanth," Becka said.

"Zanth," Ann agreed. "I got here, I don't know how, I just sort of blundered, and couldn't find my way out, and so I decided to make the best of it and I kept going and didn't know where I was so I just found this path and I guess I'll wander forever and ever until maybe I get somewhere or maybe not, and—"

"Thank you," Becka said, cutting her off. It was evident that she really was disorganized, and needed some help. "What about the bubble?"

"The bubble?" Ann glanced up, and saw another just fading out. "Oh, yes. I keep losing my thoughts, and in Mundania they really were lost beyond recovery, unless someone happened, to catch them and remind me, but that didn't always happen, and sometimes I could look for weeks and never find them again, and it was just so frustrating, and—"

"The bubble," Becka said again.

"Oh, yes. When I got into this magic land, what's-its-name, Xanadu, my lost thoughts just started to pop out in these speech balloons, like a comic strip or something, and it's been really distracting, in fact I don't know what to make of it. So I just traipse along, hoping to get somewhere, and I'm not even sure where I should look." She raised her hand to brush away a disorganized strand of hair. In the process, she interrupted the Dastard's line of sight to her bosom.

"Look," he echoed blankly. Then his wits returned. "So you're not a princess."

Ann burst out laughing. "Princess? You think I'm a princess? That's really weird, because I *am* a princess!"

Now Becka's jaw dropped. "You are?"

"Of course. A very disorganized one, of course. Maybe it doesn't count here in Xanthus, but back home where I'm lost from—you don't happen to know the way back, do you? I got lost, and I really don't know how to find my way anywhere."

Ann had dropped her arm, exposing her cleavage again, and the Dastard's eyeballs were locking in again. If they had their way, they might pop out of his head and right into the woman's frontal valley and be lost amidst the mountains. "Let me help you with your buttons," Becka said, and reached out to get the woman's shirt correctly fastened.

That restored the Dastard. Becka had been tempted to let him remain locked in, but realized that if she was supposed to help him, she had better do it. Besides, that constantly heaving cleavage annoyed her.

"What kind of thoughts do you lose?" the Dastard asked.

"Oh, anything," Ann said. "My friends tell me I'd lose the—the—" But she had lost the thought.

However, a bubble had formed, and in it was a picture of a messy tub piled with dishes. "The kitchen sink?" Becka asked.

"Yes, that's it! I'd lose the kitchen sink if I could. And sometimes at home I almost did, because I never got the dishes done on time, and, and—"

This time her balloon showed a tall stack of dishes. As she floundered, the stack tilted, then fell over. The dishes crashed, breaking, sending fragments of broken china in all directions. Some shards flew right out of the balloon, landing with little plinks on the ground.

"And you're really a princess?" the Dastard asked.

"Of course I am! You don't think any normal person could be this fouled up, do you? I must find my way to the palace, or whatever, so I can rest my maidenly feet for a while and eat some cake."

"Kiss me," the Dastard said. He wasn't much for the social graces.

"Why of course." Ann turned to him and planted her lips on his. She kissed him so hard and long that it was a wonder either of them could breathe. Becka was disgusted, but also fascinated; this was one strange and oddly aggressive female.

The Dastard seemed to be coming to a similar conclusion. He pulled his face away. "Maybe this is premature," he gasped.

"No, you seem like a fine young man," Ann Arky said. "Let's signal the stork a few times." She hauled him in again.

"Let's discuss this first," he said. Becka almost had sympathy for him. Ann seemed to be getting less disorganized by the moment, now that she had oriented on the man.

"No need, you luscious thing." Ann put a hand on her shirt and ripped it open. The balloon over her head showed the rest of her clothing being ripped off, and his too.

Suddenly Ann was standing without moving. The Dastard was also standing frozen, holding nothing. The speech balloon hovered, disconnected.

Amazed, Becka stared at it. What was happening? This was so strange that she couldn't make any sense at all of it. But inside the bubble a picture was forming, so she focused on that.

It showed the Dastard floating through some kind of limbo where nothing was quite real. Ghostly scenery passed across the background; he was evidently moving through Xanth. He was traveling back in time to unhappen something! She was seeing an unhappening happening, for the first time, maybe because it was a big enough one to require extra effort. The Dastard was looking for something, and nothing could happen until he found it.

He found it: the place and time where Ann Arky blundered into the Land of Xanth. There was a path that forked, and one fork seemed to pass through a spot in the interface so a person could get through. So the Dastard simply hauled some prickly bushes across to close off the path, so that it wouldn't be used. Then he slid back toward the present.

And Ann Arky faded out, along with her balloon. She was gone. She had, Becka realized, never entered Xanth.

"You saw?" the Dastard asked.

"Yes. You unhappened her entry into Xanth."

"I had to. She was weird."

Becka had to agree, but also had to argue. "I thought you liked her bosom."

"Yes. But the longer I talked with her, the less credible she became. She was no princess."

"It was weird the way she started coming on to you."

"It certainly was. I couldn't understand her, so I had to get rid of her. I'm glad that's done."

"But you could have—have summoned the stork with her, if you had waited just a little longer."

"I wanted to. But I never get too deeply involved in what I don't understand. It's dangerous. So I had to stop her before I lost all control."

He didn't like to lose control. That made sense. Ann Arky's disorganization could have dragged him down. The man might have no conscience, but he did have discipline. "So I guess your nexus wasn't right, this time."

He nodded. "That's the first time something like that's happened. I'd suspect she was an impostor, but she really was a stray from Mundania." He shrugged. "Well, let's move on."

They started to walk back down the path. Then Becka felt an awful chill. Something was closing in on her—something utterly horrible. But she could neither figure it out nor fight it. It was like breathing foul air: The alternative was to suffocate.

You'll get used to it, child.

What was that? It seemed like a voice in her head. But how could that be? Becka wasn't given to hallucinations.

Meanwhile, her body walked on beside the Dastard, just as if nothing was happening. She didn't know what *was* happening, but she wished he would unhappen it. This was gruesome.

Here is the word, child. I am the Sea Hag. I have taken over your body.

The Sea Hag! But that couldn't be. She was locked in the Brain Coral's pool.

I escaped. Now give me all your memories.

Becka fought desperately to free herself from the loathsome embrace of the Sorceress.

If you fight me, I will hurt you.

Becka still fought. Nothing could be worse than being Possessed by the Sea Hag, who took pretty girls and soon rendered them into worn hags. She'd rather die!

Then terrible pain flooded through her body. Every muscle, every bone was on fire. She tried to escape by turning dragon, but it was no good; the pain continued.

She found herself lying on the ground in her natural form. "What's the matter?" the Dastard asked irritably. "Can't you even walk a little way without collapsing?"

If only he knew! But her mouth curved into lying words. "Just a stumble, my pet. I'll be all right."

Her body got up and turned full girl again. It walked. The Dastard, reassured, paid no further attention.

As I said, I will hurt you. Now give me all your memories.

Becka tried to resist, but the awful pain returned, and she couldn't. She had no power, and not much will. She surrendered, letting the Sea Hag delve into her mind.

So that's what happened! I thought I should have had a body before this. He took it away before I got it. What a dastardly deed.

Yes, he had unhappened it. Now it was clear that the Sea Hag had taken over Ann Arky's body, and lost it when he unhappened the woman's arrival in Xanth. He had been far smarter than he knew, to abolish what he didn't understand. So the questing Hag had had to find another body—and had taken Becka's.

That's right, child. And a good body it is, young and pretty. It should last for years.

What was going to happen to her? Becka dreaded her likely future.

Have no concern about that, my pet. It will be far worse for you than you can imagine. Your body is mine, now, and I will use it until I'm tired of it, then I will kill it. You are doomed.

And she couldn't even warn the Dastard.

EXCHANGE OF SELVES

W ira guided them to the rose garden, where the Designated Wife, Rose of Roogna, was cultivating roses. That was of course what she did best, and they were very nice looking, sweet smelling, and magical flowers. "Hello, Princesses," she said, giving them a combined hug. They knew her, as they knew all of Humfrey's five and a half wives. Some of her roses still grew in Castle Roogna, signaling love for those who were in doubt. Uncle Dolph had used them to prove that he knew the meaning of love even at age nine.

They went to the kitchen for rose shaped cookies and rose colored tsoda pop. Then Wira took them upstairs to the Good Magician's dingy little study. They had been here, too, before, but this time it was official, and that made it much more impressive. When they formed their illusion castle there was always a dingy dark study in it, in case the Magician should ever happen to want to visit.

They lined up before Humfrey's little desk with its huge old tome. After a moment, his worn old eyes looked up from the page and slowly oriented on them.

"How can we stop that man?" Melody asked.

Humfrey didn't need to ask what man. He knew everything, because he was the Magician of Information. "This is difficult," he said. "You cannot do it at present."

"But that's all we have to do, and we must do it now," Harmony said.

"Not exactly," Humfrey said.

This was different. "What do you mean?" Rhythm asked.

"As adults you will have the capacity to deal with the Dastard," Humfrey said. "But it will be seventeen years before you reach that stage. You are correct: It must be done now. Therefore, a rather special measure is required."

"What special measure?" Melody asked.

"You must exchange places with your older selves."

The three little princesses were seldom at a loss for words or mischief, but this suppressed both parts of their nature.

Then Wira spoke. "Magician, according to the schedule, Sim is arriving. He will be here in five minutes."

Humfrey winced. "I forgot to change the Challenges!"

Now the princesses revived. "Is that our friend Sim, the son of the Simurgh?" Melody asked.

"The Simurgh, who is the wisest bird in all Xanth?" Harmony added.

"Who has seen the universe end and reappear three times?" Rhythm concluded.

"Yes, of course," Humfrey said. "The Simurgh wants him to amend his education, so she sent him here without his nanny. How will I ever change the Challenges in time?"

"We'll help," Melody said.

"If you tell us what to do," Harmony added.

"If you let us use our magic," Rhythm finished.

"But I had a different Service in mind for you," he protested.

"Okay," Melody said, her little feelings hurt.

"We'll get out of your way," Harmony said sadly.

"We were just trying to help," Rhythm said, wiping away a sweet tiny tear.

"Magician—" Wira began.

"Oh, all right," Humfrey grumped. If any person existed to whom he couldn't say no, she was the one. "Conjure yourselves to the supply room and—"

The three princesses held each other's hands, forming a ring. Melody hummed, and Harmony tootled on the harmonica that appeared in her mouth, and Rhythm tapped her toes to make the beat. They pictured the supply room, and suddenly it was around them. They didn't hear the last of the Good Magician's instructions.

This was a fascinating place. Weird things were piled up like junk. They had no idea what was needed. But that didn't stop them from proceeding. Melody grabbed an armful of little angel figures. Harmony grabbed a model of a winged monster. Rhythm grabbed a bag of tiny green tentacles. Then they made another circle as well as they could and hummed and played and timed their music, making the region just outside the moat become real around them.

The Challenge they had faced remained in place. Melody threw the angel figures into the air, and they expanded and became real angels, flying uncertainly around. Harmony put the winged monster where Ition had been, and it expanded into a fair sized dragon. Rhythm tossed handfuls of tentacles across the sig nature garden, and they landed and sprouted into full tangle trees.

"What are you doing?" A. Cause demanded. She was rising from her chair, with Ition beside her.

"We're changing the Challenge," Melody told her.

"So that Sim can use it," Harmony added.

"And here he comes now," Rhythm concluded. Indeed, a bird figure was cresting the hill.

"But there has to be a plan, organization, a point," A. Cause protested severely. "Each Challenge is carefully crafted to fit the querent."

"Too late for that," Melody said.

"We didn't know," Harmony added sadly.

"We were just trying to help," Rhythm said, a tear forming.

The severity melted. "It will have to do," A. Cause decided. "We must get away from here immediately."

The three princesses made a circle around the woman and beast, holding hands, and sang and played to make the inside of the castle real around them.

"Why hello, Anna," Rose said, surprised. "And the princesses."

"We changed the first Challenge," Melody said.

"And brought Miz Cause and Ition here," Harmony continued.

" 'Cause Sim's here," Rhythm finished.

"I dread to think what will happen," Anna Cause said.

"Perhaps you should take the princesses to a parapet, so you can watch," Rose suggested.

The princesses didn't wait. They sang and played and tapped, and the parapet became real around them. It was at the top of the castle, with a low wall at the edge.

"Oh, my," Rose said, surprised. The rose she held looked surprised too.

They looked out over the wall. The lower sections of the castle were there, and the moat, and the land beyond it. Sim was just arriving at the Challenge. He was big for a bird, but small for a roc, being about the size of a grown man though he was only five years old. He was the most beautiful and precious bird in Xanth. His flight feathers scintillated with twice the colors of the rainbow, and his beak and talons sparkled like gems. He glided to the ground in a scintillation of iridescence and stood for a moment, considering.

He evidently decided to fly over the forest of tangle trees. In fact, it was a tangle tree farm with a hundred young tanglers growing, cutting off the approach to the drawbridge. But he didn't leave the ground; the magic of the Challenge prevented him from taking the easy way past.

So he tried walking through the forest. Immediately the young tangle trees grabbed at him, showing no respect for his beauty of form. He would have been sadly mistreated, not to mention defeathered, had not the angels flown in to rescue him. They carried him gently back out beyond the forest and set him on the ground.

Meanwhile, the princesses could see other creatures working inside the moat, setting things up for the second and third Challenges while Sim tackled the first Challenge. There was a group of human people just inside the moat, and the chamber where the river had run was becoming a small forest.

Sim tried walking around the tangle tree farm, but the only way that led to the moat was blocked by the winged monster. It was full size now, and looked dangerous. Sim did not try to pass it. Instead he walked back to where the angels hovered.

"This would be easier to understand if we could hear them talk," Rose murmured.

"But Sim doesn't talk," Melody said.

"He just peeps," Harmony agreed.

"But we can understand his peeps," Rhythm concluded.

"Then perhaps you can make it possible for us to hear the translations," Rose said.

They concentrated, then sang and played and tapped, and the sound became real. The figures were far away, but it sounded as though they were close. When Sim peeped, it seemed as if he were speaking their language.

Sim was just arriving back where the angels hovered. "The winged monster says he is lost," Sim peeped. "He followed an airline and thought he was getting somewhere, but it became a nightline, and he had to leave it, and now he has no idea where he is or what he is supposed to do."

"That's too bad," the angels sang in a sweet chorus.

"Meanwhile he thinks he's supposed to stop anyone from passing, until he gets unlost."

"How unfortunate," they sang sweetly.

"So now will you carry me to the other side of the forest, so I can cross the moat?"

"No," they sang with angelic regret. "We are lost too. We found ourselves here, with no hint of where we are supposed to be or what we are supposed to do."

Sim considered. "I never heard of angels in Xanth before. Where do you live?"

"In Heaven," they chorused.

"Where is that?"

"We don't know."

Sim considered further. He was not a stupid bird. "Maybe you need to make Heaven. Then you will know where it is."

"But we have nothing to put in Heaven," they chorused.

"I think you need a nice young forest," Sim peeped. "And a guardian for your gate."

They were intrigued. "Where could we find a forest?"

"Consider this tangle tree farm. Once this Challenge is over, there will be no place for these poor trees to go. They need a permanent home. I'm sure they could make a very nice forest, with angelic guidance."

"Why so they could," the angels agreed. "But where could we find a guardian for our gate?"

"The lost dragon should make an excellent one."

"Why so it should," they agreed. "We hadn't thought of that. But maybe he has somewhere else to go."

"If he did, he would have gone there. He is lost, and needs to be found. He needs a place to call home, and a job to do."

The angels nodded. Then they set about fashioning a floating Heaven, and they took the tree farm into it. The trees became greener and brighter and considerably more friendly in that beneficent environment. Then they took the lost monster into it, and he took up his position by the pearly front gate, and was no longer lost. Heaven floated away, carrying its lovely scene, leaving the ground of Xanth bare and dull.

Sim walked to the drawbridge unchallenged. He had overcome the first Challenge. That was a good performance, considering the random nature of its institution.

"But now he faces a genuine Challenge," Rose said, watching the bird cross the drawbridge.

On the inside side of the moat sat a morose man. He blocked the main gate.

Sim approached. He tried to walk past the man, but abruptly stopped.

"What happened?" Anna Cause asked.

The little princesses concentrated, and soon the mood of the bird became real to them. "The man's talent is making others feel shame," Melody said.

"Or embarrassment," Harmony agreed.

"So nobody can get by him without being overcome by morti— morti—" She stalled out, but then the other two took her hands, and together they were able to handle the huge word. "Fication," Rhythm finished.

Sim went to the side, but there he encountered a number of disreputable men, women, and children. "Hello," he peeped.

"Get out of here!" a man cried.

"But I have to get into the castle," Sim peeped.

"We hate the castle," a wild-eyed woman said.

"And we hate you," a surly child added.

"But I'm just an innocent bird of Xanth."

"We hate birds," the man said.

"And we hate Xanth," the woman said.

Sim looked surprised. "How can anyone hate Xanth?"

"We hate magic," the child said.

"And we hate humor," the man said.

"And we absolutely detest puns," the woman said.

This set the bird back. "Who are you?"

"We're critics," the child said.

Sim stepped back, realizing that these folk were incorrigible. They hated everything except themselves, and they surely didn't feel very good about that exception.

Then a bulb flashed over Sim's head. "Do you hate that man in the chair?" he asked, pointing with a wing.

"Of course we do," the man said.

"Well, I like him. I am going to walk right by him through that door."

"We hate that!" the woman said. The group of them charged toward the seated man.

Soon they stumbled away, holding their heads, overwhelmed by shame. Now they hated themselves too.

Sim quickly walked past the motley group, before anyone noticed him, and hurried through the gate. This was almost too easy; he felt ashamed of himself.

The three princesses tittered. "Sim's fun," Melody said.

"He's a smart bird," Harmony agreed.

"And our friend," Rhythm concluded.

But now Sim faced the third Challenge. This was a forest from which lovely music came. He paused to listen, and so did the princesses, Rose, and Anna Cause.

Then he started to walk through the forest. The trees were passive, not interfering. But then a funny little machine-like thing appeared. It had a body of metal and feet of rubber, with big square glassy eyes. When it moved, it made a subdued roaring sound. It came to block Sim's progress.

"What are you?" Sim peeped.

The thing played a lovely piece of music.

"That's very interesting," Sim peeped. "Tell me your story."

He understood the music, but the princesses did not. So they concentrated, and sang, played, and beat the other music into intelligibility. Then the notes became words, and the story unveiled. Some of the words were unfamiliar or even nonsensical, but they were able to get the sense of it anyway.

Once upon a time, a Mundane forest ranger drove his car through the intangible barrier between Mundania and Xanth. There were various leaky spots in the Interface, and sometimes Mundane creatures did leak through. The land turned magical, but the ranger didn't realize it, because like most of his ilk he didn't believe in magic.

The car's front wheels rolled into a small patch of slowsand. Because it had front wheel drive, this meant that when they slowed down, so did the whole car. The driver thought the car had stalled, though the motor seemed to be running. He turned it off, got out, and peered at the front. He wasn't caught by the slowsand because it didn't extend beyond the car. He saw nothing wrong, which confirmed his impression that the car had stalled. So he walked back the way he had come, to get help.

He must have passed through the leaky spot, and then maybe it had closed up, because the man never returned. The car sat there for some time. Slowly some of the magic of Xanth seeped into the car's parts, and it came alive. It turned on its motor and slogged its way out of the slowsand. This took time, but the car had time, and after a few months it was clear. Then it was able to move at its normal speed, which was actually pretty fast.

It looked for a gas station, because it thought it was low on fuel. It didn't realize that when it came alive it had also acquired a magic talent, which was never to run out of fuel. Since it couldn't find a gas station, it finally gave up and decided to explore this odd land it was in. It met dragons and tangle trees and a girl who glowed in the night. Her name was Pearl, because her glow was thought to be pearly. Some said nacreous, but they were wrong; it was pearly. So the car's adventures were entirely ordinary, and in time it got bored.

One hot AwGhost day the car was chugging up and down hills, and began to overheat. It had learned how to handle this: It needed more water for its radiator. Thirsty, it looked for a river or pool or sea, but there were none. All it found was a pleasant seeming spring. That would have to do.

Just as the car pulled up, a harpy landed. This was a filthy creature whose face and front were those of an ugly woman, and whose body and legs were those of a handsome buzzard. She had spied the car, and naturally wanted to revile it. Harpies needed daily exercise of their cussing abilities, lest they lose their edge. She didn't recognize the species, but that hardly slowed her. "You ### hunk of $$$$!" she screeched, making the air around her blanch. Then she warmed up to some real profanity. The nearby foliage wilted, and a stump of wood began to smolder.

But this didn't bother the car. It was used to this kind of language, since its driver had used many of the same words whenever it had stalled, which it had done often. It just listened, hoping to learn some neat new term.

Finally the harpy's mouth got dry from her hot screeching, and she was forced to take a drink from the spring. The car took advantage of this break in her monologue to drink too. They finished drinking at the same time.

The harpy turned to the car and took a deep breath, the better to resume her barrage. The car turned its headlights on her, realizing that it was safer to meet the onslaught head-on. At least its paint would blister evenly, that way.

What neither realized was that they had blundered into a love spring. They fell immediately and hopelessly in love. Since they were both of age, they proceeded to summon the stork immediately. The car had never done this before, but was familiar with the procedure, because its driver had done this type of thing repeatedly in the back seat. Anyway, ignorance was no excuse, in a love spring.

The signal gave the stork a headache, but it finally delivered a baby boy machine that looked exactly like his father, except smaller: the size of the harpy. He did not resemble the harpy in any other way, except that on a hot day when he got mad and overheated, he would blow off steam by honking his horn. The horn sounded a lot like a harpy's mouth, and when blown really fiercely could make nearby foliage wilt a bit.

The baby came to be called the Autoharp, after his parents' names. As he grew, he turned out to have a special magic talent, in addition to never needing fuel. This talent absolutely disgusted the harpy, and she finally took the Autoharp into the deepest forest and left him there, hopelessly lost. The talent was to play beautiful melodies on strings that ran through his interior.

"And so I am here," the Autoharp concluded musically. "I never found my way out of the forest, until the Good Magician rescued me. Now I work for him, until I find something better to do with my mechanical life."

Sim realized that he would not get past the Autoharp as long as the little car worked for the Good Magician. He would have to find a better thing for it to do.

But what could a music-playing machine do in Xanth? Sim pondered, and came up with a really stupid suggestion. But he had to say something. "Why not join the Curse Fiends as a touring musician? They do some musical plays."

"Great!" the Autoharp played, and zoomed off to find the Curse Fiends.

Amazed, Sim walked on into the rest of the castle.

The triplets sang and played him onto the parapet with them. "You made it!" Melody cried, hugging him.

"We were hoping you would," Harmony added.

"We made the first Challenge," Rhythm finished.

"Now we must all go down to talk with Magician Humfrey," Rose said firmly.

Sim peeped. The princesses' translation spell remained in force, so they understood him. "Yes."

He peeped again: Had they seen a Mundane dog named Boss?

"Maybe in the Tapestry," Melody said.

"Big and black," Harmony added.

"With a sign on his collar," Rhythm concluded.

"I read the sign," Sim peeped. "He is looking for a home. But mine is out of his reach."

That made them all sad. But there was nothing they could do about it.

They trooped down the narrow spiral stairway into the castle. Sim led the way into the Good Magician's tiny study, with the princesses lined up behind him.

Humfrey looked up, just as if there had never been an interruption.

"Yes?" he inquired grumpily. It would be an awful day in Xanth if he ever ran out of grumps.

"How can I obtain the broadest feasible education?" Sim peeped. He needed that, in order to become the wisest bird, in the course of a few millennia.

The Good Magician glanced at Wira. "This is private," he said regretfully. "You understand."

She nodded. "The Rule of Ten," she agreed, and shut the door. They heard her departing footfalls.

Now Humfrey focused on the bird. "You need experience with two difficult realms whose parameters do not match common sense," he said without even turning a page of his tome. "The first is the Idea, best approached through the Worlds of Ida. The second is the female mystique, best approached by associating closely with several mischievous girls in a setting of mutual confusion. You will thus accompany the three princesses as they exchange with their older selves."

Sim was a very smart bird, but this confused him. "Older selves?"

"You will exchange similarly with your older self," Humfrey explained. "You and the girls will visit Ptero."

"Ptero!" Sim peeped. "The first moon of Ida, where time is geography. This should be interesting. But what of our Selves who are there?"

"They will come to Xanth to help save it from the depredations of the Dastard."

"The Dastard?"

"The girls will explain in due course."

Sim glanced at the princesses. "Of course," he peeped uncertainly. He knew them as mainly sources of mischief. Then he looked back at the Good Magician. "What is to be my Service?"

"Your elder Self will perform that, assisting the princesses in saving Xanth."

A three-way bulb flashed over the princesses' heads. "That's our Service too!" Melody said.

"Done by our older Selves," Harmony agreed.

"While we're on their world," Rhythm concluded.

"Yes," Humfrey said. "Now you must understand one thing. Your exchange must be secret; you must not tell anyone else in Xanth about it. On Ptero it doesn't matter; they will all know."

"Yes, Good Magician," Melody said.

"We'll keep our little traps shut," Harmony agreed. She shut hers, though it was exceedingly cute.

"But how do we exchange?" Rhythm asked.

"Go to Princess Ida, of course."

"Of course," Sim agreed.

But Humfrey had already buried his nose in his tome, tuning them out. They had to find their own way from the study. Fortunately they were up to it, being Xanth's smartest bird and three Sorceresses.

Rose served more cookies and drink and exotic bird seed for the four of them. Then Wira guided them out of the castle. "We wish you well," she said. She was surely curious, but would not inquire about their Answer.

The three princesses hugged her again, and Sim made a friendly peep. Then they walked out across the drawbridge. They sang and played to fashion their magic carpet, and rode it into the air, while Sim spread his wings and flew beside them. They did not discuss their mutual mission, knowing that some of the creatures of the forest had sharp ears.

They reached Castle Roogna and went to Princess Ida's room. "Why how nice to see you," Aunt Ida said, as if she hadn't seen them a hundred times before. "And Sim too. What can I do for you?"

Melody looked around. "Is this private?" she asked.

"Yes, if you wish it to be."

"We have to keep it secret," Harmony explained.

"Something about a Rule of Ten," Rhythm concluded.

"Of course," Ida agreed. "No more than ten people can successfully keep a secret. It is a magical theorem."

"But we have to tell you, we think," Sim peeped.

Ida smiled. "Then I must be one of the ten. Who else knows?"

Melody counted on her little fingers. "The four of us."

"And the Good Magician," Harmony added, using one of her fingers.

"Which makes six," Rhythm concluded, using hers.

"That seems safe. What is the secret?"

They told her about the exchange, in order to stop the Dastard. Sim was interested, because he had not known about this person.

Ida nodded. "I can effect the exchange, though this has not been done before. As you know, my worlds contain all the folk who ever existed, or who will exist, or who might exist. There are a number of worlds, because there are a great many folk to occupy them. They do contain every person and creature who lives in Xanth, but are missing the year in each person's life that matches the time they spend in Xanth. Different rules of magic apply to each world. You should find this educational."

"That is the point," Sim peeped.

"However, there will have to be some people added to the secret. Your parents, for example."

"Awww," the three princesses said together.

"Let me explain. Your grown Selves cannot simply take your places here without attracting some attention. They will need help to conceal the exchange. Princess Ivy and Magician Grey Murphy will be able to do that, but only if they know exactly what is occurring."

The three princesses reluctantly nodded. It did seem difficult to conceal such a change from parents who already seemed to know entirely too much about childish business.

"And the Simurgh," Ida said.

Sim peeped. "No. She wishes me to broaden this aspect of my education by myself. That's why she gave Roxanne Roc and Che Centaur a holiday. She does not want to know at this time."

"Excellent," Ida said. "That makes the number eight. That's comfortable. I will bring the two." She walked to a magic mirror and spoke to it. "I would like to speak with the princesses' parents at this time."

The mirror made a pattern of lines and blips, then cleared. Princess Ivy's face appeared in it. "What have those little nuisances done this time?"

Princess Ida kept a straight face. Adults were good at that. "I think it best to keep the matter confidential, sister dear."

"Remember, they're *your* nieces. We'll be there in a moment." The mirror zapped into background noise.

In precisely a moment Mother and Father appeared at the door. They looked grim. The three princesses almost felt guilty, because usually they had done something disastrous if not outright funny when conferences like this were called.

But Ida quickly set them straight. The three little princesses quailed, afraid that Mother would say NO and Father would back her up as he always did, but when they heard about the Dastard they looked thoughtful and withheld judgment.

"This does need to be dealt with," Grey Murphy said. "That Dastard is dangerous. Their mature magic coupled with Sim's knowledge should be sufficient."

"They should be safe on Ptero, since death is unknown there, and our analogues will be there to guide them," Ivy said. "And it will be good experience for them."

They were working their way around to agreeing! What a miracle.

"However," Grey Murphy said. That was a chilling signal. "There is a complication."

The princesses hated complications, because they were usually another way of saying No.

"This is true," Ivy said. That was just as bad. The three little princesses had become expert at interpreting Adult-speak.

"A complication?" Aunt Ida inquired politely. She was always polite, which meant that most folk underestimated her. The princesses had learned better. There was no magic quite like hers, though they weren't sure of its full nature.

"We shall have to add two more to the secret," Grey Murphy said.

"Four," Ivy said.

The princesses counted rapidly on their digits. "But eight plus four is over ten," Melody protested, running out of fingers.

"In fact it's twelve," Harmony said, having the wit to go on to her twinkly toes.

"That's too many," Rhythm concluded.

"Are you sure?" Ida asked the Parents. She was really on the princesses' side, as she usually was, but she never opposed other adults directly. That was perhaps her one weakness.

"We may be able to conceal the presence of adult-aged daughters," Grey said. "But not the absence of juvenile daughters."

Ida nodded. Even Sim agreed. "Others would know you were gone in the first hour," he peeped. "That would ruin the secret."

"The first ten minutes," Ivy said grimly.

The princesses exchanged three mortified little glances. That was true. The whole castle would feel the absence of mischief the moment they were gone. They couldn't expect their grown Selves to have the proper sense of mischief; adults were notorious for changing their ways the moment they joined the Adult Conspiracy.

"So we shall need to elicit the support of your little friends Demon

Ted and DeMonica," Ivy said. "They will be able to emulate two of you at a time, and that may suffice. They will surely be glad to do it."

"But that's only two more," Melody said.

Grey Murphy shook his head. "Your mother is correct. Their parents will have to know too. At least their demon parents. There will be no keeping the secret from them, once their children are involved. For one thing, they will have to bring the children."

"Yes," Harmony agreed reluctantly.

"Twelve," Rhythm said gloomily. "The secret will get out."

"Not necessarily," Ida said. "The Rule of Ten indicates that a secret *can* be breached beyond ten, not that it *will* be. If everyone is circumspect, it may hold."

The princesses hesitated, not knowing what "circumspect" meant, but pretty sure it did not describe them.

"Four of us will be away from here," Sim peeped. "Does that bring the number down?"

"No, dear," Ida said. "Because four other Selves will replace you. However, they will indeed be more circumspect, so it should help."

"Well, let's do it," Grey Murphy said. "We will notify the demons while you see to the transfer."

"It will be interesting to see our children all grown up," Ivy said.

"There is one other thing," Ida said. "Such an exchange will be wearing on the fabric of reality, so we can achieve it for only one day."

"One day!" Ivy said. "That's hardly enough for them to get their bearings, let alone accomplish anything."

"I realize this makes it difficult, but I fear they will revert automatically thereafter."

"Perhaps it is one day for each of us," Sim peeped. "That would make four days in all, for the group."

Princess Ida opened her mouth in a manner indicating an adult objection. But the three little princesses jumped in with a song and melody and beat. "A day each! A day each! Four days! Four days!"

Ida looked slightly bemused, but she nodded. "Yes, that must be it. You have made it so. Four days, then."

"Their merged talent can at times prove useful," Grey Murphy said with five-eighths of a smile. "Let's hope four days will be enough."

Ida nodded, and they departed. Then Ida turned to the princesses and

Sim. "You may find this process odd, but not uncomfortable. Each of you must focus intently on my moon, Ptero. You will find yourselves floating, but do not be concerned. You will meet your other Selves, take their hands, turn with them, then let go and continue toward Ptero, which will seem larger." She glanced at Sim. "You will touch wing-tips for the same maneuver. You will not be flying." She returned to the princesses. "That is all there is to it. This contact will be your exchange of bodies; your spirits will go on, while your other Selves will take over your bodies and cause them to expand to adult size. But you need not be concerned about the mechanics of the transfer. In effect you will be traveling to Ptero, passing your Selves along the way. Try to stay together. Once you are there, be sure to get the advice of those who live there. When your older Selves are finished here, you will feel a signal, and know it is time to exchange back. Are you ready?"

The three princesses exchanged six glances, because now Sim was included. The magic of numbers somehow made the necessary glances increase faster than the people did. They had never quite figured that out. None of them felt ready, but all of them knew they had to do it. In any event it was what the adults called a rhetorical question, which was a fancy way of saying it needed no answer.

They stood in a line before Princess Ida. Her moon swung around in front of her head. It was the size of a little ball, and was normally friendly, because it knew them. When strangers were present, it would hide behind Ida's head. It reflected Ida's moods. When she was happy, it shone brightly; when she was unhappy, clouds covered its surface and it went dark. This time it was different. It wavered and seemed to grow.

They stood fascinated by it. The tiny ball became a small ball, and then a medium ball, and then a large ball. Then it started looking like a planet. Instead of seeming to float above them, it began to seem to rise below them, as though they were flying toward it. It was a wonderful and scary experience.

Four dots appeared against the globe, and the dots expanded into floating figures. Three were grown princesses, looking lovely, and the fourth was a beautiful grown bird who was not flying. These were their adult Selves.

The four other Selves came to hover before them. One princess wore a green gown; the second wore brown; the third wore red. The bird wore nothing but feathers. He was far larger than the others, being the size of a roc. But he was no roc; his feathers shone iridescently with twice the colors of the rainbow. This was Sim's older Self; there could be no other like him. He was destined to succeed his mother, becoming the oldest and wisest creature in the universe. But that would not occur for some time—probably a few million years, or whatever. Meanwhile he was learning, and was a good companion.

They reached out with hands or wings to touch their Selves. The grips of the Selves were light but firm. They turned, as in a dance, and let go. They turned around and sank down toward the huge planet below.

Soon they saw seas and continents, rivers, mountains, and plains. As they fell closer, they saw jungles and lakes, dotted by cute little houses. They were moving toward one particular house, which grew to become a building, and then a castle. In fact it was Castle Roogna, not identical to the one they knew in Xanth, but close enough to be recognizable.

They floated right to the roof of a turret, and through it, and came to rest in a chamber on an upper floor. They recognized it: This was Princess Ida's room. And there was Aunt Ida herself. Except that she looked much older.

They were safely on Ptero. But they needed to be sure. "Hello," Melody said shyly.

"You look like Aunt Ida," Harmony said.

"But you're too old," Rhythm finished.

The woman smiled. "Hello, Princesses and Sim. Yes, I am Princess Ida. I am seventeen years older than the version of me you know on Xanth. Everyone is older, here."

"Every person on the planet?" Sim peeped.

"No. Every person here in Castle Roogna at this location. We all got older when we moved the castle to this site."

"This site?"

"Time is geography. The farther west we go, the older we become; the farther east, the younger. Your other selves needed to be twenty-one for this special mission, so we brought the castle here for the duration. Once they return, perhaps we'll move it again. We enjoy living at different ages."

The three princesses and Sim found this too confusing to digest at the moment. "But we're the same age we were," Melody said.

"Which is four," Harmony added.

"And Sim is five," Rhythm finished.

"Yes. That is the point. You exchanged with your older Selves, and now they are in Xanth at age twenty-one, and Sim is twenty-two. They are of age to handle the Adult Conspiracy, among other things. But you do not need to remain your present ages."

They stared at her, just not getting it. "Maybe we need time to assimilate it," Sim peeped.

"I think you need actual experience with it," Ida said. "Your little sister has volunteered to show you around Ptero."

"Little sister?" Melody asked.

"We don't have a little sister," Harmony added.

"Or even a brother," Rhythm finished.

"You have several other siblings here on Ptero," Ida said. "This is where every person who might exist does exist. Not all of us reach Xanth, but we have full lives here." She walked to the magic mirror and spoke to it. "Please ask Green Murphy to come to my room now."

"Who?" Melody asked.

Before the others could add their bits, the door opened and a young woman of nineteen entered. She had dark green hair and bright red eyes.

"Green Murphy, here are your elder sisters Melody, Harmony, and Rhythm," Ida said. "And their friend Sim. They don't understand about time geography. Perhaps you can show them."

"Sure, Aunt Ida," Green Murphy said. She turned to the triplets. "Hi, big sisters. Hi, Sim. Let's take a walk outside." She gestured to the doorway.

Big sisters? This girl was adult! Even Sim had a perplexed curve to his beak.

"It's all right," Ida said. "All your confusion will soon fade."

Bemused, they followed Green Murphy out.

5
SEA HAG

T he Dastard walked toward his next nexus, pondering what had passed. That Ann Arky woman had been a strange one, coming from Mundania, claiming to be a princess, coming on to him so suddenly—it was as though she had become a different person. He did not trust what he did not understand, and she had been beyond understanding. So he had abolished her entry to Xanth, and that had fixed that. But he had more than a tinge of regret, because of her marvelous peep-hole bosom. A normal girl with that configuration could have been a lot of fun. So he did not feel as good about that particular unhappening as usual. If she had changed less suddenly, been less pushy, he well might have had a fine time with her. Maybe he had made a mistake, but it was too late to change it back. Sometimes he wished he could unhappen an unhappening.

Fortunately there was another nexus not far away. Maybe that one would make up for the last. What he really wanted was a lovely princess to marry, but that was bound to be complicated. Princesses were in much demand. If he unhappened her meeting with whoever else she might marry, she might just meet someone else, so he would gain nothing. He could unhappen that meeting too, but unless it was quite recent, there would only be yet another other man. Still, he would be willing to make the effort, if he found a suitable princess.

Meanwhile the girl, Becka, walked beside him. She had turned tac-
iturn since her fall, not saying much of a word. That was all right; he
needed to be rid of her anyway, unless he found a way to get around
her dragon-enforced No with regard to showing anything interesting. He
still didn't understand why the Good Magician had sent her to him, and
he wanted to figure that out before he ditched her.

They came to a centaur village. The feeling of nexus was stronger;
it must be here. Would he get to unhappen a centaur event? That would
be a pleasure. They thought they were such superior creatures, when
they were really only crossbreeds.

He followed his awareness into the village. There were stalls and
storage bins and shelters. Centaurs were getting their hooves shod, and
practicing their archery, and studying books. They wore no clothing other
than quiver harnesses or head kerchiefs, and the females were spectac-
ular, being generally better endowed than straight human women. But
there was something different about these centaurs.

He paused to watch several of them playing a game with a ball and
an elevated basket. The object seemed to be to throw the ball through
the basket. It would be easier to do if they just set the basket down
within easy reach, and wasted less time bouncing it on the ground and
getting in each other's way. Maybe they hadn't realized that.

"They're all black," Becka said.

That was it. They were Blackwave centaurs, dark as the Blackwave
humans in their human sections, and with vertical black stripes across
their equine sections. Well, why not? They could have any colors or
patterns they wanted to. Centaurs came in all types; he just hadn't encountered this particular variety before. Meanwhile it was really interesting watching some of the females playing their game; they bounced
almost as much as the ball did.

But this wasn't his nexus. He managed to pull his eyes away from
the female players; the eyeballs made slight sucking sounds as they came
free. He walked on. Becka accompanied him without comment. Her kind
didn't approve of centaur apparel.

They came to a wall. It was blank, except for a single spot. A centaur
stood looking at the spot with a magnifying glass.

"What are you doing?" the Dastard inquired.

The centaur looked at him. As he did so, the spot on the wall faded out, leaving the surface blank. "How do you do?" he asked.

Centaurs tended to be unduly polite. "Fine. Who are you?"

"I am Kress. And you?"

"I am the Dastard. What's with that wall?"

"My talent is to make a spot on the wall. Until this morning I thought it was worthless. But I happened to be carrying this magnifying glass that I found yesterday, and looked at the spot with it, and discovered that it's really a tiny picture. So I am studying it."

This was slightly more interesting. "Let me see it."

Kress gave him the magnifying glass, and formed a new spot on the wall. The Dastard oriented on the spot. Lo, it was indeed a tiny picture. It showed a disreputable-looking man meeting a lovely green-haired princess wearing a green gown.

Becka peered over his shoulder. "Why that's *you*, Dastard. But I don't recognize the princess. Which is odd, because I know them all, being one myself."

"What?" the Dastard asked, startled.

"Nothing. I misspoke."

"What do you see?" Kress asked.

"It's me—and a lovely princess," the Dastard said, amazed. "But I never met her."

"My pictures today have all been of me," Kress said. "With my friends."

"Take a look," the Dastard said, returning the magnifying glass.

The centaur looked. "Why you are correct. This is you, and a human princess. But she is too old or too young."

"Old?"

"The green dress and green hair and blue eyes. Princess Ivy is like that. But she is thirty-one years old, while this girl looks a decade younger. So it might be her daughter, Princess Melody—except that she is only four years old. So this must be someone else."

"That's my conclusion," Becka said. "That is not Ivy. But it could be Melody—as she will be in seventeen years."

"How can you possibly tell something like that?" the Dastard asked her.

Immediately the girl withdrew. "I'm guessing, of course. The facial lines—maybe I am mistaken."

"I wonder," Kress said. "I was unable to understand these pictures before, but now it occurs to me that they are not pictures of the past or present—but of the future. I will be with my friends—and perhaps you will be with that mysterious princess."

"In seventeen years? I can't wait that long!"

"Actually, you seem to be your present age, in the picture," Kress said. "So there must be some other princess who is that age now, whom you will encounter. Soon, I should think."

This notion fascinated the Dastard. He would soon meet a beautiful princess? This was what he longed for!

"This is amazing," Kress said. "Until this morning I thought my talent was useless. Now I discover that not only is it a picture rather than a spot, it's a picture of the near future of the person closest to the wall when I make it. Instead of being pointless, my talent is actually extremely powerful. Imagine being able to see the near future! To anticipate bad events and avoid them. The prospects are mind boggling."

The Dastard had to agree. Not only was this a suitable nexus that could yield him great satisfaction, he could eliminate the knowledge of others that he was about to meet a princess. He could keep his future private until it happened.

Becka looked at him cannily. "You're going to do it, aren't you," she said.

"Yes, of course." The Dastard slid into limbo and traveled back to the day before. He tracked the centaur as he trotted outside the village. He saw Kress spy a flash beside the path, and pause to pick up the magnifying glass. He slid back to a short time before that, and slid into full reality. He picked up the magnifying glass, set it on a rock, and smashed it to tiny sparkles with a stone. It was gone beyond recovery.

He returned to the present, gratified. Becka and Kress were there, looking at a spot on the wall. "Too bad you couldn't have had a decent talent," she said sympathetically to the centaur.

"A foolish dream," he agreed. "Almost I thought—but that was a mere idle fancy. A spot is a spot, and nothing else."

They walked on. "You did it, you rogue," Becka said. "You unhappened the glass. Now he may never know."

"Precisely. You don't object?"

"Why should I object? It's a truly dastardly deed."

Was she trying to fool him? The girl had agreed not to interfere, but her disapproval had been almost tangible before. Now she seemed to relish it. That was odd, and oddly dismaying. He thought he had her safely pegged, and now she was changing, almost the way Ann Arky had.

Well, maybe she was coming to appreciate his talent, and was warming to him. He thought of asking her again to show him her panties, but they were still in the centaur village, and he didn't want the resulting spectacle. She would either turn dragon or Show her nether clothing, and neither would be worthwhile in public. But later, when he got her alone, he would ask, just in case she wasn't bluffing or teasing.

They came to an older centaur standing by a river, gazing into the water. This one wasn't black, so he must be visiting. "Who are you?" the Dastard asked.

"I am Chet Centaur. I am on the way to visit my sister Chem, and stopped by here to see if my grandfilly is keeping pace."

"Your granddaughter? Why would she be in the water?"

"It's a moderately complicated story."

"We like stories," Becka said. "Especially if they concern water."

Chet glanced at them both. "May I inquire who the two of you are?"

"I am the Dastard. I do dastardly deeds."

"I am the Sea—an innocent girl named Becka."

"Well, if you are really interested, I will tell you. Some time ago I brought shame upon my species by encountering a sea cow at a love spring. It was an unusual coincidence. I was walking alone, and the question occurred to me: How do centaurs breathe? Now you might think this is a pointless question, since I am of the centaur persuasion myself. But it caught me by surprise, and in a moment I was gasping for breath. I couldn't figure out how I breathed. Was it in the human way, with human lungs in the chest? In that case, what sustained my much greater equine mass? Or was it in the equine way, with larger lungs in the barrel of the body? In that case, what was the function of the human portion? Did I have two sets of lungs, one to breathe with and the other to talk with? That seems inefficient, and centaurs are hardly noted for their inefficiency. So it was a difficult riddle."

The Dastard was getting bored with this, but Becka seemed interested, and he was interested in her interest: Was she becoming more than a shallow child? If so, what accounted for the transformation? Maybe he would learn something useful by observing her reactions.

"Fascinating," Becka said. "Do go on, my pet."

"That riddle quickly led to others," the centaur continued readily enough. He seemed to like having someone listen. "How do centaurs eat? We seem to eat mostly human food, in human amounts, but how can that relative trifle sustain the much greater mass of our bodies? It seems that magic must be involved, but many centaurs do not believe in magic as it relates to our own kind. Some even call it obscene. My dam Cherie is one such; she hardly cares to hear of any magic talent associated with any centaurs, though in truth my sibling Chem and I both have talents. Mine is to reduce stones to pebbles called calx, which are useful in calculating. In fact, the mathematical term calculus, a special system of algebraic notations that greatly facilitate complex computations, derives from that term for pebble. Naturally I am an excellent mathematician; my talent with stones greatly facilitates this."

The centaur paused, as if expecting an expression of disinterest. The Dastard was more than ready to express it, but the stupid girl said "Do go on, Kress. This is a most interesting discussion." As if she had half the wit to understand even a calculated fraction of what Kress was saying. The Dastard himself certainly didn't. Who cared about pebbles and calculations?

Gratified, the centaur continued. "So I freely confess I do possess magic, as does my sister. She has done well in life, incidentally; she had a liaison with a hippogriff and bore Chex, one of the first winged centaurs. She in turn married Cheiron, and bore Che, who became the friend of princesses and the tutor of Sim, the chick of the Simurgh, the oldest and wisest bird in all creation."

The dope was name-dropping like mad. But there might after be something here. The Dastard was becoming less bored.

"Yes, the Simurgh is a rare bird," Becka agreed. "I have made many enemies, but have been careful never to cross her. She has too much knowledge and power."

The girl's talk was getting crazier. She was only fourteen years old.

How could she have had any experience with the Simurgh? But the centaur was talking again.

"But my history is less glamorous, though perhaps not without interest. Because I was pondering questions like these, I was not paying sufficient attention to where I was going. My right fore-hoof splashed into a small puddle. I didn't realize that it had been made by a colony of love bugs, and was a temporary love spring. It caused me to fall in love with the first female I spied thereafter. This happened to be a fat sea cow in a neighboring lake. Ordinarily I would not have given her a second glance. But suddenly I had to possess her. I galloped to the lake, plunged in, and proceeded to summon the stork with her. She seemed somewhat surprised, but flattered by the attention. Soon my passion abated—it was after all a very small love puddle—and I emerged from the lake and went home, somewhat ashamed for my lapse from centaurly standards. After all, all other species are naturally inferior, and we normally breed only with our own kind. But what was done was done, and I did not try to conceal it. My sister was very understanding; in fact she later had her own out-of-species liaison. My dam disowned me. That was painful, but I understand her sentiment."

"Forbidden love," Becka breathed raptly.

"The result was Cencow, a healthy centaur/sea cow crossbreed who had a human head, a sea cow tail, and six limbs adapted for swimming and manipulating objects. I visited the shore often to tutor him in centaurly matters, and I must say he was clever enough. I admit to having some pride in him, though I did not go out of my way to call attention to him. He grew up to breeding age, but found no females of his particular crossbreed type. So he frequented the region where the love bugs clustered, and in due course his patience was rewarded: a female griffin took an unwitting drink from one of their love puddles. She glanced up—and there was Cencow. She immediately flew across to join him. Their liaison was awkward, because she could not submerge and he could not leave the water, but love found a way, and they managed."

The Dastard tried to picture that liaison, and failed. He had to take it on faith. Becka seemed rapt.

"In due course the griffin produced three offspring. They had the form, surprisingly, of human beings, and seemed to be throwbacks to a more primitive aspect of our ancestry. Both Cencow and the griffiness were disappointed. But soon the silver lining appeared on their cloud: The three foals had remarkable talents. Merei, the first female, could change to any winged creature, and so could join her mother in flight. Mesta, the second female, could change to any sea creature, and so could join Cencow in swimming. Dell, the male, could change into any land-bound creature, and so could join me as a centaur. That was very nice."

"So why are you waiting here for your granddaughter?" the Dastard asked impatiently.

"Because I am traveling with all three of my grandfoals, and we have agreed to meet periodically and do a stint mutually afoot. Merei and Dell will be along shortly, but it is harder for Mesta to keep the pace. So I have paused here at a convenient river bank, trusting that she will appear."

At that point, magically on cue, two fat sea cows swam up to the bank. One was big, the other small. The small one poked her nose out of the water, then changed into a young mermaid. Chet reached down with a hand and caught her hand, hauling her up out of the water. As she came, she changed into a fully human girl. She landed on the ground and shook herself dry. Chet reached into his backpack and brought out a dress, which he dropped over the girl. She shrugged into it, and smiled as she adjusted her hair. "Hi, Grandpa!"

"Hello, grandfilly."

She stepped forward and gave him as much of a hug as she could manage. "Who are your friends?"

"We're not friends," the Dastard said. Seeing how well the centaur's illicit liaison had turned out, he would have been inclined to unhappen it, but couldn't; the girl was seven or eight years old, beyond his limit. And of course Chet's key event was decades ago, way beyond. How unfortunate. So he forced himself to make nice. "Have a nice walk."

"Thank you," Chet said.

The sea cow mooed and departed, having gotten her grandchild safely to the rendezvous. "Bye, Grandma," the girl called. "Thanks."

The Dastard realized that he could unhappen his dialogue with Chet Centaur, but that wouldn't accomplish anything either; the centaur had already been waiting for his granddaughter, and would meet her regardless. So this was no nexus; there was nothing dastardly he could do.

Mesta climbed up on Chet's back, and he walked away. As he did so, a griffin flew down from the sky, landed before them, and changed into another girl. "Hi Merei," Mesta called.

"Hi Mesta! Hi Grandpa!" She joined her sister on the centaur's back.

Then two small young sphinxes strode up. They had the bodies of lions, the heads of humans, and the female had vestigial wings. They were not much larger than a mundane pony. "Hi Grandpa," the male called.

"Hello, Dell," Chet replied. "Who is your friend?"

"This is Nightreven," Dell said. "She's two hundred years old."

"Two-seventy if she's a day," Becka muttered. "She starting to mature."

Indeed, the sphinx did seem to be developing a modest bosom. Not enough to cause any male eyeballs to encrust, but sufficient to show the way. The Dastard was surprised by Becka's perception.

"Actually I'm two-seventy," Nightreven said. "But that makes me close to Dell's age in sphinx years."

"To be sure," Chet agreed affably. Then Dell turned human and joined his siblings on the centaur's back, and the girl sphinx waved a wing in parting and moved on.

Chet had such a pleasant life, with his talented grandchildren. It really bugged the Dastard, but there was nothing he could do about it. Disgusted, he walked out of the village in the opposite direction. Becka accompanied him; he had half hoped she would go with one of the others, but she stuck like a leech.

They met a griffin. Like all griffins, she was the color of shoe polish. No nexus here, either. She squawked at them.

"Excuse me," Becka said.

"What?" he asked irritably.

"That's what the griffin said."

"How in Xanth can you understand griffin talk?"

The girl paused half a moment as if thinking. "Oh, I just picked it up along the way somewhere."

The griffin squawked again.

"She wants to know if we've seen—"

"She's too late!" the Dastard snapped. "Anyway, that one wasn't a real griffin. She was a girl in griffin form."

"That wasn't her question," Becka said. "She's looking for her father."

"I haven't seen him," he told the griffin. "Now go away."

The griffin squawked again.

"Yes, we'd love to hear your story," Becka told the griffin.

The Dastard inflated, but couldn't think of a retort savage enough to squish the stupid girl. What did she think she was doing? The girl had become odd and willful. He had just about lost hope of ever seeing her panties, so she had no use at all.

The griffin fell in beside them as they walked and squawked repeatedly. Becka made a running translation.

"Her name is Griselda Griffin, and she has an unusual history. It seems that many years ago, back in the year Ten-forty-three, just before the Time Of No Magic, a party of four males stopped at the Magic Dust Village, which was at that time occupied entirely by females of every type. Their males had been lured away by the song of the Siren, and then turned to stone by her sister the Gorgon. So the females carried the burden of distributing the magic dust throughout Xanth, so that its magic would be more or less evenly spread. It was a dirty job, but somebody had to do it."

"*Must* we endure this ancient history?" the Dastard demanded. "It was boring in centaur school, and it's worse now."

She ignored him and continued her translation. "Two of the visitors were human males. One was a centaur named Chester, the father of Chet. The last was a griffin named Crombie. Actually he was not what he seemed: He was a human man who had been changed into griffin form for this particular mission. He was nevertheless a handsome griffin, and so was attractive to Grinelle Griffin, who worked at the village. She had lost her husband the year before in a fight among winged monsters at Mount Rushmost, and Crombie resembled her lost mate. That was to say, he had a fine strong body, lovely wings, and a bad attitude. Grinelle couldn't resist; she had to have something to do with him. So she—"

"Enough of this dullness," the Dastard snapped. "I don't care which griffin did what to whom."

"Too bad, my pet," Becka said. "I'm interested, and I'm not accustomed to being balked, so stifle your face."

Again, the Dastard was too outraged to speak. What was *with* this idiot girl?

"So she approached Crombie. He turned out to be a woman-hater; he did not like females of any type, as he quickly and nastily informed her. A true misogynist. He was just so much like her husband! But Grinelle had learned something about dealing with balky men in the course of her marriage. So she retreated gracefully and bided her time until evening. She realized that this griffin would not be staying at the village long, so she had to act promptly. She longed to have a griffin cub to ease her sorrow, someone she could love and who would love her in return, and Crombie was her best prospect to sire it. So she brought him a cup of water in the middle of the night."

"The middle of the night!" the Dastard said. "What idiot joke is this? A griffin couldn't even carry it."

"It was a covered cup, which she carried hung from a cord about her neck," Becka explained patiently. "I thought I told you to stifle it, dimwit."

Yet again she had set him back by her amazing temerity. This was definitely not the Becka he had known.

"She used a claw to jog him awake. He opened his eyes and squawked in outrage. 'You stupid bird-brained idiot female! You stepped on me! What is the matter with you?' But instead of either retorting or fleeing, she proffered him the cup of water. As it happened, he was thirsty from his efforts of outrage, so he thrust his beak into the sealed cup and drained it. The water was unusually refreshing. Then, without so much as a squawk of thanks, he closed his eyes and settled back down to sleep. But she brushed his face with a wing-tip, causing his eyes to open and catch a glimpse of her. That was when he discovered that the water he had just drunk was from a love spring."

"Beautiful!" the Dastard said, unable to stifle his appreciation of a truly dastardly deed. "She trapped him."

" 'You treacherous winged monster!' he squawked as he realized. 'You deliberately gave me that love elixir. I'll never forgive that. I must punish you.' Grinelle merely turned her back. This really heightened his rage. 'Take that and that and THAT!' And he had at her with ferocity. But she did not protest, for each 'that' translated to a dot of the dread ellipsis, and the trio of dots sent a forceful message to another winged monster, the stork. Then she turned around and sprinkled him with water from another cup she carried, and he immediately let the matter drop, and returned to sleep. It was lethe, the water of forgetfulness. He had forgotten all about her and this nocturnal episode."

"Dastardly," the Dastard repeated. Who would ever have thought this story would turn so briefly satisfying?

"In the morning, Crombie hated Grinelle even more, because in the back of his mind he felt somehow drawn to her. He treated her yet more harshly, trying to abolish the lurking attraction he felt. For though the lethe had made him forget, the love elixir had not entirely worn off, as it normally required more than three dots of an ellipsis to wear it out. But then he went on his way with his companions, and thought no more about her, though the lingering love elixir was destined to strike again, this time with a nymph as its object. But that's another story."

"I hope this one is almost done," the Dastard said wearily. However, it had given him an idea. If he found that green-haired princess, maybe he should have some of that love elixir handy to use on her.

"Grinelle in due course, not long after the Time of No Magic, received a bundle from the stork: a baby griffin girl cub which she treasured and named Griselda. She had astonishing color for her kind: a yellow beak, red mane, and blue wingtip feathers. Only as she grew did it become evident that Griselda, though griffin in body, was essentially human in mind. She was very smart, and had a soul. She never felt completely at home among the griffins, and finally Grinelle had to tell her the truth about her origin: She had a human father. So when she was eighteen in human years, she set out to find her father. But because he had reverted to his human form, she did not know how to locate him. She realized that she would be able to find him only if he wished to be found—and how could he wish that, when he didn't know she existed? So she decided to go ask the Good Magician for help."

"Oh, no, not another Good Magician story," the Dastard said, disgusted.

"But she got lost on the way to Magician Humfrey's castle, and blundered down to the Brain Coral's pool, where it stored all manner of creatures and things, pending their possible need in some distant future.

So she made the deal with it: She would do it a service, if it would preserve her until her father learned of her existence and wished to meet her. It seemed that there was a person on the surface of Xanth who was very ill and about to fade out, who had a very special talent. This was to project a thought or an image or an emotion into the mind of another person or creature, somewhat in the manner of a night mare, but not restricted to bad dreams. She went where the Brain Coral told her, and found him: his name was Just Ice, and he had somehow lost himself and was dying of coldness. 'There ain't no more Just Ice,' he wailed as he sank into oblivion. But Griselda reached him just in time, and wrapped him in a blanket, and promised to take him to a place where he would always be warm. So he went with her to the Brain Coral's pool, and dipped his big toe in the water, and it was marvelously warm and cozy. He was glad to let the Brain Coral borrow his talent while he delved into the pool. And Griselda joined him there, finding it just as comfortable. And so they remained, for thirty-eight years. Then something glitched, and several of the stored folk were washed out of the pool, including Griselda. So, finding herself back in Xanth proper, she decided to resume her search for her father, the misogynist Crombie." Becka paused, glancing at him. "Have we seen him?"

"No!" the Dastard said. "Now go away."

Sadly, the griffin spread her wings and flew away.

"You certainly are dastardly, my pet," Becka remarked appreciatively. "You let her tell her entire story, then dismissed her with a mere four words."

"I wish I could dismiss you as readily," he said.

"I am much more of a challenge, my pet."

"You don't sound at all like the girl I met yesterday."

"I am indeed not like that girl. Come, my pet, let's seek a private place, and I will freak you out with my panties."

Suddenly the Dastard was suspicious. "You are completely different! What has come over you?"

"I'm surprised you haven't caught on by this time, pet. I am the Sea Hag."

Suddenly it fell into place. The significant change in personality. The sudden interest in the histories of other people. The Sea Hag was interested in people, because they were all prospects for her to take over, and she wanted the very best bodies. "That glitch in the Brain Coral's pool, that ejected the griffin girl—it ejected you too!"

"Indeed it did, my pet. My spirit flew to my statue and waited for a suitable prospect to pass. I took Ann Arky." Her face soured. "But then you unhappened her entry to Xanth, stranding me. That never happened to me before; usually only death deprives me of my hosts. So I took the next available young female body. This one is if anything better than the first. It's clean and healthy, and with a formidable identity." She turned dragon for an instant. "It has been a long time since I have had a man to play with. You will do until I find a better one. Come to me, my unhandsome but surely serviceable male." She reached for him.

He didn't trust this at all. The Sea Hag had Xanth's worst reputation. She was cunning and unscrupulous and bloodthirsty. How could she be trusted? He backed away. "Aren't you mad at me for unhappening your prior body?"

"Well I was, my pet. But I decided to investigate, both in the memory of this naïve child and in observation of you, and I have concluded that you are my type of man. That is to say, cunning and unscrupulous and with a taste for panties. Together we can do a great deal of mischief." She advanced on him.

There was a certain aptness in her reasoning. But the Dastard had always worked alone, and was wary of joining forces with anyone, let alone a crone like this. The Sea Hag was no cute young thing, regardless of the body she occupied; she was centuries old. That bothered him as much as anything: the fact that she had so much age and experience, making him a child by comparison. "No. Go away."

Still she advanced. "Oh, come on, my pet. I have none of the restrictions this girl had, and I have considerable experience. I can give you encounters such as you never before imagined. Here; I will show you." She turned around and hitched up her skirt.

The Dastard slid into limbo before the panties showed. He knew that such a sight, when he was unprepared, would freak him out and leave him helpless as long as the view remained. Then what would she do? It could be anything, including getting his head chopped off.

So it was better to be rid of her, however tempting her present body might be. Oh, when properly braced, he could see her panties and not be freaked out, so that wasn't a long-term issue. But he could never trust her disreputable mind. She knew too much and was too cynical, and would never be in his thrall. He needed a real girl—or a real princess.

It was better to unhappen her again. He could do so, because it post-dated his last unhappening of the girl Becka; he would not be treading on his own tracks. So he went back to the time the Hag must have taken over the girl—and hesitated. Had it been then, or could she have done it earlier, and taken a while to give any sign? It could have happened any time after he had unhappened Ann Arky.

Also, how could he stop a spirit from infusing the girl? He couldn't see it, and a simple change of direction or paths wouldn't suffice. He had to not only unhappen it, but fix it so the Hag couldn't take the girl again later.

A moment's thought yielded an answer: there was a herb that repelled loose spirits. He could fetch some of that and put it on her after he unhappened the takeover. That would make her safe.

He slid to a patch of spirit herbs and picked several good ones. He tied them together with vine, making a clumsy necklace. Then he slid to the point right after dealing with Ann Arky. There stood Becka in all her innocence. She thought that her ability to turn dragon protected her from any threat; how little she knew!

He put the necklace over her head. "Never take this off," he told her urgently. "I'll explain tomorrow." Then he slid back to the present; he never remained longer in the past than he had to, as it became wearing.

In the present, Becka stared at him. "The Sea Hag!" she gasped. "She had me! I couldn't escape. But now she's gone."

"I unhappened her takeover of you," he said. "But you must always wear those herbs, to keep her away."

"I will! Oh, it was utterly horrible. I tried to resist, but she made me hurt until I couldn't stand it. She ransacked my memory, she used my body—she was merciless."

"You remember it all?" He still wasn't quite used to her ability to remember unhappened things.

"I wish I could forget! Oh, thank you for rescuing me!"

"You're welcome. Now will you show me your—"

"No!"

That was, oddly, the correct answer. It meant it really was Becka, and not the Sea Hag pretending to be her. "What did she plan for me?"

Becka grimaced as she remembered. "She was going to—to give you my body, not because she wanted to please you, but because she wanted to control you. If it didn't work, she was going to kill you and look for a man she could control. She has no use for men, except to the extent she can make them do her will."

"That's what I thought. Keep wearing those herbs, so she can't get you again. She evidently likes your body."

"Yes. It was horrible. Her thoughts—she vaulted me right past the Adult Conspiracy in sickening detail. She's had so much experience, so ugly—she's worse than you are."

"That's why I unhappened her possession of you. I want an innocent girl, not a creature like her."

"I'm a whole lot less innocent than I was a day ago—but I'll never be like her." She clutched the herbs. "I'll never give these up."

They walked on. An outsider might have thought that nothing had happened. How wrong that impression would be!

"Will she come again?" Becka asked. "I mean, will she take some other poor girl's body, and look for us? To get back at us for balking her?"

That was an excellent question. "I think she will," the Dastard said. "She will be angry. Different as you and I are, I think we must do our best to guard against that."

The girl shuddered. "Yes."

6

THREE BIG PRINCESSES

Melody touched fingers with her four-year-old younger self. Mel Junior was certainly a cute child, in her green dress and hair, looking much like Melody herself when she traveled to From on Ptero and became five years old. In fact she looked much like Harmony and Rhythm at that age too, but not quite the same; they were said to be fraternal triplets rather than identical. That had never made much sense to her, because obviously they were sisters, not brothers. At any rate, the little ones did look almost alike, and would have been hard to tell apart without their distinguishing colors. Melody remembered a game they sometimes played, calling each other Greenie, or Brownie, or Reddie, for their hair. If the little princesses were to color their hair the same and wear matching dresses, only their eyes would give them away.

She glanced to the side. Sim Bird was touching wingtips with his junior Self too, and there the contrast was startling. Sim was the size of a roc, though he wasn't exactly a roc, while his younger self was the size of a human person. He was the prettiest bird in Xanth or Ptero, because of his iridescence, but was also uncommonly intelligent, and a pleasant companion. She was glad he was coming along on this mission, and not just because he would make travel easy. Oh, of course they could always conjure a floating carpet, but then they had to agree on its color, and tell it where to go, and it could attract the attention of Cumulo Fracto Nimbus, the worst of clouds, who would try to blow them away, and then they would have to put a magical diaper on Fracto's soggy bottom, and the war would be on. So it was easiest to let Sim handle travel, now that they had something serious to do.

Mel Junior giggled soundlessly. She must have picked up the image of Fracto in a diaper, firing off enraged thunderbolts. Melody Senior smiled; teasing the cantankerous cloud was fun.

They turned around, in their little dance of passage, and separated. They floated on toward Xanth. The vague background gradually formed into a monstrous chamber, which became a huge chamber, and then a large chamber, then an ordinary one, and finally a small one. On the way, Sim diverged, flying away from them and out a window. She knew why: He would not be able to fit in a small interior chamber when he expanded to full size. He would have to settle outside the castle.

They touched the floor and caught their balance. There was Aunt Ida, looking more like age thirty-one than the forty-eight she had been when they left her on Ptero. "Hello, nieces," she said.

"Hello, Aunt Ida," they said almost together.

"You look beautiful."

"So do you," Melody said graciously. Of course nobody that age could truly be beautiful, but part of the Adult Conspiracy was to be sincerely insincere.

"Have you been properly briefed on the nature of this mission?"

"Not yet," Harmony said. "We just understand that it's important, and that our mature talents are needed."

"Yes. There is a man called the Dastard who is going around unhappening events. That is, he travels back in time to cause something not to happen. This might be beneficial, but in his case it is not; he seems to be mean-spirited, and causes nice encounters not to happen. We fear he will progress to truly dastardly things that will imperil the welfare of Xanth, so we feel he must be stopped."

"Beneficial?" Rhythm asked. "How could it ever be good?"

"If a person fell over a cliff and died, it would be good to unhappen that," Ida said. "If she ate too much humble pie and went into a depression, an unhappening would help. Or if she encountered a bad man who—"

"We understand," Melody said quickly. "There are bad events we can't always anticipate."

"So this man could do much good, if he wanted to," Harmony added.

"But he doesn't want to," Rhythm concluded.

"Exactly," Ida said. "The three little princesses saw him doing a dastardly unhappening, and prevailed on their parents to let them tackle it, as they have formidable magic when they put their cute heads together. But it was felt that however apt they are today, they will be far better in their maturity, and there are also certain complications like the Adult Conspiracy that would limit their comprehension. So Magician Humfrey arranged for them to exchange with you, trusting that you three big Princesses would have the power of magic and social maturity to handle what may turn out to be a rather difficult and possibly unpleasant challenge."

The three nodded. "We hope our little selves enjoy their visit to our realm," Melody said.

"We shall do our very best to nullify the Dastard," Harmony agreed.

"And make Xanth safe for your future," Rhythm concluded.

Ida smiled in that manner that politely suggested that they were still four years old in her view. "Now there are certain restraints. For one thing, we shall need to keep this exchange secret."

"We love secrets!" Melody said.

"Especially when they are ours," Harmony agreed.

"But why should we conceal our exchange?" Rhythm wanted to know.

"Because if the Dastard discovers what we are up to, he will do his best to unhappen it," Ida said.

"But he can't do that," Melody said.

"And if he could, he wouldn't dare," Harmony added.

"Because we're *princesses*," Rhythm finished.

Ida shook her head grimly. "When we learned of this matter, your mother and I were concerned for the welfare of the little princesses— and for yours too, of course. So Ivy and I went to the Magic Tapestry and did a Search on changed events. We discovered that the man who might have come to marry me encountered the Dastard, and that forthcoming encounter was unhappened. Now of course I can look up that man if I wish, and I may do so, in due course; it is not easy to truly interfere with a Sorceress. But this suggests that the Dastard does not necessarily hesitate to interfere with the lives of princesses. Precisely how he could unhappen this exchange of the three of you we aren't sure, but we prefer to keep the matter private so that he never thinks to try."

The three big princesses were sobered. If the man could interfere with Princess Ida, there might be no limit to his dastardliness. His talent seemed to approach Magician level, and Magicians were almost as difficult to deal with as Sorceresses.

There was a knock on the door. Ida walked across the chamber and opened it. There were Magician Grey and Sorceress Ivy, looking barely a decade older than the princesses. "My how you've grown!" Ivy said with a smile.

Melody broke free of her stasis. "Mother!" she cried, flinging herself across to hug Ivy. She was her mother's daughter, even if her mother had rejuvenated by seventeen years. Their hair and eyes still matched.

Harmony launched herself at Grey Murphy. "Father!" She was her father's daughter, as the hair and eyes signified.

That left no one for Rhythm, so she hugged Aunt Ida. They didn't quite match, but she was still a wonderful aunt. Of course they had seen their parents and aunt at this age on Ptero, but only when the three princesses themselves were much younger, because *everyone's* age changed with the geography. So this was different. Anyway, it was fun hugging people.

Then two swirls of smoke appeared. One clarified into a lovely woman holding a little boy, and the other into a handsome man holding a little girl. The demons were arriving.

"These are Metria with Demon Ted," Ida said. "And D. Vore with DeMonica. They will be helping to keep the secret."

The little half demons were just as cute as the little princesses had been. On Ptero Ted and Monica were the same age as the princesses. "That makes ten," Melody said.

"Just enough to keep it," Harmony agreed.

But for once Rhythm did not conclude it. "Except for Sim. He makes eleven."

"And the Good Magician," Ida said. "Making twelve. We are two over the limit. This puts the secret of your exchange at risk. But this does not mean that it *will* be exposed, just that it *can* be. We shall have to be extremely careful."

Melody looked at the four new arrivals. "If you don't mind our asking," she began.

"Why is it necessary for the demons to join in?" Harmony continued.

"Do they have a need to know?" Rhythm concluded.

"Yes, they do," Ida said. "Because it is not merely your presence here we must conceal, but the absence of your younger selves. If someone notices that they are not running around the castle making their usual mischief, there will be questions."

"But we can do that," Melody said. She began to hum.

"By invoking our magic," Harmony continued, bringing out her harmony-ca.

"Like this," Rhythm concluded, beating her drum.

In a moment they sang and played and beat themselves into the semblance of their junior Selves: three four-year-old Princesses. The likeness was so good that no one would be able to tell, even though it was illusionary. In this realm they could not actually change their ages by traveling From or To.

"Not when you are out searching for the Dastard," Ida said.

Oops. They stopped their music and reverted to their normal semblance.

Meanwhile DeMonica assumed the likeness of Little Melody, with a mischievous expression. Demon Ted grimaced, then fuzzed his suit out and reformed it as a dress. Now he looked like Little Harmony.

"But I'm missing," Big Rhythm protested, in her distraction speaking out of turn.

Demoness Metria turned smoky, then reformed as her alter ego, the waif Woe Betide. Then she changed further, and became Rhythm. Now they were three.

"One of the demon adults must bring the children, for they are only half demon and can't pop in and out as we can," D. Vore explained. "So that adult can take the place of the third child. Our demonly nature enables us to better emulate the mischief of children. The other demon adult can keep in touch with others, establishing a liaison between the big and little princesses. I will now explain things to Big Sim." He popped off.

They were right: This secret needed twelve participants, even if it did put it at risk. The folk of Xanth had figured things out carefully. Even so, it could be chancy.

"We shall certainly do our best," Melody said.

"But we need a bit of advice," Harmony added.

"What is our strategy for nullifying the Dastard?" Rhythm finished.

"We have considered that," Ida said. "We see three possibilities. First, we might banish him to Ptero, or one of its satellite worlds, where he could do no further mischief."

"But would he go?" Melody asked.

"If he didn't want to?" Harmony added.

"How could we make him?" Rhythm concluded.

"We do see that as a problem," Ida said. "We hesitate to suggest this, but it occurred to us that you are quite attractive young women. It seems that his ambition is to marry a princess. If one of you distracted him, you might be able to lead him to Ptero."

"Distract him?" Melody asked, not fully pleased.

Ida pursed her lips, but evidently hesitated to answer. It seemed the matter was indelicate.

"He also seems to have a taste for the look and feel of panties," Magician Grey Murphy said, stepping into the breech. The three fake little princesses giggled, partly at the mention of the naughty word "panties" and partly at the unvoiced near-pun of "breeches." "So if one of you were to—"

"No way!" Harmony snapped inharmoniously.

"Of course," Ida said. "Princesses don't."

"What's the second way?" Rhythm asked.

This time Ivy answered. "We have managed to secure a loose soul that is in need of a host. If that soul could be given to the Dastard, it would provide him with a conscience, and he would then cease being dastardly."

"Are you sure?" Melody asked.

The imitation Rhythm expanded into D. Metria. "Some of us have had experience with half souls or even quarter souls," she said. "It will be effective." Demon Vore returned, and nodded agreement. Souls had power.

"But doesn't a soul have to be taken voluntarily?" Harmony asked.

"Suppose he won't take it?" Rhythm finished.

"It doesn't have to be entirely voluntarily," D. Vore said. "When I married Nada Naga, I got half her soul. I had no choice."

"And I got half of my husband's soul," Metria said. "Later I passed half of that on to Ted, but I remain unconscionably decent regardless. A soul is a hard taskmaster."

"But the Dastard is not about to marry anyone, surely," Melody said.

"And none of us are about to marry him," Harmony agreed.

"And suppose he sees that loose soul coming, and flees?" Rhythm concluded.

"That is our concern," Ida agreed.

"So what's the third way?" Melody asked.

"Persuasion," Ida said.

The three princesses considered this. "You mean, just talk to him?" Harmony asked.

"Trying to make him See the light?" Rhythm asked.

"This may not be as far-fetched as it seems," Grey Murphy said. "Folk who do good are normally held in higher esteem that those who do evil. We suspect that it is esteem that he most desires, though he may not realize it. If he could be made to see that he will be more respected if he uses his talent for good, he might do it."

"And suppose he doesn't?" Melody asked.

The others shrugged. "We do not see this as an easy mission," Ida confessed. "So it may be that initially, all you will be able to do is damage control."

"Damage control?" Harmony asked.

"Your magic should enable you to follow him in time and space, and perhaps prevent his dastardly deeds," Ida said. "This would be a stopgap expedient, but possibly the best you can do until one of the other options proves feasible."

"We can find him," Rhythm said confidently. "But what we're going to do with him when we catch him we don't know."

"You will have to conceal your princessly nature," Ida said. "And Sim will have to mute his feathered brilliance. Otherwise the secret will be out the moment anyone sees you."

The three princesses didn't even need to exchange a glance; half a glance sufficed. They sang, played, and beat themselves into the semblance of three mature but rather common women wearing green, brown, and red clothing, suitably dull. Their little crowns became sensible kerchiefs.

They went outside to find Sim. He was chatting with Soufflé Moat Monster. Oops—that would bring one more creature into the secret, even if Sim hadn't told him anything, because Sim was such a remarkable bird.

"Sim, you will have to be more circumspect," Melody told him.

"Or you'll give us away before we start," Harmony agreed.

"And we can't afford that," Rhythm concluded.

"Oh, I know," Sim squawked. They had not given him the power to speak in human talk, but they understood him well enough. "I explained to Soufflé."

"He did," the moat monster agreed in monster tongue, which they also understood. "I was introducing my apprentice, Chip."

"We don't see him," Melody said.

"Right here." Soufflé indicated a spot on the water beside him.

Now they spied a tiny creature. It was a sea monster the size of a chipmouse.

"He looks small," Harmony said. "Is he young?"

"No, he's full grown. He will serve duty with the imps."

"They need guardians too," Rhythm agreed. It did make sense; the imps were very small.

"But now we shall have to depart," Sim squawked.

Soufflé nodded. "Zap us."

They sang, played, and beat a magic tune, and Sim assumed the aspect of an ordinary roc bird, and Soufflé looked blank, then sank out of sight. So did Chip. They had forgotten all about the big bird's visit.

But another creature came by. "What is that?" Melody asked.

"It looks like a werewolf in wolf form," Harmony said.

"No, it's a Mundane dog," Rhythm concluded. "With a sign."

They read the sign, and learned that this was Boss, looking for a home. But they had other business, and could not help him. The dog wandered disconsolately on.

Sim extended his talons, and they grabbed hold. He spread his wings and flew a short hop over the moat, landing in the orchard beyond.

"Demon Vore told me about the mission," he squawked. "I think it would be easier if I just pecked off the Dastard's head."

"We can't do that," Melody said, horrified. "It would be unprincessly, and your mother wouldn't approve either."

"I was afraid of that," Sim squawked. "We're the good guys; we have to be ethical and decent and reasonable."

"It is a pain," Harmony agreed.

"And we have no real idea how to proceed," Rhythm finished.

"Maybe we need advice," Sim squawked.

They considered that, then Melody hummed, thinking of a source for advice. In a moment she had a direction. "That way," she said, pointing north. "Beyond the Gap Chasm."

Sim picked them up and launched into the sky. It occurred to one of them that this would make them highly visible from the ground, and someone might wonder, so they sang and played a brief tune that made them all invisible. In two and a half moments they were passing over the yawning Gap Chasm; it seemed that nothing much was happening at the moment, so it was sleepy. They enjoyed it, because they hadn't seen it on Ptero though it surely existed there somewhere; they knew it mainly by reputation. In fact all of Xanth they knew mainly by hearsay, because their only real memories of it dated from the year they were four years old. This business of not changing age as they traveled was unsettlingly weird.

There was a cloud floating just over the chasm. As they approached it, it changed, assuming the shape of a vase. Then it became the image of a frog. Then the torso of a shapely woman. It obviously wasn't Fracto; he never posed like that.

"Cloud sculpturing!" Melody exclaimed.

"That must be somebody's talent," Harmony agreed.

"And there she is, standing at the brink of the chasm," Rhythm said.

Indeed, there was a girl looking up at the cloud. She was evidently practicing her talent, having found a suitable cloud. Such magic might not be practical, but it was esthetic. Maybe someday that girl would put on an artistic exhibition in the sky.

Melody gave spot directions, based on her magic awareness of where there was advice, and soon they landed near a lovely cave. They let go of Sim's talons and walked toward it.

A swirling cloud of smoke formed before them. It formed into a handsome demon man: D. Vore. "Aren't you forgetting something?" he inquired.

"Like what?" Harmony asked.

"Like being still invisible."

"Oopsy," Rhythm said. "That would be confusing."

They abolished the invisibility and became the three garden variety women. Sim hunched down, still invisible, knowing he would never fit in the cave. Vore swirled back into smoke and dissipated.

Then Melody suffered a siege of vague alarm. She paused, trying to fathom it.

"What's the matter?" Harmony asked.

"You look as if you're seeing half a ghost," Rhythm concluded.

"Maybe I am," Melody said. "It's as if someone is looking at me. Recognizing me."

"Recognizing you!" Harmony said.

"That breaches the secret," Rhythm said.

Melody tried to clarify her feeling, but it was already fading. Whoever it was had not looked at her long. There didn't seem to be anyone here. That suggested that it was a magical observation.

But if someone already recognized her, how could they maintain the secret of the exchange? That was disturbing.

The three of them could sing and play things real, but this wasn't something they could do much about. It was not their kind of magic. It was disturbing.

"Maybe it's someone in the cave," Melody said, knowing it wasn't.

They entered the cave. It was dark, but soon a screen lighted. *Hello girls.*

"Hello," Harmony said, somewhat set back.

"We came for advice," Rhythm said, recovering.

Oh, you want Nada Naga, online.

"On line?" Melody asked, perplexed.

I will summon her. But first tell me who you are.

"We are three anonymous girls," Harmony answered.

I am not sure that will do.

"We have our reasons," Rhythm said.

They were afraid that Com Passion would not accept that, or would see through their anonymity spell, but she didn't.

I am Com Passion. I am making the connection to the Xanth Xone of Cyberia. The screen blinked. Then the lovely face of Nada Naga appeared on it.

"This is Nada Naga, advice columnist for the lovelorn," she said. "What is your problem?"

Advice for the lovelorn? The three exchanged as much of a glance as would fit in the confined space. They hadn't thought to check the kind of advice being offered. And it was becoming obvious that they couldn't get relevant advice without giving away their secret. So they were not starting their mission very well.

But Melody thought of something. "I feel someone watching me," she said. "But I don't know who."

Nada considered. "Let me get a look at you." She squinted from the screen. "My, you look almost familiar."

"I'm just an ordinary anonymous girl," Melody said quickly, wishing she had thought to change her hair color. Of course she knew Nada on Ptero; she was the mother of DeMonica. But Nada was younger and prettier here, by about seventeen years. It was disconcerting.

"Oh. Well, I'm sure it doesn't matter. You are certainly pretty enough, and that surely explains why some man is looking at you. You should be flattered instead of alarmed."

"But I don't know who he is," Melody said.

"But you do have a suspicion."

Melody realized with surprise that she did. "The Das—" She caught herself. "The dashing young man I'm looking for."

"Then go and find him, Anonymous," Nada said. "He shouldn't be hard to locate." She squinted again. "But you should prepare better. Your outfit is rather passé. You should lift your hem considerably, and tighten your blouse. Let your hair hang loose. Smile more often. I'm sure you'll make an impression on him." She frowned. "That hair—I know only three people who have green hair, and one of them is a child. Are you—"

"Thank you so much!" Melody said quickly. "You've been a great help. I'll go find him now." She backed away from the screen. Nada shouldn't be able to recognize her, but she was coming uncomfortably close. Melody hadn't realized just how bad a giveaway her hair would be; on Ptero there were others, such as Green Murphy, but here in Xanth it was much more limited.

Nada's face faded from the screen. The script print reappeared. *Would you like to play solitaire?*

Harmony stepped in. "No thank you, Com Passion."

"We must hurry to find that man," Rhythm said. They turned together for the cave entrance.

But you have hardly arrived, Passion protested. *You must stay for a nice visit.* The entrance became a solid wall.

They were stuck for it. If they used their magic to make the entrance real again, they would give away their identities. Garden variety girls would not be able to escape. "Maybe we will visit for a while," Melody said. "We don't mean to be rude."

Excellent! Then the screen flickered. *Oh. I'm getting an incoming call. Pardon me a moment.* The print held for exactly one moment, then faded. A new face appeared, one Melody didn't recognize. It was a rather pretty Mundane woman. *Why Pia-how nice to hear from you!* The script now ran along the screen below the face.

"You know I was diabetic," Pia said. "Until I got cured by a healing spring in Xanth. That actually carried over into Mundania, somehow; I was amazed and gratified. I think Nimby had something to do with it. Then I heard of someone, and I thought she must be from Xanth, and I was curious, so I thought I'd call and inquire."

Of course, dear. However. I have visitors at the moment.

Pia was embarrassed. "Oh, I didn't mean to interrupt. I'll call back another time."

"No!" Harmony cried. "Stay and visit."

"Yes, we are interested," Rhythm said. For this might distract the friendly machine from the three anonymous princesses.

Pia looked out from the screen. "Do I know you?"

"No," Melody said. "Not really." For now she remembered: They had met this woman, briefly when they were three years old. The memory had almost faded, in eighteen years.

"We are three young women looking for a man," Harmony added.

"Who stopped by to get advice from Nada Naga," Rhythm finished.

"That's odd," Pia said. "You are beginning to remind me of someone. The way you talk, more than the way you look. But—"

"No, we are nothing," Melody said desperately. Their habit of alternating speech was giving them away; they would have to break that up. Pia was remembering that, but hadn't made the connection to the children she had encountered. Yet.

"Oh. Well, if you don't mind my interrupting your visit—"

"We don't mind," Melody said. She fired a glance at her sisters, warning them to be quiet.

Please continue, Pia. Passion suggested.

Pia found her place. "Well, this person I heard of is called Diana Betic. She had the talent to make things that are sweet become less so, and those that are not sweet seem sweet, so as to increase the ease of eating things without messing up her blood sugar levels. She pretty well has to be from Xanth, doesn't she? I mean, Mundanians don't have magic talents."

"She must be," Melody said, though she didn't know what blood sugar levels meant.

"She can make other people act sweet too," Pia continued. "She has a magical monitor lizard, her pet and companion, who tells her what her blood glucose level is when he tastes her blood."

"Tastes her blood!" Melody exclaimed, appalled.

"Oh, it's friendly," Pia assured her. "I gather you don't know about diabetes."

"I never met him," Melody agreed.

"It's a sort of disease where a person's blood gets very sweet. She has to stick herself to get drops of blood, to find out how sweet it's gotten. And stick herself with needles to get it back where it's supposed to be."

"Ugh!" Melody said.

Pia smiled. "Precisely. Anyway, this Diana has a tiny lance called a lancet to prick her finger for the blood she gives to the monitor to taste. She has a pine needle for her insulin. So is she in Xanth?"

I don't know. Passion confessed.

"Well, keep an eye out for her, just in case," Pia said. "I'd like to hear from her, if she calls in. I'll tell her to go jump in a lake—or rather, a healing spring." She smiled, and faded.

The screen flickered. *Now where were we?*

"We were about to go, having had a nice visit," Melody said. Would it work?

Oh, that's right. Are you sure you won't stay for solitaire? My mouse Terian will deal the cards. A lovely young woman appeared.

"No, thank you so much," Melody said, backing toward where she hoped the cave entrance was.

Oh, well. Maybe another time. The woman shrank into a real mouse.

Melody resisted the urge to shriek. There was just something about mice. Fortunately the cave entrance was there, and she and her sisters were able to back all the way through it. What a relief!

Except that there seemed to be a mistake. The tunnel didn't lead out. It led down, and it smelled of fish.

Harmony banged into a wall. "Oh, I hurt my wrist," she wailed.

"Mine too," Rhythm said. "And I didn't even touch the smelly wall."

"We'd better go back the way we came," Melody said. Her own wrists were feeling sore.

"What, and face that mouse?" Harmony demanded.

"Wait, I've got it," Rhythm said, a bulb flashing over her head. "This is a carpal tunnel."

The others groaned. Then, annoyed, they sang and played into existence a fast ramp out of the tunnel to the ground. In a moment they were clear of it, letting the carp smell dissipate.

They found Sim, able to see him despite his invisibility, because it was their magic that made him so. "Wrong kind of advice," Melody said.

"You spoke last time," Sim squawked.

"We had some dialogue while we were separate from you," Melody said. "But I suspect our custom of alternating is about to give us away. I think we're going to have to break that up. Also, we had better change our hair colors. Too many people are starting to make connections."

Sim nodded. "That does make sense," he squawked.

They sang and played, and turned their hair colors uniformly drab. That would surely help.

"But we still don't know how to handle the Dastard when we catch him," Harmony said. "I think we need a battle plan."

"Yes," Melody agreed. "We have the soul. Why don't I try to distract him, and you hang the soul on him? Maybe we can get this done efficiently after all."

"How will you distract him?"

"I think Nada Naga gave me advice on that," Melody said. She lifted her hem so as to show more of her legs. She drew her blouse tighter. She removed the kerchief from her hair, letting it fall loose. She combed it out, so that it framed her face and settled around her shoulders. Its green color returned, but that couldn't be helped; it was hard to be distracting while drab.

"But suppose that isn't enough?" Rhythm asked.

Melody pondered. "I suppose we have to decide just how badly we want to wrap this up efficiently. Daddy suggested flashing him some panties."

"Yes, but we agreed that that would be going Too Far," Harmony said. "We're not Dawn & Eve, you know."

"Though sometimes I envy them," Rhythm said. "Dawn likes to show almost too much above, and Eve likes to show more than enough below. You must admit it works."

"Certainly it works," Harmony retorted. "But who wants men's eyeballs popping out and falling on the ground? We have standards to maintain."

"Oh, come, Mel—don't you ever want to make a man do that? Or to freak out and not be able to move as long as you flash him?"

Melody was weakening. "Well, maybe sometimes. But wouldn't it be degrading to—?"

"Not if it put him away in a hurry, and stopped his depredations in Xanth."

Melody sighed. "All right. I'll shorten my dress some more. But you be good and ready with that soul. I don't want to expose my—you know—one instant longer than I absolutely have to. And you must promise never to tell."

"We promise!" Harmony and Rhythm said together.

Melody hummed, using her individual magic to hike her dress up almost to the knees, and made her blouse half a size smaller. Each of them had magic that was close to Sorceress caliber, but two of them cooperating had more, and the three together had what was generally

conceded to be the strongest talent known. They just had to agree on
what it was they were doing at the moment.

"More," Harmony said.

Melody sighed. She hummed her skirt up to just above her knees,
and shank her blouse another half size. Since her bosom didn't shrink,
this made her blouse stretch rather tightly.

"Still more," Rhythm ordered.

Melody adjusted her dress until it was halfway up her thighs, and
made her blouse another size smaller. But the others still weren't satisfied. Harmony played and Rhythm beat, and suddenly Melody's skirt
barely covered her bottom, and her blouse developed a décolletage so
tight and low that it made walking at anything more than a sedate pace
dangerous. "Oh, come *on*," she protested. "This is ridiculous, not to
mention unbearably exposive."

"Explosive is more like it," Harmony said with satisfaction.

"His eyeballs will pop loose, bounce off the moon, and fall into your
bra," Rhythm said.

"So we'd better get rid of the bra," Harmony said wickedly. "Then
they'll fall into your panty."

"Hey!" Melody protested as her bosom abruptly lost what little remaining restraint it had.

"Don't shout," Harmony said.

"You'll tear your shirt," Rhythm explained.

Melody glanced down. Indeed, her chest was threatening to push
holes in what remained of her shirt, if it didn't leapfrog right out of it.
She tilted, trying to get things better settled.

Sim squawked: He was laughing.

"Don't do that," Harmony said, alarmed. "You must stay vertical, or
it won't be just his eyeballs that pop out and droop to the ground."

"Gee, thanks," Melody said. She was of course being teased, as she
liked to think that "firm" was a better description of her bosom, even
unbound, than "droop."

"And your rear exposure is almost freaking *me* out," Rhythm said,
giving Melody's skirt a tiny tug downward. It seemed it was unable to
cope when she bent forward.

"I'll fix both aspects," Melody said. "More height above, more depth
below." She started to restore some fabric in both places.

"No!" her sisters said together.

"You're fine as you are," Harmony continued.

"Just keep it barely confined until time," Rhythm concluded.

"Well, I don't see you two volunteering," Melody said sharply. "You have exactly the same figures as I do, you know."

"No, you're the one of us who always takes the lead," Harmony said. "We wouldn't be good at that."

"And we don't want to waste all our tedious effort to make you combine the best or worst of Dawn & Eve," Rhythm said.

Melody shook her head ruefully. This had better work, because she would expire of shame otherwise.

7

Heart of the Forest

Becka was still shuddering from the awful experience of Possession by the Sea Hag. She had never in her life felt so utterly helpless and degraded. The Hag had ruled her body and ravished her mind. And it would have gotten worse, had not the Dastard finally caught on and unhappened the Possession.

What an irony: She owed her restoration to the Dastard. She didn't like him, she didn't respect him, but he had saved her from a fate that really would have been worse than death. She wished the Good Magician had not sent her here, but she was stuck with it; she would have to help the Dastard as well as she could.

"Now I figure the Sea Hag will return," the Dastard said. "She won't be able to get your body, but she'll be back, in some other girl's body. Now I want you to do something for me I may not like."

"What?" She thought she had misheard.

"I like girls," he said. "Especially ones old enough to fill their underwear. If the Sea Hag comes in the form of such a girl, you must break it up before she gets to me. Can you do that?"

Oh. "I think so. But how will I know when it's the Sea Hag?"

"You ought to know her as well any anyone does, now that you've been in her thrall. Look for the little signals. When she says 'My pet,' or when she's too eager to summon the stork. Or whatever else might give her away. Any girl we encounter, you check her out, and don't tell me she's not the Sea Hag unless you're sure."

"But how can I be sure? She might be good at fooling me."

"No. She will be good at fooling *me*. I'm a man, and I can't see far beyond her physical appearance. Not at first. But you're a girl, and you know her. You'll be able to tell."

"I hope so," Becka said uncertainly. "If I'm not sure, I'll have to say so. I might condemn an innocent girl."

"Better that, than to let her get at us. I'll unhappen any we're not sure of. That way we should be safe."

"But you could be safe just by not letting any girl or woman get close to you."

"That's not an option. I want to marry a princess. To do that I've got to get close to her. Meanwhile, a non-princess will do to pass the time. So I'll need to get close to her too."

Becka was disgusted, but it was becoming clearer why the Good Magician had sent her. She could indeed help the Dastard. She could do what the Dastard could not: be halfway objective about winsome young women. The question was, why did the Good Magician want to help the Dastard? Why should *anyone* want to help him? He needed to be gotten rid of.

But she couldn't say that. So she would just have to do her best, though she felt like a—a—well, the necessary word was not in her young vocabulary, but it wasn't a nice term. The Dastard wanted merely to use women, for one purpose or another. She pitied the princess he might marry, if he got the chance. But with luck, no princess would be foolish enough to entertain the idea for even a quarter of an instant, let alone a whole moment.

"I'll keep watch," Becka said reluctantly.

"You don't like me," the Dastard said.

"Yes, I don't like you."

"Good. You're telling the truth. That means I can trust you. When you started acting friendly, I knew something was wrong."

"It certainly was! I couldn't turn dragon and drive her away. Thank you for saving me from her."

"You know I did it for me, not for you."

"Yes. But still, I appreciate being saved."

"You would never have been Possessed, if you hadn't come to help me."

"How come you're being honest? I know it's not because you like telling the truth."

"The lie is a valuable tool," he said seriously. "But it's tricky. I have to remember what I said before, and make sure it has verisimilitude."

"Very what?"

"Verisimilitude. That means that it seems true. It's not always easy to craft a lie that has the semblance of truth. So I never waste a good lie. I tell the truth always, unless there is something to be gained by a lie."

"And I guess you have nothing to gain by lying to me."

"Nothing at all. You're not going to be fooled into showing your panties, and at this point you're more useful to sieve out the other girls I'll meet. So why bother?"

Despite herself, Becka was getting curious. The Dastard was a jerk, but he wasn't stupid. "How about not hurting my feelings?"

"Why should I care about your feelings?"

That was right: He had no soul, so had no conscience, and no human emotions like love or commitment. He simply wanted what he wanted, for pure self interest. "So I will try to help you better than I have before."

"You're helping me because the Good Magician sent you. So you're stuck for it regardless. Your feelings are irrelevant."

Becka nodded. That was the case. At least they understood each other. Certainly his brutal honesty was better than Possession by the Sea Hag. "So where are we going?"

"I'm sniffing another nexus, maybe. It's not far ahead."

"Maybe? Don't you know?"

"Nexi aren't necessarily simple. Some are minor, some are significant. I have to study each to be sure. And since the appearance of the Sea Hag, they may even be dangerous."

"Dangerous for you, you mean."

"Of course. What else could I mean?"

"How about the people you hurt?" she demanded.

"I don't hurt anyone. I merely change events. They never know what they are missing."

He had a point. Not a great one, but it was true that he wasn't actually harming others, just denying them benefit. So as bad men went, he was mediocre.

A dim bulb flashed. That could be why the Good Magician wanted to help the Dastard. To make some use of him, since he had a very strong and devious talent. And—a second bulb flashed—that must be what that spell of Awareness Humfrey had given her did: It enabled her to remember things the Dastard unhappened. Because otherwise she might never have realized what the man was doing.

"What were those flashes?"

She was tempted to say none of his business. But it *was* his business, and she didn't want to lie, albeit for different reason than the Dastard had. To her a lie was not a valuable thing, it was a dirty thing. So she told him. "I just realized that the Good Magician must want to make some use of you, and that's why he sent me. And that he gave me a spell to enable me to remember your unhappenings."

The Dastard actually paused in his walking, looking at her. "You must be right. The old codger never does a favor for anyone without demanding a year's Service or the equivalent. So he fixed it so you could help me. But he's an idiot if he thinks I'll do anything for him in return."

Becka doubted that the Good Magician was any idiot, but she didn't argue the case. They resumed their walk toward his next nexus.

They rounded a bend in the path and saw a girl looking confused. She was dark of hair and eye and unusually pretty for her age. "Who are you?" the Dastard demanded.

"I am Nadine Naga, daughter of Prince Naldo Naga and Mela Merwoman."

"You're a princess!" the Dastard exclaimed.

"Of course. Shouldn't I be?"

"But you're young."

"I'm eight years old," she said proudly.

Becka realized that the Dastard was trying to figure out how to marry a princess when she was too young to marry. This needed to be broken up. "What are you doing here, alone?"

"I wasn't alone. I was with my mother. But she gets tired of walking on legs, so she slipped into a pond and made her tail, and I walked around exploring and then I got, well, lost. So I was wondering how to find my way back to the pool. Then you came. Do you know where it is?"

"No," the Dastard said, in his careless-of-feelings way.

Nadine angled her head, looking canny. "Suppose I show you where the leak in the Fountain of Youth is? Then will you help me find my mother?"

"The Fountain of Youth?" the Dastard asked. Becka could almost see the wheels turning in his head. He was old, at least twenty-two, and surely felt the ravages of age. If he had a secret source of Youth Elixir, he would never have to grow yet older.

"Yes. There's a leak, and the water dribbles out and forms an underground streamlet that winds secretly o'er hill and dale and comes out near an ancient farmstead known only to me. I'll show you that, and maybe more." She twitched her little skirt.

At that point Becka became suspicious, but she wasn't quite sure. Maybe the girl was just inventing a story in order to enlist the Dastard's help.

"Yes, show me that," the Dastard agreed eagerly.

It had to be the Youth Elixir he wanted; he *couldn't* be interested in the skirt. Becka hoped.

"Certainly." The girl assumed her naga form, with the body of a serpent and the head of a person, and slithered off the trail. In the process, she left her clothing behind. Becka picked up shirt, skirt, and shoes, and followed. The naga girl would need them again, at such time she changed back to full human form.

They lunged through thick and thin forest, and o'er hill and dale, and came to a farmstead in a small hidden valley. But it was hardly ancient. The house looked as if it had been built last week. The farmer's boy seemed to be about twelve years old, and his sister eleven. The crop seemed to be youthful lollipops.

"See? There it is," Nadine said.

The Dastard plowed right ahead. "How old are you?" he asked the farmer.

"Three hundred and two," the boy said. "And my wife here is two hundred and ninety-eight. We haven't seen another person for fifty years, and that was an old hag who filled her canteen with our water and hobbled away. How many lollipops do you want for your family?"

"None at the moment. I'm more interested in a drink of your water."

Meanwhile Nadine had slithered behind a young silo and reverted to human. Becka hastily returned her clothing to her. "Thank you, my pet."

"You're the Sea Hag!" Becka exclaimed.

"Curses! Foiled again." She changed to full serpent form, deserting her clothing again, and slithered instantly out of sight.

Becka ran up to the Dastard. "Nadine's the Sea Hag!" she cried.

The Dastard paused in his negotiation. "How do you know?"

She realized that he might not appreciate the significance of the phrase, "My pet" or the shaking of an underage skirt. So she tried reason instead. "She has to be. She said she couldn't find her mother at a nearby pond, yet she knew her way unerringly to this long hidden farmstead. How could she know its secret, when no one has been here for fifty years?"

"What secret?" the farmer asked. "We have no secrets here. Just good clean living and hard work keep us young."

"They don't know," the Dastard murmured appreciatively. "You're right, girl: She must be the Sea Hag. Where is she?"

"She turned serpent and slithered away when I caught on to her real nature. We'll never find her now."

"Find who?" the farmer asked.

"She's dangerous," the Dastard said. "She's probably setting a trap for us, now that she has us isolated."

"I can turn dragon and defend us," Becka said.

"Dragon? Where?" the farmer asked.

"Not from her devious devices. She might douse you with Youth Elixir and make you a baby. Then there would be no bar to her getting at me. I'll have to unhappen this whole sequence."

"What are you talking about?" the farmer asked.

Then the Dastard focused. He slid into limbo, but this time he grabbed Becka's hand and hauled her into limbo too. She hadn't realized he could do that, but it figured, because she was part of the sequence being unhappened.

They slid back and forth in limbo, watching the vague scenery pass. They located a lovely buxom woman and her daughter walking through the forest. The daughter was Nadine Naga. The woman paused at a pond, and lifted her skirt. Becka put her hand before the Dastard's eyes just before the woman's plaid panties showed, so that he didn't quite freak out. "Thanks," he said, somewhat gruffly. Becka almost thought he *wanted* to be freaked out, but of course that was ridiculous, because that would prevent him from doing the unhappening.

This was obviously Mela Merwoman. She pulled her dress the rest of the way over her head and off, then stepped out of her panties. She set them carefully on a dry rock. Then she walked into the pond. Her two nice legs became a nice tail, and she plunged into the water.

"What can I do?" Nadine asked. "I'm dying of boredom."

"Pick some posies," Mela called. "But don't talk with any strange men."

"Oh, pooh," the child muttered. "I can handle strange men, and strange women too."

"That's what you think," Becka whispered.

Nadine wandered on, picking posies. Then she paused, looking surprised, then horrified, then smug. The spirit of the Sea Hag had Possessed her. Becka understood her feelings perfectly.

They slid back to just before the Possession. They emerged into Xanth, just out of sight of the girl. "Give her a herb," the Dastard said tersely. "She'll believe you."

That was right, because her mother had warned her against strange men, and the Dastard was the strangest of men. So Becka walked out to intercept the girl.

"Hello," she called.

"Hi," the girl replied, happy to encounter someone halfway close to her own age.

"I'm Becka. I found some nice herbs. They protect me from Possession. Would you like some?"

"Sure," Nadine said.

So Becka strung three herbs on a vine and made a necklace, and Nadine put it on over her head. In return she gave Becka three pretty posies.

"I have to go now," Becka said. She knew these unhappenings had to be brief, because the Dastard didn't like to stay long in the past. Maybe it was a strain on his magic.

"Awww."

"Maybe we'll meet again." She walked back to the spot where the Dastard hid.

"Good job," he said. Then he hauled her back into limbo, and slid forward to wherever the present was. That turned out to be the forest path where they had originally met the naga girl who was the Sea Hag. But now the path was empty. They left limbo and walked on.

"You did a nice thing for Nadine," Becka said. "You freed her of the Sea Hag, and protected her from reinfestation."

The Dastard paused, reflecting. "I suppose I did," he agreed. "I didn't mean to."

Becka knew he wasn't joking. He didn't do favors for others, only for himself. He had saved Becka in order to protect himself, and saved Nadine for the same reason. So his good deeds were incidental, and did him no credit. He would be doing more dastardly deeds soon enough.

"I'm getting hungry," Becka said. "And I don't see much of anything to eat."

"And we're not near another nexus," the Dastard said.

"I can turn dragon and chomp something," she suggested. "Then you can cook some of the meat for yourself."

Another girl came down the path. She looked to be about eighteen, and was strictly average in appearance. "Okay, chomp her," he said. "She's not a nexus."

Becka shuddered, because as usual he wasn't joking. He literally had no use for people he couldn't get something from or do something to. "No. No people. I never chomp people if they aren't trying to hurt me. We'll let her be."

"Suit yourself," he said indifferently. "You're the one who's hungry."

"Hello," Becka said as they met the girl. "I'm Becka, and this is—" She hesitated, not wanting to identify the Dastard by his real name and talent. The Sea Hag would know it anyway, and an innocent person did not need to be burdened by it.

"Dashing," the Dastard said.

That wasn't a name Becka would have come up with, but she let it be. "My talent is turning dragon, and his is—is changing events."

"I'm Janell," the girl said. "My talent is exaggeration."

"You mean you tend to say things that are more than they really are?"

"No. I exaggerate things."

"Isn't that really the same thing? Like saying a berry is big, when really it's small?"

"No. I exaggerate the berry."

Becka was having trouble with this. "I don't think I understand."

Janell glanced to the side. There was a bush with a single dried up greenberry. "Like this." Janell reached down to pick the berry. As she did, it expanded, becoming a big juicy fruit. "See: Now it's this big."

"It's exaggerated!" Becka exclaimed. "This would make a meal for a person!"

"Or for three," Janell said, touching it again. This time it expanded to watery melon size.

"Then let's eat it!" Becka said, delighted. "I was hungry, and this will feed us all."

"We don't have any place to sit down and eat," the Dastard grumped.

"Let me exaggerate this rock," Janell said. She touched a stone by the side of the path, and it expanded into a small boulder. Then she touched three pebbles, and they swelled into rocks big enough to sit on.

"This is wonderful," Becka said, sitting down and setting the fruit on the table stone. She rummaged for her pen knife, but it was too small to cut the huge berry.

"Allow me," Janell said, touching the knife. It expanded into a full-sized kitchen knife. But it was dull. So Janell touched it again, and it became super sharp.

Even the Dastard was becoming impressed. He reacted in his customary way. "Let's see your panties."

"What?" Janell asked.

"He says you must have some pantry," Becka said quickly. "With all that exaggerated fruit."

"Oh. No, I simply exaggerate things as I need them, so I don't need to store them."

"What I said," the Dastard said carefully, "was for you to show me your—"

"Your talent!" Becka said. "But Dast—uh, Dashing, she's already shown us more than enough. It's our turn to show her ours. Our talent,

I mean." She rushed on, afraid of his next clarification. "For example, here's mine." She stepped away from the rock table and turned dragon for a moment, spreading her wings.

"Oh, that's impressive," Janell said. "You really are a dragon girl."

Becka turned back. "Yes. My sire is Draco Dragon. I'd like to meet him someday for more than an hour." She returned to the table. Draco didn't mind flying with her, but was always afraid she would turn girl and reveal his guilty secret to other dragons. So most of her life had been spent in girl form with her mother. That could get tiresome.

"What I'm trying to say," the Dastard said determinedly, "is that you may not look like much, but if you can exaggerate your panties the way you can other things, you can really become interesting."

"My panties!" Janell said, coloring.

"He didn't mean that!" Becka cried. "He's joking."

"I am not joking," the Dastard said in his most dastardly way. "And while you're at it, exaggerate your figure, too. Then we can—"

"It's just talk!" Becka said desperately. "He doesn't realize how it sounds."

But her protests were inadequate to stem the tide. "I think I understand him well enough," Janell said grimly. She looked at the Dastard. "All you see of me is a pair of panties to get into. If you deem them good enough."

"Now at last you understand," the Dastard agreed.

Little hard lines appeared around Janell's eyes. "And do you know what I see in you?"

Becka decided to butt out. It was becoming apparent that this woman could handle herself.

"No. Who cares?"

Janell reached across the table to touch his hand. "I see a surpassingly ugly man, with a dirty mouth."

The Dastard suddenly sprouted green warts, purple tufts of hair in the wrong places, and brown wrinkles galore. He resembled a huge toad with a loathsome disease. He opened his mouth to speak, but instead a big dead fly fell out.

"Who is already halfway to hell," Janell continued inexorably.

The Dastard disappeared. Becka understood: He was literally halfway to hell, wherever that might be. Exaggeration was versatile.

"Sorry about that," Janell said. "But I doubt he's worth your time. As boyfriends go, he's a stinker."

"Oh, he's not my boyfriend," Becka said. "I don't even like him. I'm just on an assignment to help him."

"I can't bring him back. My talent is one way. Maybe I shouldn't have gotten mad, but the way he talked—"

"No man has the right to demand a girl's panties," Becka said. "I'll have to tell him that. Maybe after this he'll listen."

"It may take you some time to find him. I think hell is a long way away."

"That won't be a problem. It's been nice knowing you, Janell. I'm sorry you won't remember me."

"Of course I'll remember you, Becka! You're a really pretty dragon."

Then Becka found herself back on the path, walking beside the Dastard, and she was hungry. He had unhappened the whole episode, as she had known he would.

"This way," he said, drawing her off the path.

They waited while Janell walked past from the other direction. After she was gone, they stepped out on the path again and resumed walking.

"You've got to stop being so blunt about panties," Becka admonished him.

"Why?"

"Because girls don't like being seen as mere walking panties. They want to think you care for their personalities."

He laughed. "Who cares about personalities? Take away panties, and all that's left is bras."

She was having trouble getting through, as she had thought she might. "Dastard, I'm supposed to help you, though I think you're an utter creep. And maybe the best way I can help you is to make you realize that you're never going to impress a princess or any other woman if you don't clean up your language."

"$$$$!" he swore.

"Exactly. If I hadn't been corrupted by the Sea Hag, that word would have freaked me out. Now why don't you try to be nice to the next girl you meet?"

"Oh, I can do it," he said. "I just don't see why I should bother."

"Because maybe you can unhappen things when they go wrong, but if you, perish the thought, should meet an available princess, you won't be able to marry her by unhappening the encounter. You'll have to impress her favorably. Your talent won't impress her, because she'll never see it. You have to do it without magic."

He looked surprised. "I never thought of that."

"Now let's try to find something to eat. You just unhappened a good meal."

They walked on, but the pickings remained sparse. This was a barren region of the forest.

One more girl came down the path. She was cute, but looked to be only five years old. "Nothing there," the Dastard muttered. "She not a nexus, and too small for—"

"So you have nothing you want from her," Becka said. "So try to be nice to her. It'll be really good practice."

"All *right*!" he snapped. "Then will you stop bugging me?"

"Yes."

"Hello, cute little girl," the Dastard called as they came within range. He sounded friendly.

"Hello, strange homely man," the child replied.

"I am Dashing, and this is Becka, who can change into a dragon. Would you like to see that?" He sounded excited.

"Yes!" the child cried happily.

So Becka turned dragon, and suffered herself to be petted in that state. The child turned out to be Piper, the daughter of Hiatus and Desiree. Hiatus was the son of the dour Zombie Master and Millie the Ghost, while Desiree was a dryad: a tree nymph. How the two had ever gotten together was a long but interesting story, and now here was Piper, the point of it all, whose talent was healing. "Not like healing elixir," she said. "I'm not that good. But I can heal some, and maybe more when I grow older."

"But why are you traveling alone?" the Dastard inquired, sounding interested. "Shouldn't you be at home with your mother?"

"No, she lives too close to the madness," the child explained. "It waxes and wanes, and gets kinda crazy, so when it does, I go visit Castle Zombie for a while. I know my way around the forest."

"You surely do," the Dastard agreed, sounding impressed. "Your mother would have made sure of that."

"Yes, she can't leave her tree, but I can. Well, 'bye, you nice people; I gotta go." And she went cheerily on down the path.

The Dastard turned to Becka. "Well?" He sounded disgusted.

"I'm amazed! You were charming. You *do* know how to do it."

"I told you I did. I just don't see the point, if there's nothing I want from her. So now we're rid of the little brat and I don't want to hear any more from you."

Becka realized that without a soul he would never see the point. "Okay."

"Now there's a nexus," he said.

"A nexus," Becka agreed, resigned. How long would she have to watch him doing his dastardly deeds?

This time it was a female troll who came down the path. "Ugh," the Dastard muttered. "No panties there."

"So maybe you should just let her pass by," Becka suggested, not wishing the mischief of unhappening on anyone, even a troll.

"No, a nexus is a nexus."

So they hailed the troll. "Who are you, ugly face?" the Dastard asked, reverting to his normal crudity.

"What do you care, crude mouth?" she responded in kind. Already, Becka liked her better.

"You have recently done something or discovered something, or have had some significant effect on something," he told her. "I mean to change that."

"I don't care if you mean to fly to the moon! If you try to interfere with me, I'll banish you."

Perhaps the experience with Janell made the Dastard cautious. "Banish me?"

"Like this," the troll said. She pointed to a nearby rock—and suddenly it was gone. "I can banish people too. Can't necessarily bring them back."

The Dastard nodded. He understood threats. He turned charming. "That's an excellent talent."

The troll gazed at him as if trying to determine whether he was sincere. Then she changed into a centaur filly. "So what makes you think I have discovered something?"

Both Becka and the Dastard stared, she at the face, he at the bare breasts. "You—are you the same creature?" Becka asked. "I mean—"

"I'm the same person, yes," the centaur answered. "Just a different form. And a different talent."

"A different talent? But—"

"But I can't control my form," she said. "I am Xena. Who are you?"

"I am Becka. I'm a dragon girl." She turned dragon for an instant. "So I know about changing forms. But that's all I do; I have no other talent, really. How can you have two forms and two talents?"

"I don't know, but I do. In this form I can see the true nature of anything. I see you are telling the truth." She looked at the Dastard. "But you—what a dastardly piece of work you are! You have no soul!"

"So what have you discovered?" the Dastard asked.

"That you have no—" Then the centaur was replaced by a clothed female with her head in the shape of a star, holding a tray supporting several bowls of soup.

"What are you now?" the Dastard asked. His interest might even have been genuine.

A mouth appeared in the star-head. "A souper star, of course. Have some soup; it's hot."

Becka was really hungry by this time, so rather than marvel where it had all come from, she accepted a bowl of blue carrot soup. It was delicious. She noticed that another bowl appeared on the tray the moment hers was off it.

"I mean, what other thing did you discover?" the Dastard said.

"Oh, that," Xena said. "It's a—"

She disappeared and was replaced by a fat trunked little tree. It danced constantly around, never rooting in one place for very long.

"This grows wearisome," the Dastard said wearily. "What is she this time?"

A wooden mouth opened in the trunk. "A hyper-bole," of course."

"What's a hyper-bole?" Becka asked.

"A very active tree trunk," the mouth said.

Then the tree trunk disappeared, and a normal seeming woman stood there. "Unless I happen to assume the form of a hyperbole," she said, pronouncing the word differently. "Then I get wildly exaggerated."

"You're making me dizzy," Becka said.

"Excess exaggeration can do that."

"Don't assume that form!" the Dastard said, alarmed.

Becka stifled a smile. He was thinking of his experience with Janell, whose exaggeration was not verbal but physical. "What's your talent in this form?" she asked Xena.

"It is to copy people. But it's not much good, because they last only a few days, and they're really stupid. Only the original has normal intelligence."

The Dastard was interested, which was not a good sign. "Can you copy yourself?"

Xena shrugged. "Sure. But the copy remains stupid."

"Let's see it."

The woman twitched, and suddenly there were two of her, looking identical.

"Which is which?" Becka asked.

"I'm the original," the left one said.

"Show me your panties," the Dastard said to the copy.

"Gee," she said stupidly, and reached down to draw up her skirt. She was actually a well enough formed woman.

"Oh, no!" Becka exclaimed, disgusted. "That's why he wanted a stupid woman."

"He won't get far," the original said. Then she and the copy changed into ogresses.

"Yuck!" the Dastard said. For the ogress's panties had the opposite effect, completely turning him off. The ogre kind was expert at ugliness, and it hardly stopped at the face.

"Me brute; he cute," the ogress said, reaching for the Dastard with a ham hand. Her smile was worse yet.

"I've seen enough," he said. "Uncopy her."

"That is not talent me got," the original ogress said smugly.

"Because your form changed," Becka said, catching on. "And as an ogress, your talents are strength, stupidity, and ugliness."

Meanwhile the ogress copy, who seemed to be of average intellect for her form, was pursuing the Dastard. "Me want see he pantee!" she cried, grabbing for his pants.

Becka's stifled smile almost tugged her mouth off her face in its effort to emerge. The Dastard was being served as he deserved. Hey, she thought—she was rhyming like an ogress!

The centaur reappeared, in both places. "I see that you are a genuinely good girl," Xena said. "But I also see that your friend the Dastard is well named."

"He is indeed," Becka agreed. But something nagged at her. She had introduced herself, but didn't think the Dastard had been named. How could Xena know his name, then?

Meanwhile the copy-centaur had caught the Dastard and was holding him to her ample bare bosom. She might have changed form, but had not forgotten her romantic interest. The Dastard seemed to be not entirely unwilling. But was that how even a stupid centaur filly would act?

"You're the Sea Hag!" Becka said.

The centaur reached for her. "I'll stifle you before he catches on!"

Becka turned dragon and chomped her hand. Xena shrieked.

The Dastard heard her. He struggled to turn within the copy-centaur's embrace, and saw. He understood. "Get over here," he cried.

Becka flew across to him, and returned to girl form as she landed. He grabbed her hand.

Then the two of them were sliding into limbo. They moved back in time and geography, locating the moment the Sea Hag infused Xena. It was not long before, as it had to postdate Nadine Naga's reversion.

There was Xena in troll form discovering a very special stream, which glowed with life. "That's the Stream of Life!" the Dastard said.

"What's that?"

"It is to healing elixir as a mountain is to a molehill. Of course nobody needs that much restorative power, so there's never been a search for it. But it would probably attract the Sea Hag."

Xena changed to hyperbole form, and reacted wildly. She dipped a damaged root into the stream, and the root was suddenly whole and vigorously healthy.

After a moment Xena became the centaur—and the centaur paused, looking surprised, then repelled, then smug. The Sea Hag had come.

They slid back to the time between the stream and the Possession. The Dastard emerged into the regular scene, and gave Becka a shove. "Introduce yourself, give her some herbs, and tell her to meet your friend where we met her before."

"You're still after her panties!" she exclaimed, disgusted.

"Two things, girl: First, she's obviously of age, so can show me her panties if she wants to. Second, those panties are too brief between changes to be feasible, so what I'm after is the nexus, which I have not yet identified."

He was right. She was being unduly suspicious and restrictive. It was not her business to police his morals. Her experience with the Sea Hag had shown her how much, much worse morals could be. Embarrassed, she walked out to intercept Xena. "Hello, Centaur filly."

"Greetings, human girl."

"I'm Becka, a dragon girl."

"So I see, and you do mean well. I'm Xena, a multiple—" Suddenly she was the ogress. "Me be torn, many form."

"You have many forms?" Becka asked, drawing on her prior experience to catch on remarkably quickly. "That's your talent?"

"Talents too, different doo," the ogress said.

"A different talent for each form? That's remarkable!"

"Mainly painly," the ogress said, looking unogreshly pensive.

"You don't like it? Well, I'm afraid I can't help you with that, but let me give you something. These herbs will protect you from some other threat. Take them." She proffered a string of herbs.

"Girl give she, gift me see?" the ogress asked, dully astonished. She donned the necklace.

"Yes. And—"

But now the ogress was the souper star. "Oh, good," Xena said through her star shaped head. "Now I can repay you. Please have some nice hot soup before I change again."

"Thank you." Becka took a steaming bowl of black potato soup and tasted it. It was just as good as the other soup had been, or rather, would be. "I think I saw you discover something a moment ago. What was it?"

"The Stream of Life," Xena said. "I thought it was mythical, but I just stumbled upon it. Well, actually I was looking for it, but I never expected to find it."

Becka was aware that time was passing. She had to get back to the Dastard. "Look, Xena—I'd like you to meet a—an associate." She couldn't push the word "friend" through her reluctant mouth. "Why don't you walk on down this path, and I'll take a brief errand behind some bushes, then I'll tell him about you, and then you can tell us everything."

"Very well," the troll said. "Keep the soup."

"Thank you." The troll walked on down the path.

Becka rejoined the Dastard, who pulled her right into limbo, then reverted to their present. They emerged walking along the path as before. Becka was still eating her excellent soup. She decided not to wonder about that too much, lest it fade away. "You took your time," he grumped.

"She kept changing form. I couldn't let on that I knew about it. Anyway, I learned that she was looking for the Stream of Life, so she must have a reason, and maybe that's why she's a nexus."

He glanced at her almost appreciatively. "That helps, sometimes I almost regret that you're underage." He glanced where her panties would show, if they showed, but of course she made sure they didn't.

"Not to mention being a dragon girl," she reminded him grimly. One of his problems—by no means the worst—was that he could not appreciate a girl or woman at all without orienting on her underwear. Age had very little to do with it. What princess of any age would ever put up with that? He ought to settle for a nymph who liked being forever chased and—what did they call it? Celebrated. Maybe she should suggest that.

They rounded a turn, and there was Xena, in her woman form. "Hello, Xena," Becka called.

"You know me?" the woman asked, surprised. "Did you see this form?"

"I recognize the herb necklace."

"Oh, of course. And you have the soup."

"Yes, it's wonderful. This is the Das—Dashing. He's very interested in what you found."

"Yes," the Dastard said. "What use do you have for the Stream of Life?"

"I want it to revive the Heart of the Forest. It's the only thing that can. For years I have searched for the Stream, and now at last I have found it. I filled a can—"

She became the centaur. "—teen with it." She stared at the Dastard. "But I am not at all sure I should tell you about it. You are not a nice man." She paused, reflecting. "But there is that in your mind that suggests I owe you a considerable favor."

How true that was, Becka thought. He had, for purely selfish reason, saved her from the Sea Hag.

"If you held your human form long enough to show me your panties," the Dastard said suggestively, "I'd show you how nice I can be. For a little while."

Xena considered. "You know my nature, and you want to get at my panties?"

"You know mine, and you want to give them to me?"

"Perhaps. It is true that no man has been interested in me after the first or second change."

Becka was amazed and slightly appalled. They were working it out! She knew she should keep her mouth shut, but it opened anyway. "But you want to marry a princess," she reminded the Dastard.

"True. But until I find one, I want to find a temporary relationship. One I can throw away as convenient. This is a prospect."

"A throwaway prospect," Xena agreed. "Your soulless candor is refreshing. I'll consider it. Certainly I wouldn't want to associate with you for very long." She became the ogress. "Me choose he use."

"Why do you want to revive the Heart of the Forest?" the Dastard asked.

"That's a separate story that perhaps would bore you," the centaur filly replied.

"We're interested," Becka said.

The souper star reappeared. Apparently the order of change was random, as was the duration of a particular form. "Soup?"

Becka had finished her prior bowl. She took another. So did the Dastard. "Tell us while we eat," the Dastard said.

"Very well," the star-head said. "The Dead Forest was once a wonderful living forest, until the Curse Fiends cursed it for obscure reason, killing all the trees. Something to do with an amorous ogre, I believe. But I live near it, and I regret that it suffers such a fate. I learned that it is not quite dead, merely dormant. In its center is its heart, and if the heart of the forest were to be revived, the whole forest would quickly recover. So I resolved to revive it. The only thing that can revive the Heart is water from the Stream of Life. I have been searching for it for years. Today, at last, I found it. Now I can revive that forest. It will be the culmination of my generally indifferent life."

Becka heard this narration with increasing distress. This was a truly worthy thing to do—and so naturally the Dastard would unhappen it, and the forest would never be revived. What a pity.

The centaur returned. "So that is why. And—" She stared at the Dastard. "And you intend to ruin it! I ought to kick your head!"

"Maybe there's another way!" Becka cried desperately. She knew that if the centaur filly tried to kick his head, he would just unhappen the event, then unhappen her project. Both together, probably, to avoid overlapping. "That dead forest has become a landmark. It's famous. People chart their courses by it. It would be a horrible shock to almost everyone if it suddenly changed. What you really want to unhappen is the dead forest itself."

The Dastard considered, surprised. "You could be right."

He was buying it! "And if you help her revive it, maybe she really will show you her p—pan—" She couldn't get the word out, in this naughty context. "You know."

Now he was definitely intrigued. "Would you?" he asked Xena.

"Oh, I think so," the centaur agreed. "In one of my forms that has them. After the Dead Forest revives. Shall we call it a deal?"

"Deal," he said immediately. He was very quick to appreciate a net gain. Of course his word was not good, but he would go along with what profited him in one way or another or both.

They walked on down the path toward the Dead Forest. Xena changed forms erratically, but maintained her side of the dialogue well enough. She did seem pleased to be associating with someone for more than a change or two. Her life was surely a lonely and frustrating one. And, Becka forcefully reminded herself, she was an adult and could do as she chose. Even with a heel like the Dastard. So Becka sipped her soup as she walked, and let it be.

In due course they approached the Dead Forest. Souper star handed Becka a flask. "Follow this path on to the center of the forest," she said. "The Heart will be there. Pour the Stream of Life water out onto it, and observe what happens."

"But I thought you wanted to do that yourself," Becka said, surprised.

"I want to be sure that it is done," the centaur said. "But I know you will do it. Meanwhile there is a nice private bower here that I think will do for the other."

"Will do for what other?" Becka asked, perplexed.

"I am bound to assume my woman form before long. We need to be ready, as there may not be much time."

"Ready for what?"

Xena and the Dastard just looked at her. After a moment, Becka blushed as deeply as she could manage. "Oh."

She turned and walked on down the path. The fire on her face slowly burned off, leaving her merely embarrassed. She wished the Sea Hag hadn't so brutally educated her about the secrets of the Adult Conspiracy. There were some things she would gladly have waited several more years to know.

She saw the dead trees on either side of the path. They were huge and gnarled and bare. This was a really gloomy region, and would have been scary were she not a dragon girl. It seemed impossible that these trees could ever live again. But she would find out.

She came to the center. This was a heart-shaped clearing, slightly raised. Obviously this was where the Heart was supposed to be. But where was it? She looked all around and didn't see it. Just this dirty mound.

She squatted and tapped the ground to see what kind of rock it was. But it wasn't rock, it was wood. This was an old, worn, weathered, battered, mass of wood, maybe the remnant of some giant ancient tree. Everything must have rotted away except the heartwood.

Heartwood. A bulb flashed. "The Heart!" she exclaimed. "This is it!"

She uncorked the vial and poured it out on the wood, spreading the fluid around. A gentle, sweet-smelling vapor rose from it. The liquid flowed across the ridges and cracks, finding its way into the crevices of the giant wooden heart. She backed away, still pouring, until the last of the elixir was gone. There had not been nearly enough to cover the whole surface, but she hoped that wasn't necessary.

The wood began to swell where the water from the Stream of Life touched it. Becka hastily got the rest of the way off it, and stood by the edge of the clearing, watching. The effect was expanding, and the surface was beginning to move slowly up and down. There came a sound, deep and increasingly powerful, as of a drum being slowly pounded, ba-boom, ba-boom, ba-boom. In fact the Heart was beating!

Becka watched and listened, awed. The heart was now a dramatically living thing, pumping its fluid through the Dead Forest. And the trees were coming alive too. Buds were swelling, leaves were growing, even some flowers were blooming. The entire forest was turning green. It was absolutely lovely.

Becka stood there, entranced by the wonder and sheer splendor of at all. What a marvel this was, the dead returning so dramatically to life. All because she had poured a few cups of healing water onto the Heart. If this was the only really good thing she ever accomplished in her life, still it was enough to give her life meaning. She was utterly thrilled.

8

PTERO

Little Princess Melody looked around. Castle Roogna looked just like the real one on Xanth, but so far the people were either too old or odd. This Green Murphy, for example: How could she be their little sister, when she was nineteen? That was positively ancient. But she did have one thing going for her: her dark green hair. Melody could relate to a person with green hair; there weren't many, apart from her mother Ivy, and Grandma Irene.

Green Murphy led the four of them out of the castle. There was the surrounding moat, and the moat monster. Melody didn't recognize the latter. "What happened to Soufflé?" she asked.

"Oh, this is Chip, Soufflé's apprentice," Green said. She called to the moat monster. "Hi, Chip!"

The huge serpent slid through the water toward them. "Hi, Green. Who're your friends?"

"He talks?" Rhythm asked, surprised.

"He uses illusion," Green said.

"Oh, you promised not to tell," Chip said.

"To talk, I mean," Green said quickly. "So folk can understand you."

"What's not being said?" Rhythm asked.

"Chip," Green said, "these are the Princesses Melody, Harmony, and Rhythm, and their friend Sim."

"But they're too young for this region."

"They're from Xanth. They exchanged with the ones we know. So is it all right to tell them about the rest of your illusion?"

The monster peered closely at the four. "They do look like them. Very well, I'll tell. My illusion makes me big, when I'm serving in a big moat."

"You look regular moat-monster size," Sim peeped.

"I'm not. I'm imp moat-monster sized." Then the illusion dissipated, and Chip shrank into the size of a chipmouse. "But this wouldn't impress an invader, so I use illusion to magnify my size and make my voice intelligible."

"Oh, that makes sense," Melody agreed. "Maybe we should do that too."

"No need," Chip said. "Just travel downtime."

"Downtime?" Harmony asked.

"I'm about to show them," Green said. "This is their first visit here."

"Oh. Have a nice visit. Beware of the comic strips." Chip slowly sank down into the water and disappeared.

"Downtime," Rhythm repeated. "Comic strips?"

"Let me show you," Green said. "Then you'll understand. We're so used to it that we tend to forget that it's different on other worlds."

"Other worlds?" Sim peeped.

"Those too," Green said. "I'll show you everything. One thing at a time."

They walked westward. "Look north," Green said, and they looked. "Do you see that it's blue?"

"Yes," Melody said. "There's a sort of blue haze."

"That's because it's cold that way. Now look south."

"There's a red haze," Harmony said. "Does that mean it's hot?"

"Yes. The farther you go, the hotter its gets, until it's just a desert. So you can always have the climate you want, here on Ptero. Now look east."

They turned to look back toward the castle. "There's a yellow haze," Rhythm concluded.

"That's the color of the past. Now look forward."

"It's green," Sim said. "That must indicate the future."

"Smart bird," Green agreed. "We refer to them as From and To. From the past, To the future." She paused. "Now do you notice anything about yourselves?"

They considered. "No," Melody said.

"Then I'll use my talent," Green said. "Which is to manipulate time so I can travel farther."

"But time isn't travel," Harmony said.

"Here it is," Green said. "Hold my hands."

The four of them touched her two hands. Suddenly they were farther west. The scenery had changed.

"What did you do?" Rhythm asked.

"I moved us two hours west. Now how do you see yourselves?"

They looked around. There was something odd about the landscape. "It's smaller," Sim said, surprised. "And so are you, Green Murphy."

"No, I'm the same size," the woman insisted.

"We're bigger!" Melody exclaimed, a bulb flashing above her head.

"So we are," Harmony agreed, staring at her sisters and Sim.

"No, we're *older*," Rhythm concluded. "We're six years old, and Sim is seven."

"Two years older," Green agreed. "So am I. In this circumstance, an hour equals a year. If you go farther west, you'll eventually become adult, and share the Adult Conspiracy. When you go back, you will return to your original age."

The three not-quite-so-little princesses were awed at the notion of fathoming the Adult Conspiracy, but didn't quite believe it. There was always a catch.

"How can this be?" Sim peeped, amazed. "Geography is not time."

"Yes, geography *is* time, here," Green said. "That's the thing about Ptero. We're not fixed in age; we can be any age we want, from baby to ancient. All we have to do is travel east or west."

"From or To," Sim peeped, showing how well he understood.

"Different magic!" Melody said. "Ptero has different magic."

"Yes. The magic of time and space. This makes my particular talent more useful."

"But how can hours be years?" Harmony asked.

"Strictly speaking, it can be confusing," Green said. "I was speaking of the time it would take us to walk this distance. It would take us another two hours to walk back, but then we would not get older, but younger. I simply jumped us two hours ahead in our schedule. My talent is not exactly to manipulate real time, but personal time. It will be simpler if you just think of geography as age."

Rhythm put her hands to her head. "I can't."

"Neither can I," Melody said. "That thought is too big for my cute little noggin."

"I can," Sim said. But he didn't count; he was destined to be the wisest of all birds. Besides, his noggin was bigger than theirs.

"Let's move farther downtime," Green said. "Your adult minds should find it easier to assimilate."

Bemused, they took hold of her hands again, and suddenly they were twenty years old, full grown. They gazed at each other, awed. "We're beautiful!" Melody said.

"Lovely," Harmony agreed.

"Phenomenal," Rhythm concluded.

"And I'm huge," Sim peeped.

They looked at him. He was now full roc-sized, a splendid avian figure.

"I'm sorry I can't take you to your age twenty-one," Green Murphy said. "But that is now your missing year."

They looked at her. "You're old!" Melody said tunelessly.

"Thirty-five," she agreed. "I can travel in personal time, in my fashion, but geography governs me too. Were your older Selves here, they would be thirty-seven."

"Ugh!" Harmony said unharmoniously.

"What a fate," Rhythm said without a good beat.

"Not necessarily," Sim peeped. "Since they can control it geographically."

"That is correct," the older Green agreed. "Age is no specter for us, as we exist at whatever level we choose. Actually, we discover delights in any age, and periodically move Castle Roogna From or To for variety."

Melody had a problem with this. She found that her new adult mind was more reasonable and rational than her child mind, but it couldn't make sense of all aspects. "If you can be any age, when do you fade out?"

"We don't. We remain indefinitely without beginning or end. We are immortal."

Harmony's mind was also more mature. "Yet you have babyhood and seniorhood. How can that be, if you never pass from the scene?"

"We are constrained by our natural life-spans," Green explained. "We can travel anywhere within them, but not beyond them. So I have been back to age two and forward to age eighty-two, and enjoyed both, and all between. But if I want to know what is beyond, I must ask someone whose life extends before mine, or after mine. Thus our geography is limited, not our existence."

"But what of us in Xanth?" Rhythm asked. By not much of a coincidence her mind too was mature. "We do grow old, and fade out if we don't get Youth Elixir. What happens to us?"

"Why you return here, of course. You are mortal only temporarily, but immortal forever."

"This does not seem like such a bad place," Sim peeped.

"It isn't. Of course it's not very exciting, either. But it's what we have. Sometimes we arrange to visit the smaller worlds, for variety."

"Those would be the other worlds you mentioned before?" Sim inquired.

"Yes. Perhaps it is time to explain about them. Ptero, as you know, is actually a moon orbiting your Princess Ida's head. Princess Ida on Ptero also has a moon."

"Oh, we didn't see it," Melody said.

"It is shy about folk it doesn't know. I'm sure soon you can see it, if you wish. It is Pyramid, with four triangular sides, each a different color. Its rules of magic differ from those of Xanth or Ptero, but are consistent to their world."

Harmony's brow furrowed. "Is there a Princess Ida on Pyramid?"

"Yes, and she has her own moon, called Torus, in the shape of a doughnut."

All four of them burst out laughing. "We hope nobody eats it," Rhythm said.

"And Torus, too, has an Ida?" Sim inquired. He was always interested in learning more.

"Yes. It is called Cone, because it is in the shape of a cone. It is filled with water, which is a mighty sea to those who live there. Land folk live on the outside, and water folk under the sea, but they can summon the stork only by getting together with each other. So there is a lot of activity at the shore."

"The stork!" Melody exclaimed, amazed. "We know how to signal the stork!"

"But you will forget it when you return to your younger age," Green said.

The three considered. "It isn't as if it's all that much," Harmony said.

"All that curiosity wasted on such a dull business," Rhythm concluded, disgusted.

"Let's learn more about this world," Sim peeped.

"I thought I would show you a comic strip," Green Murphy said.

"Didn't Chip Moat Monster warn us against them?" Melody asked.

"Yes he did," Harmony agreed.

"So naturally we're most curious about them," Rhythm finished.

"I thought you would be," Green said. "There's one not far north of here."

They walked toward the blue haze. It did not get perceptibly colder, so Melody realized that the really cold weather was probably a long way away. That was fine with her.

Before they got there, they encountered two somewhat seedy-looking adults. "Hello, Green!" the woman called.

"Hello, Zelda," Green called back.

They came together. "Who are your friends?" the man inquired. "They look like the royal triplets, but they're the wrong age."

"They *are* the triplets," Green explained. "They exchanged with their other Selves for a Xanth mission. So they're seventeen years younger now. So is Sim." She turned to the four. "These are Xander and Zelda Zombie, twins, children of Xavier and Zora. His talent is electromagnetism, and hers is slowing time."

"But King Xeth is Xav and Zora's son," Melody protested.

"We were delivered the year after," Zelda explained. "We never made it to Xanth."

"Never made it?" Harmony asked.

"Like me," Green said. "Ptero is filled with folk who aren't in Xanth. We wish we could be there, but there simply isn't room for all of us might-be's there." She looked sad.

"Can't you go to Xanth?" Rhythm asked.

"No we can't," Xander said. "We have to be taken there by the stork, and the storks don't take every person who wants to go. But we're glad our brother Xeth made good. There are not great opportunities for zombies or half-zombies there, but things are improving."

"Especially since the Zombie Master found us a world of our own," Zelda said.

"Yes, now you can all rot together," Sim peeped.

"Say, maybe we can exchange a service," Xander said.

"A service?" Melody asked.

"Here on Ptero we exchange services," Green Murphy said. "Nobody does anything for anybody else without a fair exchange."

"But you're showing us around," Harmony said.

"That is part of the exchange of services you four are making. Your friends on Xanth are surely helping your other Selves to manage there, and we are helping you to manage here."

"So we don't have to do anything for you," Rhythm concluded. "But we can for Xander."

"What do you wish?" Sim peeped.

"I thought of something I want to tell Magician Trent," the half-zombie man said. "But telling Trent here is no good, because he can't affect his self in Xanth. So I need to find a messenger to take it to him there."

"We can do that," Melody said. "Magician Trent is our great grandpa. He and Grandma Iris were youthened."

"They moved to the Isle of Illusion, where they set up an embassy to the merfolk," Harmony added.

"And they have a daughter," Rhythm said. "I forget her name."

"Irenti or Trentia," Melody said.

"Yes. She's here on Ptero. That is what made me think of this. I think he should go back and rescue his first wife, in Mundania, and bring her to Xanth."

"But she died," Harmony protested. "Awful things like that happen in Mundania."

"But a person in Xanth can visit Mundania any time," Zelda put in. "So he could cross over and catch her before she died."

They considered that. It did seem possible. "But then what about Great Grandma Iris?" Rhythm asked. "Would we have to change her?"

"You can't do that," Sim peeped. "That would be paradox. Not to mention the elimination of their daughter."

"No, we're thinking of having him rescue her now, in your present time," Xander said. "So it wouldn't change anything for you. But she would be alive, and young, and he could have her back. I don't think Iris would mind."

Melody wasn't sure of that, but didn't think it was her place to make such a decision. "We can tell him," she said. "What he does then will be his own business."

"Excellent," Xander said. "Now what can we do for you?"

The girls exchanged a glance. It was a much larger glance than usual, because they were now several times as old as they were used to. Thus it conveyed several times as much information.

"We'd like to see Mother and Father when they were little," Harmony said.

"So we can prove they messed up too," Rhythm finished.

"We were delivered five years after Princess Ivy," Zelda said. "We can go back to when she was five. But we can't take you there, because you are too young. Your territory does not extend that far."

"Maybe you can," Sim peeped. "The princesses have very special magic, if it works here."

"It does work here," Green said. "But as far as we know, no magic can enable a person to travel beyond her lifetime."

"If we sing and play it real, we might do it," Melody said. "At least in illusion."

"That would be good enough," Harmony agreed. "We just want to see them."

"Illusion," Xander said. "To recreate the scene. Based on our observation."

"Yes," Rhythm said. "You can go back there, and send what you see, and we'll see it."

The man nodded. "Maybe that will work. We can certainly try it. But it would be better to start from our home, instead of out here in the open, so we won't be disturbed."

"But we live across the comic strip," Zelda said. "You wouldn't want to go there."

"Yes we do," Melody said. "We were headed for it anyway."

"What's supposed to be so bad about the comic strip?" Harmony asked. "It sounds funny."

"It's disgusting," Xander said. Which was an odd thing for a half-zombie to say.

"It's not dangerous, is it?" Rhythm asked.

This time it was Xander, Zelda, and Green who exchanged an adult-sized glance. "No, it's not dangerous to the body. It's just something you have to experience to properly appreciate," Green said.

"But what *is* it?" Sim asked.

"The regions of Ptero are separated by no-creatures-land strips of puns," Green said. "We live in the human section, Xander and Zelda live in the zombie section, and the centaurs live in the centaur section, and so on. There are many mixed sections, where crossbreeds exist, and of course folk don't *have* to live with their own kind. The folk of the different sections don't bother each other much, because it's so uncomfortable crossing the strips."

"Because we're half-zombie," Zelda said, "our brains are half festering anyway, so we can tolerate the comic strips. So we can explore freely. But you completely human folk may suffer worse. You have sane minds."

They were acting as if mere puns were horrible. Melody thought they must be exaggerating. "Let's go see," she said.

"Every person just has to learn the hard way," Green murmured.

They walked on as a group. "There it is," Xander said.

"All we have to do is cross to the other side," Zelda said. She looked a bit pale, even for a half-zombie.

They looked. It seemed to be a thin zone of odd plants and objects. It did not look frightening or gruesome.

"Puns, do your worst," Harmony said, striding forward.

"Here we come," Rhythm said, joining her.

Melody would have hesitated, but had to join her sisters. Sim seemed to have similar reservations, but came along also.

They stepped across the vague line almost together. Nothing happened. Melody saw what looked like beans lying scattered on the ground. She stooped to pick one up. It seemed soft, so she squeezed it. There was a squirt of fluid from its end that vaporized and formed into letters: BEWARE! PUNS AHEAD.

Melody stared at it, not getting the point. Of course there were puns ahead!

"I get it," Sim peeped. "That's ampoule warning."

Slowly that registered. Melody groaned. As puns went, that was egregious.

Meanwhile, Harmony found a little package. She opened it—and everything went still. There was no motion anywhere; it was as if they were all frozen. But they weren't, exactly.

Zelda joined them. "Ah, you have opened half of a split moment," she said. "I recognize it, because of my talent of slowing time. When you open the other half, time will stand still, and you will be able to act with greatest effect."

"But I just wasted it," Harmony said, disgusted.

"That happens, in the comic strip."

Meanwhile Rhythm had stirred up a cloud of bees. They were buzzing angrily around their tree but not stinging.

"Those are wood-bees," Green said. "They have grown up to be hasbeens. That's why they can't sting."

"I feel like a has-bee myself," Rhythm confessed, appreciating the awfulness of the pun.

Sim passed nearby, and stirred up more bees. They didn't sting either; instead they banged into things, and whatever they touched sprouted a little sign saying NO CHARGE. He considered that for a moment, then brightened. "Free bees!"

Melody took another step, and suddenly she was half stuck in tar. She slipped in it and fell, getting more of it on her. Tar was everywhere, coating her clothing and limbs. "Oook!" she cried.

"No, it's tar-nation," Xander clarified. "Everything in it is made of tar. You'll just have to drag on through it."

Next to her, Harmony was stepping in a puddle. She felt something under her foot and bent to pick it up. It was a fish in the shape of her foot. "Oh, no, a sole!" she exclaimed, disgusted.

Rhythm left her bees behind and came up against a huge flat freestanding sign. BILL IS BORED, it said.

"A bill bored," she muttered.

Sim blundered into a bog in which tall thin plants with expanded muffs grew. The moment he touched one, it moved, pulling out of the bog to reveal a body below. It was a tail. "Do you know that Sean Mundane and Willow Elf summoned the stork?" it demanded. "And I'll tell you exactly how they did it!"

"A tattle tail!" Sim peeped.

"We've got to get out of here!" Melody cried. She linked hands with her sisters and charged for the nearest clear region, with Sim right beside them.

They burst out into what appeared to be a huge cave. "Oops, wrong direction," Zelda said. "This may be complicated to escape."

"Why, what is it?" Harmony asked.

"The Com Unity section," Green said grimly. "We'd almost be better off in the comic strip."

Rhythm looked around. In every direction were lighted screens. Some had print on them, others had pictures. "This resembles Com Pewter's cave," she said.

"Which suggests that these machines can change local reality," Sim concluded.

"Back away slowly," Green said. "Don't make any sudden moves. Maybe we can escape before they realize we're here."

PARTY OF SEVEN STEPS FORWARD, the nearest screen printed.

They stepped forward in unison, seven steps.

"Who or what is this?" Melody asked, alarmed.

I AM COM PULSION, the screen printed. I CHANGE THE REALITY OF VISITORS WHO DO NOT WISH TO OBEY. WHO ARE YOU?

She felt compelled to answer. "I am Sorceress Melody, and these are my sisters and companions."

"Who are the others?" Harmony asked.

In answer, words appeared in each screen, identifying them:

COM MUTE. I CHANGE THE REALITY OF TRAVEL.

COM RAD. I CHANGE THE REALITY OF FRIENDSHIP.

COM MA. I CHANGE THE REALITY OF PUNCTUATION.

COM FUSE. I CHANGE THE REALITY OF INTELLIGIBILITY—I THINK.

"Well, we can't stay," Rhythm said. "It has been nice meeting you."

Com Pulsion's print changed. VISITING TWENTY-YEAR-OLD WOMEN ARE SILENT. PARTY OF SEVEN WILL—

A flickering zap crossed all five screens. "Turn and flee!" Zelda cried. "I'm slowing their time."

"And I'm nullifying them for an instant electromagnetically," Xander said.

They turned and fled the cave. In half a moment they were back in the comic strip. The half-zombies' talents had gotten them free.

But now they had to fight their way back out of the stinking morass of puns. Melody's foot came down on something squishy. She yanked her foot up, but the squished thing clung stickily to it. She had stepped in a pun. She had to use her hand to pry it off, and then some of the squished ick got on her fingers. It stung, and without thinking she put her fingers in her mouth. That was another mistake. The taste was foul.

"$$$$!" she shouted. "####! ★★★★!"

Her sisters stared at her. Harmony turned as red as utter shame, and Rhythm's teeth fell into the bottom of her mouth.

"She's swearing!" Sim peeped.

Green Murphy looked at the remnant of the squished pun. "No wonder! That's I-be-profane. It makes a person swear villainously."

"Or a here-tic," Xander said. "It's hard to tell, in that condition."

"Stop theorizing and get out of here," Zelda said. "This way."

They followed her into a blinding light. Suddenly they were flung outward. Melody found herself sitting on the ground, the dread comic strip behind her. The others were sprawled around her.

"What happened?" Sim peeped. His lovely feathers were severely ruffled.

"I found a white hole," Zelda said. "It throws everything out."

"Thank you," Melody gasped. "I couldn't stand much more of that."

"You were right about the comic strip," Harmony said. "It's horrible."

"Yuck!" Rhythm concluded.

They were evidently in the zombie region, because the grass of the lawn was somewhat rotten, and the trees dripped slime. But it seemed wonderful. What was a little honest rot, compared to spoiling puns? They got to their feet, got themselves organized, and walked the rest of the way to the half-zombie house.

The house, of course, was something less than pristine. It reminded Melody of the Zombie Master's castle back on Xanth, only on a lesser scale. "Why didn't you join the zombies on their new world?" she asked.

"Because we're only half-zombie," Xander replied. "Anyway, it's the zombies of Xanth who need that world; we have a perfectly good region here on Ptero."

"Now let's see how we can show you your mother as a young girl," Zelda said. "I'm afraid we can't show you your father; he was in Mundania, and so he didn't appear in Ptero until he came to live in Xanth. He is limited to his adult life, geographically."

"That's all right," Harmony said. "Mother Ivy is enough."

"We can't do this with our magic," Xander said. "How are you going to arrange it?"

"We'll sing and play a picture of what you send us," Rhythm said. "We may not be able to go as far back as you can, but we can use our magic to tune to your minds and see what you see and hear what you hear."

"I'm not sure I understand," he said. "I don't have the healthiest mind."

"I think I understand," Green Murphy said. "It's not that your mind is bad, but that the concept is tricky. But I've seem them do it before, when their other selves wanted to travel beyond their life spans. They set up a connection to you, and maintain it while you travel. So it's as though you're in touch with a magic mirror."

"This is formidable magic," he said.

"They are Sorceresses, and their power squares when two of them act together, and cubes when three do. They can be formidable manipulators of time, when they try."

"That is indeed formidable," Zelda agreed. "It makes my talent seem like a spot on the wall."

"And mine seem like garden variety," Green agreed. "Though I am myself a Sorceress."

Melody refrained from reminding them that time was only one aspect of their joint talent. They could be formidable in several types of magic, when they tried. She realized that her sense of discretion was now adultish instead of childish. "We'll start our picture now," she said. "So you can see how it works."

Melody sang wordlessly—she realized with a start that humming had been her childish form of music—and Harmony played her harmonica and Rhythm beat her drum. A picture of Xander and Zelda formed in the air between them, looking exactly as they did in real Ptero half-life.

"That's me!" Xander said, startled, in life and in the picture.

"And me," Zelda said. "But I shouldn't be there; I'm not going. I'll stay here to fix a batch of pickled cookies for a snack." She turned, in life and in the picture, and stepped out of the picture. As she did so, the picture figure zipped to the real figure, and they merged.

"Very well," Xander said. "I will hike back to Princess Ivy's childhood in the human section." He left the house and started walking. The man disappeared, but the picture remained, showing him emerging from the house. Then he looked around. "Are you still there?"

"There's a picture in front of you," Green said. "Only you can see it, but it's there. Just focus your eyes on it."

"Oh, there you are," he agreed. "Right there inside the house. But you know, it will take me several hours to get there, even electromagnetically enhancing my velocity."

"I'll fast forward us to your arrival," Green said.

"Maybe that's just as well. I will have to cross a comic strip on the way there."

"Fast forward!" Harmony said. The picture wavered, because she had to interrupt her playing, but it steadied when she resumed. The others laughed.

"I'll bake those cookies," Zelda said, leaving the room.

Then they were several hours later. Melody could tell, because the hands of the decrepit clock on the wall had jumped. Zelda was just returning with a hot plateful of cookies. Green had used her talent, which was proving to be useful to alleviate boredom.

The cookies looked slightly putrid, but tasted good; they were not actually rotten. While they ate, they contacted Xander. "Are you there?" Sim peeped.

"Yes," he agreed. "Your picture was frozen for several hours; I was getting concerned." He didn't speak in words, because he was now a baby one-year-old. He spoke in goos and gurgles, but they were able to understand him.

"They couldn't update it while they were being fast forwarded," Green explained. "It will be the same when you return."

"Where are you?" Rhythm asked.

"I am in the eastern part of the human section, where Princess Ivy is six years old," he gurgled. "In fact, here she is now."

The picture oriented on a cute little girl with green hair, a green dress, and a little crown. She was, it turned out, holding Baby Xander. All girls liked babies. "She looks a lot like you, Melody," Sim peeped.

Ivy in the picture looked at him. "Who are you, big bird?"

"I am Sim, son of the Simurgh," he peeped.

"She has a chick?" she asked, cutely astonished.

"I'm from a later time," he peeped. "I was hatched in the year Ten Ninety-five. At the moment I am in the year Eleven Sixteen, visiting Xander and Zelda Zombie."

"Oh, downtime," she said. She peered past him. "Is that Zelda? She looks so old!"

"I am forty-two at the moment," Zelda agreed.

"I am your daughter Green Murphy," Green said. "And these are your daughters: Melody, Harmony, and Rhythm."

"Wow! I'll have to get on To and meet them."

"They want to see you as a child, because they never knew you then."

"They do? Well, here I am." Ivy stuck out her tongue and made a bronze cheer. This wasn't as great as a copper or sliver cheer, but it was naughty enough.

Melody and Rhythm laughed, and Harmony choked slightly on her harmonica. Ivy was like them, all right!

"Do you want to see more of me?" Ivy asked. She set the baby down and turned around. "Here's my friend Seachel. He can clone anything."

Seachel nodded. He was a tousled lad about Ivy's age. He waved his hands.

Ivy became two Ivies, and then three, and four. Soon the picture was filled with little Ivies, all making cheers: bronze, brass, or worse. But they couldn't hold their positions; in a moment they all fell over laughing. There got to be a pile of naughty little princesses buried in mirth.

Then Xander started back. Ivy obligingly carried him until he could walk competently; then, about age three, he waved 'bye to her and proceeded on his own. They decided to watch for a while, as this distant past was fascinating even in its ordinary details. But he got lost when crossing the comic strip, and wound up on a different world. It was shrouded by fog, and looked jungle-hot. Melody and the others watched, unable to help; he had to find his own way back. "Where am I?" he asked the first creature he spied.

"You're in the Xanth enclave of Planet Venus," she replied. She was a lovely tentacular monster shrouded in delicate parts by clouds. "Kiss me." She reached for him with three and a half tentacles.

"Thank you," he said, and stepped back into the comic strip. There was the usual clog of awful puns. Then he stepped out on a burningly hot surface. Fortunately his zombie feet were relatively insensitive.

He approached the nearest creature, which was a giant firedog. "Where am I?" he asked.

"You're in the Xanth enclave of Planet Mercury," the dog growled. "You look good enough to eat." It opened its formidable mouth.

Xander hastily scrambled back into the comic strip, where he was mercilessly buffeted by more horrid puns. Melody almost couldn't watch. Then he rolled out on a rather barren, dry region. The air was thin, and it was very cold.

"That looks like Mars," Sim peeped. "Mother has been there."

The fourth time Xander emerged from the strip, it seemed to be a normal Ptero region. But he was suddenly old instead of young.

"Oh, he must have somehow blundered into a downtime zone," Green said. "Those awful puns must have gotten him completely confused. That's a danger, when you get caught in too many of them."

Several birds appeared in the sky. No, they weren't birds, they were winged centaurs. They spied the confused man and circled down for a landing. They were four lovely fillies.

"Where am I?" Xander asked.

"You're in the Downtime Centaur section," one replied. "Shall we exchange introductions?"

"I'm Xander Zombie, son of Xavier and Zora. I'm afraid I'm lost."

"We are Cheline, Chen, Cherin, and Chel, foals of Che and Cynthia Centaur," the first one replied. "We'll help you find your way home, if you will tell us your interesting story."

Thus the exchange of services was made, and he talked while the winged centaurs carried the zombie back toward the time and place he had started from. He told them all about his adventures in the recent past, which they found fascinating. They turned out to be age nineteen, but were a decade downtime from him, so as they traveled east they grew younger. When each passed twelve her large bare breasts faded out and her body became spare. They also lacked sufficient power of flight to carry him, so descended to the ground and carried him there. Fortunately they were able to hurdle a thin part of the comic strip that separated the Centaur section from the zombie section. When they cantered up to his house they ranged from age nine for Cheline down to age six for Chel.

Which was the right range for pickled cookies. Zelda went out with a plate of them. Overall it was a fine visit. But the three princesses were ready to rest. Ptero was a most intriguing place to visit, but Melody wasn't sure she would care to live there.

So they sang and played an elaborate tent into existence, big enough for them, the zombies, and the centaurs, and they all had a fine time resting in style.

9

DEAD ENCOUNTER

Melody felt physically comfortable and emotionally uncomfortable, for the same reason: Her scant blouse
and skirt set her body largely free to jiggle and
bounce as it wished, and it was warmed by every ray of sunlight and
cooled by every playful gust of wind. She was afraid that if any man
saw her in this state, she would blush in places that shouldn't even be
visible. "I can't even take a long step without my panties showing," she
complained.

"Then maybe we had better abolish the panties," Harmony said.

Melody took a breath to make a horrified protest, but Rhythm spoke
first. "No, we need them to freak out the Dastard. Her bare bottom
wouldn't do a thing for him."

"So says the ludicrous Adult Conspiracy," Sim squawked cheerfully.
He, of course, was immune to the panty effect, being unrelated to any
human breed or crossbreed. He found the whole Conspiracy amusing,
having long since learned what it was all about.

"We had better go get this job done," Melody said. The plan was to
freak out the Dastard with her panties, so that the soul could catch him,
and make him halfway decent. With luck they could do it within the
hour and return to Ptero, where things were normal.

"First we have to find him," Harmony said.

"So we'll locate him in the Magic Tapestry," Rhythm concluded.

They started back toward Castle Roogna. "Aren't you forgetting something?" Sim squawked.

They circled a blank glance. "Are we?" Melody asked.

"You can't show yourselves in familiar haunts, lest someone recognize you."

"Oopsy," Harmony said.

"So we'll turn invisible again," Rhythm finished.

They sang, played, and drumbeat themselves as invisible as Sim was. Then he carried them to the roof of the castle, and they left him there and went quietly down into the upper hall.

There were three wild little princesses dashing madly along, playing Faun & Nymph without the benefit of any fauns. They simply liked running and screaming.

"Were we like that?" Melody whispered rhetorically.

"We must have been," Harmony agreed.

"We still are, when we get young on Ptero," Rhythm said.

Princess Ivy appeared, properly appalled. "Girls! At least put on some clothing!"

"Awwww," they protested in unison, and went into their room.

"No one will ever know we're gone," Melody said, satisfied.

"The demon kids are doing a good job," Harmony agreed.

"And so is D. Metria," Rhythm said.

Ivy looked around, smiling. "I hope there aren't any unfamiliar ghosts in here," she said loudly to the supposedly empty hall. "We wouldn't want our regular ghosts to get jealous."

Melody realized that they needed to be silent as well as invisible, lest they arouse suspicion. They shut up and went to the Tapestry room. Fortunately it was empty.

They directed their thoughts to the Dastard, and in a moment a picture formed of lutans riding horses hard at night, just across the border in Mundania. The poor animals were getting worn out, but the beastly lutans had no mercy.

"That's not it," Melody complained. "We're looking for the Dastard."

The scene changed. Now it showed northwest Xanth, just inside the border with Mundania. Animals were crossing, traveling from Mundania into Xanth. They were weird: cats, cows, frogs, and other mundanish beasts, in great numbers.

"Why, it's an Animal Wave," Harmony said, amazed. "Like a Human Wave, only comprised of animals."

"But we never heard of such a Wave," Rhythm protested.

Then a nondescript man appeared in the picture. He saw the animals, and disappeared. But the picture changed, following him as he reappeared at the border just as the first animal was finding a path into Xanth. He dragged a big pile of wickedly barbed thorn-brush there, blocking it off so that the animal couldn't pass.

"That's the Dastard!" Melody exclaimed. "He saw the animals getting into Xanth, so he went back to earlier in time and stopped them."

"Is he trying to protect Xanth?" Harmony asked, perplexed.

"We don't need protection from animals," Rhythm pointed out. "Their offspring will have magic soon enough."

An invisible light bulb flashed over Melody's invisible head. "He did it to mess up the animals! They were happy discovering Xanth, so he stopped them."

"What a dastardly deed," Harmony said, outraged.

"Precisely," Rhythm agreed. "That's what he does. That's why we have to stop him."

"But what was that prior picture, of the lutans riding the Mundane horses?" Melody asked.

"Maybe it related, and we didn't realize it," Harmony said.

They turned the Tapestry back to that scene, and discovered that this time the Dastard had made a hole in the interface that let the lutans out so that they could bring misery to Mundane horses. This wasn't to help the lutans, for they became gnarled and unhappy without the magic of Xanth, but to torment the horses. Another dastardy deed.

"We oriented the Tapestry on the Dastard," Rhythm said. "But we didn't tell it when. We should have specified the present time."

The Tapestry evidently heard, for the picture changed again. Now it showed the Dastard with a centaur filly. The filly was leading the way into a bower at the edge of the Dead Forest. Then suddenly she became a moderately pretty adult woman.

"What happened?" Melody asked.

"She must be a were-centaur," Harmony said. "She changes from woman to centaur."

"What would the Dastard want with a were-centaur?" Rhythm asked.

Then suddenly they saw. The woman was showing her polka-dot panties. The Dastard freaked out, but then she removed them and he returned to animation. Then—

"They're summoning the stork!" Melody said.

But just before they could do so, the woman disappeared and a tree trunk appeared in her place. The three princesses were floored. They fell in a tangle of invisible bodies.

Harmony was first to pick herself up from the floor. "She has another form! She's a shape changer."

"She must be teasing the Dastard," Rhythm said, returning to her feet. "Though she certainly had seemed willing a moment ago."

The tree trunk vanished and an ogress appeared. She remained in place, and so did the Dastard, just waiting. "What are they up to?" Melody asked.

Then the woman reappeared. She immediately clasped the Dastard.

"The changes are involuntary!" Harmony cried. "So they had to wait until she turned girl again."

"What a complicated tryst," Rhythm said, impressed.

Then something even stranger happened. The trees of the Dead Forest started to animate. Their bare twigs expanded, forming buds, and the buds sprouted leaves.

"It's coming to life!" Melody said, amazed. "The Dead Forest is no more."

"But it's a landmark," Harmony said. "It's been dead for decades."

"Which makes its transformation a dastardly deed," Rhythm concluded.

But Melody wasn't so sure. "Couldn't it be that the bad deed was the curse that killed the forest? Living trees must be better than dead ones."

"I'm sure he didn't do it to be nice," Harmony said.

"So maybe he didn't do it at all," Rhythm concluded. "It happened while he was distracted by the were-female."

That seemed to make sense. "He was coming to stop the revival," Melody said. "But the were-female distracted him with her panties, and the forest recovered."

"But *why* did it recover?" Harmony asked. "After all this time?"

"We'll just have to see," Rhythm said.

They had the Tapestry orient on the center of the Dead (now living) Forest. There was an enormous beating heart, and there stood a girl with an empty flask. They played the scene back and verified that the girl had emptied the flask on the Heart of the forest, and brought it to life. The flask must have contained healing Elixir, though there seemed to be too little of it to manage a job such as this.

They tracked it back farther, and discovered something astonishing: The were-woman had found the Spring of Life, and filled the flask with its Elixir. Then she had met the Dastard and the girl—and given the flask to the girl just before going into the bower with the Dastard.

"The Dastard knew about it—and didn't stop it," Melody said. "There must be some decency in him after all."

"Unless he goes back now and unhappens it," Harmony said.

"Maybe having told the were-woman he wouldn't, so she would show him her panties," Rhythm finished.

They decided to get on to the Dead Forest and intercept the Dastard before he could do that. They left the room and the hall and the castle quietly, and found Sim, who was waiting patiently and invisibly on the roof.

"To the Dead Forest," Melody said. "Only it has changed."

"How can it have changed?" Sim squawked as he took off, carrying them.

"You'll see," Harmony said.

Very soon they were there. The trees below were vibrant in their new foliage. Sim circled, confused. "I don't see the Dead Forest," he squawked.

"Yes you do," Rhythm said. "Isn't it beautiful?"

"But this forest is alive." Then he caught on, for he was the smartest of birds. "It has been restored!"

"And we are here in part to see that it stays restored," Melody said.

"To take out the Dastard before he unhappens it," Harmony agreed.

"Because we think he let it happen just so he could get at some panties," Rhythm concluded.

Now they saw the great Heart of the forest, powerfully beating. Sim circled down while they filled in the details they had discovered.

There was barely room in the clearing for Sim to land without touching the Heart, but he managed by spiraling carefully down. The Heart was even more impressive at close range, as it thumped steadily, majestically serving the forest. But the girl they had seen with the flask was gone; they must have just missed her.

"We'll look for the Dastard on the ground," Melody said.

"While you fly up and check from the air," Harmony said.

"We'll meet outside," Rhythm finished.

Sim nodded, taxied forward, then spread his giant invisible wings and launched into the air. They felt the down-draft of his wingbeat. Then they started walking.

"That girl must be going to rejoin the Dastard," Melody said.

"So all we have to do is follow her," Harmony agreed.

"Let's make her footprints glow," Rhythm suggested.

They sang and played, and the girl's footprints glowed, making them easy to follow. The three invisible princesses did not hurry, as they did not want to catch up until after the girl rejoined the Dastard.

Then they saw two young men walking the other way. "Maybe they've seen the Dastard," Melody said.

"We had better talk to them," Harmony agreed.

"So we'll have to turn visible," Rhythm said.

"Maybe better if just one of us does," Melody said.

"You," Harmony agreed.

"Now," Rhythm agreed.

So Melody turned visible and approached the two young men. They spied her—and came close to freaking out.

Oh, no! She had forgotten how she was garbed, with a bulging low blouse and skirt so short that it was dangerous to turn her back. She hastily shored up the blouse and shored down the skirt.

The men recovered somewhat. "Hello, fair maiden," one called.

"Hello, halfway handsome man," she replied. "I am Mel, with a talent of—of maybe appearing prettier than I am." She didn't like lying, but she couldn't tell the truth.

"I am Geo," he said. "This is my brother Graphy. We are twins who know where every place is."

"But we've never seen this forest before," Graphy said. "So we're investigating."

"I believe I can help you there," Melody said. "This is the Dead Forest. Its Heart evidently started beating again, and restored it to vitality."

"The Dead Forest!" Geo said, amazed. "This is where it is supposed to be."

"But it was so different, we couldn't believe it," Graphy said.

"I found it hard to believe too," Melody said. "But I just saw the beating Heart."

"We must verify that," Geo said. "No offense intended; we simply have to see everything for ourselves."

"I understand," Melody said. "I won't stand in your way."

"Oh, we would like to have you stand in our way," Graphy said. "Are you by any chance looking for company?"

"Not at the moment," Melody said. "Did you see a girl walking the same way I am?"

"Nobody could walk the way you do," Geo said, trying to draw his eyes from her blouse.

"Nobody," Graphy agreed, trying to pull his eyes from her skirt.

Oh. "I mean, the same direction."

"Yes," Geo said. "Her name is Becka, and she's fourteen. She seems like a nice girl, but a bit young."

"Maybe I'll catch up with her," Melody said. She walked on.

"Maybe we'll meet again, when the moment is better," Graphy said as they walked on.

"Maybe," Melody agreed noncommittally. She of course could not make any commitments here in Xanth, because she would soon be returning to Ptero.

"Too bad," Harmony said invisibly when they were clear.

"They're cute boys," Rhythm said.

"But only two of them," Melody reminded them. "And three of us."

"Still, we might look them up, back on Ptero," Harmony said.

"Two dates are better than none," Rhythm agreed.

Melody was about to say something else, when something weird happened, rapidly becoming unpleasant. Something was taking over her body! She tried to fight it, but the thing was horribly proficient and powerful. She tried to cry out, but the alien spirit stopped her mouth.

What was this? she wondered, trying to throw the thing off.

I am the Sea Hag, my pet, and now you are mine.

Melody quailed. The horrible Sea Hag was supposed to be locked away in the Brain Coral's pool.

Times change, my precious. Now give me all your memory, or I will hurt you. The awful mind crawled into her mind like a loathsome disease.

Melody fought to defend her mind, resisting with all her might. Then terrible pain flared, bringing her to her knees.

"Melody!" Harmony cried. "You fell."

"What's the matter?" Rhythm asked, concerned.

Melody's mouth worked. "I'm all right. I just tripped." She wasn't saying it; the Sea Hag was.

The others helped her up. Melody tried to cry out to them, but her jaw locked. The pain came again, less intense but quite bad enough. *I will hurt you.*

There was no question of that. The Sea Hag was notorious for stealing young beautiful bodies and wearing them rapidly out, making them old before their time. Then she threw them away by getting them killed, and went on to the next. It was the most horrible fate imaginable.

I see you understand, my pet. Now cease opposing me, and I will hurt you less. Open your memory.

Melody tried to keep her memory closed, but the hideous mind of the Sea Hag forced its way in, like the venom of a zombie cobra, hurting all the way. The filth of it was as bad as the pain of it. Melody had never imagined a mind this ugly. Her very soul was being laid waste.

You're from Ptero! the Hag thought, amazed. *"You're a princess! In fact, you're Princess Melody! And your two sisters are with you here, invisible. And you have a big bird with you too. What a collection!*

She had wrested the secrets out, in much the manner she might have dug out a living kidney with her dirty claws. Melody knew she was lost.

That's right, my pet. You are forever mine. Now stop trying to hold back, or I'll hurt you more.

Melody did not stop, and the Sea Hag did hurt her more. Why she resisted she wasn't sure; she just couldn't give in completely to this monstrosity.

Meanwhile her sisters remained concerned. "Melody, you look faint," Harmony said.

"You look pained," Rhythm said.

I will punish you later, the Hag thought. Then she focused on the externals. She made Melody's mouth smile. "I am all right, sisters dear. It is just a passing indisposition."

This was not the way Melody normally spoke. She hoped her sisters realized that, and caught on that she was not herself.

So I must use your silly mannerisms, the Sea Hag thought. *Thank you for advising me, you sad excuse for a princess.*

Melody realized that she would have to stifle her thoughts, because the Hag was too apt at intercepting them. Her only hope was for her sisters to catch on. But then what? They wouldn't be able to dislodge the parasite from outside. So all she could do was delay her utter capitulation as long as she could manage.

You're learning, my pet.

Meanwhile Melody's body was walking with increasing facility, and her sisters' concerns were abating. They came to the bower where the Dastard and Xena had been, but they were gone. Becka's glowing footprints led on. She had evidently caught up with them, and now they were all going somewhere.

They saw a four-legged black creature. *Oh, there's that dumb Mundane brute again,* the Hag thought. *He's been wandering all over Xanth, looking for a home. What a nuisance.*

Maybe the dog would smell the change in her, and so alert her sisters to her predicament.

Forget it, my pet. There is no way to tell my presence physically, because only my spirit is here. The stupid canine will never catch on.

So it seemed, for the dog walked sorrowfully on.

It was getting late in the day. *I'll wait to catch him,* the Hag decided. *He's a cunning rogue, and has unhappened my Possessions more than once. I need to be fully prepared before I brace him again.*

But Harmony and Rhythm were moving right along toward the rendezvous. The Hag had to delay them. So she made Melody's body trip again.

"There's definitely something wrong," Harmony said.

"We had better find a place to camp," Rhythm said.

They turned aside, locating a suitable spot to stay the evening. They turned visible, and Sim glided down to rejoin them, but he remained invisible because there was no easy way to conceal his great size and bright color. Melody's body harvested a hagberry pie and smacked Melody's lips over it. The sisters did not comment. The Hag realized that she had made an error; sweet young princesses did not like hagberry pie; they preferred peach or cherry pie. Then, as the Hag fashioned a nest for the night, she used Melody's mouth to speak silently to Melody.

"Now I can in time roust out your entire personal history," she spoke. "But what use is it? You're an exchangee from Ptero, so your experience hardly relates. I'm certainly not going to let you return there. So first I'll have to separate you from your siblings. I can do that tonight when they sleep."

Melody feared that Harmony and Rhythm would never realize. They would think she had gotten up in the night for a call of whatever, and gotten lost.

"You three princesses do seem somewhat naive," the Hag remarked silently. "I suppose that comes from living on an unreal world so long."

It probably did. They simply lacked experience of Xanth, where geography was not time, and people's ages were firmly fixed. They had never thought to encounter anyone as smart as the Sea Hag.

"Enough of your dull thoughts," the Hag decided. "I have to remain awake until they sleep. So I'll educate you by reviewing my early history, which is far more interesting than yours." Then she sent her memory back, way back, perhaps thousands of years—she had long since lost count—to when she had her first incarnation as a girl in the year minus twenty-two hundred. "Back then we counted years backwards," she said. "Because it was before the first official Human Wave of colonization, from which the current dating system derives. So I was a girl from minus twenty-two hundred to minus twenty-one ninety and a woman thereafter. I didn't much like it. For one thing, I didn't know I had magic. I was the daughter of two of the true first human colonists of Xanth, and they, being Mundane in origin, didn't have talents and didn't know about them. Later, of course, some of them would be breeding with assorted other species, as they ran afoul of love springs, giving rise to centaurs, harpies, merfolk, naga, sphinxes, ogres, goblins, elves, fauns, nymphs, fairies, imps, gnomes, werewolves, skeletons, vampires, and other cross-breeds and variants, populating Xanth with the hybrids we know and love today. But those other species tend to be close-mouthed about their origins, not liking to admit that their lineage was ever debased by human stock. I even recently encountered a dragon girl whose sire barely acknowledged her. But that was all in our future. We were just trying to make our living in this odd magic estate."

As she spoke, the Hag pictured that ancient land, and Melody saw it take form. It was as if she was Sea Girl, as the Sea Hag was called then, because she lived by the sea shore and gathered pretty sea shells to trade for the necessities of life. She was a rather scrawny child with a tangle of wild hair and sea-colored eyes.

On the day she was ten years old she went out as usual to seek sea shells, and found several rather nice ones. She brought them home, thinking her stern salty father would be pleased, but instead her mother was there, her eyes rimmed with tears. "Daughter, today your father was toasted and eaten by a dragon," she said. "I can no longer afford to maintain you."

"But where will I go? What will I do?" Sea Girl inquired plaintively.

"I will have to sell you to the Green Horn," Mother said sadly. "That will enable me to survive, and he will take care of you in his fashion."

"The Green Horn!" Sea Girl exclaimed, horrified. "But he's not even human! He's a leprechaun."

"No, he just looks like one," Mother said. "He's quite human in ways that count, unfortunately. He has had his evil eye on you for some time, and now you must go to him and do whatever he wants."

"How will I know what he wants? He always speaks in riddles."

"I'm sure he will make his desire known," Mother said with a shudder.

"How will I find him? He lives hidden in the deepest darkest forest."

"He will send a coach for you."

Then, tearfully, she hugged Sea Girl and sent her off with no more than half an electronic cookie, which had also been sent by the Green Horn. She stood by the trail out of the village and ate the cookie as she was supposed to. It tingled in her mouth as its current animated her.

Soon the coach arrived, orienting on the signal sent by the cookie. Many people did not have magic, but many things did, and the cookie's magic was to identify the person who ate it, and reveal that person's secrets to the one who sent it. Had Sea Girl known that at the time, she would never have eaten it; she would have fed it to a basilisk.

The coach was surprisingly fancy. In fact it was a cherry-ot, formed in the shape of a huge cherry. It rolled smartly up and the burdened beast that pulled it halted. Its red door opened.

Sea Girl hesitated. "This fancy coach can't be for me," she protested. "I'm just an anonymous orphaned waif."

"It's just a stage," the cherry-oteer told her.

Reassured, she boarded, and the coach rolled into the deepest darkest forest. Sea Girl shed a tear as she left her village. She would have shed another if she had realized that she would never see her beloved sea again. Not in this life.

Sea Girl dreaded her upcoming encounter with Green Horn, but this was because she hardly knew him. Had she known him better, she would have been properly appalled.

The ride was not easy, because a rat spied the cherry-ot and decided to eat it. The Rat Race had recently immigrated from Mundania and had taken a liking to racing. Rats would race anything, and do anything to win, and would eat the loser after winning the race. No one else liked a rat race. The cherry-oteer whipped the beast of burden cruelly, making it gallop blindly ahead, outrunning the shorter-legged rats. But the coach bounced so much it almost fell apart. Sea Girl grew nauseous, and wished the ride was over. But had she realized what was at its end, she would have been truly sickened.

In due course the coach stopped at the very deepest, darkest part of the forest. "Debouch; you're done for," the cherry-oteer said kindly. Or had he said "Debauch"? In any event, she might have wished for some other phrasing, had she understood either term.

She got out of the coach, and it rolled hastily away from that place. She stood before a ramshackle shack almost hidden in the gloom. In its poor excuse for a doorway stood Green Horn.

"So you have arrived," he said. "Now do you know what I want of you?"

All Sea Girl knew was that she didn't want to know. So she made a desperate ploy. "Don't you always ask a riddle, and anyone who answers correctly gets to flee your awful presence?"

"That's only half right," he said. "Anyone who answers correctly gets horrendously rewarded with an indescribable life experience."

"So why can't I have a riddle?"

"That's different," he said. "I bought you from your widowed mother. Too bad about that dragon."

"How do you know a dragon widowed her?" Sea Girl demanded bravely, trying to stall for time.

He answered with a riddle, as was his wont. "Who do you think sent the dragon?"

"You sent it?" she asked, beginning to be properly appalled.

"Who else, delicious girl?"

Delicious? She saw past him to the huge boiling pot on his hearth. Now she began to be truly sickened.

She tried again, twice as desperately. "So don't I rate a riddle?"

He frowned. "Very well, as it won't make any difference. No one ever answers correctly anyway. Here is my riddle: Where is my Green Horn?"

"What happens if I answer incorrectly?"

"I will do one of three things. I will curdle your milk so you never enjoy it again, or deform your knee joints so you never walk straight again, or cook you in green beer in my pot. I have already made my decision with respect to you, as it is near supper time."

Sea Girl didn't dare answer incorrectly, so she made a wild guess. "There is your Green Horn," she said, pointing directly at him.

"Curses!" he swore. "You got it."

She was foolishly relieved. "What is my horrendous reward? What is my indescribable life experience?"

"I will marry you."

She had thought that nothing could be worse than the boiling pot. Now she knew better. "I changed my mind," she said. "I take back my answer."

"Too late. I always keep my foul word. There is no help for it but that I marry you forthwith. Of course I will treat you despicably for the rest of your life, and make your worthless existence miserable, but that's only to be expected in marriage. Take off your clothes."

Worse yet. "But I'm only ten years old!"

He glanced at her, perplexed. "What's your point?"

"What about the Adult Conspiracy?"

"It hasn't been invented yet. This is the year minus Twenty-one Ninety, remember."

She realized that there was no escape. And so it was she married young, and hated every minute of it, for Green Horn was a despicably cruel husband who made her work her fingers off on the endless dull chores of the household. Once her fingers were gone, of course, she could no longer do the chores or feed herself, and soon expired in dull misery. It had not been, taken as a whole, a good life.

Even after she died, there was no respite, for her soul did not find any comfortable haven. It wandered across the landscape, unsettled. She saw the living people going about their business, and envied them. They at least had decent lives, of the sort she had not. Their children were developing magic talents—something the adults did not yet realize, but that was obvious to someone hovering invisibly near and observing. Regular people, too, could have magic!

Finally she spied a lovely young woman who seemed to have excellent prospects for marriage and all else. She wore her heart on her sleeve; everyone could see it beating there. Sea Girl couldn't help herself; she just had to try to share in it, even if it was only illusion. She floated to the woman and overlapped her body.

Suddenly her soul took hold, and the body became hers, answering to her directives. She had become the girl!

It took her some time—perhaps as long as five minutes—to realize that this was her magic talent. She could take over another body after she died! She could live her life over again.

But her marriage to the Green Horn had hopelessly spoiled her for conventional existence. She had so much bitterness accumulated that it would take several lifetimes to wear it out. So she decided to do something about it. The first thing she wanted was vengeance.

She left the girl's village and made her way to the Green Horn's ramshackle shack. "Ho, miscreant!" she called at the door. "Get your sorry donkey out here."

Green Horn appeared, astonished at the appearance of so lovely a woman. "What is your concern?" he asked, almost politely, for normally attractive women would have nothing to do with him.

"Aren't you the riddler?" she demanded, knowing the answer.

"That I am. Have you come for a riddle?"

"No. I didn't come for a riddle. I came to marry you."

He could hardly believe what he took to be his good fortune. So they were married, and on their wedding night she made him a cake of wild thyme. They had one fabulous party, and he fell utterly in love with her. He was helpless to oppose her will in any way.

That was what she wanted. She had a lifetime of contempt to return, and she returned it in good measure. She made him suffer every day, until finally he could take it no longer, and threw himself in front of a hungry dragon. Sea Girl was a widow.

But she still had too much bitterness left to just let it go to waste. So she went after another man, and treated him similarly. After she drove him to suicide she went to another. But by this time her bitterness had degenerated into corruption, and that was affecting her body, and she was beginning to look like a hag. It was harder to trap her third husband, and impossible for the fourth: She no longer had sufficient appearance.

So she retired to further bitterness, knowing that she had thrown away at least one good man who might have given her a good life, had she given him a chance. She swore not to let that happen again. So when she walked carelessly, and fell in the sea, and drowned, and her soul ranged free again, she made sure not only to seek a good man to torment, but to line up her next body, so that she would always be young and beautiful. The prospect was a child of ten, but she watched the girl become a lovely woman in the course of a few years. Then when her personality started showing, making her body ugly, she arranged to kill herself, and took the one she had watched ripen. She had found her formula for success.

The odd thing was, she never succeeded in using up her store of bitterness and ill will. After a few centuries, she didn't want to. It was just fine being the mean Sea Hag. The opinions of others didn't matter; only her personal satisfaction.

"And so I continue today," she concluded. "Though never before have I encountered so much difficulty hanging onto new bodies. That's why I have to get rid of the Dastard."

The Dastard! The Sea Hag had run afoul of the Dastard?

The Hag was surprised. "You know of the Dastard?"

Melody wasn't sure where this could lead, but she could not conceal her thoughts from the Sea Hag. Yes, she knew of that Dastard; that was why she was here. They had to nullify the Dastard before he did any more harm.

"So we both want to get rid of him," the Hag said, amazed. "Well, I will do it for you. You are a princess, with an excellent body. That is exactly what he seeks, fool that he is. I will go and marry him, and make him miserable as only I can do. I will drive him to suicide in reasonably short order."

But Melody did not want to marry the Dastard. That was absolutely the last thing she ever wanted to do.

"Tough tears, toots. You do not have a choice. This is what I have decided to do. First, we'll have to restore your appearance to natural, so that it's obvious you're a princess. Then we'll go fascinate the Dastard. That shouldn't be hard to do, with your body and my experience."

Melody gave herself up for lost.

10
DASTARDLY DEAL

The Dastard was pleased, which was an unusual state for him. Not only had he gotten into some panties, they had turned out to be fairly decent ones, all things considered. Now Xena was on her way elsewhere, and he and Becka were on their way to the next nexus.

This turned out to be a group of vaguely demon-like creatures. They were busily excavating a hole in the ground.

"Who are you?" the Dastard inquired. "In fact, *what* are you?"

One of them glanced up. "Hello, mortal man. I'm Jeorge, and this is my sister Jeorgia and my junior, Jerry. We're jinns."

"They all begin with J," Becka murmured, impressed.

"That's interesting," the Dastard said, bored. "What are you doing?"

"We're digging out a precious Jeode we located by sheer chance," Jeorge said proudly. As he spoke, it came free.

"It looks like a dull rock," the Dastard said disparagingly.

"Oh, but it isn't," the jinn said. He tapped it, and it fell into two halves. In each half was a lovely three-dimensional picture of a beautiful scene.

"This is a representation of our long-lost home," Jeorgia said raptly. "It exists only within special stones: Jeodes. We have searched for a century to find one, and now by incredible luck we have found it."

"We could search for another century," Jerry said, "and never find another. They're very rare."

"How did you come across it?" Becka asked, obviously intrigued.

"I happened to see the faintest glint from a speck on its surface in a momentary beam of sunlight," Jeorge said. "Had I not by amazing fortune been looking in that direction at that instant, I would have missed it."

"This is the culmination of our eternal ambition," Jeorgia said. "Now we can at last relax and bask in its special beauty and relevance to our lost land."

"But why don't you just go home, if you like it so much?" Becka asked.

A tear welled in Jerry's eye. "We can't," he said. "It was destroyed by a terrible storm."

"That sounds like Fracto," Becka said. "The worst of clouds."

"Yes, it was Cumulo Fracto Nimbus," Jeorgia agreed. "He's really a type of demon. The Demon Queen was so angry at this breach of inter-disciplinary etiquette that she enchanted him to take solid form for the next three-point-nine years. But the damage was done, and Fracto has long since finished his sentence and returned to his mean-spirited ways, while we searched endlessly for what little we could salvage of our home." She gazed at the scenes in the half stones. "Now at last we have our desire."

"The Demon Queen can do that?" Becka asked, amazed.

"Oh, yes," Jerry answered. "She could transform King Dor into a dor-mouse if she wanted to."

The Dastard had heard enough. He grabbed Becka's hand and slid into limbo. He went back an hour, to before the jinns spied the stone, and emerged in Xanth.

"As if I need to ask what you are going to do," Becka said sourly.

"You agreed not to interfere," he reminded her.

"I wish I hadn't."

The Dastard used a stick to scrape dirt over the tiny portion of the stone that showed, and packed it down firmly with his foot so that the beam of sun would never catch it. Then he grabbed Becka's reluctant hand again and returned to the present.

There were no jinns. They had passed this spot and never paused.

The Jeode remained hidden, and it would probably never be discovered.

The Dastard walked on, well satisfied. Becka was silent.

They came to a man working on a set of cones. "What are you doing?" Becka asked.

"Don't bother," the Dastard said. "It's not a nexus."

"So at least you won't destroy it," she retorted.

"Oh you wouldn't want to destroy this," the man said, overhearing them. "It's a very special hourglass timer."

"A timer? Don't all hourglasses time hours?"

"This one uses a mixture of quick sand and slow sand. It can be set to time any amount of time, simply by changing the ratio."

"Great!" she exclaimed. But the Dastard dragged her on. There was a nexus ahead. At least it seemed to be; the feeling was different from the usual, but very strong.

There, coming toward them on the path, was the mysterious green-haired princess he had seen in the vision of the future. She was every bit as wonderful as he had ever dreamed. Her bosom jiggled in her tight low-cut blouse, and her skirt was so short it barely covered her panties, and she was smiling at him.

"That's the princess!" Becka whispered, astonished. "Complete with her little crown."

The princess walked boldly up to them. "Hello," she said cheerily. "I'm Princess Melody. I am visiting Xanth for four days. You look like an interesting man."

The Dastard was speechless for a moment. This was partly because the last thing he had expected was for her to approach him directly, and partly because from up this close he could see down into her flexing bosom.

Becka took up the slack. "Hello, Princess. I'm Becka, and this is the—he calls himself Dashing."

"He certainly looks dashing to me," Melody said. "I think I'll kiss him." She stepped up close and planted her lovely warm mouth on his.

The Dastard was not only speechless, he was senseless. He collapsed in a heap. Only a glimmer of consciousness remained, just enough to enable him to hear their dialogue and feel their touches.

"Oh, horrors, he must have fainted," the princess cried, sweetly dismayed. She touched him with her soft hands, setting his limp body straight.

"I think he's just surprised," Becka said. "Still, I never saw him as the fainting type."

"Maybe the lip bomb helped," the princess said somewhat smugly.

"Lip balm?"

"Never mind. Why are you with him?"

"The Good Magician assigned me to help him. So I'm trying to do that, though I can't say I like it. How is it that you came here?"

"That's my business, my pet. Do you think he likes me?"

"I'm sure he does," the girl said. "You see, we saw a vision of you in his future. He—I think he started to fall in love with you then. But we didn't know who you were."

"I told you: I'm Princess Melody."

"But you can't be! She's only four years old."

There was a pause. Then there was a different quality to the Princess' voice. "That has changed. I am from Planet Ptero. I exchanged places with my younger Self so I could come here. I am twenty-one years old, and I think the Dastard is handsome."

"How do you know his name?" Becka demanded. "I introduced him as Dashing."

"You ask a lot of questions, my pet. You risk getting answers you don't like."

"You're the Sea Hag!" Becka exclaimed. "I'd know you anywhere."

And the Dastard realized she was right. His dream princess had finally come to him—Possessed by his enemy. What a dire pass!

"Well, this time I'm not going away, you sniveling brat. If you try to tell him, I'll take away your stupid herbs and Possess you again."

The threat was evidently effective, for the girl shut hastily up.

The Dastard decided to play dumb, so that the Sea Hag would not know he knew of the Possession. He groaned and stirred.

"Oh, you poor man," the princess cooed. "Let me help you rise." She wrapped her arms around his shoulders and hauled him halfway up. This wasn't very efficient at getting him back to his feet, but was very very efficient at plastering her soft bosom against his shoulder and head.

He had distinctly mixed feelings. He loved the contact, but hated the fact that it was really the Sea Hag. He had a notion how the Hag worked:

She Possessed a lovely young body, then seduced the man she wanted to hurt, making him love her. She had a long history—millennia long—of torturing the men who had annoyed her in some trifling way, or maybe just for the bleep of it, and finally driving them to suicide. He wasn't the suicidal type, but he was fairly sure she could make him miserable if he ever let her get to him.

If only he could have encountered this lovely young princess when she was herself! Of course he could unhappen the Possession, rescuing the Princess from the Hag. She should be duly grateful, and that could be an excellent start. But there was one significant problem: She wouldn't remember. The girl Becka was the only one besides himself who ever remembered an unhappening. And that was only because of a spell the Good Magician had given her. He was pretty sure the Good Magician wouldn't give the princess such a spell.

He managed to get to his feet, with the princess' seductive help. He stood unsteadily, facing Becka. "What happened?" he asked groggily.

"Princess Melody kissed you, and you fainted," the girl said.

That much was true; the kiss had been potent. Now he knew why: He had heard of something called lip bomb that blew away the one kissed; the Hag had indicated that she had used that on him. He had been intrigued by the lovely princess; now he was fascinated. The kiss had made him eager to do her bidding, if it led to more such activity.

Obviously the Hag had come prepared. He had unhappened her prior Possessions, so now she was being more careful. She had taken a body he couldn't resist, and had promptly bombed him with a kiss. She was definitely out to capture his emotion.

What she didn't know was that he had no soul. He had emotions, but was incapable of love. He wanted to marry a princess for cold practical reasons: to achieve prominence, a life of indolence, and have all the stork-summoning he wanted. Becka thought that was love, but it was merely desire for what was good for him. So the Sea Hag could not make him her love slave.

Still, she could do him much mischief. Each time he unhappened one of her Possessions, she returned with another, and if she ever decided that he was not worth her while, she would come as an ogress and smash him into oblivion. So just as she was getting more cautious about him, he realized than he had to get more cautious about her. She was dangerous.

So he would have to play along with her, until he figured out a better way to deal with her. Meanwhile, he could no longer prolong his guise of dizziness; he would have to say something. "I fainted," he agreed.

"You poor man," the princess said sympathetically. "Let me comfort you." She embraced him.

The contact was very nice. He put his arms around her; he could hardly help it. But this meant that he could see past her lovely head to where Becka was standing, for the moment out of sight of the princess.

The girl lifted a small placard on which she had scribbled two words: SEA HAG. Then she put it away.

So she had not been completely cowed by the Hag's threat. She had bided her time, and informed him of the danger when she could. She really was helping him. He appreciated that, though he had already figured it out for himself. Now they both knew that they both knew. And surely Becka understood why he hesitated to unhappen the Possession immediately. He needed to learn more about the Sea Hag, so as to discover how to abolish her so that she could not return to plague him. He could afford to delay as long as she did not realize he knew her identity.

But that didn't solve the problem. How could he get rid of the Sea Hag, without having her come back in some more dangerous form, and without prejudicing his case with the princess? Because he did want the princess. She was everything he desired, and he might never have a better chance to win her—if he just played his hand correctly.

He would simply have to play along until something forced him to act. Maybe if he got to know her better, the Sea Hag would let slip some weakness, some clue to the riddle of her nature that would enable him to be permanently free of her. It was his best chance.

Meanwhile, the princess was still embracing him. She was marvelously soft and suggestive. But if he yielded to temptation, it would be the Hag who governed him. He couldn't afford to do anything with the princess until she *was* herself. So he sought to disengage. "This place is—is too public," he said.

She squeezed him once more, pneumatically, then let him go. "I know a private place," she murmured.

Surely she did. He could not afford to go there. The form she had taken was too alluring. She would tempt him into something the princess would not forget or forgive, when she got her body back, if she learned of it, and that would ruin any future he might have with her. But how could he avoid it?

Becka stepped in. "Dashing, you can't tarry with her. You have to go unhappen something."

"No you don't," the princess said sharply. That was another give-away: The princess would not know his nature, while the Hag did. "I can show you something much better."

It was a straw, and he grasped it. "No, she's right. I have to unhappen something every day. I must do it now." That was a lie, but a really necessary one. Would she fall for it?

"But this is a huge potential unhappening," the princess Hag said, falling for it. "One truly worthy of your talent. And only I know where to find it."

Again, this would have given her away, had she not already done that: How did she know about the nature of his talent? The word "un-happen" should have confused the princess. But the Sea Hag understood it well.

"Where?" he asked guardedly.

"It's on the Isle of Fellowship," she said eagerly. "One of the tem-porary islands off the coast of Xanth. It is hidden most of the time, but I know how to invoke it. Come, handsome man; I will lead you to it."

"But the coast is far away," Becka protested.

"Then you will take us there, dragon girl," the princess said.

Was this a good choice? Was there really an island, or was this some other nefarious scheme of the Sea Hag? He would just have to find out. He wasn't accustomed to dealing with someone who was a worse person than he was. "Very well. We'll go there. But it had better be worth my while." The truth was that the notion of a really significant unhappening excited him almost as much as the prospect of marrying a lovely princess.

He looked at Becka, who still hesitated. "I can't carry two people through the air," she said.

"But you can move rapidly along the ground, my pet, can't you?" the princess said. "That will do."

The girl looked as if she wanted to protest some more, but finally changed into her dragon form. She stood there with her bright green scales with their purple tips. The Dastard helped the princess to climb onto the dragon's back, then mounted himself, using pillows plucked from a pillow bush to protect their legs. She sat before him, close and warm and excruciatingly desirable.

"West," the princess said in a peremptory tone. She leaned back slightly to touch him. "Put your arms around me, lest I fall," she murmured to him. The sweet fragrance of her body encompassed him.

The Dastard wanted to refrain, because this was seductive, but her request made sense. So he put his arms around her, and felt the supple female nature of her body. If only she were real!

The dragon hesitated, evidently not liking this, but then got moving. She chose her route, wending between trees, and made good time. But the ride was bouncy, and the princess bounced within his embrace. Her hair flounced across his face, caressing it. "Hold me more tightly, lest I bounce off," she whispered. He had to do it, though it made him want to do more than hold. She was quite bouncy already. He knew she knew this. She was trying to seduce him despite his caution, and it was getting harder to fend off the desire.

The time seemed eternal, and instant. She was so special, in his arms, yet so dangerous. How much longer could he dare to let her continue impressing him? Maybe he should just unhappen the Possession now, and take his chances on meeting the princess himself. Yet with a vengeful Hag spirit loose, what might happen? She might return to kill the princess. He couldn't risk it. At least this way he knew where the Hag was. All too well.

"Bear south," the princess told the dragon. The dragon obligingly turned that way.

The princess turned her face, almost touching the Dastard's face. "We're making progress," she said dulcetly.

That might be the problem. She really knew how to make this body perform, and he was sure it wasn't limited to casual touching. She had probably made a hundred lovely young bodies do a thousand deadly seductions.

They reached the shore. The sea stretched out ahead, undisturbed.

The dragon came to a halt. They got off the dragon's back, and the dragon returned to girl form.

"Where is it?" Becka asked, peering around.

"It interfaces with the mainland only when summoned," the Princess replied. "I am one of the few who know how to do that. So you see, you need me."

Did the Sea Hag suspect that he knew her identity? That made her more dangerous, because she might do something to him before he could unhappen her Possession. But the temptation of a really big unhappening prevented him from acting just yet. "So summon it," he said curtly.

The princess put two fingers into her mouth and made a piercing whistle. Fog swirled in, and formed into the shape of an island, complete with trees and a beach. It solidified, and there appeared a causeway to the mainland.

"I can whistle like that," Becka said.

The Dastard glanced at her. He knew she wanted to be rid of the Sea Hag as soon as possible. He agreed with her. Now that they had found the island, they no longer needed the dangerous dame.

"They are alert for intruders," the Princess said. "You will need me to introduce you."

"We can introduce ourselves," Becka said. Again, she had a point. He should play it safe and unhappen the Hag now. Of course that would mean they would not be here at the Isle, but since both he and Becka would remember its location, that was no problem.

"Ah, but are you good at lying?" the princess asked.

Becka stood mute; the Hag had scored on her weak point. Few naturally souled folk could lie well; their consciences interfered.

"Of course," the Dastard said. But it was true that a person familiar with the culture of the isle would better know how to lie to the people there.

The princess nodded, seeing that she had made her point, and led the way across.

When they reached the island, the Dastard looked back. The mainland looked like a bank of fog. Then it dissipated, leaving only endless sea.

"We can't get off this island," Becka said, alarmed.

"Oh, we can, my pet," the princess said. "When it is time. Now let's meet the denizens." She forged ahead, finding a path.

Both Becka and the Dastard hesitated. The Hag/princess had taken over their course, and this clearly made the girl as nervous as it made him. Just what was on this mysterious island? If he unhappened her now, he would not know. So he would have to wait just a little longer.

The princess paused, glancing back. "Come," she said.

They came.

There was a swirl of smoke just ahead, which soon formed into a large male figure. It was a demon. "Who are you?" he asked, surprisingly politely. "I am D. Tain."

"Thank you, Tain," the princess said. "I am the Princess Melody. This is the Dastard, and this is Becka. We have come to observe your community."

"Welcome, all three," Tain said. "I will gladly conduct you to our Fellowship Village. May I inquire whether you have any prior knowledge of our community?"

"Not really, my pet," the princess said. "We have heard that it is a very nice community, so we thought we would see for ourselves, in case we should wish to join it."

"By all means," the demon agreed. "I will tell you all about it. Its origin is way back in time, thousands, of years ago, when the land of Xanth was first colonized. It's a marvelously intricate tale, and—"

"You're stalling," the princess said. "This community formed only three years ago. Before that the Isle was vacant. You're trying to fool us."

"By no means, Princess. I am following my nature."

"D. Tain," Becka said, catching on. "He's detaining us."

"Get you gone, demon, and send us a better guide," the princess snapped.

Tain puffed into smoke, which dissipated, reappeared, then reformed into a different aspect. "And who the #### are you, woman, to give us any orders?" the new form demanded arrogantly.

Becka quailed at the obscenity, but the woman took it in easy stride. "I am the Princess Melody. And who the %%%% are you?"

The demon paused, evidently taken aback. "You can't be much of a princess, if you can say that word. I look down my long nose at you."

"I recognize you," the princess said. "You're D. Spise."

"And not at your service," the demon replied with a sneer. "I hold you in contempt."

"Then get you gone, Spise, and send us another," the princess said.

"Why should I obey any demand of yours?" Spise inquired disdainfully.

The princess merely shot him a glance. He quickly converted to swirling smoke. In a moment a third form coalesced. This one looked woebegone. "Oh, this is awful," the new demon wailed. "I can't even begin to think of trying to deceive you."

"I recognize you too," the princess said. "You are the Demon Spare."

"Yes, and I have no way to stop you from invading our fair community. What hope remains?"

"None," the princess said. "Now get you gone and send someone more useful."

The demon swirled and reformed. This one smiled ingratiatingly. "Oh, I am so very dutiful! How can I help you?"

"And you are D. Voted," the princess said. "You'll do. Lead us to the community."

"I'd love nothing better." The demon walked ahead of them, leading them.

The Dastard was impressed by the way the princess handled the demons. They had evidently recognized her as the Sea Hag, and they must have had long experience with her before. They clearly did not want to cross her. It was unusual to find a human person who could order demons around. But of course the Sea Hag was no ordinary person. It would be better to unhappen her now.

"The demons are merely a preliminary diversion," the princess murmured. "The community has other defenses."

"How can you know that, if you haven't been here before?" Becka demanded.

"Ah, but I have been here, in spirit, my pet," the princess replied.

In spirit. She had traveled around while between bodies, probably looking for good ones to Possess, and must have seen a lot. So the Hag did know about this one. So far her guidance had been good. There probably were other defenses. They still needed her.

The path opened out onto a pleasant valley with a lovely village in its center. "Here is our Community of Fellowship," Voted announced.

"It is my great pleasure to introduce you to it. Surely you will want to join."

Surely he *didn't* want to join, the Dastard thought. But it was a good pose to learn how to unhappen it.

"What's that?" Becka asked, squinting at the sun.

The Dastard looked. The sun was very bright, but squinting did enable him to look at it. Something was happening on its surface. There seemed to be small human forms lying on it or in it. Some seemed to be washing children in the flames.

"Those are sun bathers," Voted explained. "And a few son bathers, too. Here at Fellowship we love to relax, and the sun is nice and warm. Of course we have to use protective emollients and lotions to prevent sunburn."

"How do they get up there?" Becka asked. She seemed to be a curious girl.

"We have a long ladder," Voted said. "Would you like to use it?"

"No," the Dastard said, wary of the diversion. "Just get us on down to the village."

"Of course," the demon agreed. "I am entirely at your service."

They passed a palm tree, whose open hands held thyme sprigs spelling out days of the month. Beside it were two eyeballs. "H-eye, Voted!" one of the eyes observed.

"So nice to see you, Al," the demon answered.

"Well, eye try to get along with others," Al Eye said. He turned toward the other eye. "Say hi to the visitors, May," he said.

"Oh, may eye?" the lady eye asked, batting her lashes.

"You may," Voted told her. Then, to the visitors, he said: "This is the date palm. The Eyes have it. They met here when they were looking for some thyme. They are Al and May."

"Al Eye and May Eye got a date," Becka murmured.

"Let's get on to the village," the Dastard said shortly.

The village was on a deep inlet of the sea that washed against the backs of many of the houses. The villagers were going about routine tasks. What surprised the Dastard was that they were of several different species. Demons, centaurs, goblins, nagas, and merfolk were mixing freely. Normally each species associated mostly with its own type. This did seem to be an unusual community.

A centaur stallion trotted up, followed by a filly with the usual ample bare breasts. The Dastard had to fight his eyeballs' inclination to stare. This wasn't a human creature, after all. "I am Cesar Centaur," the male said. "How may we be of service?"

"You can show us around," the princess said. "We're thinking of joining the community."

She was right: She lied well.

The filly clapped her hands. "Wonderful!" she said generously. "I am Charity Centaur. I will help."

Actually the Dastard didn't want to meet a whole lot of villagers. He wanted to find out how this community had started, so he could figure out how to unhappen it. This promised to be a boring session.

"Here is Ann Chovie," Cesar said, indicating a merwoman reclining at the edge of the water. She lifted a hand to wave languidly. She had herringbone stripes along her sides. "And her husband Strate." A demon appeared.

"But he's a demon!" Becka protested.

"Of course," Charity said. "All our couples are mixed. It is the way of Fellowship."

"But I thought you—Cesar—"

"We are siblings, not spouses," Cesar said. "My wife is Glitter Goblin." He indicated a pretty goblin girl who approached, smiling.

"And my husband is Naro Naga," Charity said, indicating a naga man who slithered up.

"Oh—you mean there's a love spring here," Becka said.

"No love spring," Cesar said. "Just good fellowship."

"But this is amazing," the princess said, pretending to be amazed. "Do you mean to say that if we settled here, we would have to marry others not of our own species?"

"You wouldn't *have* to," Charity said. "But we hope you would want to. It preserves amity."

"It's weird," Becka muttered, and for once the Dastard agreed with her.

But maybe now was his chance. "How did this come about?" he asked.

"That is Ann's story," Cesar said.

They oriented on the merwoman. She was much like a mermaid, except that she was of course a saltwater creature, a bit firmer in the tail and generous in the bosom, to handle the rougher tides of the sea. "If you are really interested," she said.

"We are," the Dastard said. With luck this would give him the key to the community.

"Well, I was swimming alone, exploring the inlets of the sea," Ann said. "I found a rather interesting island I hadn't seen before. In fact it was this one; we hadn't named it then. I followed an inlet inward as far as I could, trying to see more, because I am not one of those merfolk who can change their tails into legs. Then the tide reversed, and I found myself stranded; I couldn't return the way I had come, and was in danger of getting beached. That would have been a horrible fate."

"I thought all mermaids could make legs," Becka said.

"No, no mermaids I know of," Ann said. "And only some merwomen. I'm not sure what the rule is. Anyway, as I said, I'm not one. I would have had to try to crawl over land, and it would have scratched my tail awfully. I would have trouble breathing, too; I need the support of the water to function properly. There's a fair amount of weight on my chest; it needs uplifting. So there I was, trapped in a diminishing pool, when suddenly a demon appeared." She looked around expectantly.

Demon Strate had faded out. Now he reappeared. "Aha!" he cried. "A helpless but generously endowed mergirl!"

"Eeeeek, a demon!" Ann screamed. "Whatever do you want with me?"

"I am about to demon-strate that," the demon said, ogling the exposed endowments.

Cesar Centaur inserted a comment: "The mergirl began to suspect that the demon was up to no particular good. But she had no experience with evil, and less with males, so she tried to put the best face on the situation."

Ann looked a bit worried, but was naturally too innocent to know what she might be worried about. "Can you help me get back to the sea, so I can swim merrily away?"

"I can, but I won't," Strate said, rubbing his hands together. "Instead, I shall ravish you cruelly and throw you away, seeing that you are unable to escape."

Charity Centaur put in her comment. "Now she was almost sure that the demon was planning mischief. But she was not a dull girl, so she tried to find a way to improve things."

Ann cocked her head, trying. But Strate gave her no time to ponder. He grabbed her by the shoulders and hauled her onto the bank, where her tail had no purchase. "Now it is time for you to scream helplessly and struggle ineffectively," he said. "I don't like cold fish."

"But that small delay give Ann time to think of something," Cesar Centaur said.

"You're a demon," Ann said. "You must have had endless experience with women. Don't you find it rather boring?"

"Boring?" Strate asked, perplexed.

"Doing the same thing over and over," she said. "Don't you long for something truly different? Wouldn't that be more interesting?"

"I never thought of it," the demon said, surprised. "But now that you mention it, it does seem dull. Their screams are so similar. But what else is there?"

"Why not try something truly different?" Ann asked "Something no demon has done before. Something no unsouled demon would even think of doing."

"I can't think what you mean."

"Precisely. Why not try being decent?"

"Decent?" Strate asked blankly.

"Such as treating mortal folk with respect and kindness. Helping them instead of hindering them. Being nice."

"That would be different," Strate agreed, confused. "But if I were nice to you, I wouldn't ravish you, and that would be frustrating."

Charity Centaur interjected another comment. "Ann realized that this was not necessarily simple. She would have to give the demon something for his trouble."

"Well, maybe you should try to charm me into liking you. Then you wouldn't have to ravish me. I would give you what you wanted willingly. Whatever it is."

Cesar Centaur stepped in again. "Demon Strate thought about that. He had never encountered a willing female. He hadn't realized that such a thing was possible. All the demon females were endless teases, and all the non-demon females hated being ravished. So he tried being nice to her, and to his amazement, she was nice to him in return. Very nice. It was interesting and fun. One thing led to another, and now they are married, and have a son."

A small swirl of smoke appeared. It coalesced into a little merboy. "That's my cue!" he said, splashing the water with his tail.

"And after that," Charity continued, "they named the island the Isle of Fellowship, and encouraged others to try inter-species cooperation. A number of others were interested, and so an experimental community developed. It is still growing; every month more folk hear about it, and some come to see, and a few remain. There's Charnel Centaur with Merla Merwoman, and Gizmo Goblin with Nancy Naga, and—"

"I get it," the Dastard said. "Everybody gets along, because Ann Chovie had the big idea of getting along instead of getting ravished. I think I've heard enough." This was certainly well worth unhappening; he could change the lives of dozens of folk with a single unhappening. It would be a record!

Becka tugged at his elbow. "Um, Dashing," she murmured. "Not yet."

He looked at her, annoyed. "Why not?"

"Because you can't unhappen an unhappening. If you do this one now—"

"Shut up, girl!" the princess snapped.

But she had said enough. If he unhappened the Isle of Fellowship community now, he would not be able to unhappen the Sea Hag's Possession of the princess. Because that would overlap this one. The Hag would be locked in, and he would be unable to get rid of her. It was evident that the Hag knew this. She must have learned it when she Possessed the dragon girl. That meant that she did remember some of it, despite being unhappened. That made her doubly dangerous.

But if he unhappened the entire Possession now, including their isle experience, he and Becka would retain their memories of this island, though they would never actually have visited it, and would be able to return to unhappen it later. So he could have it all—in the right order. The girl had saved him a dreadful tactical mistake.

He turned to the princess.

"Wait!" she cried. "You obviously know, but there's an aspect you haven't considered."

"What's going on?" Cesar asked, understandably confused by their dialogue.

They ignored him. "Don't let her stall you," Becka said. "She's dangerous. She threatened to Possess me again if I told you."

"And I will, you disobedient twerp!" the princess raged. "I was going to get rid of you by dumping you somewhere without food, but it's no more Miz Nice Guy."

"I don't think so, Hag," Becka said. "I ate one of the herbs, so I'll still be protected if you snatch the others. And if you try, I'll chomp you something awful. But not quite enough to kill you, so you can't escape that way."

The princess paused. Then her rage seemed to melt away. She was good at hiding her feelings. She returned to the Dastard, smiling prettily. "Let's make a deal. I have shown you what great things I can do for you. I can do much more. I can give you all the joys of this young healthy royal body. I can make you the husband of a genuine princess. But only if I keep this body."

"Don't listen to her!" Becka cried. "You can't trust her!"

"Yes you can," the princess said. "You can trust me to do what's best for me. And what's best is to have the body of a princess, and to be assured that no one can take it away from me. And so it will pay me to give you what you desire. We can give each other what we each most want. We don't have to like each other, or even to trust each other personally. We just each have to know that the other benefits most by continued association. Neither of us cares half a whit about anybody else. Self interest. That never lets a person down."

She was talking his language. He had never considered making a liaison with the Sea Hag, but it would solve the problem of making contact with the lovely princess. It would solve many problems. Did their best interests really coincide? It almost seemed that they did.

"She'll kill you in your sleep," Becka warned.

The Dastard wavered. The Sea Hag already had the body of the princess, and might simply want to lull him until she could dispatch him.

"Here is the rationale," the princess said. "This body is here temporarily from Planet Ptero. The regular Princess Melody is only four years old. The two exchanged worlds—so as to get you. But working together, we can perhaps keep her here, and eliminate the other two princesses of this trinity, and in time make Melody the only heir to the throne, so that eventually she will become King of Xanth. Then we will have all power! I can't do it alone; I need you to unhappen adverse events as they occur. Only you can do that. With you, I can achieve ultimate power; without you I can't. All my life I have wanted to rule Xanth; this is my best chance yet. So I'm not going to do anything to hurt you. In fact I'll do everything in my power, which is considerable, to make you surpassingly happy you associate with me."

She was making more sense than ever. He did want to marry a princess, and to be recognized as a great man. She could give him that. Still, inside that lovely young body was an ugly old mind. That daunted him.

"Beginning immediately," the princess said, and lifted her skirt almost to panty height. Several of the Isle males almost freaked out. "I know tricks no princess ever dreamed of. I have no scruples. In fact I rather like a good inter-gender tussle. Try it day by day, and if I don't completely satisfy you, you can still unhappen me."

That decided him. "Okay," he said. "It's a deal."

"This is a disaster!" Becka cried. But both of them ignored her. They moved together for an embrace.

It was a fitting partnership, because neither of them were inhibited by conscience. The Land of Xanth would never be the same.

11

FOR THE BIRDS

S im woke as Princess Melody stirred. He was a bird; his
senses were sharp. He realized that she probably had to
indulge in a natural function, which among human be-
ings, especially females, was considered a private thing. In fact they
seemed to prefer to pretend that they had none. She had been unsteady
the day before, perhaps slightly ill; her digestion could be upset. So the
others had encouraged her to rest, and she had retired to their magic tent
early while they puttered about doing incidental chores. The three princesses had marvelous powers, but they weren't used to camping out in
Xanth, where the rules of time, geography, and magic were different
from what they were accustomed to. So there had been details to attend
to. Sim had helped.

Now it was night, and Harmony and Rhythm were asleep. They knew
that if anything approached, Sim would be aware, so they slept easy. By
the same token, he was aware if anything departed. He gave no sign;
Melody would be embarrassed if she thought she was disturbing anyone.

The princess made her way quietly outside. But she did not go to
the area they had designated as a privy. She continued down the path,
away from the tent. What was she up to?

When it was evident that Princess Melody was actually leaving the
company of her sisters, Sim knew something was amiss. This was not

like her; the three were always together, in speech and body and spirit. She would not ordinarily leave without telling the others. She had not told them; Sim would have heard. So her mysterious mission was secret.

Could it be some kind of game? The princesses loved games. But they never deceived each other. Something must be wrong.

So Sim followed her quietly. He was as large as a roc, but few folk realized how quiet big birds could be when they chose. He set each foot down just so, and made no noise. He was invisible, so his silence made him largely undetectable. Princess Melody could detect him, of course, if she wished, but she seemed distracted.

In fact, she hardly seemed like herself. Sim knew the trifling individual mannerisms of the three girls, and Melody was not evincing hers. It was almost as if a different person were controlling her body.

That was of course ridiculous. Still, she evidently had some kind of problem, and he felt it prudent to keep an eye on her, in case he could help. He continued to follow her, silently.

Once she was well clear of the camp, Princess Melody stepped off the path, found a flame vine, and used its light to facilitate faster progress. "Now we're getting somewhere, my pet," she said, speaking to herself.

My pet? Melody had never used that term before, that he knew of. Sim had an extraordinary memory, because his mother expected him to learn everything about everything so as to become the most knowledgeable bird in the universe. Then, building on that foundation, he would have to commence the hard part: becoming the wisest bird. So he had a eye-detic memory, and an ear-detic memory, and knew exactly what he had ever seen or heard. And the only time he had heard that phrase used was by the Sea Hag.

An awful chill passed through him, that no feathers could shield against. Could it be? The Sea Hag's evil spirit took over the bodies of the pretty girls and soon rendered them into ugly women. But she was supposed to be presently confined in the Brain Coral's pool. So surely she could not be on the loose.

Meanwhile the princess was walking rapidly onward, and still talking to herself. "You are foolish, my pet. You cannot abolish me, and your continued resistance merely makes me retaliate by hurting you. You would do better to cease this quarrel and go with the flow. I will make your body do splendidly revolting things that you should find interesting.

So relax and enjoy it, since you have no choice. Do not aggravate me by futile opposition."

Sim was appalled. It was true! The Sea Hag *had* taken Princess Melody's body. This was completely unanticipated mischief. He knew of no way but death to free a person of the Hag's Possession, and of course he couldn't kill Melody.

Could the other two princesses do it? They had, collectively, the strongest magic in Xanth. Each by herself was a minimal Sorceress, and two of them together could do things only a maximal Sorceress could, but the three acting in concert could do virtually anything they might put their minds to. So the three together could surely defeat the Sea Hag. But what about two of them—when the third was captive of the Hag?

Sim put his fine mind to work on it, calculating the variables, and concluded that the other two could, just barely, accomplish it. They could drive out the Hag without killing their sister. He would return and tell them that, and they would handle it immediately. But first he had to know exactly where the Hag was going, so they could find her promptly without alerting her.

But the news got worse. The princess went to a hidden bower that the Hag must have prepared at another time, and proceeded to make herself look quite pretty in a rather cheap, exposive way. She came to look like a princess, complete with crown, instead of an anonymous young woman, but with a very tight blouse and short skirt. Then, as dawn came, she set out in a new direction. He followed, because otherwise he could lose her. The moment he knew what she would be doing, he could return to the others and acquaint them with the problem.

And the Sea Hag intercepted the Dastard. She was joining forces with him! The one they had come to nullify.

Sim recalculated. This time the result was negative: The two remaining Princesses could not oust the Hag from their sister, when the Hag had the support of the Dastard. The best they could do was stop the pair from performing more mischief, for the moment. The case had become hopeless.

He flew immediately back. Harmony and Rhythm were looking around, perplexed by the absence of two members of their party. They had not yet used magic, because they assumed it was nothing of consequence. They were nice girls, which meant they were slow to suspect evil. He had been slow too, but he had seen what he had seen.

He landed and squawked out his awful news. They were of course horrified. "We must act immediately," Harmony said.

Then he delivered the worse news: they lacked the power to free Melody without seriously hurting or even killing her, because the Dastard would unhappen anything they tried to do to oust the Sea Hag. The two had made a truly dastardly deal.

They were girlishly crushed. They had seldom before been at a loss, because their magic had always been more than sufficient to get them out of trouble. But they had never before encountered mischief of this magnitude.

"What can we do?" Rhythm asked.

Which meant it was up to Sim. He sorted through his farther memory files, and found The Little Prince. His name was Dolin, and he was eight years old. Circumstantial evidence indicated that he might know the answer. But there was a problem: Dolin did not exist.

Sim squawked, letting them know that he had a notion. Out of kindness he did not tell them the problem. He asked them to wait while he made a brief side excursion. Then he took off for Castle Roogna.

He was of course familiar with the exact layout of the castle. He landed quietly and invisibly on the roof, walked to the edge, poked his head over, and peered into the window of Princess Ida's chamber. "Squawk," he peeped.

"Why hello, Sim," Ida said, recognizing his voice. "What brings you back here already?"

"Squawk," he explained.

"What, alone? Without the princesses? In private?"

"Squawk," he agreed.

"As you wish." She angled her head so that Ptero swung into view.

He oriented on it, and felt himself shrinking. In a moment he spread his wings and flew toward the little planet. As he moved, it expanded, and a figure came from it to meet him. It was his junior self, summoned by his approach.

They met, and circled. He regretted that he could not explain, but he was sure the other would understand that there was excellent reason.

He parted, and he flew on toward Ptero. Soon he landed, and looked around. He was in the place his other self had departed from, because that was the nature of the exchange. Unfortunately that was not precisely where he needed to be. Worse, he wasn't sure exactly where he did need to be. Which meant he would have to look.

He sifted through his memory again. Ptero was where every person or creature who had ever existed, or who would exist, or who might have existed, existed. Prince Dolin was one of the mights. Sim had met him only briefly, and learned that his life was limited to youth. That meant he was always a child, never party to the nefarious human Adult Conspiracy. This fell within the territory covered by the Sea Hag, who was as unpopular on this world as on the other. Sim strongly suspected that she had been responsible for the abrupt shortening of Dolin's life. Since the Hag didn't much care about boys, there had to be special reason— and that reason might be that he represented a threat to her. That threat was what Sim needed to know.

Sim's own territory overlapped that of Prince Dolin by about four years. His range went far beyond Dolin's in the To direction, but only four years into it in the From direction. He had been four when he met Dolin, and had not at that time recognized his possible significance.

One problem was that to meet the prince again, he would have to go to his age four territory. His powers of body and mind would be accordingly diminished. But there was no help for it; he had to talk to Prince Dolin. He alone might have the answer.

He spread his wings and flew toward From. He remained invisible, which meant that he did not have to explain to anyone what he was up to. That was just as well, because the number of people aware of their mission was already over the limit of secrecy.

As he flew he grew younger. As he approached age five he saw a thick cloud covering the landscape. That wouldn't do; it would make him visible by outlining his shape.

He glided down below it, but the trees reached up to intersect it. He had to land. Fortunately he was almost there. He found a glade and settled to the ground.

He moved on, afoot. But he was unfamiliar with the local terrain, and he didn't know exactly where Dolin would be. This could take forever, and he couldn't afford to lose much time. He would have to inquire.

He saw a man walking briskly along, coming toward him. But as the man approached, Sim began to feel stiff. His joints hurt. How could he be so suddenly ill? He was normally a supremely healthy bird.

"Who are you?" he asked the man.

Unfortunately the man did not understand squawk talk. He looked around, and saw nothing, because Sim remained invisible. "Where are you?" he asked.

Sim didn't answer; he was too uncomfortable.

"Well, wherever you are, don't get too close to me," the man said. "I am Arthur Itis, and my talent makes people's joints stiff."

That explained it! Sim remained silent, and Arthur walked on. Soon the stiffness faded, and Sim was able to move freely again. He resumed walking, and encountered an ogress.

Should he inquire again? He couldn't make himself visible; it was the princesses' magic. How would an ogress react? He was now, at age five, smaller than the ogress; he didn't want her to smash him with a hamfist. But he didn't have time to dither, for all that time was geography here; he had to find The Little Prince.

"Hello, ogress," he squawked.

She paused and looked around. "With all due respect, I have to confess I do not perceive you," she said.

Sim was taken aback. This was an ogress? "I am not visible at the moment," he said. "Is this a problem?"

"Not for me, obviously, but I should think it would be for you. What manner of creature are you, if I may be so bold as to inquire?"

This couldn't be an ogress! "I am a big bird. I am looking for Prince Dolin."

"He is not far distant, but you will have to pass through a comic strip. In that direction." She pointed a ham finger.

"Thank you," he squawked. But he couldn't just go on. "You seem uncommonly well spoken for your species."

She burst into unogrish tears. "I so much want to be properly stupid, but I haven't found the secret. Do you think it's my name?"

It must be something! "Perhaps. What is your name?"

"P. R. Ogress. I want to fall behind, but somehow I keep getting ahead."

"Yes, I think it is your name. It spells progress, so you can't help getting ahead. Maybe if you could find another name you could achieve greater stupidity."

"Now why didn't I think of that? I'll try it."

"See, you're getting duller already."

He went on to the comic strip. This would be awful; they always were. Could he avoid it? He looked to the left, but that was an impassable thicket of thorns, and the clouds remained too low to allow him to fly over it. It was awful being landbound!

He looked to the right, and saw a ferocious fire. He knew it would be impossible to put it out, because it was an extension of a Xanth fire: its past and its future. He had learned that some Mundane fires had managed to cross over into Xanth, where dragons had eagerly amplified them. That was one of the nasty things about Mundania: Sometimes it exported its problems to Xanth. At any rate, there was no passage there.

Sim firmed his beak and plunged into the comic strip. He regretted it immediately. There was an awful engine sound above, and a wedge-shaped object caromed off a cloud. A shower of coins came down. What weirdness was this?

He ducked a roll of bills and collided with a soft body. It was a young woman of ordinary aspect: hair, shirt, skirt, slippers. "I beg your pardon," she said politely, as she brushed money out of her hair. "I didn't see you."

"My fault," Sim squawked. "I'm invisible." He spread a wing to fend off another flurry of bills.

"Oh. How do you do? I'm Lacky." She spat out a small coin. She seemed to have no trouble understanding him.

He decided that the truth wouldn't hurt here, as they were in the same predicament. "I am Sim, a big bird. I am trying to get across the comic strip, but this falling money is interfering."

"That's from the plane," she said. "It does its banking in the clouds." She ducked as the flying plane banked off another cloud, shaving off a curl of vapor, which coalesced into another wad of bills.

"The cloud bank," Sim agreed. He was becoming temporarily visible, because of a coating of money.

"Yes. I suppose I will have to make it go away."

"You can do that? Who are you?"

"I am Lacky, daughter of Lacuna and Vernon. My talent is to write things true, briefly." She brought out a pencil and a pad of notepaper.

"Briefly?" he asked as she scribbled. He remembered that Lacuna's talent was to change the print in books, or make print appear elsewhere.

Children didn't often have talents similar to those of their parents, but sometimes it happened.

"It doesn't last very long. That's why I had hoped the plane would pass on its own." She finished her written sentence. "There." She held up the pad.

The plane abruptly banked off one more cloud and flew away. The way was clear. "Thank you," Sim squawked.

"We had better hurry," Lacky said. "But I have lost my bearings. Which way is the other side?"

"I'm not sure," Sim squawked, for the money was now swirling into fog, confusing the scene.

"That way," a big ant said, pointing with an antenna.

"Thank you," Lacky said. She and Sim plowed on in that direction. And promptly emerged—on the side they had just left.

"That ant deceived us!" Sim squawked, annoyed.

"Oh, now I recognize its type," Lacky said. "It's an onym. It says the opposite of what it means."

"Ant Onym at your service," the ant agreed from inside the comic strip. "Suckers!"

They plunged back into the strip. But the plane was already returning. Lacky was right about the brevity of her writing. It was not for the ages. They were soon plowing through a blizzard of flying money.

Lacky stumbled into a bush with small round flat berries. She stared at it. "Maybe our luck has turned. Is this what it looks like?"

"It looks like a mint plant," Sim squawked.

"Yes—a manage mint. If we eat its fruit, we'll have authority."

"Authority?"

"Over whatever is near. Better than my writing, because it lasts longer. So we can tell the awful puns to get stifled—"

"And can get on across," Sim finished gladly.

They each took hold of a mint and pulled. But instead of coming loose, the mints clung to their branches. In a moment the bush changed shape and assumed the form of a little man. "What are you cretins doing?" he demanded angrily.

Oops. "We thought you were a mint," Lacky said.

"Well I'm not. I'm an Imp. My name is Each, and I mean what I say. Now get you gone before I put you on trial."

Sim assembled the terms. "Imp Each Ment," he squawked.

"Meant?"

"He meant what he said."

Lacky groaned. "I've got to get out of here!"

"So do I." They plowed on.

They found two paths going in the right direction. Neat signboards identified them, but the words had been smeared out except for the first letters: P and S. They paused, uncertain which one to take.

"Maybe we should each try one path," Lacky suggested. "And see which one is better. They seem to be parallel, so we can compare notes as we walk."

"I agree. My name begins with S, so I'll take the S Path." He set off along it, while she took the other.

Sim felt suddenly lighter as he stepped on the path, as though he had shed a burden. He looked across, and saw that Lacky's path was leading her into a tangle tree. Too bad for her; he was just glad that the tree wasn't along his path.

Then he almost ran into the needle cactus that was along his path. He halted just barely in time, with a squawk. The only reason it hadn't fired a barrage of needles at him was that it hadn't seen him. Yet.

"Almost got you, bird brain, didn't it!" Lacky called, laughing.

She had seen the cactus, and not warned him? She didn't care if he got hurt? This was psychopathic behavior.

Then something clicked in his mind. His own behavior was sociopathic. He was being extremely antisocial by not warning her of the danger he saw along her path. The S sign might be for Socio-Path, and the P sign could be for Psycho-Path. The paths were destroying their consciences!

"Get off the path!" he squawked, jumping off his own. Immediately the burden returned: the burden of conscience.

"Why should I?" Lacky asked, obviously indifferent to his fate.

"Because there's a tangle tree ahead."

She looked, and saw that it was so. She leaped off just as the first tentacle was reaching for her.

Then, recovering her own conscience, she was horrified. "I was acting like a jerk!" she said.

"It's the path—the Psycho—Path," he squawked. "Not your fault. Mine was similar."

"The path! I should have known that the comic strip wouldn't give us any easy ways out. How awful."

"We had better stay off any other paths we find here."

"Yes! The puns here aren't necessarily funny."

"We'll be more careful now," Sim squawked.

There was a fierce buzzing. "That sounds like bees," Lacky said nervously.

"I'm a bird. I can snap bees out of the air."

"Not if they're wood-bees or could-bees or worse."

The buzzing things came into sight. They were little horns. "Worse, I fear," Sim squawked. "Those look like hornets."

"Yes—and maybe that's good." She grabbed one from the air, put its small end to her mouth, and blew. A net flew out.

"That may help," Sim squawked, gratified. "The nets may clear a path ahead of us."

"Yes." She grabbed another, and blew its net ahead. All manner of dire puns cringed back, not wanting to get netted. They followed, and soon emerged on the other side.

"Thank you," Sim squawked. "I don't think I could have made it through alone."

"Me neither," Lacky agreed. "I was going to visit a friend, but lost my way, and had to risk the comic strip. But I had forgotten how awful they can be."

"When I return, I'll fly across," Sim squawked. "It's always worse than you think possible."

She nodded. "Well, I think this is farewell, invisible bird. May you succeed in your mission."

"Thank you," Sim squawked. "I hope your visit goes well."

"I hope so too. I don't even know my friend."

Sim paused. "How can you have a friend you don't know?"

She looked embarrassed. "I—am lonely. So I wrote that I would find my best friend soon, hoping that though my writing comes true only briefly, the message would remain, and it would happen. But I got lost in the comic strip, and that may have cost me too much time, and my friend may no longer be there."

Sim's fine mind clicked over some coincidental thoughts. "Is it possible that you would meet a temporary friend—in the comic strip?"

"Yes, that's another interpretation. I—" She paused, astonished. "I met you! You helped me get through. And now we're separating."

"We don't have to separate right away," Sim said. "I am about to go to another realm. But perhaps I can help you find a more permanent friend."

"That would be nice. Maybe I can help you in return, so that we can exchange services, as is the custom. What are you looking for?"

"Prince Dolin, who should be somewhere in this area. Do you happen to know him?"

"Yes I do; I can take you right to him. The poor boy is limited to a range of nine years." She led the way across the new terrain.

"So I understand. But I don't know what shortened his life." He followed.

"He doesn't like to speak of it. I think it was traumatic."

"I hope he will speak of it to me. We have a serious crisis back on Xanth that he may be able to alleviate."

"Xanth? I had the impression that you were native to Ptero."

"I am, in the sense that we all are. But I have a temporary mission on Xanth."

"Oh, you are one of the real-be's instead of the might-be's."

"Yes." But Sim did not care to discuss this further, lest he betray the secret, though theoretically it didn't matter here on Ptero. So he changed the subject. "This friend you seek—is it of a particular gender?"

"No, either will do."

"Is it of a particular species?"

"No, any will do."

"Then perhaps I have a candidate. How do you feel about Mundane dogs?"

"Mundane?" Her tone suggested that this wasn't good.

"They really can't be faulted for their origin."

"I suppose that's right. I understand some Mundanes are reasonably good folk. We don't see many here."

"I have encountered a good-natured dog who is looking for a home. I think he would remain longer than briefly, because he has nowhere else to go. He seems to be hopelessly lost in Xanth."

"I suppose I could consider him," she said doubtfully.

"And I think very lonely."

"Lonely," she echoed, relating.

"Try writing three words: BOSS BLACK LABRADOR."

She wrote them. In a moment the dog appeared, with his sign. He approached and gazed wistfully at her as she read the message.

She melted. "Oh, you poor thing!" she said, getting down to hug him. "You are welcome in my home!"

Boss wagged his tail and licked her face. It seemed she had found her friend.

They walked on, now a threesome. But there was a problem: Sim arrived at his blanked year. "I can't go there," he squawked.

"Oh, that's right—you real-be's have your missing time. The time in your lives when you are in Xanth."

"Yes. If the prince died there, then I will be unable to interview him about it."

"Where is your line?"

"Right here," Sim squawked. For there before him was the line that marked the missing section of his existence on Ptero, extending six months before and after his life on Xanth.

"There's no line for me. But Prince Dolin lives a little farther on. Maybe he's on the other side."

"I hope so. I believe his end was masked by my missing year, but that was a year ago, so maybe I can reach it now." Things could be tricky around a person's missing year, in part because the missing section wasn't constant; it kept moving To. "We'll have to cross together, or we'll lose our association."

"Yes." Lacky extended an arm. "Give me something to hold onto."

Sim extended an invisible wing. When she felt the feathers of its tip, she took gentle hold. Then they stepped across. To Sim it was just like taking a single step over a painted line. But suddenly he felt a size smaller: he was now four years old.

"Wheee!" Lacky exclaimed. "You zoomed me right across your year. I'm younger without seeming to have traveled the distance." She checked herself. "I was twenty-one; now I'm twenty."

"And I am four," Sim squawked. "I hope I can cope."

"Boss and I will help you. After all, you brought us together." Then she looked around. "Boss! I lost him!"

"He wasn't touching us," Sim squawked. "He must be a year To."

"Oh, I must find him before he thinks he's been deserted again."

"We can step back."

Sim extended a wing, and Lacky took it, and they stepped back downtime. There was the dog, looking around, sniffing the air, confused. "Here!" Lacky cried, joining him. He wagged his tail, relieved.

They crossed From again, this time with the dog, and resumed their trek. Boss was interested in the terrain, now that he had company.

They came to a child-sized castle, with toys scattered around it and floating in its little moat. "His parents, Prince Dolph and Princess Taplin, live in a larger castle farther along," Lacky explained. "I understand they are rather upset by the brevity of their son's territory."

"Just how did they get together?" Sim inquired. "In Xanth they did not."

"Well, as I understand it, Prince Dolph was nine years old and on his own adventure, when he came across this sleeping princess. So he kissed her, and then later when he grew up he married her, and it worked out okay. She was Princess Taplin, daughter of King Merlin and Sorceress Tapis, but there wasn't much there for her, so her mother made her a coverlet and she bit into an apple or something and slept for most of a thousand years until Prince Dolph came. That seemed to be the right decision. How is it that it didn't work out in your reality?"

"Magician Murphy came and messed it up, and an ordinary girl ate the apple by accident, and slept, and married Prince Dolph, and they had two daughters, Dawn & Eve."

"Oh, I know them! They're the same territory as Prince Dolin, at least at this end. I didn't realize that they had the same father."

"Things can get confusing, with alternate lines of history," Sim squawked. "I have trouble keeping them straight myself. I hadn't known Prince Dolin's derivation. Do Dolin and Dawn & Eve know each other?"

But her answer was cut off by the appearance of Prince Dolin. "Oh, a big Mundane dog!" he cried, delighted. He was about seven years old.

"Yes, we have come to visit. You know Sim, I think."

"Who?" the lad asked, looking around.

Oops, there were two problems. First, he was invisible, and second, he had actually met the prince a little later than this, so might not be remembered. Still, time was not the same here as in Xanth, so maybe it was just the invisibility.

"I am a big bird with iridescent feathers," Sim squawked.

"Oh, yes, now I remember. But I don't see you."

"I'm invisible at the moment. The three princesses did it."

"Oh, those little brats. They do stuff like that."

The princesses were five years younger than Dolin, so he would know them as two or three years old. He had never had a chance to see them as responsible adults. Sim decided not to try to correct the confusion about their motives. "Feel my wing, so you know it's me," he squawked. He extended the same wing Lacky had held.

The boy touched the feathers. "Yeah, that's great. I remember you were real pretty. But you didn't stay long."

"Well, I'm only four years old myself, here. My attention span is brief."

"Yeah, I guess so." The prince turned to the dog. "Who's this dog?"

"This is Boss," Lacky said. "My new friend. He likes to be petted."

"That's great!" The two were getting along well, though the dog was actually larger than the boy.

"Sim needs to talk to you," Lacky said with adult diplomacy.

"Okay."

Sim firmed his beak. This might be tricky. Death was not something nice to talk about, especially with children. "I need to know the details of your—your fading out."

"No!"

"But it's important."

"Go away!"

Lacky interceded. "Boss and I are here only because we were showing Sim where you are. If he goes away, we'll have to go too, and Boss is really enjoying your company."

The prince hesitated. Boss licked his face. "Well—"

"The Sea Hag is hurting folk in Xanth," Sim squawked, grabbing his slim chance. "We need to stop her. I'm hoping you know how."

Prince Dolin looked intently at the space Sim occupied, orienting on his voice. "I'd sure like to stop that old bag."

"I'm guessing you saw something she wanted to keep secret, so she killed you. Is that right?"

The prince grimaced. "Yeah. My talent is doing the right thing. So I was there at the edge of my range when I saw a huge monster. It was stuck in a big hole in the ground, and looked sort of unhappy, so I thought maybe I'd try to get it out. But before I got there, I saw the Sea

Hag. She was in this middle-aged body, but I knew her right away, 'cause I can't do the right thing if I don't know who's who. She was hauling along a lovely young maiden with a rope around her neck. The poor girl had her hands tied and she was crying. So I ducked back and watched. I thought maybe the Sea Hag was going to feed the maiden to the monster, and maybe I could do something to stop it, because even a girl doesn't deserve to get chomped like that. But I wasn't sure what I could do; sometimes my talent doesn't kick in right away. So I just hid and waited. I saw her park the maiden by tying her to a tree. Then the Hag went up to the monster and walked right into it. Of course it chomped her and gulped her right down; it didn't care that she was sort of stringy and sloppy. That really surprised me; I mean she did it on purpose. She didn't feed the maiden to it, she fed herself to it."

"She was killing her old body," Sim said. "She has to be rid of it before she can take a new one."

"Yeah, I caught on to that. Then there was a while where nothing much happened. The monster was just burping and licking its chops, and the maiden was quietly sobbing. So I decided it was time, and I went to untie the maiden. But the funny thing was she didn't even thank me. She just said, 'There's no hope for me,' and went right on crying. I tried to lead her away, because the monster was getting hungry again and I wasn't sure just how firmly stuck in that hole it was. Then suddenly the maiden screamed 'Noooo!' in a wailing voice. Then she stopped, and a funny expression sort of traveled across her pretty face. Then she said 'Aha! It's good to be young again.' 'But you're the same age you were,' I told her. And she looked at me, seeming surprised I was there, and bared her teeth and said 'Are you trying to interfere, you disreputable boy?' And I said 'I'm just trying to get you away from that monster.' Then she said 'That's what you think, my pet,' and she picked me up and threw me at the monster, and it gobbled me up and ended my life at age eight. Then I knew she was the Sea Hag in a new body, but it was too late to do anything about it."

There was a brief silence. Then Lacky spoke: "That's horrible. She's a really mean woman."

Dolin looked through Sim's space. "So does that help?"

Sim was assimilating the rush of information. "I think so. She threw away her old body, and her withered old soul took over the fresh young body. Because you saw it happen, she killed you. But I'm not quite satisfied. Maybe my four-year-old mind isn't quite big enough to make complete sense of it."

"If there's no way to stop her from changing bodies," Lacky asked, "why does she care if anyone sees?"

"Maybe it's like panties," Dolin said. "For some reason girls don't want boys to see them."

"Well, panties are very personal," Lacky said, tugging her skirt down a bit.

The Prince nodded. "Maybe that's *her* panties. I mean, she doesn't like to have people see her changing bodies any better than a girl likes a boy to see her changing clothing."

A bulb flickered over Sim's head, but didn't quite flash. There was something he wasn't quite realizing. Something important. What could it be?

"There is a reason," Lacky said. "If a man sees a woman's underwear, he gets all excited and wants to signal the stork with her. She may not want to do that, so she keeps her private clothing out of sight. Unless *she* wants to send a message to the stork."

Sim's bulb remained, trying to increase its glow.

"So maybe if someone saw the Hag changing bodies, they'd want to do something she doesn't want?" Dolin asked.

"Like killing her," Lacky said, and they both laughed.

The bulb finally ignited. "She's vulnerable when she's changing!" Sim squawked. "So she wants to keep it secret. There must be something that can destroy her."

"That'd be great," Dolin said. "But what?"

"She evidently went to some trouble to bring the innocent maiden to the monster," Sim squawked, working it out. "Why do that, when she could have simply thrown herself off a cliff and taken the girl immediately?"

"There must be something about that monster," Lacky said.

The prince brightened. "Now I remember. There was something else she said. When she was tying the maiden to the tree, she said 'I must restore my spirit.' But then she fed herself to the monster."

"And the way you describe it, she didn't go straight to the maiden," Lacky said. "She waited a while. Why was that?"

Sim's bulb flashed again. "Her spirit must suffer some wear and tear, getting out of one body and into another. So she needs to strengthen it. Otherwise she might not be able to take over a new body. The spirit of the owner might fight her off. So there must be something about that monster that enables her to do that."

"They do seem to have a working agreement," Lacky said. "Maybe they like each other."

"Sure, she feeds it women and boys," Dolin said. "But what does it do for her?"

Sim's bulb flashed a third time. "It guards her spirit! It helps her strengthen it."

"What, by chewing up the souls of victims and giving them back to her?" Lacky asked.

"I don't think a monster without a soul could do that," Sim said. "And my understanding is that this monster, which was stuffed in that hole by Prince Dolph in the form of a sphinx after Jenny Elf came through, so that no more monsters could come, has no soul of its own. So I don't think it could help her that way. But it might help her by guarding the spot beyond the hole where she stores souls. So nobody else could go after them. Then she can go there and get more spirit for herself, that enables her to beat down the spirit of her victim."

Lacky shrugged. "Makes sense to me. But we still can't do anything about it, because she's the only one who can handle souls like that."

"I think we can," Sim squawked. "Because otherwise she wouldn't care. If we could block off that cache of hers, so she couldn't upgrade her spirit, then maybe she couldn't take over another body."

"How can you stop her from going where she wants, when she's between bodies?" Dolin asked.

"Maybe by giving the monster a soul," Sim squawked.

The two of them looked at him, not getting it. But Sim was almost sure he had the answer. Because it explained why the Sea Hag went to that spot, and why she didn't want anyone else seeing her do it. If he was right, they could conquer the Hag. If they did it just right.

12
MONSTER

Melody was in hell. The Sea Hag had complete control of her body, and was about to use it for awful new purposes. She was lifting the hem of her skirt to show him her panties, and she was not about to stop there. She was going to ravish Melody's body, by making it do what Melody never would.

The Dastard's eyes were almost bulging from his face. The girl Becka was watching with evident horror; she at least cared about what was right and wrong. The villagers of the Isle of Fellowship were beginning to realize that something was wrong. But neither the Dastard nor the Sea Hag cared about any of that.

Melody concentrated all her remaining faint strength, and forced the hem down again. *Wretched girl—stop that! I'll hurt you!*

It was no empty threat. But Melody *had* to fight, lest she lose all. She struggled to lock the hand, holding the hem in place. Her panties would *not* be shown in public.

The Sea Hag struck. Melody was suddenly burning up with pain. She whimpered, but hung on. It was easier to prevent the hand from moving than it was to move it, so she was succeeding. For the moment.

The pain focused on the hand. It was as if it had been plunged into a bonfire. She could feel the skin baking, blistering, and flaking off. But she knew it was not real. She was close to fainting from the agony, but she would not yield. This was all the protest she could mount, and she clung to it.

"Are you all right, Princess?" Cesar Centaur asked, concerned.

"Yes. Just a muscle spasm," her mouth said.

"No it's not," Becka said. "The Sea Hag has Possessed her. The real Princess is trying to fight back."

"You lying snot!" Melody's mouth snapped. The pain eased as the Sea Hag's attention was diverted.

"The Sea Hag!" Charity Centaur said. "We have heard of her. She takes over young, pretty girls and makes them do horrible things."

"That's right," Becka agreed. "That's what she's doing now."

"Is this true?" Cesar asked the Dastard.

"Of course not," the Dastard said. "The girl is inventing it because she's jealous of our relationship."

"That's a lie!" Becka cried. But the surrounding villagers were nodding; it was the kind of thing girls did.

"Come, my pet," the Sea Hag said, taking the Dastard's arm with her other hand. "Let's depart this quaint village. The girl is welcome to remain here if she prefers."

"Don't let them go!" Becka cried. "The princess is captive. She just wants to be free. I know exactly how it is."

"Now how could you know anything like that?" Melody's mouth said. "The Sea Hag never lets go of a body."

The villagers wavered. They were reasonable people. The problem was that they were reluctant to believe evil of others, or to credit something fantastic.

"Find her sisters," Becka said. "Ask *them*. They'll tell you the truth."

"Shut your $$$$ mouth!"

The villagers were appalled by the awful word. Two females fainted, and several children held their heads in pain.

"See?" Becka cried. "No princess speaks that way. She's the Hag! Stop her until you can verify what I say."

That decided them. Several centaurs closed in and caught the swearing, struggling Sea Hag. Others surrounded the Dastard, preventing him from interfering. They conducted them to closed separate cells, and, to be fair, put Becka in a third cell. They sent out runners to locate the other princesses.

You started this, the Hag thought at Melody. *You just couldn't keep your hand to yourself. Now you'll pay.*

The pain came again, encompassing and awful. But Melody knew that as long as the Hag was distracted with her, she wouldn't think of a worse danger to her. Melody might not be able to save herself, but she might at least prevent the Hag from winning.

But the Hag caught the thought. *What's that? What are you plotting?*

Melody tried to stifle her thought, but the Hag ferreted it out. *So that's it! You cunning little schemer!*

Then she raised her voice and called across to the Dastard. "The centaurs are on their way! They will bring the other princesses. Destroy this community before they can do that."

"No!" Becka cried from her cell. "Don't do it! Then you won't be able to unhappen the Hag!"

"I don't want to unhappen her," the Dastard responded. "We have a deal. We can do each other a lot of good."

"But you can't trust her!" the girl called. "She's just using you. She'll throw you away the moment she's tired of you."

"Who are you going to believe?" the Hag called. "Get us out of this, and the princess's panties are yours."

The worst of it was that the Sea Hag was sincere. She had concluded that the Dastard was genuinely useful, and she knew how to keep him happy. She didn't have to like him; she liked nobody. But she could use him for a long time. She didn't care about the body at all; she would make it do anything she needed to, to keep things moving. So she would satisfy the Dastard early and thoroughly, so that her will would gradually become his, and he would be her puppet without knowing it.

There was a silence. How was the Dastard reacting? Was he considering sliding into limbo to unhappen that first key meeting between Ann Chovie and Demon Strate? Or would he listen to the dragon girl and let the princesses come and deal with the Sea Hag?

The cell faded away. They were standing in a glade empty of all buildings and all people except the three of them. The Dastard had unhappened the Isle of Fellowship.

Becka was crying. The girl had clearly liked the community. Melody was sorry too. The Dastard had done a huge amount of harm this time. All because he wanted to—

"To get at your pretty body, honey," the Sea Hag said, using Melody's mouth. "It's a good body, and now he's going to get it. I won't have to make you hurt any more; I'll just let him hurt you another way."

It was true: There was no worse way to hurt Melody than by making her acquiesce to what the Dastard wanted. The horror would be emotional more than physical, for all that it was a purely physical act. She couldn't stop it; even if she managed to freeze her whole body, it wouldn't stop him from having at it. She was inevitably lost.

"I'm so glad you understand, my pet," her mouth said. "I will love this; you will hate it." Then her feet propelled her toward the man.

Melody tried to resist, to drag her feet, but the Sea Hag's control was complete. She continued toward the Dastard.

He in turn approached her. "You will truly do it, Sea Hag? Our deal remains?"

"Our deal remains," Melody's mouth said. "But let's make this a bit more fun. I will free the princess' head, so you can hear her. No more than that. The rest of her body will be mine. The next voice you hear will be hers."

Suddenly Melody had her head back—and no more. She screamed.

The man paused. "You're really the Princess Melody?" he asked.

"Yes!" she cried. "Don't do this!"

To her surprise, he actually seemed to listen. "Why not?"

"Because it's not right! I don't love you. I want you to stop doing dastardly deeds."

"But that's my mission in life," he said. "That's how I get ahead."

Melody found herself somewhat at a loss. She hadn't expected him to listen, or to talk with her. She wasn't prepared. "How does it help you to do dastardly deeds?"

"It makes me feel good, because then others who were happy aren't, and I'm ahead of them."

"Why not feel good about doing good deeds?"

"Because I have no soul. I traded it for my talent of unhappening."

No soul. She had for the moment forgotten about that. So he had no conscience, no sense of decency. That explained a lot. She was wasting her time trying to appeal to any sense of honor. "But you can't get ahead by hurting others. You have to help yourself."

"I'm trying to. I'm going to marry you and be a prince."

"But I don't want to marry you!" she protested.

The Dastard shrugged. "The Sea Hag will make you."

"But you shouldn't do it!"

"Why not?"

This grows tiresome, the Hag thought. She put Melody's arms around the man and pressed her body in close to his.

"That's not me doing that!" Melody cried.

"I know. I like it anyway." The Dastard moved to embrace her.

Then there was a roar. A green dragon wedged in between them. Melody was caught up on its body and borne away. Somehow the dragon was supporting her as it ran, leaving the Dastard behind.

The Sea Hag took back Melody's head. "What are you doing, you despicable girl?"

The dragon carried her on across a stream and to an isolated glade. Then it became the girl, Becka. "I'm stopping you from abusing the princess," she said.

"You wretched thing! This is not your business."

"Yes it is. I'm helping the Dastard avoid entrapment."

"It won't work. I'll take this body back to him."

"No you won't."

"Why not?"

"Because I'll stop you."

"Foolish girl! How do you propose to do that?"

"If I have to, I'll bite you so that you can't walk. Then you'll be alive, and won't die, so you can't leave the body, but you'll be helpless."

Melody knew from the Sea Hag's reaction that the dragon girl had scored better than she knew. The woman could leave a body only by death, except in one very special case. Even then she could not desert it for another; she could leave it only briefly, and had to return to it soon.

Meanwhile the Hag was laughing, faking unconcern. "You wouldn't want to hurt the princess, you fool."

"I think I would hurt her worse by letting you have your way with her," Becka said stoutly. "I think if she could talk now, she'd thank me for stopping you."

Yes! The situation might be hopeless, but the girl had the right spirit.

"Maybe you're right," the Sea Hag said aloud. "Maybe I shouldn't try to seduce the Dastard."

But Melody knew that the Hag was merely trying to deceive the girl, to lull her so that she could grab her and throttle her. The Hag knew how to kill a person rather quickly, when she wanted to, and now she wanted to.

"Then why don't you take that body away to Melody's sisters, and tell them you have changed your mind?" Becka asked, not trusting this.

"I will. Right now."

"How can I trust you?"

She couldn't, of course. The Sea Hag had nothing but treachery in mind.

"I will shake your hand, Mundane style."

"What would that prove?"

But the Hag was already putting forth Melody's hand, and the girl was about to take it, not realizing. Melody tried to scream a warning, but could not.

The girl took the hand. The Hag gripped it tightly and hauled her forward so that she stumbled. In no more than three quarters of an instant she had Becka's neck in her grasp, and was squeezing cruelly. "Now see what your arrogance has reaped, idiot girl," the Hag hissed. "Suffer, before you die." She squeezed harder.

Suddenly she was squeezing the neck of the green dragon. The dragon's head twisted around and bit her arm. Melody felt the pain flare; it was a bad bite. She was paradoxically glad of it.

The Hag screamed and let go. "You villain! I'm bleeding."

The girl reappeared. "You forgot who you were attacking. Now I know how treacherous you are. I'm not going to let you go."

The Hag stared at her, outraged but helpless for the moment.

Then suddenly they were back in the clearing where Fellowship Village had been. Melody's arm no longer hurt; it had been unbitten. The Dastard had unhappened the whole sequence. Melody clung to the fading memory, knowing that it could be useful; as a Sorceress she could do that, though it wasn't easy.

"I'm so glad you understand, my pet," her mouth said. "I will love this; you will hate it." Then her feet propelled her toward the Dastard.

Melody realized that though she had managed to salvage the memory, the Sea Hag had not. Yet the Hag had remembered the prior unhappening, when the village disappeared. Oh—because that had been the Fellowship Community unhappened, not their own little group. The memory was lost only when a person's own experience was unhappened. Regardless, it was a remarkable talent the Dastard had, one that could do incalculable evil—or good. The man could change reality, to a degree.

Meanwhile they were replaying the earlier scene, just before Becka had turned dragon and carried Melody and the Sea Hag away. Did the Dastard himself remember? Yes, surely he did, because otherwise his talent would not be very useful to him. He would need to know what happened in one version, in order to change it in the next.

The Dastard came to meet her. "Good to see you again, Sea Hag. Our deal remains?"

Yes, he did remember. So how would he play it this time?

"Our deal remains," Melody's mouth said, following the script exactly. "But let's make this a bit more fun." She freed Melody's head.

Melody screamed, because she was sure the Dastard remembered, and would notice if she played the scene differently before he himself did.

But the man's attention was on the dragon girl. "Go forage for some food," he told her. He was trying to get Becka away, so he could have at Melody's body without interference.

"Sure. I'll take the princess with me."

"&&&&!" he swore. "I keep forgetting that you remember. You can be a real annoyance."

"Remember what?" Melody asked innocently.

"Nothing. Princess, you have the wrong idea about me. I want to be your friend."

"Then let me go," she said.

"That would not free you from the Sea Hag."

He was right. She tried another tack. "You won't really be getting me if it's only because of the Sea Hag."

"You may have a point," he said. "Explain it to me."

He was allowing her to stall for time? Could it be that there was a fragment of decency in him despite his lack of a conscience?

"You're just trying to get beyond the last unhappening," Becka told him. "Because you can't overlap unhappenings of the same events."

The Sea Hag's mind was perplexed. What was this about over-lapping? But Melody understood: It was a limitation of his power. It seemed that he couldn't unhappen the same sequence twice. So if he grabbed her body, and the dragon interceded again, he would not be able to undo it. So he was waiting until his power could be effective again.

Still, she was glad for the reprieve. So she answered. "You want to marry a princess, I think. But you would really be marrying the Sea Hag in another body. She's not a princess. So it wouldn't be real. If you truly want to marry a princess, you will have to find one who isn't Possessed by a malignant spirit."

The Sea Hag jumped back into control. "That's more than enough, my pet," she said angrily.

"Oh, you're back," the Dastard said.

"Yes, I'm back. The princess was talking nonsense."

"I'm not sure it was. She seems to have a good mind."

"Who cares about minds? Kiss me, handsome man, and take off my dress."

His eyes flicked toward the dragon girl, knowing she would intercede the moment she had to. Not enough time had passed. "Let me talk to the princess some more."

"You don't need to waste your time on that. Consider this." She put her hand to her blouse and drew it down to expose more of her bosom.

The Dastard jerked his eyes away just in time. It seemed that breasts did not freak him out as strongly as panties did, but they did have con-siderable effect. "Let me talk to the princess," he repeated.

"To what conceivable point? She is my slave."

"She's a nice girl. I like her. I want to get to know her better."

Melody was amazed. The Dastard was stalling, but he didn't have any reason to lie, since he had a fair amount of control of the situation. Did he really like her for her mind rather than her body? Or for her royalty?

"Oh, all *right*, numskull," the Sea Hag said ungraciously. She turned the head back over to Melody.

"Hello," Melody said. She smiled at him. "Thank you." She drew her blouse back up. The Hag had inadvertently freed her arms too.

"I want to get to know you better," he repeated.

"The Sea Hag has a point," she said. "If your intent is to ravish me, there's little point getting to know me."

"I like my women willing," he said. "I want them to respect me."

And he would never have respect from the Sea Hag! "Respect has to be earned."

"I don't know how to earn it."

That had to be honest! "Is it true that you lack a soul?"

"Yes. I traded it for my talent."

"I didn't realize that was possible." She forced another smile. "How did it happen?"

"It was a demon. But enough about me. What is it like, being a princess?"

The irony was that he seemed really interested. "I wouldn't know. I've been a princess all my life, so I have nothing to compare it to."

He continued to question her, and she continued to answer. He was no dummy, she realized, and now that he was trying to be nice, he was succeeding. Had the situation been otherwise, she could almost have liked him.

Finally the Sea Hag lost patience again. She took over the head. "You are boring me to death! Let's get the @@@@ on with it." She reached out to embrace him.

He drew back. "The princess would never use a word like that."

"The Princess would never #### you either," she returned. "I will. Now let's get on with it."

"True," he agreed. He put his arms around her.

The dragon charged. "Beastly girl!" the Hag raged as they were carried away again.

This time the Dastard waited less time before unhappening it. He returned to the time just before the Sea Hag had taken back control of the head. "Will you allow me to kiss you?" he asked quietly.

The Sea Hag, about to lose patience, was mollified; something was starting to happen. She held off, to see where this would lead.

Melody, remembering what had just unhappened, realized that it was best not to provoke the Hag, with the ensuing intervention and unhappening. She also realized that a similar thought was prompting the man. "You may," she breathed.

He kissed her—and she was surprised to find that she rather liked it. The man did know how to kiss.

But that was as far as it could go, and not just because of the dragon girl. They were walking a fine line here, trying not to trigger undesirable consequences.

Unfortunately, the Dastard wasn't satisfied with just one kiss. He tried for another, and when she said no, he grabbed her—and the Sea Hag eagerly made her body grab back. The dragon girl charged.

After the next unhappening, Melody suggested that they take a walk while they talked. The Sea Hag was fit to be tied, but for a reason Melody didn't quite understand, she had not quite taken over again.

There was a noise, and something was there before them. "Sister, come with us," a voice said.

"Harmony!"

"And Rhythm," her other sister said. "Stiffen your elbows; we're picking you up."

Immediately the Sea Hag took over. "The other princesses! I'll not go with you!" She raised her hands, her fingers curving as claws.

There was a faint tune, and a faint beat. Then Melody's body became light, and the Hag was unable to prevent them from picking her up. Melody floated into the air.

"What's going on?" the Dastard cried.

"I'll handle this," Harmony murmured.

"While I stifle the witch," Rhythm concluded.

"You'll do no such—" the Sea Hag cried. But then her voice faded out. She had been stifled by the magic of a Sorceress. In fact, she became invisible as the magic continued.

They had recovered Melody's body. But that would neither free it of the Possession by the Sea Hag, nor stop the Dastard from unhappening this event.

Then Melody saw Harmony become visible. She looked exactly like Melody. She was taking Melody's place—only she was not Possessed.

As Melody and Rhythm floated invisibly away, she saw Harmony on the ground, walking with the Dastard. Could she possibly fool him? Oh, yes; she knew Melody's mannerisms perfectly, and now that she had her appearance, she would be perfect. So she would make the Dastard think that she was Melody, so that he did not know that Melody and the Sea Hag were gone, and would not unhappen the exchange.

You'll never get away with this! the Sea Hag thought violently.

Melody was afraid that was true. But she really appreciated her sisters' effort to rescue her. What did they have in mind? At least they now knew of Melody's Possession, and were bringing their powers to bear. Probably the Hag had not had to fight two Sorceresses before. The situation had changed. But had it changed enough?

Soon she realized that they were not flying magically, exactly; they were being carried by invisible Sim. That had been why there was noise when the exchange was made: Sim's landing. Still, though they could take Melody and the Hag far from the Dastard, it wouldn't free Melody from her dreaded captivity.

That's right, my pet. They are bound to lose.

Yet Melody had confidence in her sisters. They must have something in mind. They were after all Sorceresses.

So am I, my pet. The only magic I ever encountered that could unPossess one I Possessed is that of the Dastard. And even he can no longer do that. Not that he wants to.

They flew to a giant tree. There, nestled in its topmost foliage, was a huge nest. That would have been made by a roc bird. Sim landed in it and carefully set them down. Rhythm became visible.

"Now Sim and I have to go fetch the one who can expunge the Sea Hag from your body," Rhythm said to Melody. "We were afraid that it couldn't be done, but we found a way. But it requires preparation and equipment and some delicacy. So we shall have to store you in a safe place while we get set up. There is no safe way down from here, so I don't think we need to tie you up."

That's what you think, my pet!

Melody tried to speak, to warn her sister that the Sea Hag had devious ways to escape. But she couldn't make a sound.

Invisible Sim squawked.

"Oh," Rhythm said. "Do you really think so? The Hag can escape by throwing Melody's body to the ground and killing her? Then trying to take over one of us instead? We don't want that! Then we shall have to find a better place. What do you think will do?"

Sim squawked again.

"A mutant lair?" Rhythm said. "All right, if you know where one is."

Sim picked them up, and flew across the forest to another location. This time he landed by a boulder at the base of a mountain. He squawked again.

"I see," Rhythm said. "Yes, this should do very well. I'll put her inside." She turned to Melody. "Sister, this is a Mut Ant nest. It has no entrance and no exit; it is entirely sealed in stone. Only sorcery can get into it—or escape it. So you should be safe here, while we set up."

Melody tried to speak, but still could not. She was silent as her sister ensorceled her into the boulder.

She was inside a hollow stone sphere: the deserted Mut Ant nest. It was of course like no other nest.

"And now, my pet, we shall depart," the Sea Hag said with Melody's mouth. "They thought I could not draw on your powers of sorcery. But of course I can. Sing us out of here, dear." She turned Melody's mouth over to her.

Melody tried to resist, but the pain started. It soon became intolerable. She didn't want to, but she had to use her magic to phase them out of the Mut Ant nest. If only her sister had realized how much control the Sea Hag had over her Possessions! She opened her mouth and sang, concentrating on the stone, thinking it into vapor. Her magic acted through her mind and voice, and the stone became cloudy, and they walked through it into daylight.

"Now turn us invisible and fly us that way," the Hag said, pointing in a direction. Again Melody tried to resist, but again the pain welled up until she couldn't bear it. If only she could resist, she might keep the Hag here until her sister returned—but she couldn't. That's what Rhythm and Sim hadn't known.

She sang again, willing her body to be invisible, and it faded. Then she sang it light, very light, until it weighed no more than the air around it, and could float. Then she sang webbing between her fingers, and feathers on her hands, so that they could catch the air. She stroked the air with those special hands, and flew up into the sky.

"Very good, my pet," her mouth said when the magic was complete. "I can see that you will be extremely useful to me, for the rest of your life. Now I will direct us to our destination." The Sea Hag took over the flying.

Melody wondered why the Hag wasn't returning directly to the Isle of Fellowship, where they had left the Dastard. "Well, I'll tell you, my pet," her mouth replied. "You have been a difficult host, and I have had to expend some considerable effort to keep you under full control and make you perform. That bitchy dragon girl hasn't helped, and neither has the magic of your stupid siblings. So I shall have to restore my vitality sooner than I would otherwise have required."

Restore her vitality? "Yes, my pet. My spirit is not limitless, and it loses some of its essence each time I change hosts, and when I have to fight to control them. So periodically I go to a secret place where I maintain a supply of spirit. I restore myself, and then I am good for another decade or so. How unfortunate that you will never have opportunity to tell anyone else about this marginal weakness of mine."

It would indeed have helped to know, for Melody would have fought yet harder despite the pain. "I know you would have, my pet. But now it no longer matters, because I am close to restoration, and thereafter you will be entirely suppressed."

They flew where the Sea Hag directed. This was to an obscure section of jungle Melody hadn't seen before. They landed, and walked forward, still invisible. Ahead was some kind of a tangle tree, or—no, it was worse. It was a monstrous monster. In fact she recognized it now: It was the monster from another world that Prince Dolph had jammed into the hole in Xanth. The hole that Jenny Elf had come through, when she first lost her way chasing her cat. That hole had been letting other things through, so it had to be plugged. Dolph had changed into a Sphinx and sat on the monster, squeezing it down until it was firmly stuck, nicely plugging the hole. No one she knew of cared to go there, because the monster was always hungry and had a long reach. But it did make an excellent plug; nothing else had come through that hole.

Yet this was exactly where the Sea Hag was taking them. Had she misunderstood? Was she going to kill Melody by feeding her to the monster, so she could take another body? "No, of course not, my pet. This body is far too good to give up casually, and my deal with the Dastard is too important to pass up. Seldom have my immediate prospects been better. But I shall need all my strength to eliminate your sisters. It has been centuries since I have had to fight more than one Magician or Sorceress at a time, and it's no easy thing."

They came to a halt safely beyond the monster's reach. "Hello, my pet," the Sea Hag called. "I have no body for you to eat this time, but I'm sure you will endure. Now I will visit you, or more correctly, the realm just beyond you." The monster, hearing her, evidently recognized her, as it waved a tentacle.

The realm beyond the monster? That could only be the other side of the hole. Melody had never dreamed of such a thing. Only the Sea Hag would have dared venture there. "Yes indeed, my pet. That's why I set up my cache there, once the hole opened up; it was the safest possible place for it. The monster of course can't interfere, because it is soulless. My spirit passes right through it without resistance. Since most folk who are any conceivable threat to me have bodies that they can't separate from their souls, they can't pass; the monster would eat them. It is utterly convenient for me."

The Hag quested around, and found a shaded spot among ferns. She lay Melody's body down. "Now I shall leave you, for a brief time, my pet, but never fear; you will not be going anywhere." With that, she stunned the body; Melody remained conscious, but was unable to move any limb or her face.

I shall return, the Sea Hag said, and her foul spirit departed. For the first time since the Possession, Melody was fully herself. It did her no good; she was locked in place. She could not call out, and since she was invisible, she could not be spied by searchers. She couldn't even cry.

But she could hear and see. Her face was toward the plugged monster, and perhaps because of the Possession she could see the spirit of the sea Hag flitting through the air toward the monster. The spirit looked old and twisted, rather than young and sweet. It went right up to the monster, and through it, and disappeared. The Hag had gone to her hoard of spirit stuff, to refresh herself.

Melody struggled, but the stasis remained absolute; she could not even twitch a toe. The Hag did know what she was doing, unfortunately.

Then she saw something coming. It was a spirit, but this one was fresh and full and esthetic. In fact it was beautiful. What a change that restoration had made! How could a creature as ugly in every way as the Sea Hag become so lovely?

"Melody!" a voice came.

That wasn't the Sea Hag. That was Rhythm! Melody tried to cry out warning, because of the returning spirit, but couldn't.

The spirit came closer, looking even more beautiful. "Melody, it's me."

Now Melody saw that the lovely spirit was attached to a body. It wasn't the Sea Hag, it was her sister! Coming to rescue her. Again. But she still couldn't respond.

Rhythm arrived. "There you are! I hadn't expected you to be invisible. Come, you are free now."

Free? Hardly.

Harmony bent over her body. "Let me explain. The Sea Hag is gone. She isn't coming back. As soon as we nullify that stasis spell, you'll be free." She brought out her little drum and beat a pattern on it.

The freeze lifted. Melody sat up, feeling gloriously free. The dreadful Sea Hag really was gone. "How did you do it?" she asked, singing herself visible. Then, seeing her weirdly feathered hands, she sang them back to normal. "I thought there was no way."

"Sim went to Ptero and found a way," Rhythm said. "We had to catch her when she went behind the plugged monster."

"But she'll come back," Melody said.

"No. She's trapped there. She can't return to Xanth."

"But how can that be? She said the monster is no barrier to her spirit."

"That was because the monster had no soul of its own. Now it does."

"It does?"

"Remember that soul we were going to give the Dastard? We had to use it for this. Now the monster has it, and is opaque to the passage of other spirits. It represents a spirit block as well as a physical block."

"I never thought of that!"

"None of us did. Except Sim. Still, we had to get the Sea Hag to go there. So we thought if we stressed her some, and then let her seem to escape, she might get careless. Then we could block her out of Xanth, and rescue you. And it worked!"

Sim, invisible, squawked. "That's right!" Melody said. "The Dastard can still unhappen this unPossession, and I'll be captive again. There's no way I can escape it, if he decides to do it."

"I hadn't thought of that," Rhythm said. "We haven't won yet."

"Indeed we have not," Melody agreed, feeling a horrible shiver.

13
CASTLE MAIDRAGON

Becka couldn't figure out what was happening. Or unhappening. Each time the Sea Hag was about to seduce the Dastard with the princess' body, Becka had turned dragon and intervened. The Dastard hadn't liked it, but she was acting to protect his interest as well as the princess, because she herself had once been Possessed by the Hag and knew that the woman was absolutely ruthless and not to be trusted. She would ruin the Dastard and throw him away as readily as she would the body of the princess, when it suited her purpose. So they needed to be kept apart if it was at all possible. But Becka wasn't sure how long she could keep this up, particularly now that it had gotten really confusing.

Princess Melody had talked the Dastard into taking a walk. Becka had followed, not interfering as long as nothing bad was happening. But then it had turned weird. A voice from nowhere has said "Sister, come with us," and the princess had risen into the air and disappeared. Then reappeared. The Dastard had been suspicious, but the princess had kissed him and said it would be all right. And so it seemed to be. Had he done a partial unhappening, only enough to prevent the princess from flying away? She wanted to ask him, but didn't think she could while the princess was listening. She didn't know how far the Hag had caught on about the several unhappenings, and didn't want to tip her off if she didn't know.

The Dastard was acting as if nothing had happened, but Becka knew he had noticed too. He surely knew whether he had unhappened anything, and he was cautious when he didn't understand something. He was not a stupid or rash man. So if this was not of his doing, then he was playing along until he knew exactly what had happened.

But there was something else odd about this. The princess was walking and talking, but she didn't seem quite the same. She had little mannerisms, and while her present ones were similar, they weren't identical. It was almost as if—

"This isn't the same princess!" Becka said. "I think it's one of her sisters."

Suddenly the Dastard stopped walking. "Bring back the Sea Hag," he said.

The princess stopped too. "Oh, you caught on," she said. "I'm Harmony, Melody's sister." A little harmonica appeared, and she played it briefly. Her hair changed color, becoming brown. So did her dress and eyes. Then the harmonica faded out. It was magic that would have seemed formidable, with anybody except a Sorceress; for her it was obviously incidental.

"You changed places?" he asked. "Why?"

"So we could rescue Melody from the Sea Hag."

"You can't. The Sea Hag will kill her before she lets her go."

"We think we can do it."

"Then I'll unhappen it."

"But you mustn't!" Harmony said, alarmed. "Possession by the Sea Hag is the most horrible thing imaginable."

"The Hag and I have a Deal. I won't let you break it up."

"And I won't let you hurt my sister," Harmony said.

"How are you going to stop me?"

The little harmonica reappeared in Princess Harmony's hand. She played a few notes. The Dastard froze in place.

After a moment, Harmony stopped playing. "That's how," she said.

The Dastard recovered. "I didn't know you could do that. Princess Melody never did."

"Melody was captive of the Sea Hag; she couldn't use her power. Otherwise you would never have gotten close to her."

"I see," the Dastard said thoughtfully. "You three are all Sorceresses."

"We are," she agreed.

"But my power will work on you. I could have unhappened your magic."

"Why didn't you?"

"I think you already know."

"Because if you unhappen me once, you won't be able to do it again for the same event."

"That's right. If I unhappened just your music, I wouldn't be able to go back and unhappen your exchange with Melody."

Harmony nodded. "I thought to trick you. You were too smart for me. But if you try to unhappen my exchange with Melody, I'll go back with you and block you."

Becka was trying to stay out of this, but couldn't help herself. "You can do that? You can unhappen things too?"

"No, not alone," Harmony said. "But I really am a Sorceress in my own right, and can block hostile magic when I have to."

"I can go back to before your arrival here," the Dastard said. "I can stop that exchange you made with your younger Selves."

But the princess was unfazed. "Two things: first, I'll go back with you, and block you there too. Second, if you succeeded, then my sister Melody would not arrive either, and the Hag would not take her over. So you would have no deal with the Hag, and none of this would matter."

The Dastard studied her appraisingly. "You're no dummy."

"Neither are you. So I trust you'll know better than to start something you will regret."

"I think you're bluffing. If you could go back and stop me, you would have done it already, and we would not be here discussing it."

Still she showed no distress. "You have been unhappening events for four years. We have been here as adults only a few days. We're not used to Xanthly concepts of time and geography, but we're learning rapidly. So you have had the advantage of experience, but on the other hand we have the advantage of numbers. When the three of us act together, we can do anything anyone can do."

"But one of you is captive of the Sea Hag."

"I think two of us could handle you," Harmony said evenly.

"Then why didn't you?"

Harmony smiled. "Now you are the one asking a question to which you know the answer."

"Because eliminating me would not have saved your sister," he said. "You have to deal with the Sea Hag first."

"Yes. But if we can't save our sister, we can certainly make you regret it. I think you would prefer not to face us when we have nothing to lose."

Becka whistled internally. The princess was handling the Dastard rather nicely. But the Sea Hag did have her sister, and that was a strong deterrent.

"What is it you want?" he asked.

"We want Melody free, and you to stop making mischief. What is it *you* want?"

"To marry an attractive princess and live in luxury the rest of my life."

"That's a pretty selfish desire."

The Dastard shrugged. "I have no soul. I can afford to be selfish."

"There is something you perhaps don't realize. If you marry any human woman, including a princess, you will inherit half her soul, which will in time regenerate to a full soul. You will then be governed by it. That will be hard on your selfishness."

The Dastard seemed taken aback. "Is this true?" he asked Becka.

"Yes, as far as I know," Becka said, surprised to be asked. "At least, I've heard of it when demons marry humans."

The Dastard considered a moment, then shrugged. "But in that event I would already have achieved my desire, so it wouldn't matter."

"It would matter," Harmony said. "You would have to act decently, if your soul was not corrupted. Your present way of life would be finished."

Then the Dastard thought of another angle. "If I married the Sea Hag, in Possession of Melody's body, would I get half *her* soul?"

That evidently set the princess back. "I'm not sure. The Hag has hung on to her withered old soul for millennia. I doubt she would give any of it away. But you might still get half of Melody's soul."

"And I might not," he countered. "The fact is you don't know."

"I don't know," Harmony agreed. "And I will do everything I can to stop you from marrying the Sea Hag in my sister's body. So will our sister Rhythm."

Becka realized that this was no bluff. Two Sorceresses working together could destroy one man, especially if they could follow him in time, as it seemed they could.

There was a sound. Suddenly two more princesses appeared beside Harmony. One wore green and one wore red, with matching hair colors.

The Dastard looked at them. "Is—?"

"Yes, I am free of the Sea Hag," Melody replied.

"How—?"

"We locked her on the other side of the plugged monster," Rhythm said.

The Dastard slid into limbo. He was making his move. The three princesses slid with him. They were countering it. Becka was carried along in the powerful swirl of magic.

They came to the time and place where the Sea Hag had been trapped. Becka saw Melody's body lie down, and a withered spirit leave it and flit toward the monster. This was how it happened.

The Dastard slid back farther, to the time just before the Hag brought Melody here. He slid into Xanth. He was going to try to warn the Sea Hag not to go behind the monster.

The three princesses slid out with him. Melody began to hum; Harmony played her harmonica; Rhythm produced a small drum and beat lightly on it. A field of power formed around the Dastard and started to make him fade out.

He slid back into limbo. The three princesses followed. Becka was again sucked along in the vortex. There was no question of the combined power of the princesses; Becka felt the surge of magic, stronger now, and knew that with each experience they were discovering how to tune their magic for greater effect. They were learning rapidly, and would soon overwhelm the Dastard. They had already stopped him from unhappening the unPossession, which had surely been the trickiest aspect of this contest.

He slid back to the time the princesses had exchanged with their younger Selves. The three went with him. This time he didn't even make it out of limbo; their magic bound him within it, rendering him helpless to interfere with their past.

The Dastard tried once more. He slid all the way back four years, evidently trying to get before the time the stork delivered the little princesses. Becka realized with horror that this ploy might work; obviously they could not go back to before the time they existed, any more than he could go back to before he got his talent.

But it turned out that they had been delivered just before he got his talent. He could not unhappen their very existence. Becka was relieved; she was supposed to help the Dastard, but her sympathy was with the princesses.

The Dastard snapped back to the present and returned to Xanth. The princesses returned with him, and so did Becka, carried along. She had never before experienced such strong magic; she felt its power like the strong current of a swollen river, carrying her along like a floating leaf. It was frightening and exhilarating at the same time; she was glad to be out of it for the moment.

"So you can balk me," the Dastard said. "But for how long? The Sea Hag said you were here only four days. After that I will win."

The princesses looked triply stricken. "He's right," Melody said.

"We have very little time to settle this," Harmony agreed.

"So we'll have to do it the mean way," Rhythm concluded.

Becka didn't much like the sound of this. "The mean way?"

"We'll have to kill him," Sim squawked. He had not accompanied them through limbo, but remained in the present scene, still invisible. Becka could see him because the princesses could, and their daunting magic encompassed her.

"I'll unhappen that!" the Dastard said.

"Not if we balk you," Melody said.

"We'll chase you until we catch you," Harmony said.

"And feed you to a dragon," Rhythm finished.

"I'm not eating him!" Becka protested.

But the Dastard was plainly worried. "Maybe we should negotiate."

"Why should we?" Melody asked. "You want to enslave me to the Sea Hag."

"No, I want to marry you. Will you do it without being Possessed?"

Melody looked stricken. Harmony stepped in. "No, she won't. Anyway, she can't; she'll be returning to Ptero soon. So that's out."

"The Sea Hag said there was a way," he said.

"Her way is anathema," Rhythm said. "Whatever it is."

"You three could make it true your way, if you wanted to."

"But we don't want to," Melody said. "I don't want to be Possessed, or to marry you. I just want to stop you from doing dastardly deeds."

But the Dastard had her number. "You don't want to kill me, either. You're bluffing."

"But we could stop you some other way," Harmony said.

"Really? How?"

"By giving you a soul," Rhythm explained.

But the Dastard was ready for that too. "You used your spare soul for the plugged monster. Now you don't have one for me."

The three princesses exchanged a triple glance. "He's right, you know," Melody said.

"But souls are divisible," Harmony said. "One of us could share half a soul with him."

"By marrying me?" the Dastard asked.

The three quailed. Obviously that was not their plan.

Becka was impressed. The Dastard was proving to be smarter than the princesses.

Then Princess Melody tackled the matter. "You have a certain advantage because you have no conscience. You can do things we can't, because of our ethics. But I think we have more power than you, and if we have to make a choice between letting you tear up Xanth or stopping you permanently, we'll stop you. We have to make that decision in the next two days, before we return to Ptero. So if you have any suggestion that might enable us to stop you without killing you, we would like to hear it."

And that, Becka realized, put it back on the Dastard. The three princesses did have more magic; she had felt its awesome power. But they also did have consciences, and that limited them substantially. Becka could feel the difference: When she was near the Dastard, there was a kind of emptiness, while near the princesses there was the goodness of their sweet souls. It remained a standoff.

"Yes, I have a compromise," the Dastard said. "Marry me, Melody, share your soul with me, and we'll both have everything we want."

"Some other compromise," Harmony said.

"That's the only one I'm interested in."

"And it's one we are not interested in," Rhythm concluded.

There was a silence. Becka wanted to help the princesses, but was supposed to help the Dastard. She made an effort to do both. "Maybe— maybe if you gave it some time," she said. "You're rejecting the Dastard without really knowing him. You ought to let him make his case, seeing as it is a viable compromise."

"No it's not," Melody said. "The gain is all his, the sacrifice all ours."

"Still, you shouldn't decide in ignorance," Becka argued. "Maybe if you know him better you'd be absolutely sure you would never marry him in a million years. But you have to find out first. It might be that he would improve with half a soul, and be—" She couldn't quite make herself say "good," and needed a more neutral word.

"Tolerable," the Dastard suggested with four-sevenths of a smile. He obviously didn't care about the soul; he just wanted the princess.

"Sim, does this make sense?" Harmony asked the invisible bird.

"Yes," Sim squawked.

"Then I guess we'd better try it," Rhythm said. "Why don't we give it one day, and then if there's no other way, we can do what we have to do."

"All right," Melody said miserably. "I will get to know him. For one day. But I'm not going to let him do any Adult Conspiracy things."

Becka turned to the Dastard. "There. You have one day. If you're ever going to win a princess, this is the time. But you have to behave."

The Dastard nodded. "Then it's a truce. For a day."

"Now we have to figure out the setting," Harmony said.

"A magic castle," Rhythm said. "With just the two of them."

"And no magic talents," Harmony said. "No unhappenings, no sing- ing things real. Just the two of you. Getting to know each other better."

"Who's going to enforce this?" Melody asked. "Suppose someone cheats?" She didn't need to clarify who might cheat; there was only one person present without a conscience.

"That's no problem," the Dastard said. "You'll be watching. You'll know if I cheat. Then the deal will be off. But let's qualify it: no magic unless the other agrees."

Melody and Harmony exchanged an uncertain glance. Sim understood why: "We need an objective judge," he squawked. "Someone who doesn't stand to gain or lose from this."

"Becka," Rhythm said. "She can watch, and judge."

"Me?" Becka asked, startled. "I'm just a dragon girl. I can't stop an unhappening, or the magic of a Sorceress."

"But *we* can," Harmony said. "If someone watches and alerts us."

"And Sim can figure out alternatives," Rhythm said. "So after the day, maybe we'll know what to do."

"But the setting," the Dastard said. "I want it limited, so she can't just run away."

"Limited to a castle," Harmony said. "A fancy one, with many turrets and terraces and chambers."

Rhythm smiled. "Are you thinking what I'm thinking?"

"Of course I am. This is our chance to animate our chocolate castle, only in stone."

"But it would take forever to conjure all that stone!" Melody protested.

"No, I believe you could do it in a few hours, as background magic, since you have the pattern," Sim squawked. "This is Xanth, where stone is common."

Becka had another concern. "You said I could watch and judge. How am I supposed to do that? I can't just follow them around."

Sim squawked. "Adapt."

Harmony and Rhythm nodded. "Beautiful!" Harmony said. "A rehearsal for a real stone castle."

"We know the design," Rhythm agreed. "All we need is practice implementing it."

"You'll need my help to make it," Melody said. "We haven't done adaptation on this scale before."

"I don't understand," Becka said.

"You will," Sim squawked.

Then the three princesses faced her. Melody sang, Harmony played her harmonica, and Rhythm beat her little drum. Magic surrounded them, becoming overwhelmingly powerful. It was as if a phenomenal storm were forming, yet there was no breath of wind. Something breathtaking was happening—but what? It seemed to reach right through her, taking hold of her very flesh and bones.

Becka felt herself changing. Weirdly. "Hey!" she cried as her hair stood out from her head and current surged through her limbs. She tried to turn dragon to escape it, but the change continued. Her body expanded enormously, and her feet spread into the ground. Her scales turned into outcrops of stone—tors or battlements. Her eyes fractured painlessly into a hundred panes of glass. She was becoming something huge and hard and amazingly intricate.

Then she realized what it was: She was developing into a castle! A big one, with endless turrets and walls and stairways and windows, and green trees growing in gardens throughout. There was a circular moat, but the castle was evidently nestled on a small hill. She had lost her eyes and ears, yet she could see and hear everything, outside and inside, via the windows and doors. She was the setting!

The three princesses stopped their music. The castle was complete. What a fantastic edifice it was!

Melody detached herself from the trio and walked to the front entrance. Her clothing became an ornate gown. She had been beautiful; now she was stunning. She crossed the drawbridge and stood by the gate. "Welcome to Castle Maidragon," she said to the Dastard.

"There?" he asked, taken aback. He plainly hated to admit it, but he was as plainly awed. So was Becka; she had never imagined that such compelling magic was possible. The princesses seemed like such delicate girls, yet they had the strength to change the very face of the local geography—or turn a dragon girl into a castle, without hurting her.

"Where else?" Harmony asked.

"But we had better dress you appropriately," Rhythm said. She beat her drum, and Harmony played her instrument, and the Dastard's clothing became a royal prince's robe. He had been halfway homely; now he was halfway handsome.

He stood on the drawbridge and looked down at his reflection. "Clothes really do make the man," he murmured.

"You will look like that all the time, if you marry a princess," Sim squawked. Becka realized that the big bird wanted it to happen, because it would immediately nullify the danger of unscrupulous unhappenings.

Unfortunately it was Melody who needed to be persuaded; the Dastard was already more than willing.

He crossed the moat and joined her. The drawbridge lifted. They were confined to their setting—and Becka could see and hear everything. She almost hoped that the Dastard would be charming enough to impress the princess, because it *would* solve the problem. Yet how could Melody ever make such a sacrifice?

"Let me show you the castle," Melody said graciously. "We have spent years working out its details." She took his hand and led him into the first chamber.

He came with her, looking almost as bemused as Becka felt. The princess was giving him her time, but in her own fashion, not that of the Sea Hag. She was doing what she was supposed to do, being the perfect hostess.

"You actually turned the girl into the castle?" the Dastard asked, looking around at the dozen or so turrets. The castle was on so many levels it was dizzying to try to comprehend in a single gaze.

"Yes, but don't be concerned; she is unharmed. We merely performed a topological technique we learned from Grandma Vadne. We will return her to her natural form when this is done."

"Is she conscious?"

"Oh, yes. She can see and hear everything that goes on here, because this is her. But she will communicate only with my sisters. We can ignore her."

"But changing a living person into stone and trees and water—"

"And much much more," Melody agreed. "Now let's change the subject. You have just one day to convince me to marry you, and you had better hurry, because I think your chances are one in a googolly."

"A what?"

"A very big number."

"I haven't heard of that number. What is it?"

"It's one we invented back when we were three or four years old. Just as we designed this castle. Originally it was a doll castle made of chocolate, called Castle Chocohol, but as we grew, we enlarged it and added details. We name it after whatever we make it from. We're rather proud of it, actually."

"The number," he said. "Exactly what is it?"

Melody made a moue. She looked really cute when she did that. "Oh, that. It's based on a googol."

"What's a googol?"

She made a flounce of impatience, her artful graciousness slipping a trifle. "Do you really want to know?"

"Yes."

"Well, it's your own time you're wasting. A googol is a one followed by a hundred zeroes. Are you with me so far?"

"Yes. Ten to the hundredth power. 10^{100}."

She paused, nodding. "You *do* understand."

"I am without conscience, not without intelligence."

Becka was getting to halfway like the Dastard. He had set the princess back right when she had expected him to be ignorant.

"Very well. A googolplex is a one followed by a googol zeroes."

"Ten to the googol power," he agreed. "Ten to the ten to the hundredth power."

"So we made the googolly, which is a googol to the googol power."

"Ten to the hundredth power raised to the ten to the hundredth power," he said. "Got it now. That is a very big number."

"It seems appropriate in the circumstance."

The Dastard had that little chance of persuading Melody? Then this exercise didn't seem to have much point.

But the man seemed unbothered. "What are the chances of your killing me if we don't marry?"

"About one in—" She paused uncomfortably. "Well, I don't know, exactly."

"Would you rather kill me than marry me?"

"I don't want to do either!"

"But as long as you do neither, we have an impasse. I'm not going to change my nature without a soul, and you aren't going to let me go. If you marry me, I'll be satisfied, and I'll have a conscience, and won't do any more mischief. So your choices seem to be between letting Xanth suffer, or killing me, or marrying me. You don't seem to want to do any of those."

Melody stared at him. "If this is your idea of courtship, it's not winning me over."

Becka saw that the Dastard's soulless rationality was not very romantic. But she wasn't in a position to advise him, assuming that he would listen.

"I don't want to win your heart, just your acquiescence."

"What about love?" Melody flared.

"What is love?"

Without a soul, he could not love. So he had no use for it. Becka saw that, but wasn't sure the princess did.

Melody turned away. "Anyway, we're proud of our castle. It has many fascinating features. The topmost turrets are good for observation; from them we can see all the way to Mundania. The trees are of many rare and magical types, not just the useful shoe trees and pie trees. The mistress bedroom is opulent, and—"

"What kind of bedroom?"

"The mistress bedroom. That's the most important one in the castle, for the mistress of the castle. Other castles may have master bedrooms, but they weren't made by princesses. Let me show you."

"I would be happy to be shown your mistress bedroom."

For a reason he surely didn't understand, that just made Melody further annoyed. Becka saw her graciousness slip another notch, but the princess pretended to be unaffected. She led the way through the entrance tower, up a spiral of stone steps, and out a back door on the third story. This led to a very long narrow stairway on the top of a stout wall. There were stone railings on either side rising to waist height, so there was no danger of falling off unless pushed. The outer rail was a battlement, so that defenders could fire their arrows at a besieging force, while the inner rail was smooth. There was an embrasure halfway up toward the next turret. Becka really liked this castle, and wished she could assume it as a third form, being a dragon/castle/girl, but of course it would be gone the moment this scene was done.

The Dastard looked out, evidently intrigued. "This is highly defensible."

"I suppose it is, though we don't have any soldiers. We prefer to spend our time in the garden inside."

He looked in, over that smooth rail. "I suppose."

They followed the steps up to the turret. They went around it on the inside, and there was a door opening into it. "We have a nice maid's room there, with her bedroom above, and a dormer looking out," Melody said. "And storage of supplies below." She turned the other way, and indicated a courtyard with a pleasant terrace and garden. "We play games there."

"I would be happy to play games with you."

There he went again, spoiling whatever faint chance there might have been for a mood. Becka wished she could give some spot advice to the man, informing him about subtlety. Girls didn't much like crude implications.

Melody hurried grimly on up the wall-stairs to the next complex of structures. This was truly fancy, with shrubs around its edge and a fountain in its center. "On the right is the chalet, where visitors can stay; downstairs is a stage for plays. The left leads up those flights of wide steps to the main chateau, where we stay. Of course there is much more."

"I would be happy to stay with you."

Uh-oh. He had finally triggered a direct response. "Stop that!"

"Stop what?"

"Stop making those suggestive remarks. I'm not sharing a bed with you, or playing any games with you, or staying with you. I'm just showing you the castle."

The man looked thoughtful. "I apologize," he said.

"I don't need your fake regret either!"

Becka knew it would take a miracle to fish this relationship out of the mire.

The Dastard looked across to another complex of structures to the left. "What's there?"

"Oh, game rooms, and the kitchen, and guest rooms. There's lots of space in this castle."

He looked farther, toward a low turret with a conical roof. "What's there?"

"Oh, nothing, really."

"Nothing?"

"Well, if you must know, it's the forbidden chamber. Its door must never be opened."

"What's in that chamber?" he asked, intrigued.

"We don't know. That's the point: It's secret. It must never be known."

"You made it, but you don't know what's in it?"

"That's right. We thought it would be nice to have a secret."

"Well, I'm curious, so I'll go look."

"Don't do that!" Melody cried. "There's no telling what's in there. It could be a hungry dragon."

"If there is, I'll unhappen the opening of the door."

"You're not supposed to unhappen anything during the truce."

"This would be an unhappening of the breaking of a rule, so that it never happened."

"You must not either break the rule or unhappen it. That's the truce." Actually the deal was to allow magic if the other party agreed. But it was obvious that Melody would agree to nothing. There might not be enough googollies in all the universe to give the man any chance.

The Dastard shrugged, seeming unperturbed. "Have it your way. What's there to eat?"

Melody waved a hand nonchalantly. "Anything you want."

"Anything?"

She flushed, for a reason Becka did not understand. Evidently the Dastard had blown yet another nonexistent chance. "Shoefly pie, then," she said abruptly. "Made from the best flying shoes." She led the way to the dining room.

They had shoefly pie. "It's good," the Dastard said.

"Thank you." But ice almost crackled off the words.

"I was making a statement of fact, not complimenting you." Worse yet.

"That's good. I didn't want your compliment."

"Then why did you thank me?"

"I was being polite."

"Isn't that the same as lying?"

She flushed again. "I apologize for lying."

The Dastard had scored, but not in any way he wanted. If only the princely clothing had brought a princely manner! Yet he still seemed unbothered. Maybe he simply didn't realize what a disaster this was. "Let's go open that door."

"What door?"

"You know which one." His eyes flicked toward it.

"No! That door must not be opened."

The Dastard considered. "Suppose we contest for it?"

"Suppose we do what?"

"We can play a game of some sort. If I win, we open the door."

"No!"

"Aren't you curious about what's there?"

"No!"

"Isn't that a lie?"

Once more she flushed. The man simply didn't realize that catching Melody in trifling nuances of deception would never make her warm to him. Social etiquette was fashioned of complimentary deceptions. "Not curious enough."

He shrugged. "Then let's play for other stakes. If I win, you kiss me."

"No!"

"Then what do you suggest?"

"Nothing!"

"So shall we just sit here for six more hours and do nothing, leaving our problem unsolved?"

Melody angled her head, studying him. "You spoke of what I would have to do, or allow to be done, if you won a contest. What if you lose?"

"Name your penalty."

"You will leave Xanth and never return."

The Dastard considered. "There's a flaw."

"What do you mean?"

"I could agree, but since I have no conscience, I wouldn't keep my word."

"Then you wouldn't keep your word to make no more mischief if you married me."

"I'm not giving my word for that. I'm just saying that I wouldn't have any inclination to make mischief, because I would already have what I want, and I would have some conscience."

"I don't trust that."

He shrugged. "Do you have a better idea?"

"No! Maybe I'll just have to take your worthless word."

"About what?"

"About leaving Xanth forever if you lose the game."

"Very well. What game?"

"We invented one to go with the castle, sort of. Will you play it?"

"Yes, if the terms are right."

"If you lose, you leave Xanth. If you win, I'll kiss you. Once."

"You kissed me before," he reminded her.

"That was when the Sea Hag was Possessing me. Now I'm in charge of myself. It's different."

He considered. "No. A kiss isn't enough. I want to marry you."

"No!"

"Then I want to open the door."

"All *right*! I win, you leave Xanth. You win, we open the door."

So he had neatly maneuvered her into making his deal of the moment. But did he have any plan to win their larger contest? Becka couldn't see any.

"Agreed. What's the game?"

"It's called Swamp Road. It's like tic-tac-toe, only different."

"Show me."

She fetched a sheet of paper, a pencil, and an eraser from the castle supplies. Her hands in the cupboard made Becka feel ticklish, but she couldn't laugh. "Here's a small sample diagram. We play it on larger ones, but this will show the way." She sketched it lightly. "This is the neighboring village, where some of the castle servants live. It is laid out in a square or oblong in a swampy area. There are nine houses, with fourteen dirt roads connecting them to each other, so they can visit each other freely. When it rains, water runs over the roads, but usually doesn't hurt them. Still, it's a nuisance, and they worry about heavy rains. None of them want to be isolated by having their roads wash out, preventing them from visiting others. So when a road-paver comes, one of them may have a road paved to a neighboring house so it won't wash away."

"This is a game?"

"Yes. I'm giving the background. When one resident paves a road, that makes the water flow less freely through the swamp at that point, so the water level rises. That washes out one of the remaining dirt roads. The homeowners panic, and pave over another road so that it won't wash away. But that makes the water rise still higher, and another dirt road washes out. The homeowners are afraid that if they don't hurry, some of them will get cut off from the rest and be isolated. That would be awful. It would mean that the swamp had defeated them."

"So what's the game?"

"One player is the paver. The other is the swamp, or the washer, we call it. They take turns: First the paver paves one road, then the swamp washes out one. If the game ends with all the houses still connected, however deviously, the paver wins; if any house or houses are isolated, the swamp wins. We mark the paved roads by darkening a line between houses; we mark a washout by drawing two lines across a road, like a ditch." She demonstrated, darkening one line and making a gap in another.

"That's it?"

She smiled grimly. "It's enough to make a good game. Let's walk through it once on the sample diagram; then we can play a serious game."

"But just darkening lines, or erasing them on paper is dull."

"We can make it seem real, via illusion, if you wish."

"Yes. Reality by illusion."

Melody hummed a tune. The surface of the table expanded enormously, until it was the size of a village, and they were standing at its edge. Rain was drizzling down on a grid of dirt roads. At each intersection was a little thatch house. There were nine houses, with the roads between them forming four squares. There were also two diagonal roads, bisecting the grid from northeast to southwest, but no diagonals from northwest or southeast. There was a total of fourteen roads. Becka was impressed again; it did look real. Some of the houses even had gardens, and toys outside, as if there were children.

"Here's how to pave a road," Melody said. She took a wand that appeared in her hand and stroked it along the road's surface. Immediately the road became hard and raised. "You can pave only an existing dirt road; most diagonal routes don't exist. And here's how to wash one out." She used the wand to make two strokes crossing the road. A ditch appeared, with water coursing through it. "Now you try it." She handed the wand to the Dastard.

He used it to pave another road, and to wash out one. "That's easy enough. But I want to see how the game actually plays."

"Yes." Melody took back the wand and stroked it across the paves and ditches, and they disappeared. "We can play as many practice games as you want. They generally favor the paver. Do you prefer to pave?"

"No. I prefer unhappening things."

They walked through a game, with Melody paving and the Dastard washing. In the end, he succeeded in isolating one house on the corner.

"So you see, that's your win," Melody said. "But I could have prevented you."

"I'm ready," the Dastard said. "Let's play a larger game."

"But there are tricks. You'll be at a disadvantage."

"No I won't. I understand this game."

She shrugged. "If you're sure." She waved the wand, and a larger grid appeared, four houses square, with twenty-nine roads connecting them.

"Larger."

She waved the wand again, and a grid of twenty-five houses appeared, with a total of forty-seven roads. The Dastard nodded.

"Let's review the terms," the princess said. "If I win, you agree to leave Xanth. If you win, we open the forbidden door."

"Yes."

She hesitated. "But you may renege, because you have no soul, and therefore no conscience."

"Yes."

"So why should I make any such deal?"

"Because you hope that I might honor the deal if I lose, and you're curious about what's in that chamber if you lose."

Melody flushed again, meaning that he had scored again. He was clearly smart enough. "All right, let's do it."

They started playing the game. Becka couldn't tell who had the advantage, so she did what they couldn't: She indulged her girlish curiosity. She looked inside the forbidden room without opening the door. It was part of the castle, and she *was* the castle, and could see anywhere within it.

The chamber was empty except for a manlike figure standing in the center, facing the door. Across the back of his shirt was printed the word FACTOR. That was all.

Becka couldn't make sense of it. This was no terrifying sight. There was no dragon or bug-eyed monster or other horrendous creature. Just this standing man-thing named Factor. Why should the princesses be so wary of him?

She returned her attention to the game. The castle was as it had been before, but the chamber with the game seemed to be as big as all the rest of it, with the rain and marsh. That illusion was remarkable. The two people were even getting wet in the drizzling rain.

The Dastard washed out a road. Melody paved one to maintain the connection to a house that was threatened with isolation. He washed out another. She went to pave another—and paused, horrified. "Oh, no!"

Becka looked. There were two houses at risk, and only one of them could be saved. The Dastard was winning.

Melody paved. The Dastard washed. And it was done. He had won.

Melody clapped her hands. The illusion vanished. They were standing in the castle chamber, looking at the grid on the table. Both were dry again, as if never wet by the rain. It did not change the fact that the Dastard had won.

"Maybe you'd rather have a kiss?" the princess inquired. Becka could not be certain whether this was sarcastic.

"No. Open the door."

"I really don't think this is wise."

"I don't care."

She spread her hands. "This way."

They went to the forbidden chamber. Melody produced a key, put it in the lock, turned it, and hesitated. "You're sure?"

"Yes." The Dastard jammed in beside her and pushed open the door.

They stood side by side, looking in. "It's the Factor," Melody said, shuddering. "The Random Factor."

Now Becka saw that the front of the man-thing's shirt said RANDOM. Still, what did it mean?

"So what?" the Dastard asked.

"There's absolutely no predicting what he will do. It can be anything, but surely something significant. And we can't stop it."

Hence the name, Becka realized. A random factor could not be anticipated.

"This is *all*?" the Dastard asked, a sneer in his tone.

The figure raised his arms, pointing at the two in the doorway. There was a flash of magic. Then the door slammed shut and the Factor became inert.

Becka was mystified. As consequences went, it didn't seem like much.

Princess Melody and the Dastard stared at each other with strange expressions. Something had definitely happened—but what?

14

RANDOM FACTOR

The Dastard stared at Princess Melody. She was lovely, and he sincerely appreciated that, but that wasn't what bothered him. He was feeling something weird, and it was somehow associated with her.

She was staring back at him, her expression changing from horrified to smug. "Do you know something? I feel better now that the Random Factor has struck and not accomplished anything. I was afraid he would turn us into toads or something."

"He didn't do that," the Dastard said. "But he did something. I can feel it."

"I can't feel anything. And you know what? I don't care. Let's go up to the bedroom and have some wicked fun."

He stared at her with downing horror. "Melody, what has happened to you?"

"Nothing! I'm just coming to my senses. Here we've been pussy-footing around, playing stupid swamp games, when we could have been having some real sport."

"I don't understand."

She shot him an arch glance. "Yes you do. I mean chasing storks."

"But you don't want to do that."

"The %%%% I don't! So are you coming, or do I have to start

without you?" She caught the hem of her gown and lifted it enough to show a fair ankle.

"But Melody, this is against everything you stand for. What of your princessly honor?"

"Princesses lead pretty dull lives. Now get your donkey in gear and go to the bedroom."

"How can you swear? How can you suggest such a thing?"

"Are you suddenly turning prudish on me, Das? Is that what the Factor did to you?"

"No. I'm not sure what he did. I just know that this is not right."

"~~~~!" she snapped. "I sure misjudged you. I thought you were a man." She drew her gown up enough to show a fair knee.

He stared at her with burgeoning horror. "You have been taken over again by the Sea Hag!"

She burst out laughing. "The Sea Hag! Ludicrous. I wouldn't let that wizened old fraud near my luscious body. Whatever gave you that idea?"

"Your swearing. Your attitude. That's the way *she* is."

Melody considered. "Well, maybe she's got a point. Certainly I learned some useful words from her, and what she doesn't know about the power of panties isn't worth laundering. Why honor foolish restrictions? But she's not here. For all I care, she can stay plugged up forever."

He peered at her. "She's really not there?"

"What the #### do you care, Das? I can do anything with my body she could have. Here, I'll show you." She put the other hand to her blouse and tore it halfway asunder.

"This—this is beyond my understanding," the Dastard said, his left eyeball glazing. "I can't think what happened to you."

The princess paused. A bulb flashed over her head. "Well, I can. Suddenly it's obvious."

"*What* is obvious?" Actually there was an answer: the left half of her bosom, as he faced her, or her right side as she would see it. Fortunately his right eye remained free. But he was pretty sure she wasn't talking about that.

She smiled smirkily. "You don't get it, do you, Das?"

That was because it was out of reach, and he was not about to step forward. But again, that wasn't what she meant. "Don't get what?"

"What the Random Factor did to us."

"No, I don't get it. This makes no sense, and it appalls me."

"Well, you asked for it, idiot," she said.

"Asked for what?" He remained baffled, but deeply concerned. He wished she would restore her décolletage.

"Well, I'll tell you, moron. *He exchanged our souls.*"

"But I have no soul."

"Now you do, dummy. You've got mine. And you know something? I feel better off without it."

"I have your soul?" he repeated blankly. But as he spoke, he realized it was true. Suddenly he cared about things like decency and fairness and justice. That was why he suddenly had compunction about taking advantage of her offer. He had a conscience. And it was evident that Melody did not. "Oh, no!"

"Why the $$$$ not? I never appreciated what a relief it would be to lack a soul."

"But we can't have exchanged souls, exactly," he said, troubled on another score.

"Why not?"

"Because it would be a one-way exchange. How can you exchange something for nothing?"

"Well, we did. You have a conscience now, and I don't."

Then a bulb flashed over his head. "Our magic talents! Did they exchange too?"

"Let's find out." She hummed. Nothing happened. She hummed louder. Still there was no result. "I've lost my talent!" she cried, alarmed.

The Dastard hummed, thinking of an illusion. It formed: a pretty flower in mid-air. "I have your magic."

"Then what the &&&& do I have?" she demanded irritably.

"You must have my talent, which I originally traded for my soul. We traded souls and talents. You must be able to unhappen things."

"This is weird," she said. "But interesting."

"Don't try to use it!" he said. "Careless use can be dangerous."

"Dangerous to whom?" she inquired.

"To anyone! To you. There are special aspects."

"Well, I'll risk it," she said. "It promises to be fun." She eyed him speculatively. "I suddenly realize that there's an aspect of experience I need to catch up on. If you don't want to go to the bedroom, we can do it right here." She ripped her blouse the rest of the way.

The Dastard realized that something had to be done immediately. His conscience would not permit him to do any such thing with her. But how could he stop her from ripping off the rest of her clothing? He couldn't even see her clearly; now both eyeballs were glazed. What a torso she had!

The Random Factor! It had made the switch; it could make it back. The Dastard wrenched his eyes clear and ran for the door, which remained unlocked, and turned the knob. He shoved the door.

"No you don't!" Melody cried, leaping to intercept him. But she was too late; the door swung open.

The Factor was there. It pointed at them—and the scene changed. It became completely weird. The door slammed shut, but they were somewhere else.

The Dastard looked around. It was clear that the Factor had not exchanged them back, for he still cared about decency, motherhood, and apple pie—but what had it done? He could not make sense of what he saw.

"Oh, goody!" the princess said with heavy irony. "It's a comic strip! Are you proud of yourself, you blithering idiot?"

"It's a what?"

"From Ptero, you numbskull. Between major residential sections are strips of the puns and characters that are too awful to allow elsewhere. We're in for it now."

"Puns?" he asked blankly.

"You don't know what a pun is? Where have you been all your life?"

"I know what a pun is. But what has that to do with this?"

"You'll see. I'm getting out of here." She turned and tried to flee from wherever they were, meanwhile drawing the tatters of her blouse up to cover her front. She was evidently too concerned about this new problem to waste time dazzling him at the moment.

But she was blocked by several odd figures. One was an animated stick bent into the shape of a capital R. It looked exceedingly old and worn, and was of antique design. It moved threateningly, and she retreated from it.

"What is it?" the Dastard asked, trying to come to her rescue.

"Don't you recognize it, you ninny? It's an R-cane."

"An arcane stick?"

"It will make me look obscure!" Indeed, the cane was trying to fit itself to her hand, so that she would have to use it.

"Oh—a pun," he said, finally catching on. As he did so, the R-cane came to his hand, and he found himself feeling rather obscure and esoteric. That didn't bother him. "It's not so bad."

She did not deign to answer. Instead she tried to run in another direction. But there she encountered a woman in a strange outfit.

"Get out of my way, weirdy!" Melody snapped. Somehow she seemed less endearing than before.

"I know where your soul is," the woman said.

Could she help? "Who are you?" the Dastard asked.

"My name is Voyant. Claire Voyant. I know where things are."

"Do you know how to exchange souls back?"

"No, of course not. That's a process, not a thing."

"Do you know the fastest way out of this comic strip?" Melody asked.

"No. That's another process, not a thing."

"Then to ££££ with you," Melody said, and plunged on.

"She's bit impatient at the moment," the Dastard explained apologetically. The princess' nice soul was making him a nicer person than he had ever been, and now he valued courtesy. Then he thought of something else: "Do you know where there is a person who will know how to undo recent damage?"

"That would be the Funct."

"Who?"

"The Demon Funct. He can shut anything down."

The Dastard realized that this would be D. Funct," another pun. He was beginning to appreciate why Melody disliked the comic strip. Still, if the demon could make the soul exchange defunct, that should help. "Where is the demon?"

"The far side of Xanth."

Oh. That was not much help. "Thank you," he said, and went on after Melody.

She was conversing with a female centaur. No, as he caught up, he discovered that the dialogue was all one way; the centaur was talking so steadily that no one else could squeeze a word in. "I just love to talk, and I never stop," she was saying. She proceeded to prove it by not stopping.

He noticed that she had a really fine bare bosom, even for a centaur. It was almost enough to make his eyeballs crystallize; they had already been roughed up by Melody's brief exposure. She noticed his noticing, and was not affronted; centaurs were extremely nonchalant about bodies. "I do have a fine bust, don't I? That's why my name is the Filly Buster." She went right on talking about other things. It didn't seem to matter to her what she talked about, as long as she never gave another person a chance to speak. It seemed to him that her name should reflect her talkativeness, but evidently centaur naming conventions were different.

By this time the Dastard was almost as eager to get out of the comic strip as the princess was. Puns were all right in their place, but enough was enough.

They lunged onward. They came to a region where pans were lying on the floor so thickly that it was hard to avoid stepping on them. Many were battered and dirty, and some were rusted. "Dead pans," Melody muttered with disgust. "Thrown away; this must be the pan graveyard."

The Dastard saw that many of the pans were labeled. One rather sick looking one said DEMIC, a nervous looking one said IC, and a tasty looking one said CAKE. He realized that these were yet more puns: pandemic, panic, and pancake. There was a flowery one labeled SY, and a half digested one labeled CREAS, a mind boggling one labeled TY, an elegant one labeled ACHE, and a very fancily illustrated one labeled ORAMA. After that he stopped looking, just trying to get past this region.

But it wasn't any better beyond the pans. There was a series of gaps in the clutter, but as he passed through them, each flashed a scene of something disgusting. "What are these?" he asked as he caught up to the princess.

"Inter-lewds, of course," she said, making him feel stupid. "Do they give you any hot ideas?" She made as if to tear off her blouse again, but moved on when he turned away.

The lewds gave way to a proliferation of paths. They twisted everywhere, like so many wriggling worms. "Maybe one of these paths leads out," he said.

"But which one?" she demanded, frustrated. To be soulless, he realized, was not to be without emotion, but the emotions tended to be shallow and selfish. As he had been.

He saw a ghoul sitting on a pile of ashes between several of the paths. "Can you tell us which path goes out of here?" the Dastard inquired.

"Tell a path," the ghoul ash replied tastefully.

"Tell a path what?"

"Read its mind."

The Dastard had the sick feeling that he had fallen into another pun. He forged on, determined to win free of this punishment.

Melody almost fell into a ragged hole in the floor. The Dastard caught her arm just in time to pull her back from the brink. "Let go of me, dope!" she snapped.

"But you were about to fall into the chasm."

"Can't you see it's a micro-chasm? I can step right over it."

Oh. He had been snared by a very small pun this time.

Ahead was a young pretty woman with no clothing. She wore a placard saying PEN NAME. "Look, a nymph!" the Dastard said, interested. The sight of nymphs did not freak men out in the same manner as the flesh of real women did, but they were fun to watch.

"No she isn't," Melody said. She swept her hand through the figure, and there was no contact: it was illusory. It was a pseudo nymph.

Was there no end to this? They struggled onward. Now he heard a kind of tapping or beeping, with some long beeps and some short ones. Overall, the sound was very sad, as though generated by an extremely regretful person. "What is that?" he asked.

"Isn't it obvious? That's remorse code."

She had made him feel like an idiot again. Obviously she had had prior experience with comic strips, and knew how they operated.

They came to a female ogre. The ogress was huge and hairy. "Me fork for stork," she said eagerly.

A sex-crazed ogress? "What's your name?" he asked.

She pulled out a plaque with her name. It said ViOgra.

The Dastard didn't even try to fathom the pun, if there was one. He moved on.

"At last!" Melody said. "Something useful." She was looking at several girls running by in their underwear. The Dastard was immediately freaked out by the sight of all those panties, but he did see that they had printing on them.

He managed to get out a question. "What are these?"

"News briefs, of course," she said witheringly.

He read the print on each panty as it flashed by: DON'T BE LOST DON'T YOU POUT JUST BE HAPPY THIS WAY OUT!

They followed the last panty, and suddenly they were back in the castle, free of the comic strip. They were next to the forbidden chamber; either they had not gone anywhere in the comic strip, or had circled around to their starting place. The Dastard collapsed to the floor, breathing hard. What an experience!

"That was fun," Melody said.

"Fun! It was awful! And you didn't like it before."

"I changed my feminine mind. Anyway, next time will be something else. Let's do it again." She headed for the dreaded door.

"No!" he cried, chasing after her. But she got there first, and pushed it open.

The Random Factor was there. It raised its arm to them. Things changed.

They were standing on a grassy slope. The sky was blue with a few pleasant white puffy clouds. In the distance were green trees, and beyond them gray mountains. It was a lovely scene, but completely unfamiliar.

"Where are we?" the Dastard asked.

"How the bleep should I know?"

The air near her shimmered, recoiling from the bad word. "Please don't use such language," he asked her politely.

She sneered. "Why the >>>> not?" Now the grass around her wilted.

The Dastard breathed deeply, feeling his ears wilt too. But he did his best to remain calm, knowing that she was baiting him. "It's unprincessly, and it's bad for the environment."

"Since when do you care about such things?" she demanded.

He realized with surprise that his attitude in this respect had suffered a profound change. "Since I got your sweet soul," he replied.

She stared at him for half a moment. "And it makes you decent, you poor slob," she said indecently. "What a laugh."

"It does make me decent," he agreed, realizing the truth of it. "Now I care about right and wrong, and about propriety. Please do not distress me and this nice region by speaking intemperately."

"Oh, stuff it up your bottom!" she snapped. "I'll speak any way I ●*●*●*●*want."

This time the grass around her not only wilted, it withered, browned, and burned. The earth below shrank and caved in, leaving a smoking crater. She shrieked as she lost her footing, flapping her arms as if about to fly.

And she did fly. She rose above the crater, her delicate feet just clearing it. She moved away from it to firm, cool ground, and landed.

Then she turned and looked back. "What just happened?"

"You flew," he said, amazed. "I thought you had lost your singing magic."

"I did, lout. You have it now—or does your tiny dim mind not remember three moments back?"

She certainly was not very endearing without her soul. Had he really been like that, for four years? He was coming to appreciate how he had annoyed her. "I really don't know how to use your talent well," he said apologetically.

"So how the bleep did I fly?" she demanded. "I couldn't have just raised my arms and done it, you know, without my magic."

She had a point. "Maybe the rules of this region are different," he said. "Let me see if I can do it too." He spread his arms and flapped them up and down, birdlike.

And rose into the air. A little. His flight was awkward and unsteady, and in a moment he had to touch down lest he crash, but he definitely flew.

"Oh, sure," she said witheringly. "You used *my* magic, clumsily."

"No I didn't. I just flapped my arms, and I flew. Just as you did."

"Oh, sure." But she didn't argue the case further. Instead she spread her arms again, and flapped, and rose a little. "Say, this is fun, in its fashion. Well, I'll be going now. You stay here, ilk." She made her way slowly across the meadow, her dainty feet just clearing the tall grass.

"No, I'm staying with you. Melody, we have to trade souls back. It's not right that I have yours." He ran after her.

"Oh, fuddy-duddy! I'm doing great without it. I want to go make something unhappen."

"No! That's a bad talent. You must not use it."

She peered down at him. "Why the **** not, 'Tard?"

Somehow that version of his name was not as sweet as "Das." In fact the very air had a singed odor from her repeated invective. "It's dangerous! You could do someone harm."

"Soo?" she inquired derisively.

She had no conscience: She didn't care about harm to others. So he tried another angle. "That talent is tricky, and it can't be undone. I mean, when something is unhappened, it can't be happened again. So you have to be careful. I always took time to study a situation, to be sure the details were straight. It took me years to get proficient at it. You're bound to get in trouble if you go at it without experience."

"Oh, pooh! You just don't want me to have any fun." She flapped her arms harder, and rose a little higher. "Now go somewhere else; I'm tired of you."

"No, I'm staying with you until we get this straight. For one thing, we have no idea where we are. There might be danger."

"Double pooh! I'll fly away from it." She flapped harder yet, achieving a bit more elevation.

"I'll stop you!" he cried, running after her.

But she was the one who stopped him. She did a little somersault in the air, so that her skirt flared up, and flashed him with her green panties. Stunned, he fell on his back, little moons, planets, and stars swarming around his head. Now that he had a nice soul, he was far more vulnerable to such naughtiness.

He fought for control. He blinked until the mind-boggling green image faded. He reached up and carefully cleared away the planets with his hand. Then he climbed unsteadily to his feet and looked around. Melody was flying toward the nearby forest. He would have to hurry to catch her; once she got into the trees, she could hopelessly lose herself.

Then he heard something chilling. It was a distant baying, as of a werewolf scenting prey. Werewolves could be all right, when encountered socially, but it was another matter when a person was at the wrong end of a hunt.

"Melody!" he called. "There may be trouble!"

"Sure there will be, if you don't stop bugging me," she called back.

The baying was rapidly coming closer. He did not like the sound of this at all. He ran to catch up with her, as he could move faster on the ground than in the air. He heard the baying closing in behind him, getting louder and uglier. He definitely did not like this.

He caught up to Melody. "Get higher!" he cried.

"Oh, po—" she started. Then she heard the baying. "What's that?"

"I fear it's a werewolf pack on the hunt."

That she understood. "Oopsy!" She flapped her arms harder, and rose a little, but probably not enough.

The Dastard looked back. Now they burst into sight: several toothy wolves, gaining rapidly. They were big ones, capable of doing a man—or a woman—real harm.

There was no ready escape. The slope was smooth, without trees. The wolves would be able to run them down, anywhere they went. Except the air. "Get higher!" he repeated desperately, and flapped his own arms.

They rose, but the wolf pack closed in on them. The first wolf snapped at the Dastard's foot; he yanked it up out of the way just barely in time, so that the teeth snapped on air with a nasty clash of sparks. Others went for Melody.

She screamed. She might have no conscience, but she was well aware of her self-interest, and it did not include getting chomped by wolves. She flapped as hard as she could, but remained barely above the questing noses. Then a wolf leaped, barely missing her. The two of them were not high enough.

"The slope!" the Dastard cried. "Go down the slope, but keep your elevation!"

They did that. The ground descended, but they did not, so they gained a bit of relative elevation. But the wolves were leaping higher, and snapping at bodies when at the tops of their leaps; only the unsteadiness of their efforts caused them to miss, and that would not last long. It was a wonder that teeth had not yet closed on flesh.

The slope angled farther. Now at last they were able to gain enough height to be out of reach of the wolves. The Dastard breathed a sigh of relief as the wolves fell back, unable to pursue farther.

Melody screamed. The Dastard looked ahead. There were large-winged figures on the horizon, coming in fast. Big birds—or worse.

In under two moments the nature of the new threat was evident. "Harpies!" the Dastard said with a shudder.

"Harpies," the princess echoed, with a similar shudder. They could not escape these through the air, but they didn't dare drop to the ground, because the wolves were still there.

"Make for the forest," he said. "Maybe we can hide there."

There was an arm of the forest within range farther down the slope. They angled for it, gaining speed by diving. But the harpies saw what they were doing, and angled to intercept them. A line of the dirty creatures formed between them and the trees.

"What have we here?" a harpy screeched. All harpies screeched; it was their natural voice.

"A lovely princess!" another harpy screeched. "With long green hair and green dress."

"A nondescript young man," another screeched. "Oh, we can have fun with him, once we get his pants off." The Dastard's princely robe seemed to have degenerated into garden variety trousers; he wasn't sure when that had happened.

"Stay away from me, you bleeping dirty birds!" Melody cried.

"She swears!" a harpy cried.

"We can do that!" another screeched.

Then there followed a barrage of bad words, such that Melody's hair was blown back from her head, and the Dastard's skin felt the heat as from a burning garbage dump. He and the princess tumbled out of control.

But the harpies dived after them, and caught them. Dirty talons pierced their clothing. "Rip! Tear! Strip! Wear!" they chanted, catching and pulling at clothing. Indeed, the material did rip and tear in strips. But what did "wear" mean?

Soon their outer clothing was gone. The Dastard caught a glimpse of Melody's underwear and freaked out again. But then that too was stripped, and the freak-out effect diminished. Now she looked more like a nymph.

"Touch her B, touch her A!" the harpies screeched. "Oh what a feel we'll have today!"

The princess screamed, but that only whetted their foul fowl appetites. "Hold her head, spread her legs; we're going to make her lay some eggs!"

"Help me!" Melody screamed hysterically.

"Leave her alone," the Dastard cried, appalled.

But they were about to do the same to him. Dirty claws held his arms and legs, spread-eagling him in mid air. A harpy flew toward him, her dirty breasts leading. "Hold him hard, hard as you can; tonight we're going to do a man!" the others screeched as their talons scraped across his mid-section. He began to comprehend what these dirty females wanted of a male.

There was no way out of this awfulness—except maybe magic. The Dastard had Melody's magic; could he make use of it here? He struggled internally as well as externally, trying to marshal his thoughts. If only they could slip away from this disgusting horde and seek shelter elsewhere.

Slip away. He hummed, and focused. Slip! Slip!

Then he slipped out of their clutches, and so did Melody. They dropped below the milling disreputable flock.

"What did you do?" she asked as they fell through the air. They seemed to be over an abyss; the harpies must have carried them here during their distraction.

"I sang us slippery." He couldn't help admiring her nymph-like bare body.

"You should have blasted them into dirty feathers!"

"No, that would not be ethical. It's not their fault they lack our values."

"You bleeping idiot!" she flared. "They're *harpies*!"

He realized that she would see no point in treating harpies decently; that was a soul-spawned notion. "We had better resume flying," he said, and flapped his arms.

She flapped hers too. But nothing happened; they continued to fall. "You made us too slippery to fly!" she cried. "You stupid doltish idiot!"

Evidently gratitude for being saved from a fate worse than death was another soul-spawned concept. He tried to sing again, to counter the spell, but before he succeeded they plunged into the cold wet water of a dark lake.

Could the princess swim? He wasn't sure, so he grabbed for her hair as it streamed past him, and clamped his teeth on a hank of it. Then he launched himself for the surface, hauling her along.

They broke the surface. "Imbecile!" she cried with her first breath. "What are you doing?"

"Trying to rescue you, in case you can't swim."

"I couldn't swim because you were hauling on my hair, you bleeping lout!"

So he had messed up again. It was difficult to help a soulless person. "We'd better swim for land," he said.

"What land, jerkface? Where?"

He had no idea. "Maybe if we make some light, we'll see where to go." He hummed, focusing on light, and in a moment the region around them glowed. He was starting to get the hang of her magic.

Melody screamed. Startled, he looked around—and saw the towering head of a sea monster.

"Moron!" the princess screamed. "You lit us up for the monster to find!"

He just couldn't stop making mistakes! He tried to think of some kind of magic to counter this new threat, but before he succeeded, the monster's head struck down and engulfed Melody. She got out half a scream before she disappeared into its gullet.

The Dastard pounded at the monster's neck with his bare fists, trying to make the serpent spit her back up. But the head struck down and around, and snapped him up too. It lifted him high, then slurped him down.

He slid helplessly down the long slick throat. Then he landed with a thunk on a pile of rotting garbage. He bounced, sliding off the mound. What was this—the last meal of the sea monster?

"Now look what you've gotten us into!" Melody cried irritably in his ear.

He looked. The light was dim, but he was able to make out a rickety building ahead of them. Bats swirled around it, and dim moonlight bathed it in an eerie glow. "What is it?" he asked, bewildered by this change of scene.

"It's a horror house, simpleton," she said. "And that's the least of it."

"What's the rest of it!" he asked, feeling like exactly the simpleton she called him.

"We're in the gourd, nincompoop!"

"The hypno-gourd? The realm of bad dreams?"

"What else, dunce?"

"But how could we have gotten there?"

"The Random Factor sent us here, blockhead."

"But you were the one who opened the door!"

"Oh, sure—blame it all on *me*, dummy!"

There were definitely aspects of her personality that did not lend themselves to easy association. He wondered again whether he had been like that, when he had been without a soul. He rather feared he had. But right now he just wanted to get them safely out of here and back to the company of the two other princesses, who might be able to help. Because it was clear that Princess Melody needed her soul back, even if she didn't think so.

"I think we should find our way back to the castle," he said carefully. "And talk with your sisters."

"Oh, who cares about them? I want to have some fun." She paused, her eyes flicking from his bare body to her own. "And it seems we are ready for that. Let's see if there's a good bedroom in there."

"No, Melody! We mustn't dally."

"Which way do you mean that?" she asked eagerly.

He realized that his statement had more than one interpretation. Her reaction was opposite to what it had been before she lost her soul. "Both ways! We must not do anything untoward, and we must get back to your sisters."

"Untoward!" she said. "That's the first time I've heard it called that. Now I'm going in to find a bedroom, because I don't want to lie down on this garbage. You can join me for a great time, or you can go to hell." She whirled around, her greenish hair flinging out, and walked to the front door of the house. The effect was electric; he wanted very much to join her, but his conscience forbade it. She was not herself, without her soul, despite her loveliness. The irony was that now that he had a soul, he was capable of selfless love, and he was feeling it increasingly for her. For the princess as she could be, when complete.

Still, he could not let her enter that dreaded house alone; there was no telling what horrors lurked therein. So he ran after her.

She yanked open the door. It groaned. She stepped inside. He followed closely.

They were in a dark hall. Then there came an eerie glow, so they could see that it led to an interior chamber. They walked down it, and every floorboard creaked. The Dastard did not like this place at all, but Melody walked right on.

He realized that in the realm of dreams, nothing was real. It was all appearance and emotion. So a person could be horrified or terrified, but could not be physically hurt. Evidently the princess had realized that, so was proceeding without fear. That was not necessarily wise. After all, the things the harpies had wanted to do to them both could have been permanently emotionally damaging even if they weren't actually physically real.

A ghost loomed up before them. It was in the form of a pirate man, with a horrendous scar across his ugly face. "Boooo!" he cried in prescribed form.

"Oh, go stuff yourself up your nose!" Melody snapped at it, brushing on by.

The ghost was taken aback. He looked at the Dastard. The Dastard shrugged; as far as he could tell there had been no defect in the performance. "Sorry," he murmured. "She's just not in the mood."

Not perfectly reassured, the ghost faded out. The Dastard couldn't blame it for being disgruntled.

They came to the inner chamber. This turned out to be huge. In fact, it looked bigger than the whole house from the outside. But in the realm of dreams, such things were commonplace. After all, the whole house was theoretically inside the stomach of a sea monster. The chamber was a ballroom, with an enormous chandelier shedding weirdly colored light on the spacious empty scene below.

Music started, and ghostly couples coalesced, dancing gracefully. The men were in black suits with long tails; the women were in flowing dresses that flung out when they whirled. They all looked quite competent. The overall effect was beautiful. The Dastard realized that it was the soul that enabled him to appreciate that beauty; he would not have cared about its elegance, if he even noticed it, before getting re-souled.

"There's a stairway on the far side," Melody said. "Come on." She started across, walking right through a ghost couple. Obviously she was not picking up on scenic elegance.

There was a sighing scream, and the music stopped. The couples faded. The chandelier dimmed and went out. The two of them were left in an almost completely dark chamber.

"Spoilsports," Melody muttered, pausing. "Well, who needs you? All I want is a bedroom and a naked man." She took a step forward.

And screamed. She had stepped into a hole. The Dastard leaped to catch her as she fell. He hauled her back to the firmer floor near the hall. She halfway tumbled into his arms, panting with alarm over her narrow escape. Even in its disarray, her body was sleek and smooth and delicious.

"You're all right now," he said reassuringly.

"Get your hands off me, jerk," she snapped.

He let her go. Appreciation, too, seemed to be a function of the soul. He was learning a lot about soul properties, now that he had one and she did not.

If everything in the dream realm was illusion, why had she almost fallen into the pit? Maybe the fall was illusion too, but still terrifying.

He squatted and reached forward across the floor. The boards were twisted, and there was indeed a hole there—one that had not existed before. How could that be?

"Make some light, dunderhead."

He hummed, thinking of light, and it came. Now the full specter of the chamber was revealed: The floor was mainly a pit into which the floorboards had long since fallen. There was a glisten of water showing below the tumbled wood. There was no safe way across. The walls were festooned with cobwebs, and the chandelier looked as if it was about to drop into the pit. The illusion had not been the pit, but the ballroom floor.

"I think we had better leave this house before it collapses on us," he said.

"No. I came here for a bedroom, and I will have it. The ghosts had no trouble getting around."

"The ghosts aren't real."

"Neither is this whole house! If they can use it, so can we."

He was uncertain of the validity of her logic, but did not wish to quarrel. "Maybe if we showed them some respect—"

"Respect! For *ghosts*?!"

"Well, it is their house. We are merely visitors here."

"What do you want to do—dance with them?"

She was being sarcastic, but it gave him a notion. "Yes, maybe we should join them in their dance. To show that we appreciate their ball."

"Give me strength," she muttered disdainfully. But then she performed another emotional reversal. She was good at that. "Well, then, let's get with it, oaf." She held out her arms, dance fashion.

The Dastard could have wished for a more appealing invitation, but reconciled himself to the situation. He stepped into her embrace, setting his right arm carefully around her slender waist and taking her right hand in his left, in the classic ballroom dance position. For the first time in his life, he was glad the centaur tutors had made him learn that form. As he did so, the music resumed, the chandelier illuminated, and the ghostly dancers reappeared. They whirled across the intact floor, their extending shadows making artistic patterns across the walls.

The living couple moved out onto the main floor, dancing carefully. As they did so, ghostly costumes appeared on them, and they were clothed. He wore a tailed suit and dancing shoes; she wore a flaring gown, tiny slippers, and a sparkling diadem in her hair. The Dastard felt strong and competent and graceful. Princess Melody became a softly supple woman, embracing him, absolutely beautiful.

They were ideally matched. Their steps were perfectly timed, their feet touching the polished floor just so. They moved among the other dancers in a serene pattern, weaving their way through the sublime tapestry of the dance.

He studied her face, appreciating the lines and planes of her beauty. She had become part of the ghostly splendor, and if he had not yet fallen completely in love with her, he realized he was getting there.

Her face turned to his face, and her exquisite eyes met his. This scene was enchanting, and she was enchanting him. He tried to fight it, but was powerless to resist so divine a tide.

"Kiss me," she murmured.

He bent his head down, and their lips approached each other. They touched, and the glory of that contact radiated out to transform his being. He seemed to be floating.

When he regained his sense of position, they were on the far side of the ballroom. "The stairs," she whispered.

Oh. Yes. He danced her to the side, and into the alcove that was the stair landing. But when they stopped, the scene began to fade. The decrepit house faded into view.

"Dance, dope!" she said urgently. That rather spoiled the mood. She was making nice only to fool the ghosts, just as he had made nice in the past only when he wanted something he couldn't get any other way. He had a lot to answer for, these past four years.

They danced in place, at the foot of the stairs, and the scene returned in full pomp. Then they incorporated the stairway into their dance. He lifted her to land two steps up, then leaped to join her. They twirled in place, then repeated the process, ascending. The main dance on the ballroom floor continued; the ghosts didn't mind where they were, as long as they danced.

The second floor was well appointed, with a carpeted hall and fine old pictures on the walls. They danced on down to the nearest door, opened it, and found an ideal bedroom. They danced in, and continued their dance beside the bed.

"You are a handsome man," she said, smiling.

"Thank you." He knew he wasn't.

"And smart."

"Why are you complimenting me?"

"I want to have some fun with you before I leave you for other entertainments."

She was being as brutally honest as he used to be, not from any sense of integrity, but because she didn't care about his feelings. She didn't care what was right or wrong or moral, or for him. This was just a passing thrill, and of a type he could not ethically accept. "We must get out of here."

"Not yet." She let go of his hand and began to draw down the gossamer décolletage of her gown.

He was awfully tempted, but he knew she would never be doing this if she had her soul. "No—we must leave now."

"I think not." She drew the neckline down farther, uncovering rather more than was seemly. The odd thing was that the effect was more startling than her full nudity had been before. Clothing had magic, and it wasn't limited to panty magic.

"We have to," he said desperately. He knew that the only way to stop her was to get her out of here. He had developed a notion how to accomplish that—if it worked.

She shrugged. "All right." She let go of him and danced in place.

He hardly dared feel relieved. He knew she could not be trusted. "Then let's go right now."

She reached down to catch the hem of her gown. "How do you propose to do that?"

"I think I can use your magic to conjure us to the next setting, as we leave this one. With your cooperation we can return to the castle."

She hoisted the hem, showing a dainty knee. He had resisted that sight before, but now she was concentrating, and the lure was much stronger. "Really?"

"Yes. All we have to do, really, is wake from our mutual dream. That can't always be done from inside the dream, but I think in this case—"

Suddenly she lifted the dress up to her waist, showing her ghostly panties. But he was already turning away, having anticipated this mischief, so managed to avoid being freaked out. He clamped his eyes shut, turned back, and lunged for her. He wrapped his arms around her slender torso.

"Well, that's more like it," she said. She thought he was overcome by desire to signal the stork with her. Actually that was something he very much wanted to do, but he was managing to suppress the urge. She embraced him in return. "Now just carry me to the bed, and—"

He started humming, concentrating on Castle Maidragon. He carried her toward the bed—then beyond it, toward the window.

"Now wait a minute," she protested. "That's not the bed."

"We're leaving the scene," he said, standing before the window. "We can jump out, and—"

"Oh no you don't!" she cried, struggling. "First we're getting our clothes off, and—"

He tickled her. She screamed, being super ticklish, as an innocent princess had to be. With luck, she wouldn't remember in time that she was no longer innocent. Her arms flailed wildly. He resumed humming, then leaped through the window, carrying her along.

They landed in the hallway outside the Factor's door. The Dastard was on the floor, with Melody on top of him, their arms and legs hopelessly entangled. They were back in their original clothing.

"Well now," she said. She shifted around so that she could kiss him. "This may be as good a place as any to do it. There's no garbage here."

"No!" he cried. "You have to stop this! You wouldn't do it if you had your soul."

"But I don't have my soul," she replied in a reasonable tone. "So it's all right." She yanked down her blouse, half stunning him with another naughty glimpse. Had his eyes focused on both halves of her flesh, he would have been gone.

He scrambled up, staggering, and managed to turn his back before succumbing. "I won't look at you."

"Then I'll just have to open that door again," she said.

"No!" He turned, trying to catch her and stop her, but she hoisted up her skirt and freaked him out with her panties. His eyes glazed over, blinding him; all he could see was a blaze of mounded green.

She embraced him again. "One last chance, Das." She kissed him.

"No!" he cried a third time, though it was all he could do to force the word out.

"Then the hell with you." She let him go and walked away. She was going for the door, and he was unable to recover fast enough to stop her.

"Harmony!" he called. "Rhythm! Stop her. Abolish the castle!" Did they hear him? Did they know what was going on?

Then the castle began falling apart. The hallway collapsed, but the stones that fell on them lacked substance; they were becoming cloudstuff, then dissipating. Soon they stood in the forest, and the girl Becka was emerging from a pile of misty rubble.

"We couldn't interfere while you were in the comic strip," Harmony began.

"Or in the gourd," Rhythm concluded. "It might have trapped you inside."

"I could see the Random Factor," Becka said. "But I couldn't stop you from opening that door. That was awful."

Rhythm turned to Melody. "What in Xanth were you trying to do, sister dear?"

"I was trying to have some fun, for a change," Melody replied. "Especially since I never got my bra back."

The Dastard had thought something was missing from her apparel, but hadn't caught on what it was. Not that the knowledge would have done him much good.

"But you were trying to seduce him!"

"Exactly."

"Remember, she has no conscience now," the Dastard said. "She doesn't care about propriety, just the pleasure of the moment."

"We have to change you back!" Harmony said to Melody.

"But we don't know how," Rhythm said.

"I can tell you how," the Dastard said. "Simply unhappen the exchange."

"Yes!" the two princesses agreed together, clapping their hands.

"But there's one problem," he said.

"There is?" Becka asked.

"Yes. Melody has to be the one to do it. I would, but I no longer have that power."

"And I'm not going to!" Melody agreed, laughing. She sounded almost like the Sea Hag.

"Sister dear, we can make you," Harmony said grimly.

"We are two to your one," Rhythm agreed.

"First you'll have to catch me," Melody said, and slid into limbo.

"Don't let her get away!" the Dastard cried. "She can do incredible damage with my talent."

"But it's hard to follow her, with only two," Harmony said.

"We had three before," Rhythm said.

"You have three now," the Dastard said. "As long as I have her conscience—and her talent. If you will guide me in the use of her magic. I am clumsy with it by myself, but with your help I can be of real assistance. I want to do what is right."

"Yes!" they agreed, and the three of them slid into limbo, carrying Becka along.

15

PRINCESS WILD

Princess Melody's first aim was to get away from her sisters, because she knew the power of their magic. Two could indeed overcome one, but the one had to hold still for it. They had learned that when playing tag, long ago. Now with her power of unhappening, she didn't have to hold still. But she would have to be alert, if she wanted to have any fun. Too bad the Dastard had been such a drag; she might have shown him a trick or two she had picked up from the Sea Hag, there in the horror house.

Where could she go? What could she do? She searched through limbo, finding her control much better now that she had the Dastard's talent. When the three of them had balked him, they had succeeded only because they had been unified, merging their magic talents. They had not known enough of this odd magic to initiate changes, just to track him and stop him. Now she intended to make some real mischief. She just had to find suitable situations for it.

She saw the Land of Xanth in a half-real form. There were forests and fields and lakes and mountains and villages. The first four didn't seem to offer much, so that left the last. So she zeroed in on a village, and slid out of limbo. She stumbled as she re-entered Xanth, still getting her limbo-legs, as it were, but had no other trouble.

She stood before a gnarled old woman. "Hello," she said. "I'm Princess Melody, looking for a good time."

"Well, you won't find it here," the woman replied. "I'm Jean Gnome, and I know that everything is predetermined by what you start with."

Melody was not in a mood to brook much balking. "Nothing is predetermined! I'm a princess, and I will do as I please."

The gnome woman gazed at her with disconcerting intensity. "You will do exactly as your set interior pattern dictates. You cannot change what you are."

"And what do you think I am?" Melody demanded.

"A young woman destined to love a soulless young man."

"Love!" Melody exclaimed. "I don't love the Dastard! I don't love anyone. Love is for fools."

"Well, you are bound to in due course. It is written in your pattern."

Fed up with this, Melody slid back into limbo. She cruised through it, gaining proficiency, until she spied a nondescript man. He was sitting on a pillar of salt, and carving a crystal from a chunk of salt. Maybe he would do for some incidental fun. She slid out before him, adjusting her clothing to show some extra flesh.

"Hello. I am Melody. Who are you?"

"My name is Peter," he said dully. "Salt Peter."

"You look as if you haven't summoned many storks lately, Salt."

"That is true."

She lifted her skirt part way. "Would you like to?"

"No."

This caught her with half a surprise. She did not recall meeting a man who did not want to summon storks immediately, if not sooner, though most managed to control their urges somewhat. "Maybe you just haven't encountered the right willing woman." She hoisted her hem another notch.

"I'm just not interested."

He was beginning to irritate her. So she tried the crash course. "Well, take a look at this." She hauled her skirt the rest of the way up and flashed him with her panties.

He looked, and shrugged. He didn't freak out. What was the matter with him? Princessly panties could freak out a dozen men at a time.

So she plumped her bottom down on his lap. "Are you sure?"

Then a weird thing happened. She lost her own interest. She no longer cared at all about storks.

"It's my talent," the man said. "I can't turn it off."

"Your talent is disinterest in storks?"

"Exactly."

Disgusted, she slid back into limbo. She moved on until she saw an old woman gathering herbs. She slid out before her. "What are you doing?"

"I'm gathering warts, of course," the woman said.

This did not seem very promising as entertainment. "What kind of warts?"

"Worry warts."

"What kind of wart is that?"

"I'll show you." The woman threw a handful of them at her.

Melody tried to duck, but several of the warts struck her. They stuck to her body and wouldn't rub off.

Suddenly she was worried. Were her sisters about to catch up with her? What about that frustrating Dastard? Was he going to try to get his talent back? Would she ever find anything really interesting to do, now that she was free to do it? Worries beset her.

Suddenly she realized why. "The worry warts!" she cried. "They make me worry!"

The old woman cackled gleefully. "You had to ask, dearie."

"Get them off me! I don't want to worry."

"They don't come off, dearie. You have to wear them off."

"Wear them off! How do I do that?"

"By resolving whatever they make you worry about, dearie. There is no other way."

"Yes there is," Melody said. Then she unhappened most of her encounter with the woman, but sliding back to just before she threw the warts. "What kind of wart is that?" she asked again.

"I'll show you." But this time Melody intercepted the woman's arm and caused her to drop the warts on herself. "Oh, see what you've done, you awful girl!" the woman screamed. "I'm hopelessly worried!"

"Too bad," Melody said unsympathetically, and slid back into limbo. She would remember to stay clear of worry warts.

Then she realized that this was the first time she had actually used her talent to unhappen something. It had just come naturally. It was handy. But she remained bored. So far, being without a soul wasn't as much fun as she had thought it was at first. She needed entertainment; her life had little meaning without it.

She saw a child walking along a path. Maybe she could seduce a child. That would be a gross violation of the Adult Conspiracy, therefore surely fascinating. She slid out of limbo and landed in front of the boy. "Hello," she said.

"Go away."

"But I want to show you something."

"I'll show *you* something." He gestured—and a bug was buzzing in her face. She yelped and stepped back, and it buzzed on past.

"What was that?" she demanded.

"A bee, of course," he said.

"Oh. Well, I was about to—"

"Look at your foot."

She looked—and screamed. There was a spider on it. She kicked violently, but it clung. Finally she grabbed a big leaf and scraped it off. "Where did that come from?"

"That's my talent—conjuring small insects," the boy said proudly. "I love to make women scream."

Disgusted again, she slid back into limbo. When would she ever find something fun to do?

She saw a mountain. It was tall and round, with a curl of smoke at its top. She recognized it: Mount Pinatuba, the irritable volcano. Now that might have potential.

She circled around it, orienting. Limbo was a way to travel in both space and time, as they had discovered when pursuing the Dastard, to stop his dastardly deeds. How naïve they had been; dastardly deeds were the most fun. She wanted to do some herself. But what could she come up with? She knew that Pinatuba had a short temper, and when it blew its top it could put out so much dust it would cool all Xanth by one degree. But it hadn't blown its top in years.

Well, suppose she went back as far as she could, and aggravated it? Made it blow—several years ago? That would unhappen the peaceful existence of the region, and be worthy of comment. It would make her life meaningful, for a while.

She slid back, back, as far as she could, almost to the time when she and her sisters had been delivered by the stork. She couldn't go any farther, both because she had to stay within her lifetime, and because the Dastard's talent was limited to when he had obtained it from the demon. But that was good enough; it could cool Xanth for four years, and maybe even bury some villages in ash or lava. Maybe then she could even move forward a couple of years and do it again.

She emerged beside the mountain. Time to get started. "Hey, Pinhead Tub!" she called. "You think you're something? I've seen better cones on eye scream!"

There was a low rumble, and a heavier puff of smoke from the cone. The mountain heard her, and it wasn't pleased.

But this was just the beginning. "Is that the best you can do, Pinny Tubby? I thought you knew how to smoke."

This time the rumble was stronger, and the smoke shot up toward the sky. Oh, yes, the mountain was heating up.

"I heard you could cool all Xanth, when you tried," she called. "I don't believe it. Maybe a local region."

The plume of smoke shot higher, and the sides of the mountain shook with indignation.

"Maybe just the land right in sight of you," she continued.

A boulder shot up and collided with a cloud, fragmenting it into frightened wafts of mist.

"A little patch right next to your base," she said.

This time a shower of rocks shot up, and lava began to overflow the brim. Pinatuba was really ready to blow.

Harmony appeared. "Stop that!" she cried.

"Make me!"

Rhythm appeared beside her. "We will."

Unfortunately, they could. So as they advanced on her, Melody slid back into limbo. Her sisters would not dare to follow immediately, because the mountain was ready to blow in a moment, and they would have to pacify it. She wondered how they would do that. Well, it was their problem.

She slid forward in time, as that was the only way to go from here. She remained unsatisfied, because she hadn't actually done a truly dastardly deed; her sisters had caught up too quickly. But maybe she could hide from them, and have time to do something worse before they found her.

She saw a woman looking her way. This was odd, because she thought she was invisible in limbo. So she stepped out of it. "Were you seeing me?" she asked.

"Not you specifically; I just knew that there was something in the area that related to my talent." The woman's eyes were penetrating.

"Who are you?"

"My name is Destiny."

"What is your talent?"

"Destiny. I can change a person's destiny."

Now Melody understood. She slid out of there immediately, wanting none of that. She wanted to keep her destiny in her own hands.

She quested farther, ranging across time and space, looking for fun. It was surprisingly hard to find. Here she had this great talent, and complete freedom; why wasn't she happy with it? Why did she feel somehow unfulfilled?

She saw a young man. She decided to give him no chance to resist. She slid out before him, opening her blouse. "I have something for you," she said.

He looked at her, surprised. "I see you are in need of healing."

This was not the reaction she had expected. "Why do you say that?"

"It's my talent. I can tell when it is needed, and you need it badly."

"I don't need any healing. I'm in a fine fettle. I just want to have a good time."

"I disagree. You can never had a good time, until you are healed. Here, let me try." He reached out his hand.

Now she hesitated. There was something here she didn't understand. "Why do you say that?"

"Because my talent is healing human souls." He caught her hand. "Just let me see, now—" he broke off, astonished. "I can't heal yours!"

She jerked her hand away. "Why not, dumbbell?"

"Because you have no soul! How can this be?"

She didn't answer him; she just slid out of there. She didn't want her soul fixed any more than she wanted her destiny changed.

She coursed along, increasingly frustrated by her inability to find the fun she sought. There had to be something, somewhere, that she could really mess up.

She spied a cave. That looked like Com Passion's residence; it might be really fun to unhappen the sickeningly friendly machine. She could go in and range back, to discover when Passion appeared, then see if there was anything she could do about it.

She slid out of limbo before the screen. Immediately Passion's mouse appeared, squeaking. "Eeeeek!" Melody screamed; five E's was standard in such situations. She had forgotten about the little animal.

Mouse Terian assumed human form. "What can we do for you, Princess Melody?" she inquired.

Melody collected her wits, which had gotten scattered. "Nothing. I'm going to slide back in time and unhappen you and Com Passion."

She tried to slide into limbo—and could not. What was the matter? This hadn't happened before.

Then she saw Passion's lighted screen. *Princess Melody remains in place and explains her curious statement.*

Oh—the machine was using her ability to change reality inside her cave. Melody had forgotten about that. Now she was stuck in something dull.

She had to answer. "The Random Factor in Castle Maidragon exchanged my soul with the Dastard, so now I have his talent of unhappening and no soul. I'm looking for fun, and that means storks or mischief. So I'm going to do you some mischief, by unhappening your existence."

"But you're a nice princess," Mouse Terian protested.

"Not any more. Now I just want to have fun."

We shall provide you with fun, the screen scripted.

"I'll provide my own," Melody said. She tried to slide into limbo, but was balked again. What a frustration! If only she had remembered about the machine's magic.

We shall play cards.

Worse yet. Melody normally had no interest in cards, and she had less now. "I would really rather not."

Princess changes mind.

"What game?"

"We know three card solitaire games," Terian said. "One of them can be played with another person, and we have played that one with Com Pewter and his mouse Tristan. But that grows a trifle familiar, after two years. We are glad to have a new player; this should add novelty."

"But I don't know any card solitaire games."

"We shall teach you."

Melody wanted to get out of here, but she couldn't figure out a way to change her mind again. So she sat down at a table that appeared, and Terian sat opposite her, and explained to her the rules of a game called Klondike. What they actually played was Double Klondike, with Terian playing for Passion. After Melody lost one game, they played another, and another. She always lost, which didn't improve her mood.

"Is there any way out of this?" she demanded irritably.

"Why yes," Terian said. "If you teach us a new card game we can play, we shall let you go."

Melody considered. Cards weren't used in Xanth, as far as she knew, but the three princesses had encountered a Mundane in Ptero who had carried a deck. He had shown them how to play a game. Maybe that would do.

Melody took the deck. "This is War," she said.

Princess changes mind.

"No, I don't mean war with you," she said quickly. "I mean that's the name of the card game I know. War."

Mind restored.

"Thank you. This is how it is played: Divide the deck into two even parts, from which each player deals one card."

They divided the deck, and each turned over her top card. Melody's was 5♣; Terian's was 9♥. "Your card is higher than mine, so you win this battle, and take both cards. Put them in a pile beside the other."

Terian did that. Then they dealt two more cards: J♠ for Melody, 10♦ for Terian. "This time I won, so I take both cards," Melody said.

The third time they dealt, the cards matched: 7♥, 7♠. "Now we have a war," she said. "Deal three cards face down on top of your seven, and I will do the same. Deal the fourth one face up. The higher card wins them all."

They dealt, and this time the cards were 3♣ and 2♥. Melody won. "That's all there is to it," she said. "You keep playing until all your cards are gone. Then you take your discard pile and play that. Eventually one player will win all the cards in the deck, and that's the winner."

Terian nodded. "This seems to be an interesting new game."

Princess departs, doing no unhappening here.

Relieved, Melody got up from the table.

Harmony and Rhythm appeared. "Come with us, Melody," Harmony said.

Melody slid into limbo, fleeing them. The two of them could pursue her, but could not stop her from using this magic. She quickly left them far behind.

Where could she go, where they would not follow? Where they would not think of looking for her.

"Castle Zombie," she breathed. Nobody went there if it was not absolutely necessary.

She slid to the castle. There it was, just as weathered and slimy as it was on Ptero. She would surely be safe here.

She slid through its outer wall and through the interior. She knew that the zombies stayed mostly outside. That was just as well; she didn't want to meet a zombie. But the Zombie Master's wife Millie the Ghost was nice. Of course it would be a real accomplishment to unhappen her relationship with the Zombie Master, but that was impossible; that went back about eight hundred fifty years. Millie had not actually been a ghost for about the last fifty-seven years.

She found Millie's chamber. Millie was there—with two guests. Well, maybe something about them could be unhappened. She would make nice until she learned enough to act. That was the way the Dastard had done it, actually; she was coming to understand him better, now that she had the same talent.

She slid into the chamber. "Three greetings," she said.

The three looked at her, startled. "And who might you be?" Millie asked.

"Princess Melody." Now she recognized the visitors. "Hello, Jenny Elf and Breanna of the Black Wave." She had recognized Jenny because she had pointed ears and four fingers, and Breanna, of course, was black.

"But Princess Melody is only four years old," Jenny protested.

"And she's in Castle Roogna," Breanna said. "I saw her there, scarcely an hour ago, before riding the carpet here."

"What you saw was an emulation," Melody said. "Probably done by her friend DeMonica. I am the real Melody."

"But how is this possible?" Jenny asked.

"The three little princesses had a mission that required adult control," Melody explained. "So they changed places for four days with their grown selves on Ptero. I'm Melody Grown."

"Their mission?" Breanna asked.

Melody realized that further details could really mess up the secret mission. Therefore she gave them. "To stop the Dastard from unhappening things. He was traveling in time and interfering with past events, so as to change the present. Only we three princesses could stop him. But enough of this; I'm blank on current events, because on Ptero our year is blank six months either side of the time our Selves live in Xanth. What are you folk up to?"

The three exchanged one old and two young glances. Then they exchanged shrugs. "I am getting ready to retire next year, with my husband," Millie the Ghost said. "Justin Tree and Breanna of the Black Wave will be assuming our places here."

Melody realized that she must have missed more than six months worth of events; she hadn't been paying attention. "Justin Tree? How can a tree do anything?"

"He's not a tree anymore," Breanna said. "Any more than Millie is a ghost. He's a young man. We'll marry next year when I'm eighteen, and move into Castle Zombie. We'll take care of the residents."

"You mean the zombies?"

"We prefer to call them living-impaired."

Melody decided not to debate terminology. "How did you get together with Justin Tree? Why are you taking up with the living-impaired?"

"It's a long story, but I love to tell it. Two years ago I—"

"Thank you." Melody had little patience with long stories. She already had what she needed: the time span. She would go back two years and see what she could unhappen. There would surely be a way to stop Breanna and Justin from meeting, and to prevent them from taking over Castle Zombie. That would be a terrific unhappening. With luck it might send the zombies on a rampage that would horrify all Xanth. "Why are you here, Jenny? I should have thought you would have found your way home to the World of Two Moons by now."

"No, her cat Sammy can find anything but home," Millie said. "So she could never go back."

"Actually that's no longer true," Jenny said. "My home is now in Xanth, so that's what Sammy can't find. Sammy could find the World of Two Moons if he wanted to. But we don't want to, anymore."

Could she find a way to unhappen Sammy Cat? No, he had been with Jenny too long. "That doesn't explain why you are here at Castle Zombie."

"Breanna's my friend. She helped me find my husband. So Jeremy and I accompanied—"

"Jeremy?"

"Prince Jeremy Werewolf—my husband. We met two years ago, when—"

"Thank you." Now she had the time scale on that relationship too. So Jenny Elf was now a princess. Melody could ruin that in short order. She made ready to slide into limbo.

Her two sisters appeared. "Oh no you don't, Melody," Harmony said. "We're taking you back to Ptero now."

"You can't," Melody retorted. "I have no soul."

"You will have to take yours back," Rhythm said. "Then you will be the sweet sister we have known so long."

"The sweet nothing sister!" Melody exclaimed disparagingly. "So limited, so dull, so boring. I'd rather have fun."

Millie, Jenny, and Breanna were staring at her as if she had said something weird. Well, who cared about them? She slid into limbo and fled the castle.

There was no sense going after Jenny and Breanna now; her stupid sisters would expect her to do that, and have them covered. She had to surprise them, and go where they would never expect. Where could that be?

A bulb flashed over her head. Princess Ida, at Castle Roogna—they would have to return to her to exchange back with their younger Selves in good order, so no one would expect her to go there voluntarily. Maybe she could find a way to mess up the return, and leave her younger Self stuck on Ptero. That would serve the little brat right. Without a soul she was pretty sure she couldn't go, but they might find a way to give her one, so she had to run some interference. She would see what offered.

She slid to the castle. There was Princess Ida's chamber, and there was Princess Ida herself, sitting quietly with her moon peacefully orbiting her head. How tiny that world looked from Xanth! Would it be possible to steal that moon, and hide it, so that they couldn't return to it? Probably not; there was a whole lot of magic associated with it.

She left limbo and landed before Ida. "Hello, Auntie dear," she said sarcastically.

"Hello, Melody," Ida replied, seeming unsurprised. "I wonder—did you ever meet my child on your world?"

"Oh, you mean Idyll? With the talent of suppressing all thought? Sure, we know her. What about her?"

"I was just curious. Perhaps some day she will come to me in Xanth."

Melody realized that Ida had no way of directly knowing folk who lived on her worlds, because she was the one person who couldn't go there. Too bad she hadn't thought to deny her aunt the information. Oh, well, it didn't make a whole lot of difference. "So how are you doing, Auntie dear? Not that I care."

Ida gazed at her. "So it is true that you have lost your soul. That's unfortunate."

"No, that's great. Now I am free to do anything I want."

Ida's gaze seemed sad rather than hostile. "And what do you want to do?"

"To have fun. To make mischief. To ruin people's lives."

"Why should ruining other lives make you feel better?"

"Because my life is not ruined, so I'm better off than they are."

"But wouldn't you have more fun helping others?"

Melody stared at her. "Why should I do that?"

"Doing good normally makes people feel good."

Melody laughed. "What a crock of spit!"

"Didn't you like doing good when you had your soul?"

"I had no idea what a drag that soul was until I lost it."

"Yet you do not seem to be happy now."

"Well, I would be, if I could just get my stupid sisters off my tail."

"But you always liked being with them."

"That was before I shed my soul. Now I am objective, and I see how deadly dull my life was. We never did *anything* dastardly. Now I know better."

Harmony appeared. "In fact we came here to stop dastardly deeds from being committed," she said.

"Oh, fudge!" Melody swore, and slid into limbo.

And bounced. Dazed, she stared at the invisible wall that shut her off from it.

"Rhythm is barricading that entry," Harmony said. "You can't use it to escape us any more, Melody."

"Curses! Foiled again," Melody muttered. She fled physically out the chamber doorway, and slammed the door behind her. She ran down the hall. Where could she hide?

She looked back, and saw the door opening. She ducked into the next chamber, and shut its door quietly, so that her sisters would not be able to tell which one it was. Then she turned around and surveyed the chamber.

There was a woman with lovely long hair sitting at a table, facing away, writing something. She was so intent on her business that she had not noticed Melody's entrance.

"Rapunzel!" Melody cried, going to the table. There could be only one person with hair like that.

The woman looked up. Her face was hideous. "No, I'm her twin sister, Repulsive. Who are you?"

"I am—" Melody hesitated. Maybe it would be better to conceal her identity, so that Repulsive could not give away her hiding place. "A visitor. What are you doing?"

"I'm preparing a question to ask the Good Magician Humfrey. It's my one chance of a lifetime, so I'm making sure not to waste it."

"You want to know how you can become as beautiful as your sister?"

"Oh, no, I'm satisfied with my appearance. After all, it is quality of character that counts."

"What a crock of—" But she caught herself. "That's nice," she said insincerely as she sat down opposite the woman. "What's your question, then?"

"It's complicated, which is why I'm trying to phrase it carefully. So he won't give me some technically accurate but useless answer. I have to make it so that he has to be responsive. If I mess it up, I'll never get another chance, and will go to my end cruelly frustrated, knowing I could have had my Answer and lost it. So this is absolutely vital."

"What is your question?" Melody repeated restlessly.

"Well, back in historical times, in the year Ten Forty-Three, in the Time of No Magic, all the magic suddenly left the Land of Xanth, making it just about like drear Mundania. I understand it was an awful time, for about a day, before the demon Xanth returned, and the magic was restored. The lesser demons became mere whirlwinds, and magic plants wilted and sagged, and the people lost their magic talents, and—"

"What's the question?" Melody asked again, about to explode with impatience. She already knew all about the Time of No Magic; it was part of history. The centaur tutors taught the dull details to all human children.

"Well, I'm coming to that. The thing is, the magic is supposedly conveyed by the magic dust. It leaks from the Demon Xanth's being into the surrounding rock, and as that shifts and weathers it reaches the surface, and the good folk of the Magic Dust Village arrange to waft it into the air so that it spreads widely, refreshing the whole of the Land of Xanth. It's a slow, steady process, taking eons to run its course. Wherever that magic dust goes, there is magic, but there's only so far that the winds can carry it, so Xanth is the only land where there is much magic. Even the Demon Xanth himself, when he visited Mundania in another body, had to get some magic dust delivered so he could perform magic there. He—"

"What's the bleeping question?" Melody snapped. She knew all about the magic dust, too.

Startled, Repulsive finally got relevant. "How could there have been instant loss of magic, when the Demon Xanth departed this region? Why didn't the dust hold its magic, the same as usual?"

Melody paused, considering. She had never thought of that. Repulsive was right: The magic should have lasted at least a millennium after the Demon Xanth departed. Certainly it would have been good for a mere day, just about undiminished.

But she didn't see how she could use this situation to her advantage. So she explored it a little more, making nice. "So are you going to go to the Good Magician's castle, and struggle through the stupid challenges, so you can ask your careful question?"

"Oh, no, I don't have to do that. I was in a position to do him a small incidental favor, a while back, so he said he would Answer one question for me, and I could use a magic mirror to reach him. That's why I'm here." She indicated a picture on the wall, which Melody recognized as one of the castle's magic mirrors. Such mirrors weren't common; in fact Castle Roogna and the Good Magician's castle and maybe Castle Zombie were the only places she knew of where they were.

A black bulb flashed over Melody's head. She had an idea. She could help herself hide, and mess up Repulsive in the process. She needed just one other aspect to fall into place. "Repulsive, what is your talent?"

"Making masks," the woman replied.

Ideal! "Can you make face masks?"

"Yes, that's the kind I usually make. But they last only a few hours before they fade. So I usually make them for children at parties."

"Make masks of my face, and yours. Then you can pretend to be me, and I'll pretend to be you."

"But we are not children. We don't need to play such games."

"But wouldn't you like to be a lovely princess for a while?"

That got to her. "Yes. But I wouldn't pretend to be something I'm not."

"It's a game, simpleton—uh, a simple game. To see how long you can fool people who know you. And I'll see if I can make them think I'm you. We princesses love to play such games." That much was true.

"You're a princess?" Repulsive asked, astonished.

Oops—she had not revealed her identity before. No help for it now. "Yes. Princess Melody."

"But she's only four years old!"

"I'm her adult self, from Ptero. We switched places. For four days. I have to change back soon, but I want to have a bit of fun before I do."

"Oh. I suppose you would. Very well." The woman studied Melody's face, concentrating. In a moment a flexible mask appeared between them.

Melody plucked it out of the air. It looked just like her, except for the blank eyes. They would come alive when the mask was worn on the face. "Now make one of your face."

"I need to see a face, in order to copy it."

"Look in the mirror, dummy—er, dumpling. A magic mirror doesn't have to do magic."

"Oh, yes, of course." Repulsive got up and went to the mirror. As she approached, its picture cleared and it became a straight reflective surface. She concentrated, and soon formed a mask of what she saw. She brought it back to the table.

"Now let's see what we can do," Melody said, forcing a sincere smile.

She put the Melody face mask on Repulsive, and arranged her hair around it. "Of course your hair will change color to match," she said, hoping it was so. Rapunzel's hair could do that.

"Yes." The hair turned greenish. Now she looked remarkably princessly, except for the lack of a little crown.

Melody removed her own crownlet, and set it carefully on the woman's head. "Now you are a princess," she said. "Go see who you can fool. I'll stay here until you have had a chance to get clear."

"Yes." Repulsive walked to the door, opened it, and went out. The rest of her did not look as princessly, but most people looked mainly at the face, so it should be all right.

Then Melody got to work on her own hair. She had some dirt she had picked up somewhere; she rubbed it into her hair to make it brownish rather than greenish. Too bad she couldn't simply use magic, but she could cope. She fitted the mask carefully, studying herself in the mirror. "Pretty good," she murmured. "This should fool Humfrey."

The Good Magician's face appeared in the mirror. "You called?" he asked grumpily.

Oops—she had inadvertently invoked him by speaking his name before the mirror. Well, she was prepared. "I'm Repulsive, with my Question. Why did the magic fade instantly, in the Time of No Magic?"

The gnome-like man nodded. "That is an impressive Question, Repulsive. I'm glad you did not waste your chance. Let me check in the *Book of Answers*." He glanced down, reading. "Ah yes. This is because each of the major Demons has its own magic ambiance, and they compete for dominance. When the magic of Xanth was no longer buttressed by the presence of the Demon Xanth, the magic of the neighboring Demon Earth damped it out. The magic was still there, but suppressed by the more powerful field. When the Demon Xanth returned, his field extended throughout its former region, and the magic dust became fully operative again." The mirror went opaque; the Good Magician had returned to whatever other business he had. Such as staring at his monstrous tome.

Good enough. Now she had to get out of here, in the guise of Repulsive, before her sisters caught on to the ruse. With luck she would be hopelessly lost in the jungle, and they would be unable to find her before they had to return to Ptero. Then there would be no one stopping her from doing ever more dastardly deeds. She would make the Dastard look like a piker.

He'd be stuck on Ptero too, because he had her soul, and it was really the soul that traveled there. She almost let out a fiendish cackle of glee.

That reminded her: Maybe she would do the horrendously dastardly deed of releasing the Sea Hag. Now there was a woman of significance. The Hag had a soul, but it was so warped that it had no conscience left. Melody had come to know the Hag pretty well during her Possession, but had not before appreciated her qualities. Maybe they could make some deal similar to what the Dastard had made.

She pushed the door cautiously open and peeked out. The way seemed clear. She stepped out and walked boldly down the hall toward the exit. Everyone would take her for Repulsive, departing after getting her Answer.

A figure stepped into the hall before her. It wore her face. It was Repulsive, returning. "Hello," the other said.

"Good riddance," Melody said, and brushed on by.

But the other followed her. "Wait! I need to change back, so I can ask my Question, and get the Answer of my life."

"Oh, too bad," Melody said. "I already used your Question."

"You what?"

"Only I forgot what it was, so maybe I asked the wrong one. I asked why do ogres crunch bones, and he said because they are hungry, and not to call him again. He seemed oddly disappointed; maybe he had expected more of you." She moved on.

Repulsive seemed stunned. "You wasted my Question? The one my whole life revolves around?"

"Oh, stop whining," Melody said smugly. What a lovely lie she had crafted on the spur of the moment! The front gate was ahead; she would soon be out.

"I couldn't believe it," Repulsive said, tears beginning to ruin her mask. "I thought no one could be like that. But they were right."

They? "Who?"

"Us," Harmony said, stepping out to bar her way through the gate.

Oh, no! Melody whirled, but Repulsive was barring her way back. She tried again to slide into limbo, but it remained blocked. They had caught her.

Well, it wouldn't do them any good. There was no way they could make her take back her stupid soul.

16

SACRIFICE

B ecka watched Castle Roogna from the orchard. "I've always liked castles," she said. "Except for one thing:
They have moat monsters instead of dragons guarding
them."

"Squawk?" Sim asked invisibly.

"Oh, it's nothing against moat monsters. I get along with them just
fine, when I'm in dragon form. But they sort of monopolize castles. My
dream is to someday have my own castle, that I can live in as a girl,
and guard as a dragon. The best of both, really. Though I must admit it
was sort of fun being Castle Maidragon. That's a fancier castle than I
ever imagined. That will be in my dreams for years, with all its fancy
turrets and walls and chambers and gardens and things. I just loved it.
And that Random Factor—what a secret!"

"Squawk."

"That's right, Sim. The way Melody and the Dastard changed when
their souls were switched is amazing. He became a decent man, and she
became a mean woman. In fact, I think he was less indecent without a
soul than she is. I got to know him halfway well, and he wasn't really
bad, just, well, indifferent to the rights and feelings of others. He would
keep his part of a bargain if he made one. The others hardly believe
what I tell them, until they see for themselves. Now that he has a bor-

rowed soul, he's amazingly decent. Maybe he's trying to make up for everything he did before. But I hope this is the last stop; you've had to carry me around too much, so I can talk to them."

"Squawk."

Becka jumped up. "You're right—they're coming out. This time they've got Melody."

Melody walked out, with Harmony on one side and an unfamiliar, ugly woman on the other. They were holding her arms so she could not escape physically. Rhythm and the Dastard, of course, were in limbo, blocking her off there. What a handful the wild princess had turned out to be, with the Dastard's talent and without a soul.

"Take us to the glade," Harmony said as they reached the orchard.

Sim curved his talons so that the four of them could fit inside an invisible temporary enclosure. Then he spread his wings and launched into the air, carrying them all.

They landed at the glade. Then they made spot introductions. "This is Becka the dragon girl," Harmony said. "And Repulsive, Rapunzel's sister, who happened to get caught up in this. Sim is invisible. Rhythm and the Dastard are in limbo. Now we have some work to do."

"Lotsa luck, sister dear," Melody said sourly. Even her appearance had changed; she looked—Becka had to delve into the terminology that her Possession by the Sea Hag had caused to infest her mind—bitchy. Her eyes were wild and her lip tended to curl. It was clear that she was not to be trusted. At the same time, there was a certain challenging beauty in the way she flung her hair, thrust her bosom, and twitched her rear. No man would be safe near her.

Harmony spoke to Sim, Becka, and Repulsive. "I must go into limbo to relieve the Dastard. The three of you must make sure Melody doesn't escape physically, while Rhythm and I keep her out of limbo. The Dastard is the one who must do what has to be done. Don't interfere."

What did they have in mind? They must have worked out a plan of some sort, but why would they let the Dastard, of all people, implement it?

Harmony disappeared. In a moment the Dastard appeared. Becka was struck again by how handsome he had become. It wasn't just the princely costume; it was the soul. He had been a cad; now he had the aura of goodness. He nodded to the others, then addressed Melody. "I am going to try to persuade you to take your soul back, Princess. Then you will be as you were."

"The bleep I will," Melody retorted. "You can keep my old soul; I don't want it back." She, in contrast, had the aura of indifference verging into badness. She most resembled a disreputable peasant girl pretending to be a princess.

"Listen to me, Melody. I had a soul once. Then I spent four years without it. Now I have a soul again. I know both sides of this situation—know them well. You don't want to lose your soul."

"The bleep I don't. For the first time in my life I have perfect freedom—and the magic to exploit it. I'm staying the way I am." In fact, Becka realized with a shock, she was coming to resemble the Sea Hag.

"You have freedom—but not satisfaction," he said. "You have a chronic hunger that you can't ever abate. You can only keep feeding it, and never come to the end of it."

"Oh, pooh! I could satisfy it if I ever got the chance without being pestered by my cloying sisters."

"No, you could not. I had four unfettered years to satisfy my hunger, and it only got worse. Nothing was ever enough. Now, at last, I know why."

"Why?" Melody asked derisively.

"Because what I really craved, without knowing it, was my soul back. Now I have yours, and I understand what I lost."

"You lost your scruples. You lost your chains. Now you're serving a new mistress, as bad as the Sea Hag. Worse, because it makes you think you like it. You can keep it."

"No, you must take it back."

"Why?"

"Because it is your soul. It belongs to you, not to me. It is your most precious possession."

"I tell you I don't want it! So why don't you just go away, and consider it a fair deal: You have what you want, and I have what I want."

"No, that must not be." Becka was amazed at the Dastard's patience. He was addressing Melody politely despite her repudiation of decency.

"Listen, frog brain: If you really found my soul so &&&&ing precious, you'd be eager to keep it."

He shook his head. "How I wish I could keep it! But the fact that I have it means that I understand why I can't keep it. The only soul to which I am entitled is my own, and I forfeited that four years ago."

Seeing that she wasn't persuading him, Melody tried another tactic. "It really doesn't matter, you know. We can't change back. The Random Factor changed us, and he never does the same thing twice. So it's academic; there's no way."

"There is a way," he said.

"Really? How?"

"You must go back and unhappen the first opening of that forbidden door. Then the exchange will never have happened, and you will never have lost your soul."

She stared at him. "You're right! That would do it." But she reconsidered immediately. "Except that I can't unhappen my own life before I got the talent."

"You can if I cooperate. The moment my talent comes back to me, I will complete the unhappening. Together we can do it."

She nodded. "So it may be possible. But I'm not going to do it." She returned to her prior tactic. "If you think it's so great having a soul, why are you so eager to give it up?"

"Melody, I do not want to give it up. I wish I could have it forever. It's much better than my own soul ever was. But I must return it to its proper owner."

"This is ludicrous. You say you are determined to get rid of what you most want to keep. Why should I believe you?"

"Because I have your soul. It provides me with a conscience, and so much more."

"More?"

"It makes me aware of the awfulness of the way I was before. I am chagrined that I can never undo the damage I have done. My remorse knows no bounds."

"Oh, pooh! You never really hurt anybody. You were never violent. You never tried to force anything on a girl."

"Oh, but I did. Becka can tell you how I tried to kiss her and see her panties."

Melody burst out laughing. "You call that criminal? All men try to do those things. Want me to kiss you and show you my panties? &&&&, Das, I'll stuff them in your face!"

Still the Dastard did not react to her baiting. "That won't be necessary. I still wish I could atone for what I did. I can't. All I can do is see that it never happens again."

"What a nothing you have become! You were a piker before; now you're zilch. The Sea Hag could have made a man of you." She shot a sidelong glance at him. "That must be it! I think you want to get rid of the soul so you can be free again. To go fetch the Hag and get really wild. You've fooled my sickly sweet sisters, but you can't fool me."

That was a shot that made Becka take stock. Could it be true? Yet the Dastard was being so honest now that she found it hard to believe. Melody was also right about him never being truly criminal before; his deeds had been dastardly rather than vicious. The Sea Hag had been truly ugly—and the Dastard had not trusted her. So now Becka had to believe that he was really trying to do the right thing.

The Dastard paused. Then he asked "What motivates you, Melody?"

Surprised, she evaded the question. "Why do you want to know?"

"Because your answer will enable me to clarify mine."

She shrugged. "I want to have fun. I want to mess up other peoples' lives. I want to freak men out. I want to signal the stork, and never get a delivery." She lifted the hem of her skirt. "Are you interested?"

"Yes, but—"

"But what?" she asked, lifting higher. "I have got your number, Das: You cannot tell a lie. You *are* interested."

Becka could see how the man's eyes began to sweat. She realized that a beautiful bitchy woman could make quite an impression. That was another thing she had learned from the Sea Hag—and probably the Hag had taught it to Melody as well. Those legs were formidable, much sexier than they had ever been when Melody had her soul. Still, the Dastard fought visibly to maintain his equilibrium. "But I know it's not right."

"Because of that stupid soul. Well, I don't care what's right. Take a good look, fool." She hauled her skirt all the way up to show her panties.

But the Dastard, warned by her prior lift, closed his eyes before getting freaked out. "I don't need to look at you, Melody; I just want to talk to you."

"Let me go, and you can have my body," she said. "I know you want it."

"Yes. And I would have taken it, when I had no soul."

"Now I have no soul, and I'll give it to you. I just want to get out of here." She continued to hold her skirt up, just in case he peeked.

He didn't. Becka marveled at his control. *She* would have peeked, from sheer curiosity, had she been a man. "You asked me a question. Now I will answer it. You define fun in terms of gratifying your immediate desires. But that can never satisfy your long-term welfare. My quest, now, is for the satisfaction that comes from meaning and love."

"Here is love," she said, waving her lifted skirt. The suggestion was so strong it made his closed eyelids blush.

"That is sex," he said, his breathing heavy. It was evident that he couldn't handle much more of this. "Love is immeasurably greater. Just as meaning is immeasurably greater than accomplishment. True happiness can be achieved only by these routes."

"Love," Melody repeated thoughtfully. "It is true I don't have that. Maybe it would be nice."

"Yes, it is the most wonderful thing a person can experience," the Dastard said fervently. Becka knew he was sincere; he had never spoken like that before. She could almost love him herself; his possession of a soul made him lovable. In fact, the soul gave him an aura reminiscent of the power of the magic she had felt when the three princesses had adapted her into the castle.

But of course Melody couldn't see it. "How do you know?"

He hesitated. "Maybe that's not relevant."

"Sure it is. You say love is the greatest. So you must love someone. Who?"

He yielded. "You, of course. As you are when you are complete. Now at last I understand the way of it."

She burst out laughing. "Well, I don't love *you*, you idiot! You won't even look at me." She waved her skirt again, fanning air past his face. A trace of glaze began to form on his closed eyelids.

"I know you don't," he said sadly. "And when you recover your soul, and are able to love, I won't be there, even if you think of me."

"You'll be out of here, free again. Unhappening things galore."

"No. I will be gone. I will not do any more harm. I will pay for those terrible four years the only way I can."

"What do you mean, gone?"

"I will die," he said simply. "So that I will do no more mischief."

Becka was shocked. What was this?

"What do you mean, die?" Melody demanded. "People don't just die."

"They do when they have taken poison. I will die before this day is done. I must return your soul to you before then."

Poison! He had done that? Becka realized that he must have. Harmony and Rhythm could have gotten it for him, and agreed that this was the way it had to be. It had obviously been his decision, because of his mortification over his past deeds. He was sacrificing his life for what he believed was right. To restore Melody, and abolish the soulless Dastard.

This got to the princess, despite her lack of soul. "Why in Xanth would you die, just as you get free?"

"Because, with your soul, I appreciate why I must not be allowed to resume my dastardly ways. I have done immeasurable harm to innocent folk, and I grieve that I can never undo it. At least I can ensure that the harm stops."

"Oh, pooh! It's fun doing mischief. I've hardly had the chance, yet. At least I got Repulsive." She glanced at the woman, who nodded sadly.

"And how do you feel about that?" the Dastard asked Melody.

"I feel great! I want to do more of it."

"How does it help you to hurt her?"

"It makes me better than her. And when I get the chance, I'll mess up everyone else, so I can be best of all."

"And when you are the best in all Xanth, what then? Will you be happy?"

"Of course I will! Isn't it obvious?"

"It seemed so to me, before I got your soul. Now I know that I was not capable of true happiness, only of the momentary illusion of it. I would rather die decently, than live soullessly."

"Well, you can throw away your stupid life if you insist. I'll never be such an idiot."

He shook his head. "You must live, Melody, and you must take back your soul. Otherwise it will be lost when I die, and that would be an unconscionable waste."

"I will live, but I won't take back my soul."

"I know it's no use appealing to your finer sensitivities, because you lost those with your soul. But I speak from greater experience in this respect than you have. Soullessness is a desolate business; it is not for you, Melody."

"Will you stop wasting my time with this nonsense? Once my sisters have to exchange back, I'll be free, and you can't stop it."

"Melody, what can I do to persuade you?"

"You can help me to pass the time interestingly. Open your eyes." She still held her dress up.

Becka know that if he did open his eyes, he would be lost, because her panties would freak him out. Their mere proximity had already weathered his face somewhat, turning it faintly green in emulation of the panties. But Becka couldn't interfere; the princesses had made it clear that this was strictly between Melody and the Dastard. Becka's role was only to prevent Melody from leaving physically. So she had to watch the disaster unfolding.

"If I open my eyes, will you open your ears?" The Dastard asked.

"What do you mean?"

"You want me to see your body, knowing that it will freak me out. I want you to see my point, trusting that it will persuade you to do the right thing. I will look if you will listen and try to understand."

Melody shrugged. "Okay, jerk," she said insincerely.

Becka wanted to cry out to him not to do it. But she had to stifle her voice, and hold back a tear.

He opened his eyes. They saw her panties. They turned green and began to glaze over. He was definitely freaking out. Becka hated to watch.

"Come here," Melody said smugly.

He came to her. He could not do otherwise. She had mesmerized him.

She put her arms around him. "Now we shall take off our clothes," she said.

But she had brought him too close. He could no longer see her panties. The glaze chipped off his eyeballs and his gaze cleared. "Now you must listen," he said. "You agreed to."

"I lied. Take off my clothes."

It was obvious that though he was no longer freaked out, his contact with the princess put him in her power. He began to remove her blouse. But as he did, he spoke. "What you are experiencing is the onset of a life without values. You have a hunger that is not really for food, a longing that is not really for power, a desire that is not really for the stork. You can try to oblige these cravings, but they will never satisfy you. Your appetites can be indulged endlessly but will never be sated. The more you struggle to fulfill them, the less happy you will become, until at last you are left with only the misery of your own emptiness."

"That sounds like a curse," Melody said. "I spit on it. Now take off my skirt."

He had to do her bidding. Becka wished she could go and put the princess's clothing back on, but she had to stay clear no matter what happened. "It *is* a curse—the worst possible one," the Dastard said. "The curse of meaninglessness."

Melody seemed shaken by the notion of a curse. She had evidently experienced just enough of it to have some doubt. "So you say that if I do with you what I am about to, it won't make me happy?"

"Did depriving Repulsive of her Answer make you happy?"

Now she stood without clothing. "No. It wasn't enough. But if I can make bigger mischief—"

"It can never be enough, Melody! I know; I have done endless mischief, and never found peace."

"So how do you say I can find peace?"

"Take back your soul!"

Melody laughed. "Nice try, fool. I know better. Very well, stand still while I take off your clothing."

He stood still. "Maybe a compromise. If you took it back for just a minute, to see if it does what I promise—"

She paused with his shirt off. "For just a minute? That might be interesting. But it's a trap: I can unhappen the Random Factor only once. I can't unhappen an unhappening. You know that. So I'd be stuck with it."

Becka marveled at the neatness of the trap. But the princess hadn't fallen for it.

"There may be another way," the Dastard said. "Hold me close. Then the soul I bear will overlap your body, and you should be able to get the feeling of it. It is after all your soul. If you don't like it, you don't have to take it."

Melody considered as she got his trousers off. Becka had to avert her gaze; she couldn't afford to see a naked man. "Okay, I have to get pretty close to you anyway, to signal the stork. I'll try to tune in to my soul for a moment. But I want a deal."

"A deal?"

"You didn't think I'd do what you want for nothing, did you? I want to get you off my case. If I don't like the soul, you and my sisters will have to let me go. Immediately."

Becka's heart skipped half a beat. Melody was putting everything on the line! If they agreed to that, she could win, and they would lose. All Xanth would lose. He couldn't agree to any such condition.

"I agree," the Dastard said.

Oh, no!

"That's not enough. My sisters have more magic." She looked around. "Show yourselves, Sisters dear. Agree."

There was a pause. Then Harmony slid out of limbo for a moment. "I agree," she said reluctantly.

Rhythm appeared. "I agree too."

Then both were gone, still guarding limbo. Had they all gone crazy? They were handing victory to the one without a conscience.

Melody looked at Becka. "And you, dragon girl. And the others. You all have souls, so will be bound by your word. You all must agree."

Amazingly, Sim squawked agreement. Repulsive spoke. "I agree."

They had to know something Becka didn't. What could she do? "I agree," Becka said, turning back to face them. Fortunately the man was facing away from her.

"This will last only as long as it takes us to summon the stork," Melody said. "I will overlap my soul, and then be gone."

Both of them were naked. The princess stepped into the man, wrapping her arms around him, flattening her body against his. She kissed him, hard. There was a faint shimmer as they turned in place.

Then she pulled her head back. "Oh my gosh! I *feel* it. Not a lot, just a little. It's like a distant lovely melody. Like the sun coming out faintly after a storm. It's calling me. I miss it. I want it. I must have it back." She paused, then came to her decision. "I'm going to take it back!"

"Unhappen the Random Factor," the Dastard said. "I'll help." Becka could view his face now, and was amazed to see a tear on his cheek. He knew what he was losing. Everything: soul, woman, life.

Then suddenly the two of them were standing fully clothed. The tears were on Melody's cheeks, but she was lovely in a way she had not been a moment before. "Oh, that was horrible!" she cried. "How could I have been that way?"

"$$$$!" the Dastard swore. "We didn't finish with the stork!"

Melody looked at him. "I suppose I do owe you that. You gave me back my soul." She started to remove her blouse.

"No!" Becka cried. "Don't do it!"

Melody looked at her. "Becka, I have my conscience back. This man has given up the most valuable possible thing for my sake. I must give him something before he dies."

Becka realized that the other two princesses remained in limbo, guarding it so that the Dastard could not escape that way. She and Sim were supposed to see that he did not flee physically. He had to remain here until the poison killed him. This unhappening had been quite selective: The soul had changed, but not the poison. But this was awful. "No! I'm supposed to help him, not kill him. There has to be another way."

"Sure," the Dastard said. "Let me go."

Then a bulb flashed over Becka's head. "There *is* another way! The demon—the one who traded for his soul. Maybe the demon will trade back."

Melody stared at her, brightening. "That would do it."

"I don't want to trade back," the Dastard said.

Melody stepped into him and put her arms around him, so close that her soul overlapped him. "I'll hold him here," she called to the others. "Find the demon! Bring him here."

Sim squawked: "You can't just fetch a demon. You have to summon it by name."

"What's the demon's name?" Melody asked the Dastard.

"I'll never tell!"

Melody squeezed closer to him. She nuzzled his ear with her sweet lips. "What's the name?" she breathed.

He tried to resist, but there was something about her proximity that weakened him. Maybe it was her soul, overlapping him, reminding him what once had been. "Demon Test," he muttered.

"On our way," Harmony's voice called from limbo.

Becka saw that Repulsive was gone. She realized that since the exchange of souls had been unhappened, Melody had never had the Dastard's talent, so had not fled to Castle Roogna and stolen Repulsive's Question and Answer. Repulsive should have had her interview with the Good Magician by now, and been happy, never knowing what else had happened.

But the primary participants remained: the Dastard, the three princesses, Sim, and Becka herself. It seemed that an unhappening affected the primaries very little. So somehow they had carried through much as before, and were still here as a group. She didn't understand all the intricacies of it, but it was the way it had been with other unhappenings.

Melody still held the Dastard. "Soon you will have your soul back," she said.

The man struggled, but obviously felt the soul, and it made him weak. "The joy of you," he breathed. "I gave you up. I can never have you again. You are not my soul. Now I must die."

He was embracing Melody but speaking to the soul!

"Maybe not," Melody said, kissing him. "I have seen what you can be, when you are souled. You sacrificed yourself for me. You were manly and decent and lovable. I didn't care then, but now I remember, and now I do care. I believe I could love you. Take back your own soul, and come to Ptero with me."

Becka stared, understanding. Melody's memory of the Dastard with a soul, and of his sacrifice, was bringing her the love that had seemed impossible. The googolly had been matched.

"You would do that?" he asked, amazed. "When you don't have to?"

"I may not be as smart as you are," Melody told him. "But I'm not stupid. You can be a good man. And will be, when I marry you and share my soul with you. Again."

A demon appeared. "Who summons me?" he demanded.

Melody did not let go of the Dastard. "Will you trade back with him, D. Test?" she asked. "Take back the talent of unhappening?"

"Sure I will," Test said. "It was a bad deal for me. His soul is dingy and worn, while the talent is great."

"Then do it," Melody said.

"He has to agree," Test said. "Otherwise it won't work. And of course he won't. Why would anyone give up such a talent?"

"Tell him you agree," Melody said to the Dastard.

But she wasn't holding him closely, and so the soul no longer overlapped him. "I *don't* a—"

She kissed him again. "We can do a lot of this, when you are souled," she murmured. "We can play Faun & Nymph, on Ptero, without end."

He still tried to defy her, but she kept kissing him, and little hearts formed around their heads. Becka doubted that any man in Xanth, with or without a soul, could resist such persuasion for very long. "I agree!" he gasped at last.

Test threw something at him, and caught something in return. Then he vanished.

Harmony and Rhythm appeared. "You may have lost your talent, but we still have ours, as part of our magic," Harmony said.

"We can slide into limbo," Rhythm agreed. "And unhappen things, now that we have learned how. But we're not going to, except for some good purpose."

The Dastard stood still. "My name is Anomy," he said. "But I have to tell you, my soul isn't in a class with yours. It's not nearly as nice. And my natural talent is that of having stupid ideas; it's not in a class with yours either. I'm nobody."

"On Ptero we need very little soul," Melody said, finally letting him go. "Because our world is so small. I'm sure yours will do."

"But you have every good reason to hate me."

"You're right: That *is* a stupid idea."

He seemed to be at a loss. "How so?"

Melody smiled. "Must I explain it again?"

"Maybe you must. I just can't seem to believe that a princess would really want to be with a nothing man like me."

"When you had my soul, you did everything you could to give it back, though you wanted to keep it. You sacrificed yourself for me. That gave me reason to love you, though I didn't appreciate it until I got my soul back. Come to Ptero with me, and be what you can be."

The hearts circling his head had not quite faded. Now they grew brighter. "Oh, Melody!" Then he collapsed.

"But he's dying!" Becka said, remembering.

"Oh, that's right," Harmony said.

"But we can fix it," Rhythm concluded.

Melody went to join them. They linked hands, and sang and played, and a bottle appeared. Melody caught it and offered it to the man. "Drink this."

"What is it?" he asked weakly.

"The antidote," Harmony said.

"We conjured it," Rhythm concluded.

Anomy tried to take the bottle, but was too weak, so the three princesses got down beside him, lifted him up, and poured the medicine into his mouth.

The effect was immediate. Strength returned, and Anomy sat up with their help. "I feel much better."

"It's strong medicine," Melody said.

He glanced around at them. Harmony was closely supporting his left shoulder, Rhythm his right shoulder, and Melody his head. He was still half buried in princesses. "That, too."

Sim squawked: It was time to go to Princess Ida, to make the return exchange.

"But how can I go, when I didn't come from there?" Anomy asked.

"You will exchange with your Self who is there," Melody said.

"If that were my idea, it would be stupid."

"Fortunately it's not your idea," Harmony said.

"It's *our* idea," Rhythm concluded.

They gathered together, and Sim carried them to Castle Roogna. Princess Ida was expecting them; she came out to meet them in the orchard, so that Sim would not be inconvenienced. The huge bright bird also became visible. He was amazingly beautiful.

The exchange was not very dramatic. The five of them stood in a circle, and faded, and then became clear again—in much reduced size. Sim was as big as a man, instead of as big as a grown roc. The three princesses were children, only four years old. Anomy was a boy of five.

"Who are you?" little Princess Melody asked the boy.

"Why are you here?" Harmony asked.

"Are you a prince?" Rhythm concluded.

"I'm Anomy," he said. "I got switched with my adult Self. I don't know why. Maybe it was one of my bad ideas. I'm not a prince. I'm nobody special."

Becka realized that none of them remembered the past few days in Xanth. They were really different people; they had not been here.

"Well, maybe you'll be a prince someday," Melody said with unconscious prophecy.

"Let's play tag," Harmony said.

"And you're it," Rhythm cried, slapping Anomy as they all bolted for the nearest pie trees. The boy chased after them, glad to play the game.

That left Becka and Princess Ida. "I think you understand that you must not speak of the events of the past few days," Ida said.

"Yes, of course. I guess I'd better go home."

"You have accomplished your purpose," Ida said.

Becka paused. "Oh, that's right! I went to the Good Magician to ask what was my purpose, and he said to effect the welfare of Xanth. Then I had to go help the Dastard, as my Service. I almost forgot how it started."

"You did help," Ida said. "Without you, this adventure might have had a very different outcome."

Becka nodded. "Maybe so. I'm glad it worked out, but sort of sad it's all over. It's going to be dull, going home again. Mother really doesn't need a teenager underfoot, especially not a dragon, and of course Father Draco doesn't either. I can't turn girl when I'm with him, because he's ashamed of my human element. There's really no place I can be completely myself."

"Perhaps that return can be delayed."

"Delayed? I can't stay on this adventure; it's over, and I can't even talk about it."

"The Big Princesses appreciated your help, and left a job for you. But it will require some upkeep."

Becka was blank. "Job? Upkeep?"

"What they left can't be moved, and needs a hostess, and guarding."

"I don't understand. They didn't leave anything; they just exchanged and went back to Ptero."

"There was one more event you were not aware of."

"There was?" Becka realized that it was possible.

"If you will change forms, I will show you where it is. Then perhaps you will understand."

"Uh, okay," Becka said doubtfully. She turned dragon.

The princess got on her back and gave her directions. Becka walked rapidly there. Whatever it was, it was deep in the jungle. There was no path; she had to forge through almost impenetrable thickets. No one would find his way here by accident.

They came to a glade. In the glade was an extremely fancy castle.

"Maidragon!" Becka cried, turning girl as she beheld it.

"It lacks a hostess to occupy it, and a moat monster to guard it. There is a chamber that must not be opened, and travelers might not understand. The Big Princesses thought perhaps a dragon would do for the outside, and a person for the inside."

"They want me to stay here?" Becka asked, awed.

"If you would be so kind. Of course the Little Princesses don't yet know about this, but I'm sure they would like to visit it, and perhaps others would too, like your parents, if we could be sure it was properly maintained. By someone with discretion."

Becka gazed at the castle, slowly appreciating the significance of the "job." It was really a gift. She had a new home. For both her forms.

Author's Note

S omething weird happened while I was writing this novel. I was gaining on the years-long backlog of reader suggestions. I call it the pun list, though actually suggestions are of all types: puns, characters, situations, corrections, whatnot. Sometimes I can base a whole novel on a reader suggestion, though most often reader's notions have only peripheral effect. They are like nuts in fruitcake: They add to the richness of the mix, but one nut will do about as well as another. At any rate, I was racing along, trying to use the oldest notions first, starting with ones from mid 1996, and moving erratically forward, crossing off whole pages as I completed them, when suddenly it happened. I caught up. In the first week of NoRemember, 1998, every single listed reader notion had been used or committed. That is, two were slotted for the next novel, *Swell Foop*, as they were too significant to be used for minor scenes in the present novel. Then more piled in as the novel ended, and by the time I write *Foop*, there may be a hundred. But I want it known that, for one brief shining moment, the list was caught up. It may never happen again.

Otherwise the news is mixed. Florida, like the rest of the world, has felt the impact of global warming, which means not an even gentle rising of temperatures, but at times devastating changes in the weather patterns. Our tree farm is on a peninsula in Lake Tsoda Popka, and the water rose and rose until we judged that two more inches would flood our drive. Then it stopped as spring floods gave way to summer drought and fires. Our trees would be finished if any fire reached them. But none did, and finally the rain resumed, and we were okay. Except that by then it was the hurricane season. The rule is this: Every storm first forms its eye and looks for us. Then, like a bowling ball rolling down the alley, it tries to knock off our pin without stumbling over other pins first. The trick is to stay over water as long as possible; that's the source of heat-energy. That means sliding across the Atlantic just south of Florida, into the Gulf of Mexico, then curving north and looping into the Florida Suncoast from the west. It's a tricky shot, and most don't make it; their eyes are too blurry to watch us constantly. But oh how hard they try! We were nervous as bleep about Georges as he completed the first part, but then he made too wide a turn and just missed us. Later Mitch revved up to a terrifying one hundred eighty MPH, but then wobbled and fell into Central America, not catching Florida until he was only a shadow. So we survived that season too. But the folk in the path of those storms had a rough time, and it's no joke. There is bound to be more of this in the future. Not only does global warming make for worse storms, they do more damage because of overbuilding on the coasts, and deforestation inland. There's too much to hurt, and too little to hold the ground in place.

My personal life proceeds in its petty pace. I exercise by jogging and working out with hand weights, and though I remind myself that the point is health, not numbers, this summer I got into a streak of especially fast jogs, in the course of which I broke all my prior records despite the heat. Remember, I'm not running four-minute miles here; eight minutes is more like it. But I am writing this at sixty-four; what do you expect? I didn't like the tension, worrying about when the streak would end, so when I was away from Florida in the course of this novel, thus interrupting it, I let that be it, and now am deliberately pacing my jogs to be one to two minutes slower. That's much more comfortable, physically and emotionally.

As offshoots of my exercise I also bicycle and practice archery, and those have become something of incidental hobbies. I gave up my regular bicycle in favor of a recumbent bicycle, and also got a traveling rowing cycle, that has no pedals, just handlebars/oars. Now my wife and I are considering a four-wheel cycle, almost a pedal car, so we can ride together. The thing is, as folks get older, balance gets less certain, and falls can do more damage. As we lurch toward retirement age we grow more careful, necessarily. It's much harder to fall from an adult trike or four-wheel cycle. No, I didn't say I was retiring, just that I'm at the age when others do. I'm a workaholic who will be halfway through a good novel at the time I kick the bucket. There's a perennial rumor that I have died, to which I reply not that I know of, but I do recognize the likely consequences of age. So, in time, my jogs will become walks, and my two-wheelers will go to three or four. As for the archery: Once I cranked my compound bow up to sixty pounds pull, I felt that was sufficient; when I miss the target, the arrow can go a bleep of a long way and get lost in the forest. I'm getting more accurate now, and rarely miss the target, which helps. I also still use a left handed reverse-curve bow, so as to balance the exercise. I've learned how to repair my battered arrows, and they are lasting longer. I recently saw a sale on Bear arrows at half-price, so bought a dozen. Rather than cut them down to proper size, I decided to use them full length of about thirty-three inches, and they work well enough. I suppose if I were a competitor I'd be more choosy, but I'm a permanent duffer, using what I have. I like to experiment, and I have learned things about the dynamics of arrows of different lengths.

We have a big dog, named Obsidian, who has grown to almost ninety-seven pounds of eagerness. She loves to ride out with my wife to fetch in the junk mail, but on Sunday there is no mail, so I have taken to walking her then. I made a path around the tree farm, and we do about a mile and a half loop, rush and sniff, rush and sniff. She seems to have no in-between gear, except toward the end, when she tires. It gives me a chance to check the trees. I see that we have a sinkhole, only about three feet deep, but about a third of a mile long, that has slowly taken out whole lines of our pines. Some are tilting, some are dead. I suppose it could be an underground stream, though we are only about five feet above the water table. Well, it's better than the kinds of sink holes elsewhere in the state, that suddenly swallow houses and highways. I tease Jenny Mundane's mom about how they should move to Florida and build on a sink hole.

During this novel we made a trip to attend a reunion of the alumni of Goddard College in Vermont, where in the 1950s I became a vegetarian, met the girl I married, and got my degree in creative writing. I'm still a vegetarian, still married to the girl, and still writing, so it seemed appropriate to attend. We met a number of lost friends, and I did a brief reading from my just-then-published novel, *Zombie Lover*, and we saw the expanded campus. But a cold wave arrived just in time to catch us; we went suddenly from a night's low of 74°F at home to a daily high of about 55°, with frost at night, and had to wear all our changes of clothing in layers and still feel cold. Probably this is the last time; we don't like to travel, and it disrupts our dull routine. I lost two weeks writing time, and I really do like to write. I wrote it up in detail in my regular column for the Hi Piers Page at www.hipiers.com, for online readers who like to keep current. Hipiers.com is the ghost of our old 800 HI PIERS shop, which has shut down.

One other thing happened during this novel. I had minor surgery on my back. I do mean minor: There was a suspicious patch developing, so rather than gamble, the doctor cut it out. There were four stitches, covered by a Band-Aid. It turned out to be benign.

Sometimes I make sure things are carefully explained in my fiction, so readers can't get confused. But that can annoy some, who don't like to think I'm treating them like idiots. So, in *Yon Ill Wind*, I didn't do that. Ever since I've been getting queries and complaints: Why did I kill off Chlorine and Nimby? What a downbeat ending! What happened after that? How come they appear in subsequent novels, if they're dead? Sigh; I suppose I should have explained in that author's note what I thought was clear from the context: Nimby needed a single tear of love or grief for him, from someone who did not know his identity or its significance, in order to win his contest and save Xanth. Chlorine shed that tear. Thereafter Nimby restored her to full health and beauty, and carried her away to the nameless Castle for something like an endless honeymoon. No, I don't know whether they got married first, and that will set off some other readers. One chewed me out for having Sean and Willow, in that novel, share a room before marriage. The Adult Conspiracy really is alive and well in Mundania as well as Xanth.

Now for the present novel. There were some miscues, such as when one reader suggested a dragon girl, and I explained that had already been done elsewhere, then next day I discovered that I had already agreed to have one in this novel. Okay, so I added to the credit for that one, but

I wish I had been able to let the second reader know at the time. Some good ideas had to be used very briefly or even offstage, because the novel goes where it goes and I can't follow up on every good notion. I also had a problem with Becka, the dragon girl: I felt the situation was too close to the chapter I had in *Zombie Lover* where Breanna of the Black Wave has to foil the cad, Ralph. So I thought Becka had better walk on stage, and then offstage soon. But the willful girl wouldn't go. So she stayed to the end of the novel.

Characters do that; they can have wills of their own. But overall I think the reader notions integrated well, and here they are, roughly in order of their use in the novel:

Talent of having stupid ideas, Sorceress Tapis returns—David Hoover; D. Test—Thomas L. Bruns; Sand wench—Lisa Saenz; Crack pot—Sarah Walker; Pee-nut—Rich Stabile; Ding Bat—Eitan Bernstein; Becka—Becky Bell (dragon/girl also suggested by Jenifer Trapp); Melody Irene Human—Melody Irene Poole; Melody Irene's story—Monica Meyerhardt; Phantom pregnancy—Kyle Johnson; Tell the Sea Hag's life story—Sarah Curran; Surprise's used talents replenish, eventually—Greg Rimko; Ho, with selective amnesia—Michael Meilstrup; Ghost King Warren's talent of creating ghosts—Kiel Van Horn; Jade—Ashley Colvin; Mac/Mike/Mal—Michael Kenny; Og and Not-Og, Green Horn—Barbara Hay Hummel; Half soul in the wind—Jessica Housmann; Gargoyle socks—Jessica Mansfield; Fray Cloud—Laura Slocum; Waxing poetic, Bears—Brenda Toth; Boss Black Labrador—Greg Kennedy; Imp ass—Craig Yoder; Thyme varieties—Donovan Beeson; Eck Sray—Monica Ramirez; Situation Magnification: a mother's talent—Caven Boyd; Pay phone—Chris Efta; See-saw, See saw convention—Samantha Holsinger; Pair-it—Matthew Aharonov; DeMonica's talent of identifying springs, Names of the denizens of the Isle of Fellowship—Nicole Mortimer; Smoke screen, cold snap, talent of controlling tangle trees, River bank lien—Vincent Tardo; Human/nightmare crossbreed—David Chapman; Compact disc, Dow Jones—Andrew Katon; Petition collecting signatures for a cause—Red Plana; Literate—Dorcas Bethel; Sim to have adventure—Crystal Tung; Cat tails—Marshall Porter McConahy; Snooze button, How?LL the who-what-where-wolf—Anna Bryant; Novella—Bentley Gettings; Chain smoker, Pack rat, Diabetic puns—Tiffany Stull; Pyrite, gneiss—Dane Woodwand; Pun-kin pies—Brittany

Nelson; Sheet rock—Chelsea Bagwell; Pun dial—Brandon Banks; Tooth paste—Stephen Andrew Humphris; Tangle tree farm, Nadine Naga, Trent and Iris move to Isle of Illusion, Swamp Road Game—Erin Schram; Angels in Xanth, Shun tree—Wes Lescelius; Lost winged monster—Kory H. Kuhlmann; Talent of making folk feel shame—Peter Landwehr; Characters who hate Xanth—Suzanna Otting; Autoharp—Tovah Veats; Talent of glowing in the night—Elizabeth Pearl; Interface—Peter Landwehr; Litterbug—Monica Ramirez; Ann Arky, with thoughts in word balloons—Donovan Beeson; Green Murphy—Erin Schram & daughters Sharayah and Fiona; African centaurs—Anna Dunster; Kress Centaur—Pisces Elf-Man; Chet Centaur follow-up—Katie Gates; How do centaurs breathe?—Wayne Donahue; Love bugs make love spring—Will Howard; Merei, Mesta, Dell—Amber L. Logue; Nightreven—Anthony McKee; Small young sphinx—Rich Stabile; Griffin story (with a nice picture of Griselda)—Nicole Dubuc; Project a thought into a mind—Bentley Ray Gettings; Project an image into a mind—Christ Efta; Project an emotion into a mind, human or non-human—Elizabeth Lay and Michael Gettings; Just Ice—Addy Taylor; Cloud sculpturing—Elizabeth Pearl; Sea serpent the size of a chipmouse—Garrett Rasmussen; Nada Naga advice columnist—Alexandra Bonyun and Sara Bruce; Carpal tunnel—Stephen Lott; Xander and Zelda Zombie—Susan Hatfield; Trent and Iris' daughter Irenti or Trentia, Bill Bored—Nicole Mortimer; Trent go back for his first wife—Mackay Wilford; Ampoule warning, split moment—Miguel Ettema; Wood-bees—William Crow; Free bees—Kellie Phillips; Tar-nation—Jamie Jacobs; Sole, Dor transformed into dor-mouse—Ellie Smith; Sean and Willow summon the stork—Michael Bui; Tattle Tails, P. R. Ogress—Katie Moran; Com Unity—Tom Redman; Com Pulsion—Ron Leming; Com Mute, Rad, Ma, Fuse—Anonymous; I-be-profane—Tamsyn Cunningham; Here-tic—Nick Hartgrove; White hole—Jessica Grider; Boy with talent of cloning—Chelsea Bagwell; Xanthlike regions on other planets—Daniel Bensen; Che and Cynthia's foals—Natalie Tran; Fountain of Youth leaks—Amber L. Logue; Talent of exaggeration—Janell Wolfinger; Piper—Nathaniel Scheidemen; Xena—Laurel Ritscher; Talent of banishing things—Sebastian Erdelt; Talent of seeing the true nature of anything, Souper star—Kelsey McHugh; Talent of copying folk—Billy Banks; Heart of the Forest, Rat race—Mike Henderson; Lutans riding horses hard at night—Vicky Wilson's sister.; Animal Wave—Julia Hendrickson; Geo & Graphy—Tom Redman and Nick Pengilley; Cherry-ot—Shaisa Noah; Wearing heart on sleeve—Raymond Gramney; Wild Thyme—Jennifer S. Katz; Jinns with J names—Jay Adkisson; Demon Queen makes Fracto solid, Quick & slow sand timer—Tim Healey; Sun bathers, Al and May Eye—Ken Brooks; Child of original Princess and Prince Dolph, in alternate history—Scott Sherbine; Arthur Itis—Emily Trum; Florida fires become Xanth dragon fires—Doug Abel; Planes banking in cloud banks—Daisy Mae; Lacuna's child with talent of writing coming briefly true—David Gustafson; Ant Onym—Jonathan Cuny; Manage mint, Why instant loss of magic, in Time of No Magic?— Gavin Lambert; Imp Each Ment—Tandy L. Dolin; Horn-net—Charles Becker; Socio and Psycho Paths—Lindsay Penner; Talent of doing the right thing—Romeo D. Mejia; Monster unplugs hole (actually I used it differently, but this was the source of the notion)—Marisol Ramos; Mut Ant—NKen; Most of the puns of the Random Factor's comic strip, plus Jean Gnome, Salt Peter, Worry warts—Ruth Taylor; Talent of conjuring small insects—Gabe Duran; Destiny—Connie Hedrick; Talent of healing human souls—Tracie Aldrich; Zombies called "living-impaired"—John Schick; Sammy Cat can now find the World of Two Moons—Katie Gates; Ida's child, with talent of suppressing all thought—Jennifer S. Katz; Repulsive, Rapunzel's ugly twin—Natalie King.

That does it for this time. I finished this novel NoRemember 29, 1998. Harpy reading, folks!